Venus Fly Trap

Also by Emma Medrano

Nothing Serious

Venus Fly Trap

EMMA MEDRANO

MICHAEL JOSEPH

PENGUIN MICHAEL JOSEPH

UK | USA | Canada | Ireland | Australia
India | New Zealand | South Africa

Penguin Michael Joseph is part of the Penguin Random House group of companies
whose addresses can be found at global.penguinrandomhouse.com

Penguin Random House UK,
One Embassy Gardens, 8 Viaduct Gardens, London SW11 7BW

penguin.co.uk

Penguin
Random House
UK

First published 2025
001

Set in 12/14.75pt Bembo MT
Typeset by Falcon Oast Graphic Art Ltd
Printed and bound in Great Britain by Clays Ltd, Elcograf S.p.A

The authorized representative in the EEA is Penguin Random House Ireland,
Morrison Chambers, 32 Nassau Street, Dublin D02 YH68

A CIP catalogue record for this book is available from the British Library

HARDBACK ISBN: 978–0–241–70358–8
TRADE PAPERBACK ISBN: 978–0–241–70359–5

Penguin Random House is committed to a sustainable future
for our business, our readers and our planet. This book is made from
Forest Stewardship Council® certified paper

MIX
Paper | Supporting
responsible forestry
FSC
www.fsc.org   FSC® C018179

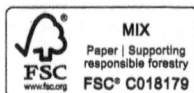

If you see yourself in this book, it was written for you.

Love her, love her, love her! If she favours you, love her. If she wounds you, love her. If she tears your heart to pieces – and as it gets older and stronger, it will tear deeper – love her, love her, love her!

Great Expectations, Charles Dickens

The body lies where she left it.

He's on the floor in the middle of the room. He died with his eyes wide open, staring at the ceiling. It's not the blood that gives away the fact that he's dead; it's the eyes. You never notice someone blinking, but it's so obvious when they stop. His eyes are dry and blank. They're grey and foggy, the pupils melting into the brown to create a blurry mess. Despite that, he might be better-looking now than he was alive.

He has started to smell. It's an odd scent, but it's vaguely familiar; almost like the time last summer when she took a pack of beef stir-fry strips out of the fridge and forgot about them for a few hours. It's warm. The windows are closed and the air feels hot and heavy. She pinches her nose shut. It's not a pleasant smell.

But it is a pleasant sight.

His arms are outstretched like he's making a snow angel in his own blood. It's spilled out on both sides of him, the puddle bigger than when she last saw it. It isn't spreading any more, but the poor wooden floors will never be the same.

Her mind itches with the sense that something is missing. Is there something she should do? A non-religious mark of respect, some sort of symbolic send-off to an afterlife that may or may not exist?

'I'm sorry,' she says.

She cringes. It's only a half-lie anyway; she isn't sorry

I

that he's dead, but she is sorry it had to end this way. It did, though. There were no other options.

She crouches down next to him, careful not to touch the pool of blood. She takes his wrist. The skin is cold. She puts two fingers to the place where his pulse should be, even though she knows there won't be one. She finds herself stroking his wrist, briefly wanting to take his hand, briefly wanting it all to have been a bad dream. Thank god it wasn't.

She stands back up and takes out her phone. She takes a deep breath to prepare herself. One final time she goes over the script in her mind. There will be no room for mistakes. She gives herself a shake and dials 999. She makes herself sob, and she pretends to be confused when she gives the address. The operator on the other end does his best to console her and keep her calm. He has no idea her hands are steady and her eyes completely dry.

Cat had left another mess for me to clean up.

I stood in the doorway looking at the carnage in the kitchen. It would have been fine if I didn't need breakfast, but I was already famished. There was no point asking Cat to clean up after herself. She was, of course, still asleep. Cat never woke up before eleven, though most often she didn't emerge from her bedroom until noon.

There were pots on all four burners on the hob, bits of food dried to the insides. Crumbs all over the counters and a used chopping board covered in onion skin. An empty bottle of wine. Bowls and plates stacked so high in the sink you could barely get your hands underneath the tap.

I'd heard them the night before, cooking, blasting indie music I didn't recognize until past midnight, talking and laughing. The shattering of glass followed by hysterical cackling. I saw now that the broken shards of a wine glass had been swept into a corner of the kitchen, to be disposed of by someone else.

I have never enjoyed mess. If I hadn't been so desperate for a place to stay, so pleased at the suggestion that we become flatmates, I would have made more of an effort to ask Cat about her cleaning habits before I moved in. It was too late now.

I filled up the dishwasher and scrubbed the stubborn dry pieces of food from the pots, which had been there long enough to become one with the metal. I put on a pair of plastic gloves to pull the food from the drain and poured bleach all over the sink, then thoroughly wiped down all the counters and the hob and the inside of the micro-wave. I placed the wine bottle in the glass-recycling bin and sat on my knees on the floor to sweep up every piece of glass.

It took me half an hour to make the kitchen presentable again, the hob clear, the counters clean, the stainless steel shining. My stomach was rumbling. I made myself a bowl of porridge and put it inside the microwave.

'Good morning,' said a voice in the doorway.

I turned. Henry the Eighth was standing there in only his pyjama bottoms, with a bit of stubble he hadn't yet shaved off. It always grew so quickly. His cheekbones always looked so sharp. I hadn't heard him enter.

'Good morning,' I said.

Henry did not apologize for the mess or thank me for cleaning it up. He took out two bowls from the cupboard, a jug of milk from the fridge and a carton of chocolate cereal. Two bowls. That meant Cat was awake too. We danced past each other in the kitchen, carefully avoiding any physical contact and apologizing under our breaths for standing in the way. He prepared their breakfasts and left before mine was done.

The first time I called him Henry the Eighth, it was almost an epiphany. The combination of their names together had seemed so familiar: Catherine and Henry. I registered it and said it out loud. 'Henry the Eighth.'

It felt fitting. Henry was young, muscular and handsome now, but I could see a future version of him that had stop-ped watching his diet and going to the gym, that had grown complacent and had a leg that stank, and that replaced one pretty young woman with another when he grew bored.

Cat had laughed more than I had expected. She told me it was a better nickname than I even knew, because he was also the eighth guy she'd ever been with. 'Of course, the others weren't called Henry, though I think one might have been.'

She twinkled her eyes and looked at me. 'Which Catherine am I?' she asked.

I considered carefully. 'Catherine Howard,' I said eventually. Because there must have been something about her, to catch the eye of a king the way she did, and I'd never met someone who had *something* as obviously as Cat does.

The nickname has stuck.

After the microwave beeped, I took my breakfast and went back to my room. They were both in the lounge by then. He was sitting and Cat was splayed across his lap, facing my direction. Her nipples were visible through her thin nightie, her legs smooth and hairless. Even without make-up and with her hair frizzy, she was gorgeous. They were the model of straight white coupledom.

I should have brought up the issue of the messy kitchen. She didn't mention it. She did not say good morning. Cat smiled dreamily, distractedly, straight at me. She raised her hand for a small wave. I waved back. I did not say good morning either.

I went into my bedroom and ate breakfast at my desk.

I had a meeting with my dissertation supervisor that day. We met in his dingy little office in the philosophy building. The window was open to help with the oppressive summer heat, but the room still smelled suspiciously like he made a habit of smoking in there. His name was Robert; he was an

American in his early fifties. He had a photograph on his desk that looked to be twenty years old, of him and his wife and a toddler that must be grown up by now.

'Welcome, Louise, welcome,' he said. 'Sit.' He gestured to the chair across from his own and began to gather the books on the desk into a pile in the corner.

'I must say,' he said, 'I'm quite excited to be your supervisor. You've always provided excellent work, and I look forward to hearing what you have to say in a less structured setting.'

'Thank you,' I said. 'I was happy to get you as my supervisor as well.'

He smiled awkwardly. 'That's good to hear.'

I wondered if he wanted to fuck me. Not that I believe every man wants to fuck me, but I know how men look at women. It's always a consideration. They assess you like you're cattle they're about to purchase, even if you're not for sale.

'Do you know what you want to write about?' he asked.

'The categorical imperative,' I said.

Robert put his hands together and placed them under his chin. I imagine not too many people are keen on writing about Kant, for good reason. Cat hated him. So did I, to be fair. But while it inspired revulsion in people like Cat, it spurred something else in me. A desire to fight him. A drive to prove him wrong.

'Anything more specific than that?' Robert asked.

'I'm going to argue against it,' I said. 'Specifically the formula of universal law.'

'On what grounds?'

'I haven't decided yet.'

'Well, it's quite a good start. How would you feel if we

met again in, say, two weeks' time? Hopefully by then you'll have a clearer direction.'

In the evening Cat knocked on my door. I'd just finished working out, and I hesitated to open it in my leggings with my face red. Working out was always a chore; I couldn't stand to do it in a gym, which is the definition of sensory overload, with the loud music and dropping weights and the crowds of sweaty bodies. At home, however, I always risked getting detected by Cat, which felt a lot like being caught masturbating. Cat didn't need to exercise to keep her stomach perfectly flat. It felt embarrassing to admit that I did, and my body still didn't come close to hers. I followed online workout videos specifically for people with down-stairs neighbours – no jumping involved.

But Cat knew I was home. I had to let her come in. She sauntered inside with a wine glass in one hand, gliding along the floor and over to my bed, sitting down on it. Cat always drank from a wine glass, even if drinking water or orange juice. Her manicured nails tapped on the glass thoughtfully.

'Working out?' she said, glancing at my attire.

'Just wanted to move for a bit,' I lied.

Every woman has told this lie. None of us is working out because it's fun or feels good.

'I need some of your motivation,' said Cat, even though she didn't. 'Have you decided what you're doing for your dissertation?'

'Cunt?' she said, frowning, when I told her. She always called him 'Cunt' instead of Kant. 'Well, you're a better man than I, Gunga Din.'

'I'm arguing against him, of course.'

She nodded. 'Of course. Can I do your make-up later?'

7

She cocked her head to one side and observed me as if she was taking notes.

'Why?' I asked. 'I'm not going anywhere. I was just about to get in the shower.'

Cat was still in her nightie, but she had put on mascara, lined her eyes, and applied a pale pink lipstick that matched the outfit.

'We're having a party tonight.' She took a sip from her glass. 'Will you come?'

Other people might let their flatmate know in advance that they were having a party. I'd long ago stopped expecting that of Cat. I was no longer surprised when she informed me of a party hours before it was due to start.

I thought about attending. I hadn't planned to do anything tonight, and my brain requires quite a bit of time to process it when plans change. At first I panic, struggle to breathe, go over a hundred reasons the original plan was better in the span of a few seconds. Then I get angry, feel a strong desire to claw and scratch and bite to maintain my plan and not allow it to change. Still, I never enjoyed it when Cat was having her monthly party and I was lying in my room trying to stay out of it. I would have to push my desk chair under the doorknob because there was no lock. Once I was lying on my back in bed when a drunk stranger managed to stumble into the room; he didn't realize I was there until I spoke up. It felt like a violation, like he had just seen me naked. Of course, I wouldn't be able to sleep either. They would be laughing and talking and playing music until the early hours. Sometimes the neighbours from downstairs came up to knock on the door and Cat would have to persuade them not to call the police, promising the music would be turned down. It might be, for a minute or two, until someone asked why the music was so low and someone else turned it all the way up again.

'Sure,' I said. 'When will people start showing up?'

After my shower, I sat on the edge of my bed while she powdered my cheeks and rubbed eyeshadow on to my eyelids. Her face was so close to mine, closer than I think it had ever been before. There was a crease on her forehead from the concentration, her teeth biting into her lip. She was not wearing foundation, and she put none on me. Cat never needed foundation. Her skin was silky smooth and evenly coloured. Mine was not quite so flawless; I could not afford the kinds of face treatments she could. I did not have the money to inject my face with my own blood or cover it with gold. Cat said nothing about my blemishes and blackheads, even as she stared straight at them.

She dabbed her own lip gloss on my lips. It tasted like I imagined she would. She patted it with a finger and I felt the sudden urge to suck her finger into my mouth. Would she tell me to stop?

I didn't do it, of course. I had always been attracted to Cat, but I knew she wouldn't be interested. Besides, it's best not to make a move on someone you live with. You don't shit where you eat.

'You're beautiful,' she said softly, almost whispering.

'You're a good liar,' I said.

It was true. I had heard Cat tell many lies, and her tone never changed, her face never twitched.

She smiled and shook her head.

When I left my room half an hour later, the party had started. I had purposely waited until around twenty people had arrived, so the gathering would be large enough that we wouldn't have to socialize as one big group. No one notices you in a crowd that big. It was already nearing ten, so I sighed, because there was no chance I would get to sleep on time. I go to bed at midnight, and before that I have to wash my face and read for half an hour to make sure I don't lie awake for ages staring at the ceiling. At least it was Friday.

I pulled down the bottom of the too-short skintight dress I was wearing. Cat had left it on my bed to borrow. In her world that meant I never had to return it. If I tried, she'd wave me away and say she hadn't worn it in ages so I might as well keep it. The dress was maroon, which was one of the colours she'd said suits me. With my bland hair that was somewhere between blonde and brown, and what was apparently my rosy undertone, she'd declared me a 'cool summer' and spent hours telling me what colours that meant I should wear. While I appreciated the effort, I'm still not sure what any of it means.

I'd tried to tame my hair, but that's a battle I've never won. It remains frizzy no matter what I do to it. It doesn't grow past my shoulders whichever products I use or however often I get it trimmed, so I usually keep it short, to make it seem intentional.

The volume of the music was still low enough that people could chat. I strained my ears to recognize one of the poppy eighties songs my mum used to blast when I was little. Cat never used the same playlist for her parties. She curated a new one for each occasion, all linked together in some way that always felt obvious but was often undefinable.

I spotted her across the room. She was wearing a short black-and-white corset dress with bell sleeves, like a

Victorian dress that had been cut off below the hip. She looked like she'd forgotten to tell everyone else that this was a costume party. She looked breathtaking.

Oliver was nearby. I was happy to see him. He raised his hand at me and waved. He was standing by himself, drinking straight from a wine bottle, looking gorgeous in a purple shirt that perfectly complemented his brown skin.

I went over. He didn't hug me; Cat was the only one who always insisted on hugging me. Oliver knew that I despised hugs. At most he'd give me a peck on the cheek, if he was very excited. If it wasn't for Cat, he would've been my best friend. Not that I'd ever tell him that, of course.

I'm your second-best friend? he'd say. *Second to what, her? Is she aware you're supposed to be best friends?*

'Can I have some of that?' I asked.

'Be my guest,' he said.

I took the bottle and drank.

'You look beautiful,' he said.

'Thank you,' I said. 'Cat lent me the dress.'

'Really? Did you check what brand it is? You might sell it for a few hundred.'

'I like it,' I said.

Even though it was a little too tight, which made my stomach protrude. Even though it kept riding up, so that I had to pull down the bottom every once in a while when I walked. This probably wasn't noticeable to anyone else. The ceiling light was off, and the LED strips on the walls tinted everything purple.

'Her entire personality is such a ridiculous display of wealth,' he said. 'There's a piano in your lounge, Louise. Does she even play the piano?'

Someone I didn't know was tipsily playing around at it

just then, pressing random keys in ways that didn't harmonize with the music flowing from the speakers.

'She does,' I said.

I liked to hear it softly from out in the lounge when I lay in bed at night, on the evenings when she was home by herself, without any friends or Henry.

'I don't trust anyone who can afford to have a piano in their lounge,' Oliver said.

He was from a similar background to my own. At the time he supported himself through a successful OnlyFans. Until I met him, I hadn't been aware that gay men were into OnlyFans, but it turns out they are. In the end, men are the same, regardless of sexuality.

Cat had spotted us now, and she came bounding across the room as if we hadn't seen each other in ages.

'Oliver!' she shrieked.

'Cat!' he yelled back.

She threw her arms around him and he lifted her up.

'Oh my god!' he said. 'You look wonderful!'

He put her back down on the floor. 'Thank you!' She smiled at me. 'Always a relief to receive the seal of fashion approval from the gay.'

'It's well deserved,' Oliver said.

'Well, you look absolutely dreamy yourself.' She batted her eyelashes at him. 'You're sure you're not bi?'

It was hard to look away from her when she was flirting, even when it wasn't aimed at me, even when I knew it was a joke.

Oliver put out his hands in an apologetic gesture. 'Alas. Though it's lucky for your Henry, isn't it?'

Cat put a strand of her hair behind her ear and laughed. 'Oh, he doesn't have to know.'

I was reminded that Henry existed. I searched for him in the crowd as Oliver and Cat chatted, and spotted him sitting on the couch speaking to a man I didn't recognize.

'Well, I should be going,' Cat said. 'I need to play hostess and whatnot.' She gripped Oliver's hands tightly and looked him straight in the face. 'You have a good time, both of you. Let me know if you need anything, anything at all.'

With that, she was gone, leaving behind only a faint cloud of her perfume.

'I don't understand how you can live with her,' Oliver said. 'She's so intense.'

'She's not always like this,' I said.

'Come, let's dance,' he said.

No one else was dancing yet. Parties with Cat and Henry's friends sometimes felt like socialite events rather than what I'd always imagined student parties would be like. People were just talking; I'm sure some were discussing politics. I didn't have much to compare this to, though. I hadn't been to many parties in my life. I've never been the kind of person you invite to anything.

'I'm not drunk enough to dance yet,' I said.

'So drink more.'

We had a bit more of the wine he'd brought, and then I took him into the kitchen to find something else. People rarely brought their own bottles to Cat's parties, but she supplied plenty. She offered wine and champagne and expensive liqueurs. The bottles were all over the kitchen counters at this point. Cat's parties always felt spontaneous and unplanned; there were no decorations, no one was invited more than a week in advance, no dress code. Somehow there were still always drinks and snacks available and there was always a new playlist to dance to.

In the fridge I found a six-pack of Henry's beers. I always imagined he liked to drink beer to feel closer to the working class, like a proper man. I poured two of the cans into two of his beer glasses. Oliver joked that their expensive ways were rubbing off on me. They weren't, but I knew how to blend in.

'Stay close to me,' Oliver said, as we were going back into the lounge. 'Stay close to me all night.'

I squeezed his arm. 'I promise.'

They're not going to eat you, I wanted to say, but I wasn't sure that was true.

I kept my promise and held on to him as we ran into another girl I knew from class, Deirdre. Her false lashes were so long they hung over her eyes and gave her a sleepy look, and she talked to Oliver about the philosophy of language and looked out across the room as he explained, as if she wasn't listening at all. I stayed out of the conversation and determined from his tone when I was supposed to laugh.

Meanwhile Cat was drifting through the room, making people laugh and making me jealous. I wished I had just some of that charisma and a quarter of her friend circle. Well, actually, maybe a quarter would be too much.

After an hour the mood to dance finally hit us, meaning we were tipsy, so Oliver and I danced, tight together like we were a couple. Bumping into others on the dance floor without apologizing, simply exchanging glances to acknowledge each other's presence. Other people took our lead, or they were also feeling the effects of the alcohol. The music was all from the eighties: Kate Bush and Bon Jovi and the Bee Gees. We danced and danced and danced.

I was drunk when Cat joined us, throwing her hair around and laughing, swaying along to the music with her face aimed up at the ceiling and her eyes closed. She was definitely drunk. When she looked at me, her eyes were red. Her cheeks were flushed. 'Lolo,' she said, the nickname only she had ever called me. She held my hips as we danced, and she told me I was *so, so sexy*, whispering it into my ear like she'd lost her voice in amazement. Her mouth was so close to my ear I thought she might nibble at my earlobe.

Henry threw himself into the mix, pulling Cat to himself. She melted against him, her hands roving over him the way they'd just been touching me.

'Isn't she gorgeous?' she said, slurring her words.

He made eye contact with me above her head, his gaze burning into me. He looked at me like we shared a secret. Smirking with a soft nod.

'She is,' he said.

I believed him more than I believed Cat. He used to tell me that all the time when I was fucking him.

2

Cat and I met about a month into our master's. We had a seminar on moral philosophy together, and for the first few sessions we didn't talk to each other. I always noticed her, though. She spoke more than anyone else. She always looked glamorous, while the rest of us showed up in sweats and messy buns. Cat was so eye-catching that every time she entered the room or I spotted her somewhere on campus I felt as if I'd glimpsed someone famous.

The first time we spoke, she asked if she could sit next to me and then did so without waiting for an answer. I instantly wondered if I had toothpaste in the corners of my mouth. She smelled just like how I'd imagined she would: fresh and clean and botanical. I'd thought she would be less perfect up close, that she'd have pores or that her hair would be frizzy, but none of that was true. That day she was wearing a top with romantic sleeves which exposed her shoulders, her hair dripping with tiny pearls.

'I can't sit next to the girl with the mullet again,' she said. 'She always asks the most stupid questions.'

I'd thought the girl with the mullet was her friend. They hugged every time they saw each other and would walk out of the seminar chatting and smiling. I had wondered why, though, because the girl with the mullet did ask the most ridiculous questions.

Cat sighed. 'God, I sound like an absolute bitch, don't I?'

The girl with the mullet came into the room. She saw

Cat sitting at the far end of the table, and I watched as her gaze drifted over to me, occupying the only seat next to Cat.

'Hey, Cat,' she said.

'Hi!' said Cat.

She smiled so wide I couldn't believe it was fake. She sounded so cheery. The girl with the mullet sat down far away from us, and the smile faded from Cat's face instantly. I couldn't help but stare. I'd tried to do what she was doing; I'd tried to pretend to care about people I couldn't give two fucks about; I'd tried to look like I was listening when I wasn't, and every single time I was called out on it. Everyone knew just how cold and unusual I was.

She turned back to me. 'I'm sorry,' she said. 'I didn't introduce myself. I'm Cat.'

'Louise,' I said.

'Louise,' she said. 'I love your sweater. Where did you get it?'

My cheeks felt red and hot at the compliment. Usually only men ever complimented me, and that's different. It's nothing like being complimented by a woman as beautiful as Cat.

'I can't remember,' I lied, because it was a charity-shop find, and Cat carried her laptop in a Karl Lagerfeld bag.

'Well, it's gorgeous,' she said, opening said laptop. 'Cool colours really suit you. By the way, though, there's a bit of foundation on the sleeve.'

I covered the sleeve with my hand. She was right, of course. There was a patch of beige on the sleeve of my white sweater. I wondered how many other people had seen it.

Cat winked at me. 'We girls have to look out for each other,' she said.

After the seminar, she asked if I was going anywhere for

lunch. I suspected she was stalling, based on the fact that the girl with the mullet was lingering in the doorway.

'I don't know,' I said.

I had planned to go nowhere for lunch. I didn't eat lunch; I couldn't afford three meals every day, and lunch was the disposable one.

'Do you like Greek food?' she said. 'There's this Greek place I recommend to absolutely everyone; no one's ever been disappointed.'

I'd woken up that day in the cheap room I was renting in a flat I'd found on Gumtree. By lunchtime I was eating a souvlaki next to Cat. I felt like I was still asleep and dreaming, but I refused to pinch myself. She talked for ages about everything and nothing. Most notably she also asked me about myself. She asked where I was from, and I told her I'd grown up two hours away by train. I didn't mention that this was the furthest I could have moved for uni without my mother dying of stress.

'Do you live in halls, then?' asked Cat. 'Or with friends?'

I laughed at this. Living in halls was the worst thing I could possibly imagine, but I wouldn't call my flatmate a friend. That morning he'd crossed a line, and so I found myself spilling everything to the gorgeous stranger who'd bought me souvlaki.

Mason worked in a pub. He left dishes in the sink every night, and he didn't own a Hoover or a mop. I stopped wearing white socks because within a few hours they'd be black underneath. I could have lived with that, but it wasn't the worst of it.

Mason once asked me if I owned a vibrator and if that was what he'd heard from my room the night before. It was, of course, but I lied. I stopped masturbating because I didn't want him to hear it again. The morning I met Cat, he'd sat me down and told me he thought I should pay more of the electric bill because my showers were longer than his. Apparently he'd spent a week timing them.

When I told him I wouldn't be doing that, he said there were other arrangements we could make. There were other ways I could make up my share of the bill. He winked at me. I wouldn't have been as offended if he'd suggested I could sleep with him in exchange for the rent money, but just the electric bill? I was worth more than that.

I recounted all this to Cat. She stared at me with wide eyes and put her hand over her mouth. At the time I thought she was exaggerating, but I would come to realize she was probably being genuine. Something like that would never have happened to her. I'm not sure she's ever been catcalled. Despite her striking looks and the way that she dressed, despite how men stared, she exuded something that made them keep their mouths shut.

'I have a spare room,' she said. Like she was a deity sent here to help me.

'Are you looking for a flatmate?'

'Not looking, exactly. My parents wanted to use it as a guest room when they come to visit, though I'd much rather have you there. They can stay in a hotel.'

I stared at her in astonishment. I'd never imagined having a spare bedroom that you didn't need to use or rent out. I knew people existed who did, but it caught me off guard how casually Cat spoke about it. As if everyone could choose between a spare room and a flatmate that not so secretly wants to fuck you.

'Your parents own the flat?' I asked in disbelief.

I had heard about these mysterious students whose

parents could afford to purchase flats for their children, flats that would then go on to be rented out to others or simply stand empty until they felt like having a holiday in another city. Then they'd remember, *oh, how convenient, don't we own a property over there? Is anyone staying in it?* Like housing was Tupperware you sometimes lent out.

'Oh, no,' Cat said. 'I own the place. My parents just paid for it. Hold on, I think I have some pictures I could show you.'

I didn't need to see the pictures to know that I would say yes. Of course I would. Fate was never this kind to me. I expected her to show me a box room with just enough space for a single bed and a desk. That would be more than enough if it came with the promise of not counting every second as I showered, if it meant living with this fairy-like creature with exposed collarbones, wearing so much jewellery she even had it in her hair.

It was not a box room. The room she showed me was larger than any lounge I'd ever had growing up. It was already fitted with a king-size bed and a wardrobe, and it had large bay windows with floor-length curtains.

'Are you interested?' Cat asked.

I knew there was no way I could afford to live with her.

'How much do you want for it?' I said.

'You know, I hadn't thought about that. Let's check the average rent online.'

I stared at her as she typed it into the search bar, amazed that she could be so unaware of the world around her. The area name she typed in was one so expensive I never would have dreamed of living there.

'My goodness,' Cat said. 'That's quite a bit, isn't it?'

The average for a single room in a shared flat was several hundred pounds beyond my budget.

'Hmm.' Cat looked at the screen and carefully applied some balm to her lips. 'Well, I wouldn't feel fair charging you that. It's not as if I need the money. How about we do two hundred per month? Since we've been friends for two hours.'

I couldn't believe my luck. I also couldn't believe she already considered us friends.

Nearly nine months later, I woke up in that room the night after the party. Oliver was next to me in bed, stripped down to his boxers, with one of my pillows between us like a barrier. I was still wearing the dress Cat had lent me. The room was hot and the fabric stuck to my skin, my body slick with sweat from the thick duvet.

I thought of the place more as Cat's than a flat we shared. The changes I'd made to my bedroom had been minor. The only signs that I lived here were the desk covered in sketchpads, the books on the bookshelf and the storage box I'd turned into a mouse cage. Perhaps I would have felt less like a house guest if I paid more rent.

I got out of bed and looked at myself in the full-length mirror. I hadn't taken off my make-up the night before, and the products that Cat had so carefully applied to my face were now smeared across it. The mascara was creating dark circles around my eyes, the eyeshadow faded. There were marks on my white pillowcase. Oliver snored.

I checked on the mice in their cage. I couldn't remember if I'd fed them before I collapsed. They were both awake. Pip was grooming herself on top of their nest, and Squeak was digging a hole in the bedding.

'Hello, babies,' I whispered.

Squeak immediately came running over towards me,

climbing up a branch and putting her nose to the mesh at the top of the cage. Squeak was sociable. She would always come towards me when I was near, and she would climb up my arm as soon as I put my hand in there. Run up and down my entire body trying to make it to the floor, and sit on my hip grooming herself. I was not fooled; there was no real affection there, I was nothing but a climbing frame to her. Pip, on the other hand, was cautious, suspicious. She didn't take treats from my hand for the first few weeks, instead watching me. She rarely ventured up my sleeve, preferring to stay on ground level. But with her I felt loved. She groomed me sometimes, the bonding ritual mice perform on each other. Squeak never sat still long enough for me to touch her, but I could rub Pip's face for several minutes and she'd sit there and enjoy it, her teeth grinding with contentment. She watched me now, as she always did.

I opened the cage and fed them, fending off Squeak's attempts at escape, until she relented, grabbed a piece of food and retreated into one of the old toilet rolls I had thrown in there.

'*Guten Morgen,*' said Oliver, who was always learning a new language.

I turned around. He had got up on to his elbows and squinted sleepily at me.

'Good morning,' I said.

'You look a fright.'

'So do you,' I replied.

He sank back on to the pillow with a hungover groan.

'Get up,' I said. 'I need to go to the library.'

I walked him home on my way there, pushing my bicycle. His sunglasses covering his eyes, he went into a little independent coffee shop near university and bought himself some coffee. We said goodbye outside his flat, and I hopped on my bike and rode down to the library to force myself to do some dissertation-related reading.

Campus was quiet this time of year, the period after exams but before the undergraduate graduations. People who have a reason to be elsewhere tend to leave university when they can. I was not one of those people. In the library I took the stairs up to the annex and went searching for a copy of the *Groundwork*. If you're going to argue against Kant, it's the only book you need to read; the arguments write themselves. Unlike the rest of the library, the annex wasn't well organized. Books overflowed from the shelves and the signs that had once signalled where to go had long since peeled and faded. There were no windows in here, but the dim light from the ceiling lamps was just enough to help me make my way.

The old books were badly catalogued and many had no tags on the inside that would alert anyone if I grabbed one and went outside without checking it out. I ran my fingers along the spines, enjoying the changes in texture and the grooves where one book transitioned into another.

It only took me a few minutes to find a copy of the *Groundwork*. Pages came off in my hand when I opened it; I picked them up off the floor and matched the page numbers to the book to put them back in the right place.

The rest of the library was likely to be occupied, so I chose to stay in the annex and found myself a couch. Being around people is tiring. I'm always conscious of them, aware of every effort I have to put into standing up and walking around and the facial expressions I make. Not that I think everyone is staring at me, but they might be.

I read, and I remembered exactly why Cat called Kant

'Cunt'. The sentences were so long, running on and on as if he thought commas and full stops were interchangeable. The language was archaic and convoluted. He wrote with far too much certainty about the way the world works for someone who had never left Königsberg.

When I'd had as much Kant as I could handle, I took out my sketchbook and drew his face as I pondered. Drawing had been the only thing that kept me sane in school. The sound of the pencil against the paper could bring my heart rate down to a normal level when other students were too loud, the lights too bright or the lessons too unpredictable. I gave my drawing of Kant far too much lip filler.

My phone rang. It was my mum. Of course it was; I had a therapy session on the coming Monday. She would need to make sure I hadn't forgotten. I rolled my eyes. I had not forgotten, but I hadn't planned to go, either. Now it would be impossible to pretend it had slipped my mind. Mum has always thought I'm much more scatterbrained and forgetful than I am. Every time there has been an event I didn't want to attend, a job she wanted me to apply for that I wasn't interested in, homework I had no intention of doing, I would tell her I forgot. *It completely slipped my mind*; *I just happened to miss the deadline*; *god, what an idiot I am* . . . Every Christmas she purchased a new calendar for me.

I let the phone go to voicemail anyway. Usually I would force myself to pick up once a week. That was about as much as I think she would be willing to accept in terms of me ignoring her. Not even a minute later her texts rolled in.

Just wanted to make sure you don't forget therapy on Monday! You know how important it is, Louise.

Also, I'd really like to hear your voice, could we do a short phone call when you have time? Just a quick one.

I let out a deep sigh. There was no way to avoid either her or the therapy session.

Funnily enough, Mum was the reason I started studying philosophy. When I was little, she always called me philosophical. I was an inquisitive child, and I found a way to question everything. Why did I have to say thank you if someone did something nice? Why did I have to say it in a certain tone of voice for it to sound genuine? Why did she get to tell me what to do? She would laugh at me, sometimes amused and smiling. Sometimes bashful and blushing, throwing an awkward glance at the people around us. Sometimes exasperated, with her hands on her hips and a shake of the head.

'You're a little philosopher, aren't you?' she would tell me.

When I asked her what a philosopher was, she couldn't quite tell me. She hummed and mulled it over, started her explanation and stopped and started over again. *Well, you see – It's someone who –*

When I was around nine, I took it upon myself to figure it out. I asked Mum to use our laptop, an ancient thing that took ages to start and which had to be turned off after an hour at most so it wouldn't overheat. Mum kept it in a cupboard, so rarely did we actually use the thing. I placed it on the kitchen table and started googling philosophers. I came across all the classic old names of white Western men who thought they had the whole world figured out. All the internet was able to tell me was that a philosopher was someone who studied philosophy. So what was philosophy? It sent me down a rabbit hole I was still digging my way out of.

I came home in the evening and heard the piano as soon as I opened the door. It sounded beautiful. Light and airy, like dancing in dewy grass holding hands with the fairies. I listened from the entrance hall for a little while. As soon as I bent down to take off my shoes and the wooden floor creaked beneath me, the piano went silent.

I had never seen Cat play. It seemed an inconsistency to me; Cat, so full of confidence, the life of every party, the loudest voice in any room, unwilling ever to play piano in front of me. I would hear her playing from my bedroom at night, when she assumed I was asleep, or I would be able to listen from the entry hall like this, if I had been silent enough in closing the front door. Everything was quiet now, and I imagined us both just waiting, still, like terrified little mice, neither of us moving a wink. Only a wall separating us from each other, both of us waiting for the other.

It had been nice to hear her playing. It meant Henry wasn't there.

I took a deep breath and went into the lounge. Cat had cleaned up from the party, mostly. There was a large bin bag in the corner of the room, and she hadn't wiped off the liquid rings from glasses on the coffee table.

'You don't need to stop for me,' I said.

Cat was still sitting on the piano stool, with her back to me, but her head turned slightly in my direction. She had a soft smile on her face.

'You know I don't like it when people can hear,' she said.

'I don't know why you care,' I said. 'You're clearly good at this.'

'Yes, but not when someone is listening. I never am.' She slid to the side and patted the stool beside her. 'Come, sit.'

Cat didn't come to you; she told you to come to her. It didn't matter to her whether you did or not. She didn't need you to. You simply did what Cat said.

I sat next to her. She was looking down at the piano and pressed one key with one of her fingers, over and over, a light sound escaping every time.

'I'm worried I was embarrassing last night,' she said.

'What makes you say that?' I asked.

'I said some silly things, didn't I? I think I should apologize.'

'Why?'

I looked at her face, but she didn't reciprocate. I wanted to hear her say it.

She blushed, shook her head. 'I called you "sexy", didn't I? I acted like I was flirting with you.'

Of course, she hadn't actually been flirting with me.

'That's OK,' I said.

'It's not. I don't want you to think that I . . . well, not that I don't . . .' She trailed off and bit her lip.

'What?' I whispered.

Not that I don't. It felt like she was about to say something momentous.

Instead, she looked at me and smiled. 'Nothing.' Her voice went high and returned to its natural state. 'Shall we have dinner together? I was planning to make chicken parmigiana.'

'You don't need to cook for me,' I said.

'You need a proper meal,' she said. 'What else would you be having, porridge?'

'Don't be ridiculous. Porridge is for breakfast. I would've had some ramen.'

I said it with a straight face, just the way I knew she loved.

She giggled. 'I won't have you eating ramen again,' she said. 'I'll cook. It's decided.'

We hung out in the kitchen as she cooked. When I moved in, I thought we'd be the kind of flatmates that were strictly flatmates. Instead, Cat had insisted on cooking for me and the two of us watching a film together every week. She invited me to something almost daily; she always had plans. I typically accepted the ones that were affordable and didn't involve other people. We'd gone shopping, we'd been to the cinema, we'd had study dates in the library.

She played music on her phone, showing me a new band she had discovered, while I doodled in one of my smaller sketchbooks. I didn't much like their sound, but I pretended to. Cat likes emotional indie music with meaningful lyrics. I prefer music that doesn't force you to think. It needs to be loud and someone should ideally be screaming.

While she was chopping garlic I checked the time.

I was supposed to be doing a FaceTime call with Alistair that night. Per his request, in-person meetings were once every two weeks and video calls once a week. It wasn't going to happen that evening, though. I had already said yes to spending it with Cat, which meant there was no chance I would be free any time before one a.m. I messaged him to let him know, promising I would make it up to him when I could. Wink emoji.

Cat wanted to watch *Strangers on a Train* with me. She was always watching something black and white from the fifties in those days. I said yes, of course. As far as Cat knew, I loved those kinds of films too. I told her my favourite film was the one where Greta Garbo plays Queen Christina of Sweden, which was released before the Second World War. She was impressed that I would know about it, let alone enjoy it. Even Cat hadn't watched that one. Neither had I, obviously. I looked up these things online, secretly and frantically, because she made me feel like I should have known about them all along.

'How is your dissertation coming along?' I asked, putting my sketchbook to the side and feeling useless as she chopped an onion. I had offered to help, but Cat didn't accept assistance if she was cooking.

She sighed, bringing the knife down with force. 'It isn't,' she said. 'Not yet.'

'You're doing psychological egoism, aren't you?' I said. 'Remind me what it is?'

Cat chopped the onion into tiny, tiny pieces as she explained. 'It's the idea that you can only be motivated to do something if it's in your own interest. That true altruism doesn't exist.'

'And what's your take?' I asked.

She shrugged. 'I think it's on to something.'

'But what about charity?' I said. 'If I give some money to a homeless person, that's not in my best interest. It leaves less money for me. But people still do it.'

'Yes, they do it,' Cat said. 'But they do it because they want the people around them to consider them a good person. Or because doing something good for someone makes them feel good about themselves. There's no such thing as true altruism.'

'So the reason you offered to cook for me –'

'Is entirely selfish.' She smiled a wicked smile. 'I have two chicken breasts that expire today.'

We ate on the couch in front of the film. Her eyes were big and wide the whole time, not even looking down at her plate as she rolled the spaghetti around her fork and ate it the Italian way. I didn't much like chicken parmigiana, but that was yet another thing I didn't tell her. I didn't live on ramen and porridge because I couldn't cook; I did it because they were foods I enjoyed, foods that were safe. They always taste the same; you can't mess up the seasoning and end up with something way too salty. Every bite is consistent with the last – no pieces of fat or chewiness. Besides, food is food. I didn't care enough about it to waste time cooking. I forced myself to eat Cat's cooking, slowly emptying my plate.

She sat with her head on my shoulder and laughed. Oliver would say it was rude and inconsiderate of her not to realize that I didn't enjoy physical contact with people. What he didn't know was that Cat was the exception.

3

Mum had one condition when I told her I wanted to go to university. She didn't make me promise that I wouldn't have careless sex or party too hard; she didn't ask that I fund everything myself with student loans and scholarships. All she requested was that I sign up with the university counselling services, and then she would let me leave home.

I obeyed. Back then, Mum made me feel fragile, full of carefully contained insanity that might spill out at any moment. For my first year I was as good a therapy patient as I was a student. I took notes in the sessions. I did all the workbooks my counsellor gave me. Every night I wrote in my diary, noting down thoughts and feelings to bring up in my next session. I was willing to put everything under her magnifying glass, reading way too much into my dislike for a particular film or my attraction to someone or other. Was it because he had the same accent as my father, who I hadn't had a close relationship with since I was about five years old? Maybe it was just because he was devilishly handsome and extremely charming, but what did I know? If the therapist said something, I listened carefully, nodding along to her every suggestion.

During the second year, I was tired of all that. My studies were getting more intense, and I didn't have the time or the energy to work on the project of my mental health. It had become clear to me that I wasn't as unstable as my mum had made me feel. I had been living on my own for a while by then, managing my studies all right, and nothing bad had happened. I hadn't slit my wrists, and I hadn't had a crying fit in a shop. In fact, I hadn't had a crying fit in a shop since I was a child. Did I really need therapy? I had also realized that Mum would never find out if I didn't go, so I began to skip sessions. Soon enough, I stopped making new appointments altogether. I said I simply felt I didn't need therapy any more, and the overwhelmed university counselling service was happy to be rid of me.

In the third year I lied to Mum about still going. I made up stories about discoveries I had made about myself or topics we'd discussed in the sessions. It went well, until it didn't. Once, when she was visiting, I needed some space and told her I was going to a counselling session. Half an hour later, we bumped into each other in H&M. I tried to convince her my appointment had been cancelled. Mum, suspicious as always, demanded to see some sort of booking confirmation or evidence of me still attending. I had nothing to provide. A screaming match ensued, the biggest fight we'd ever had.

When I decided to do a master's, I accepted that it would involve going back to counselling, if only to keep the peace. I still skipped sessions, but Mum was more involved now. She knew when my appointments were, and she would ask about it more often, keeping track to make sure I went. That's why I found myself once again sitting alone in the small waiting room next to two empty chairs. I used the time to draw in my sketchbook. I've always found drawing a better form of therapy than talking to people.

'Louise.' Susannah stood in the doorway of her office, smiling softly. She always smiled at me as though she'd just had to give me some awful news. At least she was less over-bearing and intense than my counsellor during undergrad.

I followed her into the room and sat down on the chair across from her desk.

'I was disappointed not to see you last week,' she said.

'I'm sure you weren't,' I said. 'It gave you an hour off.'

She chuckled. 'We don't get time off here. If someone cancels, there's plenty of paperwork to do.'

'I had a migraine,' I said.

'Goodness,' she said. 'Those are terrible. Do you know what might have triggered it?'

'Are you suggesting I'm stressed?'

She looked at me. 'Are you?'

'No,' I said.

'Would you like anything to drink?' Susannah asked.

'I'm all right,' I said.

I know you are supposed to say 'thank you' after offers like that. I know how phrases like 'please' and 'thank you' and 'you're welcome' work. I just think they should be voluntary.

'How are you otherwise?' Susannah asked. She opened the top of her Thermos and took a sip.

'I'm perfectly fine,' I said.

She eyed me as if she suspected me to be lying, as she always did. I wasn't. I usually didn't.

'You're still taking your medication?'

I frowned. 'Of course I am. Why are you asking?'

'I was only wondering. It's been quite a while now, and I was thinking you might want to discuss your medication with the psychiatrist again. See that you're on the right dosage and all that. We could book you in for that, if you'd like.'

35

I knew she was lying through her teeth. She didn't want to reassess my medication. She wanted to know I was still stable, that I was still taking it. The way you check a dog's mouth for the pills to make sure it's actually swallowed them. I swear, you spend a few months as an inpatient in a mental health unit at seventeen and people will always have you labelled as mentally unstable and a danger to yourself.

'If I have to,' I said.

'You don't.'

'Then I'd rather not. My medication is fine. I take it every day.'

'I was just checking,' she said. She grinned at me. 'I want to know you're doing fine, Louise.'

I held my arms out to my sides. 'I am.'

I then remembered to smile to make it more convincing, because no one who's been an inpatient in a mental health unit wants to go back.

Susannah still didn't look quite convinced. She raised one corner of her mouth and made a note in her little notebook. I wished I could see what she was writing.

'Are you seeing anyone?' she asked.

'No. You know I'm not.'

'I know I asked you a few months ago, but I thought the answer might have changed.'

'It won't,' I said. 'I've already told you. I'm never dating again.'

Susannah looked at me. I didn't want her to probe this further. The question always annoyed me, and the answer had never changed in all the time I'd seen her. It had been many years since I'd made the choice that romance was not for me. For some reason people never believed me. They always chuckled and shook their heads; they winked and said,

Oh, you'll find the right person one day. That was the problem. I might find the right person, but I absolutely shouldn't.

'Well,' Susannah said, 'sometimes we change our minds, is all.'

You should pray I never do, I thought.

'I don't,' I said. 'I'm quite determined.'

'Help me help you,' she said. 'That's all I'm here to do, Louise.'

'You're here to spy on me for my mother.'

Susannah pursed her lips together. She stared at me for a moment and then made another note. She was probably writing that I was paranoid. But Susannah couldn't care less about my romantic life. Mum would be the one who was worried. Mum was always monitoring my relationships for hints of love, worried that history would repeat itself.

'I hope you don't actually mean that,' Susannah said, still writing. 'You know everything you tell me is completely confidential.'

Unless, of course, I told her anything that might indicate myself or someone else was in danger. *Susannah, I know everything about confidentiality.*

'I didn't mean it,' I lied.

'I'm here to meet someone,' I told the waitress.

'What's the name?' she said, smiling genially.

I looked over her shoulder into the restaurant. I could already see him. He sat at a round table in the middle of the room, staring down at his phone. No doubt he was texting me. I was a couple of minutes late. I'd been sketching and lost track of time; I'd needed to recover after my session with Susannah, but Alistair was a very punctual man. I always disobeyed him a little bit; he liked to punish me.

'He's right there, actually,' I said. 'Thank you.'

I made my way over towards him. My phone buzzed in my clutch. My new dress flowed around my feet and made me feel like I was floating across the room. It was exactly the sort of dress he would pick out for me. There was a slit on one side, and it showed plenty of cleavage. I had to wear nipple pasties to keep my boobs looking good. It was the perfect blend of classy and sexy; glamorous enough to allow me into a place like this, revealing enough that he could stare at me throughout dinner. The tag on my neck was irritating me something awful; I couldn't stop thinking about it. But I'd left it on. I would return the dress after tonight. I would rather have the money.

'Hello,' I said.

Alistair looked up. He smiled, delighted.

'You're late,' he said.

'I know.'

I bent down and kissed him on the cheek. I pulled out my chair and sat down.

'You look gorgeous,' he said.

I grinned. 'I know.'

I was wearing one of Cat's necklaces. It dangled so beautifully into the exposed cleavage between my breasts. It was likely a proper brand, something that used solid gold and real diamonds. She was so blasé about letting me borrow things like that. She probably wouldn't notice if I never returned it; if she did notice, she wouldn't care.

His eyes wouldn't leave my chest. He stared at me, transfixed, and licked his lips like he was preparing for a good meal.

'Are you wearing my other gift too?' he asked.

'Of course I am,' I said.

'How does it feel?'

I leaned across the table and placed my face next to his ear. 'It feels incredible,' I whispered.

His breath hitched. If I'd put my hand on his crotch right then, I would've felt a hard-on.

I'd lied again, but he could never tell. His other gift was inside my arse. I couldn't feel it very much at all. I was only aware of it because I felt compelled to clench every time I moved, to avoid it dropping to the floor in the middle of this fancy restaurant. There was a chandelier, for god's sake.

'Did you take a picture like I asked you to?' Alistair said.

I positioned my leg against his under the table. 'I forgot.' I batted my lashes. 'You can see it later,' I said sweetly.

'Christ,' he moaned.

Alistair was not a bad-looking man, especially for a white guy well over fifty. He was old enough to have wrinkles and for his hair to be greying, but he had a hard body and a face a little bit like Pierce Brosnan's. That's why I chose him, why I replied when he messaged me on the website. We had an initial video call, and I was surprised that he looked exactly like his pictures.

He was wearing a suit tonight and the top button of his shirt was open with just a glint of his silver chest hair peeking out. I made sure to look at it longingly and bite my lip. I knew it would drive him wild to think I wanted him as badly as he wanted me. After seven months of this arrangement, I knew exactly how to get him going.

'Are you ready to order?'

There was a waiter at our table now with a small notepad.

'Oh,' I said. I pulled my leg back from Alistair's and he cleared his throat. 'I haven't had a chance to look at the menu yet.'

'There's no need,' Alistair said. 'I've decided what we'll be having.'

I raised my eyebrow, a hint of disapproval on my mouth, but I didn't mind. He could choose what I would eat if he wanted to. It was part of the power play, or it was part of his punishment for me being late and for 'forgetting' to take a picture of my arse with his butt plug in it. Either way, he gave me enough money that he could do whatever he liked. If the food was bad, I'd make some noodles at home.

'Go on, then,' I said. 'What are we having?'

One of my favourite things about our arrangement was the predictability of it. We always followed the same routine: dinner and a hotel. I never had to be anxious about surprise plans.

That night we took a taxi to the hotel. I'd never seen Alistair's home. He might have had a wife, or children, or both. I never asked. It didn't concern me what he did with the rest of his life. I didn't care about being the other woman. A cheater is a cheater, whether you say no to them or not. He'd have found someone else if it wasn't me.

I hadn't been lying to Susannah when I said I wasn't seeing anyone. Alistair didn't count. What was happening was purely sexual. And financial, of course. We didn't meet on a dating site. We met on a site where men with money look for women to spend it on, and where women who want money find men they're willing to fuck for it. We laid out our expectations and negotiated the terms for the relationship before we ever met in person. In my opinion, all relationships should be that clear-cut and honest.

He held his hand on my lower back as he checked us in. The receptionist glanced at me as she took his details and tapped at her keyboard, nodding her head at what he was saying. I smiled at her. I knew what we must look like: him so much older, me in this gorgeous dress and an expensive necklace, my earrings glittering in the light, with my hair pulled behind my ears. It was always women who seemed to care; men never did. Women sneered at me as if it was their own husband I was with. Hell, for all I knew, it might be.

'Thanks,' Alistair said, accepting the key cards she'd slid across the desk towards him. 'Have a great night.'

'You too,' she said.

He chuckled as we walked away, leaning his mouth close to my ear. 'I certainly will,' he whispered.

I laughed, not because it was funny, but because he wanted me to.

We took the lift up to the top floor. The room was large, with a king-size bed with expensive satin sheets. It was one of the nicest he'd taken me to, much more luxurious than any hotel room I'd ever be able to afford myself. I walked over to the windows and looked outside as Alistair took off his coat and shoes. You could see the whole city from here, the lights standing out against the black night, the cars emitting rays of yellow, orange and red.

'This is incredible,' I said.

I could feel his breath against my neck now, his hands at my waist.

'I've been thinking about you for a week,' he said.

He kissed my neck and ran his hands over my arse. I leaned back against his crotch, and I could feel how hard he was. My lower stomach tingled with anticipation. He gripped my hair suddenly, balling it all up into his hand. He pushed my face against the cold glass and I gasped at the shock of it.

'And you made me wait,' he said. 'Didn't you?'

'I did,' I said, smiling. 'I'm sorry.'

'You don't sound very sorry.'

'I could show you how sorry I am.'

'Was it intentional?'

I twisted my face so I could just about glance back at him. 'Maybe.'

'Then yes,' he said. 'Show me how sorry you are. But first, show me how beautiful my other gift looks in you.'

He led me to the bed by my hair and I obliged. We were a good match, he and I. We mostly enjoyed the same things, and I was kind enough to allow him to do the things I didn't enjoy too. Even kind enough to pretend to love them. This was one of those things. His grip was too hard, pulling at the roots of my hair and angering my scalp. *I'll allow it*, I thought. *The man has suffered enough tonight.*

He bent me over the bed and finally let go of my hair, using both hands to pull my dress up. He tugged my pants down and let them drop to the floor around my heels.

'Oh my god,' he said. He stroked my arse like he'd never seen it before.

The butt plug was gorgeous, I had to admit. It was a dark red with a diamond in the middle. I had quite enjoyed wearing it; it isn't every day one gets to walk around with a diamond in one's arse. Alistair gripped it and started turning it around. I could feel it move inside me, and the sensation was not unpleasant.

'Oh,' I said, and giggled.

'Does it feel good?' he asked, his voice husky and low.

'Yes,' I said. 'Please touch me.'

'Nuh-uh. I think you deserve a bit more punishment.'

*

He ordered me an Uber home afterwards. It was already past one a.m. when I walked in through the front door, careful to be as quiet as possible. I felt pretty satisfied. The food, though not my usual cuisine, had been decent. The fucking had been more than decent. He'd even said I could bring my vibrator next time; he'd like to torture me with it. I was very excited at the prospect.

I stepped into the lounge with my heels in my hands and stopped. Henry was there. He was sitting on the couch and the TV was on with no sound. We simply looked at each other.

It was probably the first time we'd been alone together since he stopped sleeping with me and started sleeping with Cat. I wasn't sure which one of us was avoiding the other. We'd never had much to talk about anyway.

Honestly, I wasn't even sure if I liked Henry. It was better that way, because it's hard to accidentally catch feelings for someone you don't like. He met my two criteria: he was handsome and he didn't want a relationship, so we had had fun for a while. I suppose most people would change their mind about relationships after meeting Cat.

'Can't sleep?' I asked.

'I was waiting for you, actually. You were out late. I wanted to make sure you made it home safe.'

'And if I'd stayed out overnight? Would you have been awake all night waiting for me?'

He laughed. 'I'd probably have given up at some point.'

Which was just the Henry I knew. His affections only stretched so far, if affections were what they could be called. I didn't know what to say, so I was silent.

'You look nice,' he said.

I wondered if he was still attracted to me, if he was

thinking right now about what was underneath my dress. My body used to drive him wild. That isn't something you can will away, is it? I still found him quite attractive, his hands especially. I could watch him cooking and get distracted by the veins on the back of his hands, and the fingers he'd done such wonderful things to me with.

'Thank you,' I said. 'Is your girlfriend asleep?'

I watched a slight smile grow on his face. His eyes drifted downwards to my dress, and he looked amused.

'She should be,' he said. It sounded so suggestive.

Yes, I thought, he was still attracted to me. Henry and I had never talked about our past since he started dating Cat, and Cat and I had only occasionally and briefly touched on it, but there was no doubt in my mind that part of him still wanted me.

'Then we should stop talking,' I said. 'She's a light sleeper.'

Cat and Henry's relationship was, like many things, my fault. They met because I brought him to Cat's birthday party, just a few weeks after we moved in together. She was radiant that day, her dress a bright bubblegum pink that perfectly matched her outrageous lipstick. I could've eaten her whole, and I suppose it was no surprise that Henry was also enchanted.

The surprise came from her being enchanted by him.

'Well, hello,' she said. 'You must be Louise's little anarchist.'

Which was the way we'd referred to him in those days, on account of his philosophical interests and his confusing admiration of Stirner. 'Going to see the anarchist?' she'd say with a wink and a smile, because we'd both agreed that any other term for someone you're regularly having casual sex with is far too awkward.

'Unless she has another one, I suppose I am,' he said,

laughing softly. I could have given him a worse nickname, I suppose. 'Are you the birthday girl?'

'I am.' She held out her hand for him. 'I'm Catherine.'

We both expected him to shake it; instead he took her hand and kissed the knuckles, as if we were in a Regency romance novel.

Cat chuckled. She met my eyes like she was assessing my reaction.

'It's a pleasure to meet you, Catherine,' Henry said. 'Louise has told me a lot about you.'

Cat smiled. I couldn't quite tell what it meant.

'Only good things, I'm sure,' she said.

'No,' Henry said. 'Terrible things.'

She laughed loudly. It took me by surprise. Her laughs were usually controlled, carefully executed, delivered at the right time at exactly the right volume with precisely the right level of enthusiasm. Another thing I envied about her.

'Then I suppose you've heard that I'm sustained entirely by devouring annoying men and spitting out their bones,' she said.

'I'll try my best not to be annoying, then,' Henry said.

She smiled lightly. 'Don't,' she said. 'I'm very hungry.'

Afterwards she would take me aside and ask if it would be odd if she asked him out.

No, there were no feelings involved.

We weren't exclusive, were we?

No, and we never would be.

4

A few days later I was sitting on my floor drawing when Cat knocked on the door.

'Lolo? Can I come in?'

'Of course.'

I closed the sketchbook so she wouldn't see; I'd been drawing Maisie. I often did, just to make sure I never forgot her face. I still knew where to place every mole. Cat wasn't meant to know about Maisie. I turned myself around to face her and she sat down on my bed.

'Do you have a boyfriend?' Cat asked, her gaze roving across my room as if everything there was more interesting than my face.

'No,' I said.

I'd never told her that I was romantically celibate; Oliver was the only one who knew. Even him I hadn't told voluntarily; it had all spilled out of me when I was too drunk for my own good. Of course, she didn't know about Alistair either. She should have, but she'd never questioned how I paid my rent or how I sometimes wore the same brands as her. Did she truly think my mother, a single parent who worked as a teacher, was supporting me? Perhaps she did. It seems like something a rich person might think.

'Do you have a girlfriend?' Cat asked.

I laughed. 'No,' I said. 'Why?'

'Henry said you came home very late last night in a nice dress,' she said. 'He was struggling to sleep. He said it looked like you'd been on a date.'

I didn't know which one of us he'd told the truth to. He had more reason to lie to her, but I knew for a fact he had insomnia.

'I had been,' I said. 'But I'm not dating anyone regularly.'

She nodded her head and hummed softly. 'But you do like girls, don't you?'

She said it as if I hadn't already told her long ago. Maybe she didn't remember. It was the sort of fact that was irrelevant to her, that she'd forget as soon as the conversation was over.

'Yes,' I said. 'What's with all the questions?'

'Well . . .'

She pursed her lips and grabbed one of my cushions, picking at it as I waited. It felt so strange to see her tongue-tied and awkward. Cat was the sort of person who was never embarrassed about anything. She'd told me when she'd had diarrhoea, for god's sake.

'Henry had this idea,' she said. 'Really, it's quite silly. It's just an idea.'

I felt as though she wanted me to interject here, but I didn't know what she wanted me to say. I didn't, because I was curious to see what she would go on to talk about. She was blushing, her cheeks pink under the hair hanging over her face.

'He said he'd like to have a threesome,' she said.

Silence.

'Ah,' I said.

'With another girl,' she said. 'Obviously.'

I nodded. I'd once asked Henry if he'd ever sleep with a guy, and he'd replied, as many straight men do, that if the right one came along, he might. It was another one of those things he said to sound refined and progressive. Of course he'd never actually have sex with a man, or let a man have sex with his girlfriend in front of him.

'Apparently it's on his bucket list.' Cat rolled her eyes. 'He said he's always wanted to try it, so I suppose I kind of agreed to it?'

'Do *you* want to do it?' I asked.

She shrugged. 'I'll try anything once.'

'I've never had a threesome,' I said. I thought she was asking me for advice.

'Really?' she said, looking at me.

I nodded again.

'Would you like to?'

I thought about it. 'Maybe. Wait,' I said. 'Do you mean – with you?'

She nodded quickly.

'Oh,' I said.

I pushed the sketchbook away from me. It felt uncomfortable to have this conversation so close to a drawing of *her*.

'It's all right if you don't,' Cat said. 'But you seemed like the obvious choice. I'd like it to be someone I could relax around, you know? And I'm not usually into girls, but I think you're gorgeous. I'm pretty sure Henry agrees.'

I wondered if there was something pointed in that last remark, a dig at our sexual past with each other. Cat knew about that, of course; it was the reason they met. She'd never given any indication that it bothered her. Was this why they'd chosen me? I didn't have the capacity to consider that for much longer. I had far too much to think about already.

It wasn't the first time I'd been invited to a threesome. For a bisexual woman, I was quite lucky I'd only been invited to three so far. But this was Cat. I'd never expected anything like this from Cat.

49

She had just said she found me gorgeous. Not just gorgeous but an exception to the fact that she was usually attracted only to men. But Cat was much prettier than me, much sexier than me, much more confident than me. If she'd gone to a club with this suggestion, there would have been any number of women desperate to take part in this threesome. Cat looked like a nymph. Her red wavy hair always flowed effortlessly over her shoulders. Her eyes were shaped like a cat's and were a blue so mesmerizing I could drown in them. She had freckles spread across her face like a constellation of stars. She moved through the world like it belonged to her, hips rolling on her legs. She was way out of my league.

She covered her face with one hand. 'I'm sorry,' she said. 'It's so embarrassing. Pretend I never said this.'

'No,' I said quickly. 'It's not embarrassing. I . . .'

'No, it is. I mean, why would you even want to? When I'm just me, and you're so – you.'

My heart skipped a beat. I'm sure my eyes went twice their usual size. Cat – perfect, gorgeous, wonderful Cat – didn't think she was good enough for *me*.

'Me?' I repeated, the word coming out hoarse.

She groaned, now covering her face with both hands. 'You know, so beautiful, so hot, experienced, confident. Do I need to continue?'

Had we, at some point, switched places?

'Cat,' I said.

She opened her fingers a crack, peering out at me through them. I opened my mouth to explain how I felt the same way about her, and the words got caught in my throat. She'd always been the one who was good with words, never me.

And the drawing of Maisie was still there, like a presence.

'Can I think about it?'

And I thought about it constantly. I weighed up the pros and cons in my head as I thought about kissing her collarbone and sliding my hands up and down her smooth thighs. As I thought about biting her lip and putting my fingers between her legs. As I thought about her whimpering and shaking in an orgasm.

Pros: I'd get to fuck Cat.

Cons: threesomes never work out. Someone always gets jealous or feels excluded. A threesome with a straight couple is vaguely exploitative, no matter how nice the girl is. The guy will always be there, objectifying you for your sexuality. My relationship with Henry was complicated enough. I lived with Cat; I couldn't afford for things to go badly or become awkward between us.

But – I'd get to fuck Cat.

'You're not listening to me, are you?'

Oliver looked at me from across the table, his fork in his poke bowl. I had stopped listening once he told me he'd met a new boy. Oliver fell in love easily, and it usually happened about every two weeks. I had more important things to consider. Like how Cat looked naked.

'Of course I'm listening,' I said.

'Really?' said Oliver. 'What's his name?'

'I'll joke about this in my best man's speech at your wedding,' I said. 'I'll say how you fell in love with so many boys I didn't even bother to listen when you told me about this one, because I never thought it would last.'

He shook his head and moved his fork around in his food.

'Do you even care about the guys I see?' he asked. 'Good friends do.'

'Is he good at blowjobs?' I said.

'The best.'

'Then that's all I care about. I know you're in good hands. Or, rather, a good mouth.'

'Louise! *Salope!*'

He picked up something from his bowl and threw it at me. I ducked to the side easily. Luckily for me, Oliver had terrible aim.

'Come on,' I said. 'You're going to make the waiters hate us.'

Oliver grumbled and shook his head. 'What are you thinking about?' he asked.

I shrugged. 'Nothing.'

'Yes, you are. You're preoccupied by something. What is it?'

I knew I couldn't tell him about what Cat had suggested. I knew I definitely couldn't tell him what I was thinking about doing.

I could still clearly remember the day I'd let him in on the fact that Cat and Henry were dating, back in the early days of their relationship.

'You're serious,' Oliver had said, staring at me with big eyes. 'Your flatmate is dating your ex?'

'He's not my ex,' I'd said, squirming. 'We were just hooking up. It was casual.'

'So your flatmate is dating the guy you used to hook up with. That's a recipe for disaster, Louise.'

I'd kept the news from Oliver for a month after they met, until it was official and even I could tell it wasn't casual. Henry was in our flat all the time by then, his and

Cat's laughter always carrying through the rooms. Their dressed-up date nights began to be replaced by evenings on the couch in their pyjamas, with Cat not even wearing make-up.

'And you're not planning to move out, are you?' Oliver had said.

'Of course not,' I'd said. 'I like it there. Besides, I can't afford to move anywhere else. We live well together. And, I promise, it's not going to be awkward. I had no feelings for Henry. He had no feelings for me.'

Oliver narrowed his eyes at me and clearly didn't believe a word.

Now I looked at him and imagined how judgemental he would be if I told him of the latest development. He'd be furious with me. He would think I was an absolute fool for even considering the idea.

He would try to talk me out of it, but I knew his opinion wouldn't sway me. Instead, it would only make it worse when everything ended in disaster and I had to go to him for support. I'd have given him the ammunition to say 'I told you so.' He wouldn't have needed to comfort me; he would've been perfectly within his rights to leave me to deal with my own mess, to say he'd tried his hardest to make me change my mind and I hadn't listened.

No, it was better to say nothing and cause chaos without the guilt of knowing he had been right all along.

'I'm thinking about Kant,' I said.

'Never mind, then. I don't need to hear about that.'

'I know, I'm sorry. Will you tell me again how you met him? I promise I'll listen this time.'

5

It took me three days to make up my mind. Decision made, I sat down next to Cat on the couch as she read a book.

'Why do you want to do it?' I asked.

She didn't ask me what I was referring to.

She looked over and smiled softly. 'What do you mean?'

'You said Henry has it on some kind of bucket list. I'd like to know why *you* want to do it.'

This was what my answer depended on. I wasn't doing it for Henry, after all.

'Well.' Cat chewed on her lip, closing the book. 'The truth is I've always wanted to try it. Being with a woman. And the way things are going with Henry, this might be the only way I'll ever have the opportunity to.'

I ignored the gnawing feeling in my chest at the implication that she and Henry would be together long-term. I focused on the fact that she wanted to be with a woman. That she wanted to be with me.

'I'd like to do it,' I said. 'If you still want to, that is.'

There was a thoughtful expression on her face, and she sighed before she met my eyes again.

'You don't think it's a silly idea, do you?' she asked. 'It won't be very awkward afterwards?'

'I don't think so,' I said. 'We wouldn't have to make it awkward.'

A sudden desperation clawed at me from the inside. If I'd been a decent person, I would've assured her that it was all right if she had changed her mind, but I'm not very decent. The night before, I'd dreamt about her naked in bed with her legs spread, beckoning me with her hand.

'It's not awkward now, with Henry, is it?' I said.

'No, I suppose you're right.'

She was so clueless. If this thing between Henry and me didn't classify as awkward, I didn't know how she defined the word. We tiptoed around each other in that flat, trying never to make eye contact so we didn't have to speak.

Cat took my hands and held them tightly. She wiggled her entire body excitedly.

'I'm nervous,' she said. But she seemed to be enthusiastic about the idea again.

I watched her lips. Her touch was electrifying.

'Me too,' I said.

'I've never been with a girl before,' she said. 'Promise you won't laugh at me?'

'Of course I won't.'

In that moment I wasn't thinking about the fact that Henry would be there too. I was only thinking about Cat.

'What was your first time like?' she asked. 'With a girl.'

I didn't like to remember. I didn't like to think too much about Maisie. There were days that could still prevent me from being able to get anything done whatsoever, leave me tethered to my bed.

I took a deep breath. 'It was very romantic,' I said. 'It took us some time to get there, but when we did – it was heavenly. It was.'

'Do you prefer girls?' Cat asked.

I thought about the question. It was more about people than gender to me, more specifically about one person. No one had ever compared to Maisie.

'I don't know,' I replied honestly.

Cat hummed and nodded her head. She held out our intertwined hands and looked at them, allowing the light from the window to shine in between the gaps.

'I feel so wild,' she said softly. 'But this is our time to be wild, isn't it? Before we get too old for it. Before we get married and have children.'

'Yes,' I said, even though I had no plans to do either of those things.

'You'll still be my friend, won't you?'

Cat looked into my eyes. Hers were the perfect blue. Mine are the most average hazel you could imagine. There is nothing about me that stands out the way that every part of her does.

'Always,' I said.

She smiled. The eye contact lasted for so long I was painfully aware of it, and I forced myself to maintain it and not look away. Was she going to kiss me? There was something unsaid in this silence, something about the way she held my hand that felt different. If she was going to kiss me, I decided, I was going to kiss her back. If she didn't stop kissing me, I wouldn't stop kissing her. I didn't care that she was in a relationship. I'd have sex with her on this couch without letting the idea of Henry hold me back.

Her gaze fluttered quickly down to my body. I was inadequate next to her. She had lovely full D-cups and a toned stomach. I wasn't fat, but I wasn't skinny. I was flabby. I had some excess weight which didn't settle nicely on to only my bum and breasts. My body was shaped like a door, while hers was shaped like heaven. I couldn't believe she saw anything in me worth having.

'I'm going to tell Henry you said yes,' she said suddenly.

The moment was over. The eye contact was broken. There would be no kiss.

Her fingers slipped out of mine and she stood up, walking over to her bedroom door.

I could hear her humming something as she stood in her room with her phone in her hands. I knew I could still change my mind, but only for as long as Henry didn't know. Once she'd told Henry, there was no backing out. I couldn't tell you why this was the case, but I knew it to be so.

And yet I said nothing.

He texted me not even an hour later.

The last messages in our chat history were about when he'd show up for that birthday party. I remember reading them as I got ready. Cat asked him out the same night, and they had their first date a day or so later. He never told me anything. We never had the talk about our relationship, nothing that resembled a break-up. We'd had nothing that resembled a relationship.

For the first time in so many months there were new messages in our chat.

Cat told me, the first one said.

I'm glad you said yes, the second one said.

I wished there was an emoji, a winking one, or the one with the hands over the mouth. I wished there was anything I could use to try to decipher his meaning. There was nothing.

I toyed with the idea of messaging him back that I wasn't doing it for him. I wanted to tell him that I wanted to sleep with his girlfriend.

In the end I left him on read.

*

It's a bit odd, organizing a threesome. Sex isn't usually something you plan, but it's harder for spontaneity to handle it when there's more than two of you.

Cat started out by suggesting Saturday afternoon. I said that was fine with me. Henry was going to a concert. Tuesday? Cat asked. *How strange to have a threesome on a Tuesday*, I thought, but I said I was free. She then realized she'd forgotten about a trip to the French Riviera she was taking with her family. As one does. How about Friday when she came back? But I was going to watch a play Oliver was in on Friday.

Cat acted as messenger throughout this whole process, relentlessly trying to make our schedules line up. I never spoke to Henry directly. I considered that it might be easier with a group chat where we could all speak to each other, and then I realized how ridiculous the idea was. It made me laugh to imagine a group chat for such a purpose. It was better to let Cat handle this.

I had never been much interested in 'preparing' for other sexual encounters. I allowed them to happen. This felt different. I couldn't tell if it was because there were two other people involved or because it was Cat, but I had to take it seriously.

I asked Alistair for some money to buy new lingerie. What I had was a bit washed out or had small holes in inconspicuous places. Things that no man ever notices during sex. But Cat had an attention to detail like no one else I knew, and never more so than with clothing. Alistair was happy to supply a few hundred for the cause. I told him I needed something to wear for the next time I saw him, and it wasn't a lie. He didn't need to know that Henry and Cat would see me in it first. I went to the most expensive lingerie shop in town, a place I'd never been to before. Ann Summers was usually good enough for me. Primark also has surprisingly decent lingerie. But Cat was not an Ann Summers kind of girl, and she'd certainly never stepped inside a Primark. I went high-end instead. I created a purple set with a bralette, a thong and suspenders. I eyed the thigh-high socks as well, but I couldn't find a pair that matched the shade of everything else. That day I spent more on lingerie than I did on rent for the month.

I watched a lot of porn. It was nothing new for me to watch porn, though I know women aren't supposed to admit that. The FMF category was one I hadn't much explored before, but now I studied it religiously. I watched porn fully clothed, without touching myself, so carefully focused that I barely even got aroused. Like I was preparing for a test, I made mental notes of sex acts you could perform with three people. I came up with numerous ways to occupy myself in those awkward moments when the other two are going at it, so that I would never have to sit on the side not knowing what my place was.

I'm usually a shaver, but I waxed. I wanted no stragglers and none of those embarrassing shaving rashes. My skin needed to be perfect all over, clear and soft and hairless, just like I expected Cat's to be. Cat was professionally waxed at regular intervals, but that was a luxury I couldn't afford. I bought wax strips in the pharmacy and held my hand over my mouth in the bathroom when I pulled them off one by one, leaving my skin red and raw and sore.

'How is everything going?' Robert asked in our next dissertation meeting. 'Do we have a clearer direction yet?'

The truth was that I'd barely thought about my dissertation since Cat had popped the question.

'Not yet,' I replied truthfully. 'I've been compiling some sources and reading through them.'

'That's a good start,' he asked. 'What have you been reading?'

Online articles with tips and tricks for threesomes. The best ways to make a woman come.

I bullshitted my way to an answer, dropping the names of the writers he'd previously recommended to me, throwing in some sentences about what I knew about Kant and what I'd seen in the summaries and abstracts I'd briefly glanced over. Robert nodded and listened.

When Cat came back from the Riviera, her skin was darker and her hair was lighter. She looked like a goddess. I'd looked at her holiday pictures all week, imagining how her skin would taste of sunscreen and saltwater, thinking about her all alone on fresh white hotel-room sheets.

It had been odd to have the flat to myself. I didn't have to worry about making noise during my workouts, and I tended to leave my bedroom door open and wander around in my underwear to keep myself cool. Still, there was clearly something missing, something so significant it almost felt like a different flat. I expected to see her around every turn, and the morning she came back, I woke up far too early and lay in bed waiting for the door to open.

She told me everything they'd done over the kitchen table. A new gold bracelet dangled on her wrist as she spoke.

'You haven't been, have you?' she asked.

I shook my head.

'I do recommend it,' she said, as if the only reason I hadn't gone was that I wasn't sure the French Riviera was worth it.

'I'd love to go,' I said.

'You'll have to come with us next time,' she said. 'Won't you?'

'If you'll have me,' I said.

I didn't doubt that Cat would insist on me staying with her family. She'd never been the stingy sort of rich person. On my birthday, a week after I moved into the flat, she had bought me a Faber-Castell pencil set worth over a thousand pounds, just because she'd seen me doodling in my sketch-book and knew I 'did art'. Even so, a trip to the Riviera would be expensive. Alistair might be willing to spend some extra money on me, though.

'I've been thinking about you a lot, you know,' she said.

'Oh?' I said.

'You know, our little plan.' She was drinking bubble tea, the first thing she'd bought after getting back from the airport, and she moved the straw around in her cup. 'I masturbated, thinking about it.'

I looked at her face. I have never been very good with tones or expressions; there have been many times when I have taken sarcasm for seriousness. Oliver was always making exaggerated statements that took me aback before I would realize he didn't mean them. This time, though, I was sure. If I tried to judge it from the expression on her face or the tone with which she'd said it, I would have guessed that she was being serious. I knew this couldn't be. She had made a joke. She had been sarcastic. She couldn't have honestly told me something like that.

I laughed.

Cat didn't start laughing, which made me feel I'd some-how got it wrong. I do that often. I felt the anxious flutter in my chest that I always do in these situations.

'Sorry,' I said.

She looked completely serious. 'It's all right,' she said. 'Are you looking forward to it?'

I didn't want to appear pathetic and desperate. They would make fun of me afterwards; they would laugh between themselves about how badly I'd wanted it.

'Yes,' I said. 'I am.'

I didn't tell her about the porn I'd been consuming, the lingerie I'd bought, the pain I'd put myself through to remove all traces of body hair.

'I've been meaning to ask you,' she said, reaching out for a stray strand of hair hanging over my face. 'What do you like?'

Her hand didn't move after tucking the hair away. She rested it on my cheek. I could hardly speak.

'What do I like?' I managed.

'In bed – you know? I want us all to enjoy ourselves.'

I swallowed.

Cat withdrew.

'You're blushing.'

I put my hands on my cheeks. They felt hot.

Cat looked at me, biting at the end of her straw. 'You're submissive,' she said. 'Aren't you?'

It didn't feel much like a question.

'Yes,' I said.

'Do you like being punished?'

I put my knees together. My crotch was tingling.

'Sometimes,' I said.

I forced myself to look up at her again. She was watching me, her head cocked to the side.

'Do you like telling others what to do?' I asked.

'I'm quite versatile.' Cat grinned widely. 'We'll have fun.'

6

The day came. I tried to maintain my normal routine, but I ended up staring at the laptop screen instead of reading anything. I was supposed to exercise, but our plans would mess up the usual time I did it, so I showered early instead, to ensure I was clean. I drifted around in my room and realized I'd forgotten to have lunch, but I wasn't hungry anyway.

Henry arrived. They talked in the lounge as I sat on my bed and waited for one of them to get me.

The new lingerie wasn't the most comfortable. The thin straps and lace dug into my skin, rubbing against me when I moved. At least it looked good. I didn't imagine I would be wearing it for long. I'd put on a nice top and a skirt and done my make-up, with foundation and lightly winged eyeliner.

I hadn't taken my medication that day. Yes, I knew I wasn't supposed to ever skip it, but it had such a terrible impact on my libido. Since I'd started taking it, becoming aroused only happened spontaneously once in a blue moon, or else I had to force it and then struggle to get wet. I didn't want that to be the case with Cat. I wanted to feel everything. It was fine to skip just one dose.

My hands were shaking slightly. I held them up in front of me. Was it very noticeable? Not if I didn't look at them carefully, no. My sex toys were in a bag on the floor. I wasn't sure if I was expected to bring them. Either they would find it fun or they would think I was way too strange and over-enthusiastic. I've always been too strange and over-enthusiastic.

Henry might also be offended. I'd never tried to use anything while I was with him, and some men do see vibrators as competition. I've always thought it's just smarter to see them as partners. Why compete when you'll never win?

There was a knock on my door.

'Louise? Are you ready?'

'Yes,' I said. 'I'm coming.'

I stood up and walked over to the door. Cat was outside.

'Your dress is nice,' I said.

'Thank you,' she said. 'I got it during the trip. You look lovely too.'

Henry was sitting on the couch, pouring us all a glass of red wine.

'Hello,' he said. 'Would you like one?'

He'd already poured three of them, so there was no point rejecting it.

'Thank you,' I said, taking a glass. 'What are we drinking?'

'It's a bottle I picked up a few days ago. Especially for the occasion.' He winked.

Cat laughed. She took a glass and sat down next to him, very close, their thighs pressed together. Something about the way she did it felt possessive, like establishing ownership. Maybe it was the fact that she looked at me while doing it. I took the hint and sat in the armchair.

Henry wasn't looking too bad himself. He was wearing a white shirt that was unbuttoned a fair way down, with the sleeves rolled up to his elbows. His dark hair wasn't as carefully swept back as usual, a few strands hanging over his forehead. I'd almost forgotten that he was this good-looking.

He raised his glass and smiled. 'To an unforgettable night,' he said.

We both touched our glasses to his and took our first sips.

I've always hated the taste of wine, and this was no exception. It took all I had to keep myself from making a face as I forced it down my throat.

We were quiet for a bit. I've always been unsure what topics are suitable for a conversation you have right before sex.

'Say,' Henry said, looking at me, 'you haven't happened to see my phone anywhere?'

'No,' I said. 'Why?'

He shrugged. 'I've lost it.'

He was so unbothered about this fact, as if losing a phone was equivalent to losing a hair tie.

'He's convinced he lost it here,' Cat said. 'But we've turned the flat upside down and haven't found it.'

'I could've sworn it was here,' he insisted.

'We would have found it by now,' Cat said, like a mother.

'I'll keep an eye out, I suppose,' I said.

Henry shot me a smile. 'Thanks. It's no matter. I'll order a new one.' He reached over to the table to top up his glass.

We silently watched him do it. At some point one of us was going to have to make a move, but no one ever teaches you how a threesome starts.

Henry took a sip. 'Have you ever done something like this, Louise?'

I raised a brow at him. 'Because I'm bi?'

'No. Because you're open to things.'

It was true. There was rarely something I said no to trying. I might decline to do it a second time, but I was always willing to try. I'd told him, when we were sleeping together, that I'd tried bondage on a few occasions and that I'd be happy to do so again.

'No,' I said. 'I've never done anything like this before.'

Cat rose. 'Stand up,' she said, looking at me. She smoothed out her dress and put her wine glass on the table.

I did as she'd told me to. She came up to me and we stood facing each other. I looked at her freckles up close. She moved some hair out of my face.

'Thank you,' I said quietly.

Henry stayed on the couch, watching us. He was still holding on to his wine glass. Cat leaned in so close I could smell her. She smelled like vanilla, and I could feel her eyelashes fluttering against my face. She kissed me. Of course, she was an excellent kisser. She devoured me, her hands on both my cheeks.

I pushed into her hard, forcing my mouth against hers, as she bit my lip. Like a warning.

She pulled away. Her head was cocked slightly to the side, her eyes considering me. I was already breathing heavily, my legs weak. She smiled softly and placed her thumb on my bottom lip. 'What do you want me to do?' she asked.

Her voice was too loud to be aimed at me. I had forgotten Henry was in the room.

'Take off her clothes,' he said.

I looked over at him. His jaw was set hard and his crotch bulged in his jeans.

'Is that all right?' Cat whispered into my ear.

She felt like Cat again in that moment, not like this sexual being, not the seductress who'd reduced me to weakness with only a kiss.

I nodded, so she grabbed my tank top and slipped it over my shoulders. She gazed down at my breasts before she continued, subtly biting her lip, and I realized she wanted me as badly as I wanted her. This wasn't a show for Henry. She wriggled my skirt down my legs, and I looked at her arse as she bent down. I made unintentional eye contact with Henry as he took another sip from his glass.

Cat stood back up. Her cheeks were flushed. She put her hands on the clasp of my bra and I felt it unhook, the support disappearing beneath me. I was exposed, wearing only my knickers. There is always that moment, the first time you're naked in front of a new person. *Is this good enough? Do you still want to fuck me?* I knew what the answer was in Henry's case. But he wasn't picky; it was Cat I worried about.

'Now undress her, Louise,' Henry said.

I swallowed hard. I reached behind her for the zip of her dress. 'May I?'

'Yes,' she said breathlessly.

We looked at each other as if we were pretending he wasn't in the room. I don't know if she was doing that, but I certainly was. I kept him thoroughly out of my line of sight. I pulled down her zip, exposing the tanned skin underneath. I'd seen it before, in her bikini pictures on social media, on the balcony when she wanted to sunbathe. This was different. She had no bra on. Her pants were red and lacy, transparent enough that I could see her pubic hair through them, dark and scraggly. It surprised me. I had expected her to be clean-shaven and smooth; she was always so carefully polished in every aspect of her appearance.

I let her dress fall to the floor.

'Henry,' she said softly.

'Go ahead,' he said, like he was giving her permission.

She cupped my breasts with her hands, staring at them with desire. I lost my breath and almost fell over. Her hands were cold against my skin, but I liked the way they felt, the contrast between my warm insides and her coldness. Her hands began to move and her fingers reached my nipples, caressing and rubbing them. I let out an involuntary sound, almost a squeak. As she rubbed one nipple, she dug her fingers into my other breast.

It didn't feel like it usually does the first time you have sex with someone. There was none of the awkward exploration or the things that you have to gently guide them away from as you encourage them to do what you actually want. I wondered if they had talked about this beforehand. Had she asked Henry what I liked, and had he told her? He'd brought me to orgasm many times. There was something unbelievably attractive about the idea of Cat having such consideration for my pleasure.

She leaned down to my breasts and kissed one. Her breath was hot, and I was so wet already. Her tongue moved over my nipple and she looked up at me then, her eyes hungry. She smiled around my nipple as she sucked on it, as if she was pleased by the expression on my face. My entire body felt like jelly and I sank into the feeling of her tongue.

Her hand moved into my pants. I felt a finger on my clit, and it was like I'd been struck by lightning. The fingers slid downwards, and the whole time she stayed watching me, her eyes intently gazing into mine, like she could see into my soul. I thrust myself into her hand, pushing my most sensitive parts on to it to feel as much of her as I could.

'She's wet,' she said.

She had moved her face, leaving behind a hollow around my nipple, an emptiness that ached and cried out for her.

'Good,' Henry said.

I'd almost managed to forget he was there.

His glass clinked on the wooden coffee table. 'Should we go into the bedroom?'

Cat looked at me with a raised brow like a question.

I nodded, unable to speak.

'Let's,' she said. She withdrew her hand and stood up, bringing a finger to her mouth and sucking on it slowly, maintaining eye contact with me. She licked her lips and smiled. 'You taste good,' she said.

Henry was standing up now, waiting for us. Cat walked first, and he went behind her, slapping her once on the arse. She giggled. I went into her bedroom last, just in time to watch her turn around and fall backwards on to the bed. I trailed after her like a starving person following the scent of food.

'Louise,' Henry said, gripping my arm.

I turned to face him, and he leaned in to kiss me. It was nothing like kissing Cat, stirring only a fraction of the desire and the longing I had felt at her touch. He tasted like the wine he'd been drinking, sweet and rich, a flavour I hadn't enjoyed. Still, he knew what I liked. He touched me as he kissed me, running his hands up and down my body. I liked having my waist stroked, my buttocks caressed, and he knew that. I kissed him harder to let him know what I wanted, but he denied me the satisfaction of touching those places I most wanted. My pussy ached. My nipples were standing erect. As I pressed myself against his body, he laughed at me. He grabbed me by my hair and pulled me away from himself.

'You're really desperate, aren't you?' he said. 'Isn't she?' he said to Cat.

I looked over to her. She was sitting up now, chewing on one of her fingers and staring at us. I'd worried about jealousy, but there was nothing in her eyes except desire.

'Yes,' she said. 'She's absolutely dying for it.'

Henry smiled at me. 'Do you want me to fuck you?'

I nodded. Still holding my hair in one hand, he used his other thumb to stroke my lips. He forced my mouth open and stuck his thumb in, and I sucked on it like it was his cock.

'I think you should learn to be more patient,' he said.

He took his thumb out of my mouth and pushed me down on to my knees. My clit was throbbing, crying to be touched, but I would have to wait. It would only make it feel so much better when I finally got what I needed.

I unzipped his trousers and pulled them down. He was hard. He was slightly above average in size. Well, I don't know what the average dick size is, but he'd told me so multiple times; I suppose it was important for his ego. He undid the buttons of his shirt and I looked up at him. I smirked at the sight of his face. He looked so strained, a vein on his neck standing out, his mouth closed tightly. He was as desperate as I was, if not more, and it was my turn to make him wait. I slowly pulled down his pants and let his cock pop out, eager to stand to attention. It had been a while since I'd seen it.

I started by licking around the tip. He let out a low, almost animal hum. I wrapped my entire mouth around him and went down slowly, only a little. He moved to go in further, but I pulled my head back to stop him. He'd teased me enough to deserve it. The next time, I went deeper and he made the choked sound of modern men who've been taught by porn that they're not allowed to make noise. I loved to push past that boundary for them.

I sucked his cock the way he liked it. I let him hit the back of my throat and gag me a couple of times, as his hips started to move with me and set the pace, as he lost his ability to control himself.

'Is she good at that?' Cat asked.

'God, yes,' Henry said.

I glanced over at her. She'd taken off her pants and was touching herself, rubbing her clit as she watched us. We made eye contact. The sight of her drove me wild. Distracted, I forgot to control the pace. I gagged, and Cat smiled, her breath quickening ever so slightly. The whole time I blew him, I didn't look away from her. Her eyes drifted from mine to his and she nodded, like she was confirming that she liked this, like she was telling him she wanted us to keep going. So I kept going.

Henry eventually grabbed my head again and directed me away. He turned to Cat, smiling. 'Don't worry, darling. We won't be neglecting you.'

She lay back again. 'Good,' she said. 'You know I never would've allowed it.'

I stood up and looked at her body. There was a dip in her hips that I'd seen in her pictures from the Riviera. She had a small tattoo over one hip, a fine line of a rose. I leaned down and kissed it.

She wiggled under me. 'That tickles,' she said.

I licked it instead. Her breasts looked gorgeous this way, round and perky.

Henry took off his shirt. He still had the abs I remembered, and the muscles on his arms were visible as he pulled his shirt off. He'd always been so obsessed with the gym.

'Touch her,' he instructed me. A wink. 'She loves that.'

She looked at me from where she was lying. 'I do,' she said.

I didn't need any more incentive. I sat down on the bed and put my hand on her pussy. Her entire body tensed at that first contact. I found her clit and started to rub it, and she whimpered exactly the way I had wanted her to.

73

Henry lay down next to her and began by kissing her, then moved down to her breast, kissing and licking one nipple while rubbing the other with his hand.

'Oh my god,' she whispered, her voice breathless.

I experimented with different patterns, moving from strokes to a circle, adjusting my pace, checking her bodily reactions for guidance. It was the circling that made her buck against my hand almost instantly.

'Fuck,' she said. 'Just like that.'

I started moving faster. Henry kept doing what he was doing, and we toyed with her as her breath quickened and her moans became louder.

'Oh my god,' she said softly, and then she cried out and she was shaking.

I didn't stop. I couldn't stop. I moved with her as she came and convulsed against my hand. The sounds she made were glorious, as if she'd never felt anything like this before.

'Lolo, please,' she said.

I finally stopped, and she sank down, gasping. Then she laughed.

Henry grabbed her throat and kissed her, hard.

I watched, letting my hands drift down her smooth legs and looking at her little rose tattoo. My fingers were so slick with her.

'Who should I fuck first?' Henry asked.

He had his gruff sex voice now, the one that sounded so harsh compared to his usual tone. He was no longer a posh English boy but someone who would use that voice on you in an alleyway and you'd do everything he told you to.

'Me,' Cat said, speaking almost into his mouth; their faces were still so close together.

He smiled. 'Then I'll fuck Louise,' he said.

She laughed exasperatedly and shook her body like a child throwing a tantrum, all for show. He got off the bed and opened her bedside table, presumably to take out condoms.

Cat sat up and looked at me. 'Come here,' she said.

I crawled towards her.

'Lucky girl,' she said. She started to kiss down my neck and I tilted my head to give her easier access. 'Thank you,' she whispered, loud enough for only me to hear.

She kissed and sucked and bit, and I hoped she would leave a mark. I'd love to see a little hickey in the morning and know it had come from her. I wouldn't mention it. We'd walk past each other in the flat or spend time together on the couch, and she'd see it and know it was from her, and I wondered if she would bring it up first. I sighed in enjoyment, to let her know to continue.

Henry started touching my clit. It was electric; it almost made me jump. It ached so badly to be touched. Keeping his thumb there, he slid a finger inside me. 'You weren't lying,' he said to Cat.

It had gone in so effortlessly. Maybe it was due to my lack of medication; maybe it was thanks to Cat. I didn't care. I moved backwards on to his finger. He moved it inwards and upwards and hit exactly the right spot. I gasped.

'There it is,' he said.

'Do you like that?' Cat whispered in my ear.

'I love it,' I said.

She nibbled on my earlobe and then kissed my mouth again, holding me by the chin.

Henry inserted another finger, and it felt colder. Gentleman that he was, he'd added lube. I felt myself expand around him and I wished he'd go faster. I tried to rock myself

75

back and forth on his fingers, but he grabbed me by the waist and held me still.

'Be patient,' he said.

'Do you want to eat me out?' Cat said.

I nodded, breathless, and I would've pleaded for it, begged for the taste of her.

She spread her legs in front of me and carefully moved my hair behind my ears.

'There you go,' she said.

I started by kissing the insides of her thighs. They were wet and sticky already, and I lapped up the salty taste. As I started kissing her lips, Henry took his fingers out of me. As I flicked my tongue against her clit, he started putting himself inside me. Slowly, gently, he filled me up. I couldn't help but moan.

'Do that again,' Cat said quietly.

So I did, moaning my breath on to her, and she shuddered. Cat had probably never had a girl go down on her, and so she'd probably never had someone as good as me. Not that I consider myself an expert, but I've always thought girls are better at knowing what girls want. I went as slowly as Henry fucked me, deliberately edging around her clit, occasionally letting my tongue brush – just brush – over it. She already sounded like she was enjoying it; her breathing was strained and interspersed with soft whimpers and quiet moans.

Henry went faster, his hands firm around my waist, one of them occasionally smacking my arse. I sank into the feeling, let him set the rhythm for the way I ate his girlfriend out. Faster. Circling my tongue around that sensitive part. She sounded as if she were about to cry.

I felt her getting closer, sounding the way she had before

she came the first time, her thighs slowly starting to squeeze the sides of my face, like she wasn't aware she was doing it. It was intoxicating. The way Henry fucked me had never felt so good. I heard sounds from myself that didn't usually come out involuntarily, as I lost myself in the way he felt.

'Fuck,' Cat said. 'Fuck, don't stop.'

She was grinding against my face, her hips lifting off the bed.

'Fuck,' she said once more, and then she bucked.

I loved how quickly she came, how easily, like her body was full of secret buttons I could press to achieve my goal.

I came harder than I ever had before. I'd never managed to from penetration alone, with nothing touching my clit. This was something else altogether. It went through my entire body, reverberating inside me, like every muscle tensed and then released at the same time. For a moment I wasn't aware of anything besides that feeling. I didn't know what my body was doing. I didn't know what sounds I was making. I just knew suddenly that I was lying next to Cat.

She looked at me, panting, her chest rising and falling, and she laughed.

Henry was wanking himself off like he couldn't help himself.

Cat looked over at him. 'Henry, stop,' she said. She sat up and grabbed his arm. 'I need you to come inside me.'

He peeled off the condom.

'Lie down,' she said.

He ended up next to me, and I kissed him just to have something to do. I felt delightfully spent and I couldn't bear the thought of being touched again. My vulva was throbbing from the intensity of the orgasm. So I kissed him, my hand stroking his chest.

Cat climbed on top of him and slowly lowered herself on to his dick, her eyes closed and her face aimed upwards.

'Oh my god,' Henry said. 'Cat, please.'

She started to ride him, bouncing herself up and down at a steady rhythm. I watched her. She was the sexiest thing I'd ever seen. Her rose tattoo was barely visible in the crease of her hip. She looked into my eyes. I felt that I should look away, but I didn't. I couldn't. Neither did she. He was a stuttering mess, biting his lips and digging his hands into the bedsheets. Cat was a goddess on top of him, a bringer of pleasure unlike anything anyone had ever experienced before. She knew every part of his body, every movement needed to bring him to climax. When he cried out, she lowered herself up and down a few more times, much more slowly, and smiled at me the whole time.

7

I slept in my own room that night. We spent a while lazily lying in Cat's king-size bed, our naked, sweaty bodies touching at random places. But it wasn't big enough to hold all three of us overnight, and I have always been particular about the conditions I need to be able to sleep.

When I woke up in the morning, I'd been having sex dreams the whole night. I desperately needed a shower. It was earlier than Cat usually woke up, but I heard soft voices and chuckles from her room when I walked to the bathroom. I covered myself in my towel on the way back, as I always did, but it felt silly now. They had both seen me naked.

When I got back to my room, they were having sex again. It wasn't the first time I had heard them; our rooms were adjacent, and the walls were not thick. I usually put on headphones and listened to something to avoid hearing it. Not because I was embarrassed; I wasn't. I knew they were fucking, and they knew that I knew, so why should we have to pretend otherwise? It just felt like the respectful thing to do.

I wondered if I should still do that now. Part of me knew that I should. But I didn't want to. I had heard so much more yesterday anyway; they had invited me into their bed, I had made her come – what was so bad about hearing it? I sat on my bed and listened. They fucked like teenagers who'd just discovered sex. I was tempted to knock on the door and ask if I could join them.

*

Mum called me as I was cleaning out the mouse cage that day. I'd popped both the mice on my desk with one of their hides to get them out of the way. Squeak explored the desk while Pip stayed in the hide, suspicious of the outside world.

It had been a couple of weeks since I had last spoken to my mum, so I had to pick up. I don't dislike her, but if she hadn't given birth to me, I suspect we never would've had more than one conversation.

'Hi, my love,' she said. 'How are you doing?'

'I'm good.'

'How's the dissertation coming along?'

'I'm still in the planning stages.'

'Is that where you're supposed to be?'

I sighed and rolled my eyes. The worst part of having a teacher as a parent was the fact that she always cared much more about my schoolwork than other parents seemed to.

'Yes,' I said. 'That's exactly where I'm supposed to be. What have you been up to?'

Mum liked that question, and I liked asking it. She thought I had learned to finally show an interest in her daily life, while what I had actually realized was that it was a great way to get through these conversations. If she started talking about herself, I wouldn't have to share anything or answer any invasive questions. Half an hour later, enough time would finally have passed that I could say I had to go but that it had been lovely talking to her. She wouldn't know anything new about my life. Honestly, I wouldn't know anything about hers either. I'm good at pretending to listen.

As I cleaned the cage, Mum talked about work and about my aunt Denise, who had apparently recently been diagnosed with breast cancer. I'd only met Denise a couple of times, many years ago, and knew they weren't close, so I had no idea why my mum knew that Denise had cancer or why she thought it so crucial to share it with me. She'd been a smoker all her life, of course, is what Mum told me, and I hummed sympathetically.

'Anyway,' she said, 'I recently read this book I thought you might like. It was written by a woman with autism.'

Oh god, I thought, *here we go*. Mum and I used to have things to talk about. We'd watch films together or gossip about the neighbours. She'd know what was going on in my school and I'd know what was happening at her work. Now we tried to keep up a conversation by talking separately about things the other had no knowledge of or interest in learning, until she inevitably brought up the one subject she knew was still relevant to me and that she believed I would be delighted to hear about.

'Really?' I said, forcing my voice to sound interested. 'What's it about?'

'Well, it's mostly about what it's like living with autism; it's an autobiography.'

'Mum, why would I want to read about living with autism? I know what it's like. I do it every day.'

I was ten years old when I was diagnosed. For a girl, that's lucky. Especially for a girl who's now 'high-functioning'. What that means is that neurotypical people can't spot me. I've never had someone ask me if I'm autistic or sympathetically tell me they have a cousin with autism. When I told Oliver, he started laughing because he thought I was joking. When I clarified that I wasn't, he asked me what it meant. He said he'd thought he knew what autism was, but if I had it, then clearly his understanding was a little bit off. I appreciated the honesty.

I was diagnosed early because back then I wasn't 'high-functioning'. My teachers at school knew something was wrong and they had meetings with Mum and sent me to sessions with the school counsellor, who asked me questions like she believed I was being abused. Did my family ever get very angry with each other or with me? Did Mum leave me alone a lot? Did I know what sex was?

I didn't have friends. I didn't interact with my peers. In my teenage years I met Maisie and managed to make a friend, but at ten I had been a hermit of my own making. I would raise my hand in class when the teacher asked questions, but I didn't make conversation with my fellow students. I had lunch by myself at my own table, drawing in my sketchbooks. During free periods, I didn't spend time with the others. I had a specific corner in the hallway where I planted myself on the floor, crossed my legs and spent hours drawing.

It wasn't that I was being bullied. No one had ever been mean to me, which I now understand is incredible because of just how strange and out of place I was. God, adult me would've been tempted to bully me. On the contrary, the others did make attempts to include me. They tried to start conversations. I was invited to a few birthday parties. They never said a mean word against me, at least not when I was in the room. And no, I wasn't lonely, because I was disinterested in them, as later therapists would theorize. They would suggest that I had different interests to my peers and that I was mature for my age, and that I just didn't have enough in common with them to be interested in lasting friendships.

The truth was that I simply didn't know how to interact with the others. I wasn't scared or anxious around them. I was simply bereft. I thought I knew how to answer their questions, but my answers always seemed to be wrong, resulting in awkward laughs and bewildered expressions. If I wasn't asked a question, I didn't know how to participate in conversation at all. What did one say when talking to people? I just didn't know. And what did people do with their friends? I didn't know that either. None of it came naturally to me. I felt like I'd been dropped into a game with rules I couldn't understand.

The school counsellor realized that I had a perfectly normal home life, apart from the absent father, which really wasn't that extraordinary and which didn't bother ten-year-old me in the slightest. That's also when she realized that she was out of her depth and referred me to a proper psychologist. I was diagnosed. Mum cried after the appointment, but she did it behind her closed bedroom door so I couldn't see. It hurt to know that she was so disappointed in me, that she was sad to have me as her daughter.

Before that day I saw her as someone I could go to for help, someone I could express my feelings to, even if she might not understand them. Other people were confusing, and when my father was still in the picture, I mostly remember him being annoyed with me. Mum was the only person I would voluntarily spend time with. But more than a decade later I still remembered how I'd felt outside her bedroom door as I listened to her sobs. Every time she told me she'd heard something about an autistic person or read another book about autism, I thought about how she'd cried that day.

'You don't have to be so hostile,' she said. 'I know that you know, but sometimes it's nice to know there are other people who share your experience, isn't it?'

'I suppose so,' I said. 'What's the name of the book?'

She told me, and I didn't make any effort to remember it.

*

Cat was gone for most of the day. She and Henry went to brunch, which I saw when I checked her socials. I found a nice selfie from a few months ago on her account, and I used it as a reference to draw her. I stared at the drawing afterwards and wondered how anyone could be so beautiful that art can't capture it. It didn't convey her spark; it didn't contain any of the sheer confidence she radiated.

When she came home, she was alone. There was only one set of steps.

I hovered at my bedroom door. I wanted to speak to her; it felt important, in order to establish normality again, to ascertain that last night had changed nothing. My heart hammered with anxiety. Would she decide that something was different? Had she already determined that it would be way too absurd for me to stay and that I would have to move out? Alistair would probably be able to give me more money for rent, but I didn't want to move away from Cat.

I took a breath and went out to talk to her anyway. She was in the kitchen. She had three full bags on the counter and was unpacking them.

'Hello,' I said.

She turned to me like she hadn't heard me until now. 'Hi,' she said. 'How are you?'

She was wearing a large sun hat, the brim of which wobbled with her every movement.

'I'm good,' I said.

'Did you sleep well?' She smiled a smile that seemed to allude to the night before.

I chuckled. 'Like a baby.'

'God, me too,' she said, lifting a large carton of milk out of the bag. 'I was exhausted.'

I wondered how much of this food she would end up

wasting. Cat liked to keep her fridge fully stocked, but she only cooked for herself and occasionally for Henry or friends, which meant she had to go through it once a week and throw away everything that had gone bad.

She lifted a large watermelon out of one of the bags. 'Would you like some?' she said. 'I'm cutting this one up.'

'That would be great,' I said.

She took off her hat and swept her hair to the side. It was almost as if she did it purposefully, intentionally revealing the mark on that side of her neck. I wondered if I had left it there. Seeing it almost propelled me towards her; it filled me with an urge to kiss and lick and bite at it, to touch her, to reach out my hand to her.

I didn't. Instead, I stood there waiting for her to speak, doubting more and more that she would bring it up at all. She chopped up half the watermelon on her wooden cutting board, sliding the slices into a bowl, leaving the other half on the counter. I could see it bleeding its thick pink juice on to the marble, running towards the edge, dripping slowly to the floor. Cat turned around, holding the bowl with a big smile. 'Let's eat on the balcony,' she said.

We went out, me holding the door open for her.

The balcony wasn't very big. It could just about hold the two chairs Cat had put out there, which you had to press yourself against the railing to walk past. But it was nice and sunny, and we sat on the chairs with the bowl of watermelon between us. Cat dug in immediately, the juice running down her hands and her wrists.

Watch your dress, I wanted to say, but Cat was never bothered about stains. I have a compulsion to scrub with stain remover and water every time there's a mark on a piece of clothing or on my sheets, desperate to remove it before it manages to set. Cat would shrug and put it into her laundry hamper until it was full, with no rush at all. I don't think she knows what stain remover is. If there was still a stain after she'd washed it, she'd count the item as ruined and throw it away without regrets. She'd replace it within days if it was something she liked, but usually she would say she was done with that piece of clothing anyway. Cat was easily bored with clothes. I bet every charity shop surrounding our flat was filled with her cast-offs.

'What are you thinking about?' Cat asked. It was one of her favourite ways to start a conversation.

'Nothing special,' I said.

'Did you have fun last night?' she said, very casually.

I suddenly felt that any answer I gave would be embarrassing.

'Yes,' I said. 'I did. Did you?'

She looked at me, smiling, and licked the watermelon off one of her fingers slowly.

'I loved it,' she said. 'I actually loved it a lot more than I thought I would.'

I smiled back. 'I'm glad.'

'You were amazing, Louise. It was so hot.'

I found it difficult to swallow and even more difficult to maintain eye contact with her. I looked away instead. I considered how it would feel to speak to her that way. Could I tell her in such a frank and loud voice that she was the hottest thing I'd ever seen? Could I tell her just how badly I'd wanted her? No, that would be entirely out of place. It would feel absurd. It would feel like telling a parent about a one-night stand.

'I'm glad you said yes,' she said, reaching for another piece of watermelon. 'Go on, have some.'

I went to grab a piece and our fingers met in the bowl. She smirked. I grabbed a slice of watermelon and took a bite.

Cat seemed to have finally found a slice that was good enough for her. 'Henry liked it too,' she said. 'But of course he likes most things. My boyfriend when I was sixteen could last longer than him.'

I laughed, choking on the watermelon.

'Henry's not so bad,' I said.

'I know you think that.' She winked at me.

There was nothing jealous or underhand in that sentence, only suggestion. Like she was teasing me about an embarrassing kink and not her own boyfriend.

'Honestly, so do I,' she said. 'He gets it done, you know. He's eager to please.'

We'd never talked so openly about sex before, and it made my stomach stir. *I'm eager to please too*, I wanted to say. *Let me prove it to you.*

To keep myself from blurting it out, I changed the topic to the least sexy subject I could think of: philosophy.

'Do you really believe what you're writing your dissertation about?' I asked. 'About true altruism not existing at all?'

Cat accepted the change of conversation. 'Of course,' she said. 'I don't waste my time saying things I don't mean.'

'OK,' I said. 'Imagine I was walking down the street at night and it was completely empty. There's no one else around, except for someone who seems to have fallen and passed out, who's just lying there on the ground unconscious. Are you saying there's no chance I would help them? Because no one is going to see me do it and think I'm a good person. They themselves aren't going to know because they're unconscious.'

'People would know afterwards,' Cat said. 'You could be

in news stories and all that. Maybe the person you help is a millionaire who will give you all their money.'

'But what if none of that is the case?' I said. 'All right, imagine that I was out doing something I shouldn't be doing, and it's not in my best interest to ever let anyone know that I was on that street at that time. If I helped, I would have to remain completely anonymous and leave before the ambulance arrived. I couldn't tell anyone I'd done it. Would I still not do it?'

She glanced over at me with one brow suggestively lifted. 'What were you out doing?'

'Never mind that,' I said. 'What matters is that it's conceivable I could still be motivated to do it. To call an ambulance and then leave like a secret guardian angel.'

Cat nodded. 'Of course you could.'

'Exactly. And what reason is there for me to do it? I would benefit from it in no way at all. All I'm motivated by is this stranger's well-being. I don't even have a stake in that well-being; I don't know them. It's not like helping out a friend or family member.'

'Helping them would make you feel good,' Cat said matter-of-factly. 'It would make you feel happy and worthwhile to have done it. It would prevent you from feeling the guilt you would experience if you'd kept walking.'

'But it would only make me feel good if I cared about them in the first place. That means it's not self-interested at its core. If I didn't care about them at all, I wouldn't feel guilty if I left. I wouldn't feel good if I helped.'

'Whether you can care about other people or not is irrelevant,' Cat said, flicking away a seed from her watermelon, sending it flying over the balcony railing. 'I think you can. But that doesn't automatically translate into motivation. I can care about my mother plenty without feeling the slight-est motivation to help her feel better by listening to her menopause complaints. No, I'm only motivated to do that if I care enough about her that it would make me feel good if I listened. So what motivates me isn't my care for her, but how that care makes me feel. Ergo, we still have psycho-logical egoism.'

For a few seconds we were silent, except for the sound of her slurping her watermelon.

'I think you're wrong,' I said.

She shrugged. 'Feel free to prove it. I'm always happy to change my mind.'

8

Robert sighed and smiled at the same time, like I was an annoying child he couldn't help but love.

'Louise,' he said, 'you do understand we don't usually allow students to change their topic this far into the semester? And that's for good reason. We don't want you to be overwhelmed and stressed when you realize how little time you have left to complete the dissertation.'

It was a week after the threesome. The same day Cat and I had that conversation on the balcony, I emailed Robert my intentions. I wasn't going to write my dissertation about Kant any more, I was going to write a conclusive refutation of psychological egoism. He'd promptly told me it wasn't possible to switch now. I'd promptly said I would do anything I could to be allowed to. Eventually he had agreed to this meeting.

'I know,' I said. 'But I'm doing this at my own risk. I'm fully aware of the time constraints and I'm prepared to deal with them. Plus, you know most of the others haven't started researching theirs yet either. I won't be behind at all.'

'I'm your supervisor because of my expertise on Kant,' Robert said calmly.

'I'm still staying in the general field of moral philosophy,' I said. 'You know enough about the subject.'

We stared each other down. There was a clock in the room that I could hear ticking, ticking, ticking.

'Fine,' he said, punctuated by another sigh. He held up his hands in defeat. 'All right.'

*

It would've been a shame if I'd been unable to convince him, because I'd already cycled to the library and checked out all the books I could find which included any moral philosophy. They were now stacked on my desk.

I was in a good mood when I got home. I put my bicycle away and went upstairs, excited to tell Cat the good news. She was already in the lounge; I could hear the TV as I hung my key and took off my jacket.

I opened the door. She was sitting cross-legged on the couch with a Domino's pizza in front of her and a box of garlic bread at her side. There was a tub of Ben & Jerry's melting in the middle of the coffee table. She was wearing her pyjamas – a tank top with a pair of short shorts – and no make-up. She was watching *Gilmore Girls*. She only watched *Gilmore Girls* when she was upset, and I'd never seen her order Domino's before.

'What's wrong?' I asked.

Her face scrunched up immediately. She started sobbing, still holding a slice of pizza.

'We broke up,' she said. 'Henry and I broke up.'

I was stunned, and I just stood there for a moment, recognizing the reality of what she'd said. And the first thing I thought wasn't: *Oh no, poor Cat*. My first thought was: *Cat is single*.

'Oh my god,' I said. 'I'm so sorry.'

I rushed to her side and sat down next to her, carefully lifting the garlic bread from the couch so neither of us would accidentally sit on it. Her shoulders shook with the tears. She put her head against my chest and wrapped her arms around me, and I hugged her back. I was acutely aware of the pizza slice she was holding, wondering if it was dripping grease on to my top that very moment, but I suspected I shouldn't say that out loud.

'What happened?' I said, stroking her back.

She sobbed against my shoulder. 'I don't want to talk about it,' she said.

I couldn't help but wonder if it was something to do with me. If it was somehow caused by the threesome. It had only been a week; the connection seemed obvious. For the first time I considered what it would be like to be with her properly, just the two of us.

'Of course,' I said. 'You don't have to.'

Had Henry done something bad? Part of me felt a tug towards being the protective friend who was furious with him for making her cry like this. Part of me didn't care what he had done. Part of me was grateful to him.

What is wrong with me? I thought. *My best friend is crying about her break-up and I'm thinking about what that means for me. I'm thinking about whether I can get with her now.*

I shook my head and felt ashamed, trying to get every thought like that to leave my mind. I had to take care of Cat.

I'd never seen her cry before. Not because she was resilient, but it just seemed to me that she'd never had reason to cry. She'd always received good marks. No one she knew had ever died. She'd told me that the last time she went through a break-up, she didn't shed a single tear; she was just happy the relationship was over. She dumped him and he was the one crying into her voicemail at two in the morning while she was snogging someone new.

'You'll be OK,' I said. 'Let's do something together tonight. I'll stay right here with you. What do you want to do?'

She inhaled deeply and pulled herself together well enough that she stopped crying. She sat back and straightened her back. 'Can we watch something terrible and drink?' she said, her eyes red and blotchy.

Despite that, she was beautiful. She cried like you do on camera, controlled and calm, with a perfect expression the whole time.

'Of course,' I said.

I went into my room and quickly messaged Alistair.

I'm sorry, I won't be able to come tonight. My friend is going through a break-up and I need to be there for her. Rain check?

Alistair was usually understanding about these things. He'd had to cancel on me a couple of times, never giving a reason, always feeding that suspicion of mine that he was married.

Do what you have to do, he replied. *But I will expect you to make it up to me.*

Of course I will, I said. *Think about how you would like me to do it.*

That night Cat was mine, entirely mine. I went out to buy wine for us at Tesco; I doubted she had ever had Tesco wine before, but she didn't complain. She was eating Domino's, for god's sake.

I put the ice cream in the freezer for her until she wanted it; it already felt so soft when I held it. We watched *Hot Fuzz*. She'd never seen it before, which amazed me. I exaggerated my amazement to make her laugh, acting like she'd committed some crime against British comedy.

'But Simon Pegg is in it!' I said.

'Who?' she asked.

I gasped. 'Don't tell me you don't know who Simon Pegg is. Cat! We have so much to catch you up on.'

This was the kind of film Maisie and I had watched together. She'd never liked any genre other than comedies.

She'd introduced me to every classic, and we'd watched them with our heads resting on each other's shoulders, sharing bowls of popcorn.

Cat giggled on the couch, but even as she laughed I could see the pain in her expression. She laughed with her face, her body remaining upright and stiff.

She let me have as much of her pizza as I wanted. She didn't even have an appetite, she said. 'Oh, I'll be so bloated tomorrow,' she said.

'Why does it matter?' I asked. 'No one will see it. Eat the pizza.' She laughed at that too.

She didn't cry once during the whole film. She didn't laugh as often as I did, but I accepted that. There were laughs at the important bits, which was good enough. During quiet periods, I would look at her and her eyes seemed glazed over, as if she wasn't watching the film at all. She wouldn't be smiling any more; she'd simply be sitting there, looking as if she was thinking about something else, her mouth twitching every once in a while. Then she'd lean over and reach for the wine bottle, drink straight from it and sit back down, smelling of alcohol, with her lips moist and reddened.

She cuddled into me, lying in the crook of my armpit. I didn't mind the physical contact. It almost felt nice. It almost felt like it had with Maisie.

After the film, I asked her what she'd thought.

'It was fun,' she said, sounding slightly disorientated.

'Are you sure? You don't seem like you enjoyed it.'

'I was just thinking. I was thinking a lot.' She drew a circle on my leg with her finger.

'Did Henry do something?' I asked.

'No,' she said quickly.

There was a pause.

'Did you do something?'

'Louise,' she said, and sighed, 'sometimes things just don't work out. It doesn't have to be anyone's fault.'

'You're right. I know.'

But it wasn't an answer to my question.

'I think it might be nice to be single,' she said, her voice full of faux cheer. 'It's been a while now. What's the dating market like?'

'Terrible,' I said.

She laughed at that. 'I love your honesty,' she said.

'Thank you.'

It's never been a conscious choice for me, never something I considered a personality trait. I just don't know when to lie, the way other people seem to. I've always wished I did. Cat might find it endearing, but it had got me into trouble many times.

'Are you seeing anyone?' she asked.

'I told you. I see people casually sometimes.'

'Is Alistair one of them?'

I choked on my wine. She wasn't supposed to know that name. I'd never told her about him. Oliver was the only person who knew, the only one I was certain wouldn't judge me for our arrangement. 'How do you know his name?'

She nodded to my phone on the coffee table. 'You have a message from him that came in when you were in the kitchen. It's quite suggestive, so don't try to tell me it's your dad.' Her tone was sharp.

'You know I don't talk to my dad,' I said, trying to change the subject.

I'd barely heard a word from him since the divorce. I was five years old when he cut me and Mum off like we'd never

96

existed, started over and made new, less defective children with a wife I've never met.

'That's not an answer,' said Cat.

I rolled my eyes. Her cheeks were rosy now, the way they always were when she'd been drinking. She took another large sip from her glass. 'You can tell me, you know,' she said. 'Are you seeing him?'

'It's a bit complicated,' I said. 'But yes, essentially.'

She nodded. 'What does he do? Is he a student too?'

'No, he's in . . .' I couldn't come up with a convincing lie on the spot, but I knew I would give myself away if I told her the truth. 'He's in business,' I admitted, because it was too late to go back. People our age are not in business.

It's a vague term, but I didn't know more than that myself. I didn't know what industry he worked in or what his role was. It wasn't among the topics we usually discussed.

'In business?' Cat said, eyes narrowing. 'How old is he?'

'Come on,' I said. 'He's not that old.'

She didn't look convinced.

'I'm not sure,' I said. 'Over forty.'

She'd said I could tell her, so I did. I tested out the waters with something simple: I was seeing an older man.

'Forty?!' she exclaimed.

I squirmed. I'd misjudged. Cat stared at me, mouth open. She was appalled. 'What are you doing with someone in his forties?'

Cat could lie about anything, so there must be a reason she wasn't bothering to hide the disgust in her voice.

'He's rich,' I said. 'Or rich enough. He paid for these.' I gestured at my earrings. They were solid gold, diamonds dangling from my earlobes.

Cat let out a gasp. 'Oh my god,' she said, her mouth moving into a smile. 'Lolo, do you have a sugar daddy?'

'It's not like I call him that,' I said defensively.

She laughed, but she visibly relaxed, nodding, taking another sip of wine. 'You're a wild card,' she said. 'You probably want to check what he messaged you, then.'

I took my phone and opened the message.

I'd like to fuck your arse. How does that sound?

'Shit,' I said. 'I'm so sorry you saw that.'

'I've seen worse than that,' Cat said.

I put my phone back on the coffee table, the message left on read.

Cat frowned. 'You're not going to reply?'

'Not right now,' I said.

'Mmm, because he'll be expecting something sexy back, and you don't want to write it in front of me?' She nodded knowingly. 'Makes sense.'

'He won't mind waiting,' I said.

'Would you mind if I replied for you?' she said.

I stared at her. Again, I wanted to determine that it was a joke. The words sounded like a joke. Her tone did not.

'I'm serious,' she said, like she'd been reading my mind. 'Let me reply. I bet he won't be able to tell.'

'OK,' I said, laughing.

I could feel adrenaline coursing through me as if we were doing something dangerous, something big. I unlocked my phone for her and handed it to her. While she typed, I couldn't even see the screen. She could be telling him anything and pressing send before I even know, I thought, and it thrilled me.

'Here,' she said. She put one finger on the send button with finality and handed the phone back to me.

Just thinking about that makes me need to touch myself.

As I watched the screen, the message was marked read. Within seconds Alistair was typing again.

What about your friend?

I showed it to Cat.

'Say "screw her",' she said. 'Say "screw her and screw me instead".'

She laughed at her own joke, and I laughed too, feeling vaguely tipsy. I wrote the message just like she'd asked me to, not pausing to question if it would sound like me or arouse his suspicions.

'This is fun,' Cat said.

Why would you say that after cancelling our meeting? Alistair said. *That's not fair.*

'Let me type,' Cat said.

She wrote out, *Because I want you to punish me.* She showed it to me before she sent it.

'I just want to make sure,' she said. 'I don't know what your dynamic is or what kinks he has.'

'No, it's fine,' I said.

'Excellent,' she said. 'You know, it's true. A rebound does work wonders. Thank you, Alistair.'

I laughed.

'Look, he's writing again,' she said.

Fuck, Alistair wrote. *You're being very bad tonight. You're making me very hard, and what am I supposed to do about that without you here?*

Cat wrote again. *I wish I was there. There's so much I could do to you.*

She reached over for the wine and refilled her glass. 'Why didn't you tell me about him?'

'I don't know,' I said. 'I was worried you'd judge me.'

'Why would I judge you?'

I shrugged. 'It seemed like you did for a while there.'

'I mean, yeah. But that was when I thought you were genuinely into this old guy. I understand now, though. I respect it. Girl boss and all that.' She smiled at me. 'I don't ever want you to feel like you have to hide things from me,' she said.

I smiled back at her. She was right. I should have trusted her. I should've known that I could.

'Let's keep going,' Cat said.

And for the first time since I'd come home and found her she seemed genuinely happy.

'OK,' I said.

9

Two days later Oliver and I were studying together in the library, or rather I was studying and he was sitting opposite me with his books open, refusing to shut up.

'Do you know why they broke up?' he asked.

'No,' I said, keeping my eyes trained on my laptop to signify that I was busy. 'She didn't want to tell me.'

'That sounds dramatic,' Oliver said, delighted.

I shrugged. 'It didn't sound that way. She said that sometimes things don't work out.'

He'd probably be thrilled if I told him that we'd had a threesome only a week before. Was it a coincidence? Who knew, but it was certainly juicy.

'Well, I think it's for the best,' he said. 'I don't like Cat, but I like Henry even less. I'm happy for her.'

'There's nothing wrong with Cat or Henry,' I said, eyeing him.

'Sure there isn't,' he said. 'Except for the fact they're both Tories.'

'They're not,' I said, even though I wasn't sure.

I was fairly certain Cat didn't vote Tory, because I didn't think she voted at all. Given Henry's affinity for Stirnerian anarchism, I wouldn't have been surprised to find out that he swung that way, but I had no evidence that he did. Oliver simply equated being rich with voting Tory, and Cat's family was disgustingly rich.

'Henry's dad is a Labour MP,' I said. 'It wouldn't make sense for him to vote Tory.'

'Unless he has daddy issues.'

Which he did, of course. I didn't tell Oliver this. Henry's mother had hopped off to Dubai after the divorce, and he'd been stuck with a father who treated him like a dog he didn't have time for. You want to spend some time together? Not now. I'll put you in boxing classes instead. You're feeling sad and want a hug? I'm busy, but I'll buy you a car. As if keeping a child happy was as simple as throwing money at them. Henry had been head boy at his school and got nothing but A's throughout his education, and that definitely sounds like someone with daddy issues to me.

'He messaged me,' I admitted.

Oliver's eyes were big and wide. 'What? Henry?'

I nodded. 'He asked me if she was all right. He told me to take care of her.'

Oliver opened his mouth into an incredulous gape. 'As if he would care!'

I shrugged. 'Maybe he does.'

He rolled his eyes. 'Maybe he wants to get back to fucking you. In the room right next to his ex-girlfriend's. Have I *mentioned* how messed up your living situation is?'

'You have,' I said exasperatedly. 'Multiple times. It doesn't matter. Even if he wants to, I'd never do it. And now that they've broken up, I doubt I'll ever see Henry again. Is that good enough for you?'

Oliver didn't respond. I tried to go back to my studying, reading the abstract of an article I'd found online, trying to figure out if it contained anything that would be useful to my dissertation. It was hitting me that I'd spent several weeks on research that I now wouldn't use and was starting over from scratch. Studying with Oliver hadn't helped matters; I'd glanced over at his notebook and seen that he was already planning out the structure of his dissertation.

'What are you reading?' he asked. He nodded at my books with his chin resting on his hands. 'That's not Kant. You're not procrastinating, are you?'

I rolled my eyes. 'Are you calling me the procrastinator right now?'

'I'm taking a break!'

I laughed. 'You're right. It's not Kant. I've switched my topic.'

'To what?'

'I'm going to write a rebuttal of psychological egoism,' I said. 'To prove Cat wrong.'

He grimaced at me. 'You don't need to write a rebuttal of psychological egoism. Hasn't it been disproved already? Is there any philosopher who still believes in it?'

'Cat does.'

'Well, I'm sorry to say, but there have been plenty of good arguments made against psychological egoism, so if she's not convinced yet, I doubt you'll be the one to change her mind.'

'There's no harm in trying, is there? Besides, I was an idiot to choose Kant in the first place. I don't want to spend the next two months reading him.'

He nodded in agreement. 'I hear that.'

'Now, I'm trying to focus,' I said.

But it wasn't to be.

'Hello,' said a voice next to him.

'*Salut, mon amour*,' Oliver replied.

I reminded myself of what the boyfriend's name was: Mateo. I looked up and saw him for the first time. He was handsome, slightly above Oliver's league, with a Mediterranean appearance. Tanned skin, dark curly hair and black facial hair.

He slid in next to Oliver. My friend looked happy in his company, which was all I could ask for. His face lit up looking at Mateo, but I had seen his face light up in that same way for many other guys.

'Hi,' Mateo said.

He had a slight foreign accent, and I remembered that he was French. That would explain why Oliver was so passionate about French at the moment, when his bouts of language learning didn't usually last more than a few weeks before he switched to a new one.

'Mateo, this is Louise,' Oliver said.

I plastered on my friendliest face and repeated the lines I'd learned for situations like this. 'Nice to meet you. I've heard a lot about you.'

'All good things,' Oliver assured him.

Mateo laughed awkwardly. I liked that about him. I'm always suspicious of people who are too confident and comfortable in the company of strangers.

'What are you guys up to?' Mateo asked.

'I was trying to study,' I said, 'but your boyfriend wasn't letting me.'

Oliver waved me off. 'Louise is my best friend,' he said, 'but we were just talking about *her* best friend and her recent break-up.'

'Cat's not my best friend,' I said. 'You are.'

Oliver smiled at me like he thought I was lying. 'You're so sweet,' he said. 'But she is.'

'Do you want to go get something for lunch?' Mateo asked.

'Yes,' I said, not wanting to get into Oliver's rivalry with Cat. 'Let's.'

*

That night I heard Cat crying in her room. It surprised me. Cat had been doing well since the break-up. The next day she'd emerged from her room without a hangover, wearing make-up and with perfect hair, and cleaned up the mess we'd made the night before. Since then she'd seemed fine. She had friends over that day, entertaining them in the lounge while I hid in my room. I'd never much liked her friends, and I didn't want to give them the opportunity to realize that they didn't like me either.

Until now, no more tears had been shed. I was already in my pyjamas. It was late, and I'd been going to the bathroom to brush my teeth when I heard the soft sobbing. I didn't know how to approach it. I've never been good with emotions or at comforting people; my skills in that area only go as far as patting them on the back and waiting for them to finish crying. Every time Oliver went through another break-up, he reminded me how terrible I was at this.

But I didn't feel right letting her cry on her own. I knocked on the door.

The crying stopped instantly.

'Cat?' I said. 'Are you OK?'

I heard a snivel. 'No,' she said. 'I'm sorry.'

'Can I come in?'

'Yes.'

I opened the door slowly. It felt like I was walking into a room with a scared baby animal that I must not upset. Cat was lying in bed. I couldn't see her face in the darkness, but I heard a sharp inhale and I imagined her cheeks were streaked with tears.

'What's going on?' I asked, sitting down on the edge of her bed.

'I miss him,' she said in a shaky and unsteady voice. 'Every night when I go to bed, I miss him so much.' She started to cry again. 'It's fine in the day, but, Lolo, at night, when I have nothing else to do, I can't think of anything but him.'

She probably thought I had a heart of ice, but it wasn't true. I had cried this hard over someone once. I had missed someone this badly once. There was no doubt in my mind that I had loved Maisie more than Cat and Henry had ever loved each other. Our relationship had been special. It had wrecked me. It had hospitalized me. It had ruined my opinion of love for ever. I knew what Cat felt, better than most. I put my hand on her head.

Cat turned her face to me. My eyes had adjusted enough to the light now that I could see her eyes, wet and pleading.

'Will you stay with me tonight?' she asked. 'Sleep in here? Please. I don't want to be alone.'

I smiled quickly. 'Of course.'

I started to lie down and she moved to the side to give me space.

'No,' she said. 'Lie down this way. I want to be able to hug you.'

'OK,' I said.

I lay facing away from her and she cuddled into me from the back, taking the position of big spoon. It felt so comfortable and so familiar, even though it was something we'd never done before. I could feel her breath at my neck.

'Have you ever been heartbroken?' she whispered.

'Yes,' I said without hesitation.

'Would you tell me what happened?'

I squeezed my eyes shut at the pain of those memories. The memory of me and Maisie lying face to face on my childhood bed and her reaching out to touch my cheek, just moments before our very first kiss. The memory of Maisie climbing through the attic window of her home and turning around to gesture for me to follow. The memory of the two of us sitting on that roof as the sun rose and she asked me, 'Isn't this the happiest you think we'll ever be?' I'd thought she was right.

'Louise?'

Why was I hesitating? I couldn't actually be considering telling her.

Not even Oliver knew what had happened with Maisie, only that, whatever it was, it was the reason I'd stopped dating. That time of my life was too sensitive, like poking at it might make history repeat itself. Might make me become the person I was back then. I knew she still existed; I could feel her sometimes in the shadows of my mind, observing, tugging for a certain action I had to stop her doing.

But it was Cat. How could I ever keep anything from Cat? She'd practically begged me not to.

I didn't consciously come to a conclusion. I don't remember deciding to tell her. But, before I knew it, I was speaking.

'I had a girlfriend when I was sixteen,' I said. 'Her name was Maisie.'

Next to me, Cat held her breath. 'What happened?'

'She died.'

For so many years, this was the moment I'd dreaded, and that had kept me from telling anyone. The moment when they'd inevitably mess up by trying to convince me how sorry they were. The moment I would turn into someone else entirely in their eyes. The moment they would say the wrong thing.

But Cat didn't say the wrong thing. She didn't ask how Maisie had died. She didn't say she was sorry.

Cat squeezed me. 'Tell me about her,' she said.

I hadn't been able to tell anyone about Maisie for so long. She'd occupied my mind for years without anything slipping out. I'd never realized how much conscious effort it was taking, how tired it was making me. I wanted to tell someone about her. So I did.

'She was a really special person,' I said. 'She could always tell exactly how you were feeling. I've never met someone who understood me like that. She always knew what to say. She was never confused by my emotions or thoughts. They always made sense to her.'

My voice broke and I shut my mouth. I wouldn't allow myself to cry.

'Thank you for telling me,' Cat said quietly.

We lay in silence for a few seconds. She pressed her face into the back of my head.

'I don't think anyone will ever love me like that,' she whispered. I almost couldn't make out the words.

'That's ridiculous,' I said. 'You're one of the most wonderful people I know, Cat. You're incredibly intelligent and funny, and you're beautiful and caring. There are so many people who love you.' I took a deep breath. 'Including me.'

I wasn't in the habit of telling people I loved them. I don't think I'd said it to anyone except Maisie in my whole life. Cat wasn't shy about these phrases; she handed them out like smiles or handshakes. She had casually told me she loved me the night I moved into her flat.

'You can't believe how excited I am,' she'd said. 'We're going to have such a great time living together. I love you so much.'

I'd simply stared at her, slowly blinking in surprise. Even rarer than me telling people I loved them was other people telling me they loved me. I wasn't sure I could remember my own mother saying it to me. I wasn't sure anyone except Maisie was capable of feeling that way about me.

It had almost been awkward, dodging her expressions of affection. I often wondered if she'd noticed, if it wounded her. If it did, she never said. If it did, it was never enough to make her stop saying it to me.

She gave me another squeeze. 'Thank you, Louise,' she said. 'You're the best friend anyone could ask for. I love you.'

I took one of her hands and squeezed it back. I couldn't bring myself to say it out loud. It felt even more taboo now, when I had slept with her, when I was lying in her bed with her arms around me. It felt like an even bigger confession, one I wasn't ready to make. She's only been single for a week, I reminded myself.

'You don't need to thank me,' I said. 'This is what friends are for.'

'I'm very lucky you're my friend,' she said. 'I'm so happy you're in my life.'

It made my whole body tingle. She pressed herself closer to my back, her pelvis pushing against my arse. I could feel her breasts, her firm and beautiful breasts, touching my upper back. I wondered if she was once again wearing that tiny white tank top.

'Louise,' she said.

I would've responded, but it didn't sound like a question or a call for my attention. I would've responded, but her hand was slowly moving down my stomach, and I couldn't think of a single thing to say. My pyjama top was cropped, and I felt her hand against my bare skin, warm and soft. Her entire bed smelled like her, like the lotion she slathered her body with after every shower.

She slipped her hand into the waistband of my pyjama shorts. For a moment I didn't breathe. It felt like any movement might make this end, like it was fragile. I felt her lips, softly, against the skin on my neck. I held very still.

Her hand moved further down, inside my underwear, her fingers reaching for my pussy. I moved into her hand, lifting myself upwards so that her fingers fell on to my clit. I could hear her breathing heavily right next to my ear. She touched me in a slow, languid, rubbing motion that went up and down, her fingertips so soft they were barely grazing my skin. I closed my eyes and thought of nothing except the sensation of her hands on me. Heavenly, tender, the pleasure growing with each second, the strokes becoming ever so slightly firmer, or maybe my body becoming more sensitive. It ached how slow she was, how teasing. It ached, and I wanted more, craving firmness, needing pressure.

I moaned unintentionally. She stopped. We lay there in stillness, her hand still inside my underwear, her body still pressed against mine. *Please*, I thought, *keep going*. I felt desperate, like a feral animal.

Her hand moved upwards faster than it had gone down. As it left me I wanted to grab on to it and make it stay, like I was running for a train and could see it slowly pulling away from the platform.

'I'm sorry,' she said. 'I'm sorry. I don't know why I did that.'

'It's OK,' I said quickly.

It was too late. She had pulled her hand away entirely and she kept both hands to herself now, firmly away from me, though her mouth was still on my neck.

'I'm sorry,' she said again.

'It's OK,' I repeated.

I wondered if she would ask me to turn over. If she did, I would do it, and I would kiss her. I wondered if she would explain why she had done that. I wondered if she would keep going. I so desperately wanted her to keep going.

'I think I need to sleep,' she said.

My insides were cold with the disappointment. I was still throbbing from her touch. If she hadn't asked me to stay tonight, I would've needed to go to my own room and masturbate frantically.

'OK,' I said. 'Let's sleep.'

I spent most of the next day at the library, only coming home in the evening. I hadn't spoken to Cat; she'd been asleep when I woke up and hadn't woken when I left her room and got ready for the day. I'd let her sleep, hoping she would text me at some point during the day. She hadn't.

When I came home, I understood why.

There was a guy with her on the couch. She was laughing loudly, her face aglow. I stared at them in the doorway to the lounge, knowing she'd already heard me come in, knowing she was deliberately ignoring me while she finished laughing. The guy looked at me and gave me a small wave. Cat finally turned her head slightly in my direction, still grinning widely.

'Louise,' she said. 'This is Paul. Paul, this is my flatmate Louise.'

'Hello,' Paul said.

He was uglier than Henry. His teeth were too big, and uneven. I didn't like the way he said nothing to me except that hello, simply staring and smiling, then returning his attention to Cat.

'I'd never have the balls to say anything like that,' she said, wiping the tears from her eyes, still laughing at their private joke.

'Of course you would,' he said. 'Don't be modest. You have more balls than I do.'

'Oh, do I?' Cat said, laughing again.

Paul laughed too.

I was invisible, holding the bag of groceries I'd got myself for dinner. They continued talking to each other. I carefully observed how close they were sitting: too close, almost touching. When she laughed, she put her hand on his knee.

I went into the kitchen. I was confused and restless. As I boiled the water for my noodles, I paced back and forth. I tried to listen to their conversation and I tried to make sense of what was happening. Was this a date? Was he a friend? No, I'd met all Cat's friends, and I'd never seen Paul before.

By the time I left the kitchen with my dinner in a bowl, they weren't speaking so loudly any more, and they weren't laughing. Their voices were soft and quiet. If she had looked over at me, I would've given her a facial indicator that I was confused and I wanted to know who this guy was. It would've been light-hearted, though, the same way you look at a friend when you see them making out with a stranger in the club. But she didn't look at me.

Neither of them looked at me at all.

I spent the whole night in a confused and angry daze, listening to the rise and fall of their voices and the peals of her beautiful laughter. I went through all Cat's social media accounts and looked at the hundreds of accounts she followed, searching for someone named Paul. I could find nothing. Maybe he wasn't big on social media. Maybe they'd just met. I drew the closest thing I could get to his face with only my memory as a reference, and I scribbled over it until his face was covered in black and the pen broke through the paper.

He didn't leave that night. I was still awake when I heard them retire to her room. He wasn't even sleeping on the couch, then. Was Paul gay? Oliver's gaydar has always been better than mine, but Oliver wasn't here to help me.

They were quieter in her room. I kept waiting to hear the sounds of sex, for panting and moaning and the banging of her headboard. I heard nothing. There was the occasional soft giggle or the creak of the bed, and I strained my ears even more, trying so hard to catch something else. Were they just having a sleepover? Were they fucking very quietly? Had they already done it out in the lounge? Had they done it before I came home? I thought about Paul's malformed teeth along her thighs, between her legs. I thought about her closing her eyes to pretend he was someone else, to imagine that someone more handsome was with her.

I was unable to fall asleep. I lay awake, obsessively listening, every nerve in my body on edge, unable to wind down in any way. *This is ridiculous,* I told myself. *Why would you care if she's sleeping with him? You wouldn't want to hear it anyway. It has nothing to do with you.*

But last night she'd touched me. I could still feel her phantom fingers between my legs, her wrist between my skin and the waistband of my trousers, her breath against my neck. How could she do that without even speaking to me about it? How could she do that and then fuck someone like Paul? *If* she was fucking Paul, I reminded myself. She probably wasn't. They were probably just friends. He was probably gay. Cat wasn't quiet during sex.

I was seething. I knew I shouldn't be angry, but I was. The night before, she'd made me expect — something. I wasn't quite sure what, but it certainly wasn't us returning to normal as if nothing had ever happened. I'd told her about Maisie. That wasn't something I could come back from. That should have changed everything.

And she'd told me she loved me. Now she was in the next room with Paul, as if I didn't matter at all. As if he was better in bed than I was. As if he would ever treat her better than I would. I felt so alone in my rage. I wanted to text Oliver, but I knew he'd laugh at me. He'd be confused, and then he'd laugh at me. This would make no sense to him unless I told him everything, and if I told him everything, he would judge me and say I'd placed myself in this situation, and he'd say he'd told me so.

I opened up my chat with Henry. His last messages still sat unanswered. It was bold of him to have sent that second text, the one about looking after Cat, when I had never replied to the first. Well, now I was going to reply. Now I was going to tell him how Cat was really doing.

I told myself it was because it would make the break between them even more solid. Maybe he'd take it as a sign that she'd moved on, so he should forget about her. Maybe, hopefully, he'd feel jealous and angry that she was already sleeping around. If I was being honest with myself, though, I think I just wanted someone to share my anger.

I typed out a message to Henry. *There's a guy sleeping in her room right now.* No value judgement, no indication of what I wanted him to do with that information. That didn't concern me. He could feel however he wanted to. I was an impartial messenger.

Oliver would've told me I was only after drama. Oliver would've told me there was no reason to send that message and I shouldn't do it. But Oliver wasn't with me in the bed that night, just a wall away from Cat and Paul doing whatever they were doing. So I sent the text to Henry and finally tried to sleep.

10

He was there the next day. I don't know when Paul left and Henry came back, but that's how it happened.

I had heard the voices in her room when I went to grab lunch. One male and one female, sounding serious. I had assumed it was Paul, and wondered if they were having the post-sex conversation about whether this was a one-time thing or not.

But when I heard someone come into the kitchen and turned around, it was Henry. He'd had his hair cut shorter.

He smiled at me. 'Good morning,' he said.

'Hello,' I said, still staring at him in surprise.

He sheepishly held up a glass. 'Just came to get some water.'

'OK,' I said, stepping away from the sink to allow him access. 'Sure.'

He ambled past me and filled up the glass in complete silence. I thought maybe he'd bring up the text I'd sent him in the middle of the night; it had probably been already past two a.m. That must have seemed odd to him. But he didn't speak, so I followed his lead. He walked back to her room and I watched him from the doorway. I thought I could still see the imprint of Paul's arse on our couch.

Later that day she knocked on my door. I was spending time with the mice, allowing them to run up and down my arms. Squeak was taking full advantage of this privilege, while Pip preferred to grip on to my sleeve and chew on it aggressively.

Cat sat down on the floor next to me and looked at them, smiling.

'They're such curious creatures,' she said. She pointed at Pip. 'I like her most. She's feisty.'

'She's the smart one,' I said. 'Her name is Pip.'

Cat snorted. 'I like that. And this one?'

'That's Squeak.'

She held out a finger to Squeak, who was sitting on my shoulder and sniffed it with great interest.

'Hello,' Cat cooed.

I knew she hadn't come in here to see the mice. She'd never shown enough interest in them to even learn their names.

'She's more sociable,' I said about Squeak.

'I think she's like me,' Cat said. 'And the other one is like you.'

I thought about this and decided she was right. Pip had my thoughtful nature and cautious reclusiveness. Squeak had Cat's lust for adventure and appetite for attention, her aptitude for social interaction, drawing people to her like a light draws moths.

'You know Henry was here earlier,' Cat said.

'I was going to ask,' I said. 'Did he have some things to pick up?'

'No,' Cat said, keeping her attention on Squeak and not looking at me. 'He was here for quite a while, talking.'

I waited for her to continue. She didn't. She stroked Squeak with one finger, and Squeak skittered away, displeased at being touched.

'What were you talking about?'

Cat cleared her throat. 'We're back together,' she said.

The break-up had lasted eight days.

'Hmm,' I said.

I wanted to punch myself. Just like it was my fault they had got together the first time, it must have been my fault they had got back together now. My text *had* made him jealous. Jealous enough to go back to her so no one else could have her.

'I hope you don't think I'm foolish,' Cat said.

'Why would I think that? I don't even know why you broke up in the first place.'

'Well, the reasons seem silly now. I suppose that's why we're back together.'

She doesn't actually care if I think she's foolish, I thought. She just wants me to know that she has considered the possibility and she knows her actions could be seen that way. She wants to prevent me from being able to say that it is foolish and she can't possibly have thought this through in the one day since she was lying next to some other guy.

'Who's Paul?' I asked.

'I told you, he's a friend.'

'Did you sleep with him?'

She looked at me. 'Why would you care if I slept with him?'

'I don't care. It's your life. I was just wondering.'

'It sounds like you do care.'

I have never been very good at monitoring my tone. It isn't something that comes to me naturally, the way it does to neurotypicals. When I experience difficult emotions, I sometimes forget to put in the effort. Because it is effortful, the constant vigil I keep over my facial expressions and tone, the thought process that goes into every smile and twitch. I had evidently failed to sound unbothered and disinterested.

'I just find it strange how he was here last night and now you're back with Henry,' I said.

'It's not strange,' Cat said.

'Did you want this?'

It took a moment too long before she replied. 'Why wouldn't I?'

'Why did you hesitate?'

I made myself look at her. She was staring at her lap. She was subdued and quiet, not smiling, not ecstatic. As if getting back together with Henry was a compromise, an adjustment she'd made that wasn't quite ideal.

She shrugged. 'I don't know what you want me to say,' she said.

'I want you to be sure of what you want,' I said.

Cat rolled her eyes. 'I know what I want,' she said. 'But you can't always do what you want, Louise.'

I blinked. It felt like an admission that I'd been right, that she didn't want this. I should've been able to be surer about that. I've never been sure of anything if it isn't spelled out for me.

'What does that mean?'

Cat scoffed and shook her head. 'Nothing,' she said. 'It's nothing.'

She stood up and left the room.

'Are you feeling depressed at all?' Susannah asked.

I blinked and brought myself back to the present. I'd been thinking of other things. I'd been thinking of Cat in particular. I didn't know if Susannah had said anything else prior to that sentence. 'Why do you ask?'

'You seem distracted and a bit . . . a bit downcast, I suppose.'

'I'm not,' I said.

She peered suspiciously at me, as if she expected me to tell her everything if she just gave me enough time. 'Are you sure nothing has happened?'

I'd had my first meltdown in years after Cat and Henry got back together. They used to be more commonplace, especially in the time after Maisie. But I hadn't had a single meltdown since I had started university, and it had made me feel very adult. It had made me feel not completely disconnected from all the other students, less like a toddler unable to control their emotions. I had no longer been someone who needed to be dragged kicking and screaming out of supermarkets by an embarrassed mother or removed from the classroom to sit on the floor in the hallway and scream.

Then Cat and Henry got back together, and it was my fucking fault. Drawing wouldn't help. Playing with the mice wouldn't help. I wasn't conscious enough to think of anything that could help.

I knew I was crying a lot, and I knew I was hitting the floor with my hands and banging my head against the wall. There wasn't much else I knew. As soon as it was over, everything that had occurred slipped out of my mind. I found myself sitting on the floor of my bedroom, rocking back and forth with a headache, my breathing laboured. It was frightening just how thoroughly I'd lost control of myself. I looked down at my hands and found that they were shaking. I wondered if I had ruined anything, if I had wailed loudly enough for Cat to hear me.

The aftermath was almost worse. This was the part of myself I hated most.

There was no way I was telling Susannah any of that. I knew she would try to be understanding, but there are things that normal people do and there are things that they don't. Things that set you apart. People always say there's no wrong way to express your emotions, but show them an autistic meltdown and they'll recoil with disgust. If I was too honest with Susannah, I ran every risk of being sent back to the inpatient unit.

But she was right that I might now seem depressed. I had been so exhausted since the meltdown, feeling as though I was trudging through water.

'I'm sure,' I said. 'I'm absolutely fine.'

They had Henry's birthday party at our place. I made sure to ask Oliver to be one of the first to arrive. Still, by the time he did, a dozen or so of Cat and Henry's upper-class friends were already there in outfits more expensive than my student loan, speaking with cut-glass accents about nothing but themselves.

'Now, tell me,' said Oliver, 'what on earth is going on?'

'I'm just as confused as you are,' I said. 'Come, we can put your coat in my room so it's safe from everyone else.'

'Thank you.'

We went through the lounge to get to my room. Cat and Henry were entertaining as if their relationship was as strong as ever. They stood at the centre of the group of people in our home, each holding a glass, his hand on her waist. Soft classical music played in the background, muted enough for conversation, boring enough that I knew Cat had made this playlist according to Henry's tastes instead of her own.

Once Oliver had thrown his coat on to my bed, we went back to join the party, standing at the edge of the group. Nothing about the decor indicated that this was a birthday party. Cat and Henry wouldn't do something as tacky as blowing up balloons or hanging a plastic banner on the wall. I eyed the selection of fancy-looking canapés on the dining table, but no one else had dug in yet, and I was not going to be the first.

'Mateo couldn't come?' I asked.

'He works in a pub,' Oliver said. 'He's at work right now, *desafortunadamente*.'

'What a shame,' I said, even though I was happy I had him all to myself.

'He would've made this more bearable, that's for sure.'

Cat was ignoring me. She had been since we'd had that little spat in my room a couple of days earlier; she'd said good morning to me on a few occasions, but we hadn't had a full conversation. At the time, it hadn't felt like enough to warrant the silent treatment. Now I wondered if I'd said something worse than I'd thought. She looked at Oliver rather than me and waved at him.

'Happy birthday,' Oliver said.

Henry nodded. 'Thank you very much.'

'Anyway,' Cat said, 'what were you saying?'

'I was saying,' Henry said, 'that I disagree with you.'

'Ah, well, then maybe we should move on.'

Someone laughed.

'Philosophy does have real-world applications,' Henry said. 'It's an excellent tool for determining the best course of action or our choices in life.'

'So if you believe Stirner,' Cat said, giving him an amused look, 'you do whatever you want at all times with no regard for other people.'

Henry smiled at her and put his thumb on her cheek. 'And if you're a psychological egoist,' he said, 'you always act in your own interest.'

As he spoke, I grabbed some glasses and poured both myself and Oliver a gin and tonic. The alcohol was plentiful tonight. Oliver stood with the crowd and looked so very interested, his brows furrowed and his head nodding softly. It almost made me laugh, and I bumped his side with my shoulder.

'You don't need to be a psychological egoist to do that,' Cat said. 'We all do it. That's the point. It isn't a matter of believing you should only do what's in your own interest; it isn't ethical egoism. It's not meant to be a guiding light for morality; it's meant to be an analysis of human behaviour.' She shrugged. 'As far as I see it, there are no other real-world applications for philosophy.'

'What about Mills on race?' Oliver said, and they both looked over at him. 'If the question of what race is was just about analysing human opinion, all we'd need to do to figure out the answer is ask people. But we don't have an answer. We need to think about it. We need philosophy to help us.'

'Thank you, Oliver,' Henry said, like he'd been proven right.

'Well,' Cat said, 'the problem is that none of that matters very much, because we don't use philosophy to help us form those opinions or to help us make decisions. It doesn't matter how much the academics argue about it, the average person doesn't care. When we look at someone, we think, "That's a Black person," because they look a certain way. We don't think about the fact that appearance can't be all that determines race, because a white-passing person could then be white despite their entire family background being something else. We don't then think, "Well, if it isn't appearance, what else is it?"'

Henry rolled his eyes and sighed. Then he turned to me. 'Louise,' he said, 'what do you think?'

'I think Cat's right,' I said. 'People don't think through their actions or their opinions, and even if they did, they'd hardly bother to read through countless philosophy books on the subject to consider all the possible answers and arguments.'

'So philosophy's entirely useless?' said Oliver.

'Yes,' I said. 'The only question is why we're studying it at all.'

It's often the first thing someone asks when you tell them you're studying philosophy. Why would you choose *that*? As if we're all unaware it makes us completely unemployable and fails to prepare us for the real world in any way whatsoever.

The thing is, I didn't choose philosophy. I've spent my entire life doing it, trying to figure out how the world works, what's right and wrong, what people expect of me and what they don't.

Cat smiled. She took Henry's arm. 'Let's stop talking about philosophy,' she said. 'I'm sure every science student in here is positively exhausted with us.'

People laughed, and she smiled genially. It was Henry's birthday, but Cat was the one they were here to see, I was sure of it. Someone asked her about her recent Riviera trip, and she was happy to launch into the details I had already heard so many times. Henry jumped in a couple of times with comments clearly meant to show everyone that he too had once been to the French Riviera. Henry had travelled nearly as much as Cat, but his stories were never very exciting.

Oliver leaned in close to my ear. 'I think he cheated on her,' he whispered.

'What makes you say that?' I whispered back.

'Come on,' he said. 'Do you think he'd pass up the opportunity to fuck someone else if it appeared?'

I drank my drink silently.

The crowd gradually grew to more than twice its original size, but the party remained tame. There was no cocaine being passed around on the china handed down from Cat's grandmother. No one was outrageously plastered. The music continued being instrumental and slow enough to almost put me to sleep, nothing like the booming techno of modern nightclubs.

I hung out with Oliver. He introduced me to Chloe, a girl he knew from his class on gender and race. She was cute and unmistakably queer, the side shave and nose ring giving her away. I was relieved to find someone else who didn't look like they'd stepped out of one of those charity galas for rich people.

The three of us talked about a terrible Netflix show we'd all seen, about a lesbian teenage vampire who falls for a lesbian teenage vampire hunter. I was pleasantly tipsy and delightfully entertained by the conversation. We'd all hated the show, but while I had only managed to watch two episodes and Oliver had turned it off twenty minutes into the pilot, Chloe had sat through the whole first season.

'Why ever would you do that?' Oliver asked, sincerely appalled.

'You wouldn't understand,' Chloe said. 'Gay men get representation everywhere these days, but women who like other women don't have that privilege. Especially not women of colour.'

'That's not true,' Oliver said. 'Not since *Orange is the New Black.*'

'It is, though,' I said. 'Us queer women fight for our scraps of representation and we migrate in a huge flock from one show to the next when they kill off our only lesbian.'

Chloe nodded. 'Yes, because the only times we ever do see ourselves on film and TV we have to die.'

'That happens to us too,' Oliver said.

'Just accept that you have male privilege,' I said.

'I'm gay *and* Black!' Oliver exclaimed. 'Doesn't that make up for the fact that I have a penis?'

Chloe looked at me and smiled. 'Does it?'

I pursed my lips and thought about it. 'Hmm,' I said. 'Depends whether you're read as gay by others, I suppose.'

'Very valid,' Chloe said. 'It's more like masculine privilege.'

'God knows I don't have that,' Oliver said. 'So am I fine? Can I re-enter the conversation?'

'No.' I booped him on the nose with one of my fingers. 'Still too male.'

He rolled his eyes. 'Fine. I'll try to make up for it by getting us some more drinks.'

I talked to Chloe while he was gone. She was obviously flirting, her eyes drifting down to my lips while she licked her own, her gaze suggestive and warm, her compliments generous. I asked her how she knew Henry, and she told me that she didn't but she was flatmates with one of his friends. Said friend was a straight guy. I offered my condolences for what I assumed must be her terrible living conditions, and she laughed. She said it wasn't too bad after she'd taught him how to dry himself after a shower without leaving the bathmat wet and turning it mouldy. And after she'd taught him how to stack a dishwasher.

She couldn't stay long; she said she had an essay due the next day. By the time she left she'd put her number into my phone. Oliver hadn't come back yet; either he was pre-occupied elsewhere or he'd also been able to tell that Chloe was flirting and was giving us some privacy.

I felt very tired and had a slight headache. The lights were too bright and every sound was very loud. A laugh from the other end of the room sounded like nails on a blackboard. It grated on my brain. I knew this meant I needed a break, so I went out on to the balcony.

The air out there was cool and relaxing. I leaned against the railing and closed my eyes, letting the breeze chill my face. It was hot and burning from the heat inside, the bodies tightly packed together in the summer night.

The balcony door slid open and I opened my eyes again. It was Henry, a packet of cigarettes in his hand.

'I didn't realize you were out here,' he said. An obvious lie. He'd only needed to look through the window to see me. 'Do you mind if I join you?' He held up the cigarettes as if he wanted to reassure me that he had a legitimate reason.

'Not at all,' I said.

Of course I did mind, but I didn't want to start an argument with him on his birthday. He didn't like his birthdays. I remembered that. He'd once drunkenly told me his dad got him the same model of VR glasses two years in a row when he was a teenager. I wondered if he'd ever confided in Cat like that. It had been rare that he was vulnerable with me. Maybe he was different with her.

He held a cigarette in his mouth, cupping it with one hand while he lit the lighter, to avoid the wind getting to the flame before it could take hold. The balcony felt smaller than ever. We were standing so close together. He always seemed taller when it was just the two of us.

Henry slowly exhaled, a plume of smoke exiting his mouth.

'I thought you were meant to have quit,' I said.

'As far as Cat is concerned, I have.' He had a glint in his eye and a smirk at the corner of his lips. He took another drag.

'So you only smoke in secret,' I said. 'Do you like keeping secrets from Cat?'

Henry laughed, the smoke billowing from his mouth and nose. He held his hand out to the window behind us. 'I'm not very good at it, am I?'

We were in full view of the entire lounge, and she was right there. Her white dress made her stand out in the crowd. She was speaking to Oliver, holding on to both his arms, and she was laughing. As if she could sense that I was looking at her, her eyes drifted over to me. I felt admonished, as if the look she was giving me was meant to convey that I had done, or was about to do, something wrong.

She looked away first, returning her attention to Oliver, speaking animatedly in the way she always did with people she wasn't particularly close to. The people she was never quite as subdued or relaxed with as she was with Henry and me.

I looked away too. 'I haven't said happy birthday yet,' I said. 'So happy birthday.'

'Thank you,' he said. 'I think I'm past the point of caring about birthdays.'

'I think you pass that point when you turn ten.'

He smiled softly. 'No, I think I cared until I was about fifteen.'

He took another puff of his cigarette, the butt glowing against his face. He breathed out. 'I wanted to thank you for sending me that text.'

'Why would you thank me? I wasn't doing you a favour.'

He raised a sceptical brow at me. 'No?'

'No. I was just telling you a fact.'

'And there was no particular reason you thought I should know that fact? There was no ulterior motive?'

'No,' I said.

'Well,' he said, 'thank you either way.'

'Is it the reason you're back together?'

'I thought you didn't care what I did with that information.'

'I don't. Just curious.'

He put his forearms on the balcony railing and looked out at the city. 'I suppose you thought we'd broken up for good,' he said. 'But you won't be rid of me that easily.'

'Why would I want to be rid of you?'

He glanced at me out of the corner of his eye. 'Maybe you don't,' he said slowly.

I said nothing, because he'd been right. I did want to get rid of him. I did want them to break up again, permanently this time.

Done with the conversation, I walked back towards the door. The way he was standing made it nearly impossible not to brush against him, but I squeezed myself as far away as I could. I wasn't sure if Cat was still watching, but it would look suspicious if I checked.

I slid the balcony door open and went back inside. The flat smelled distinctly of weed. It was still incredibly warm in there. There was a sheen of sweat on Cat's forehead when I sidled up next to Oliver.

'There you are,' he said.

'I just needed some air.'

Cat smiled. 'Don't we all?' Some of her red lipstick had rubbed off, leaving a spot of pink visible in the middle of her mouth. She looked over at Henry. 'He's smoking again,' she noted.

'Is he supposed to have stopped?' Oliver asked.

'Yes,' Cat said. She looked at me. 'What were you talking about out there?'

'Nothing,' I said. 'I just wished him a happy birthday. And I asked about the smoking.'

Cat nodded. She forced her lips into a smile again. 'Well, we —' she looked at Oliver — 'were just discussing the hot new boyfriend. You've met him, haven't you?'

'I have,' I said. 'Only once.'

'Do you approve? Is he good enough for our Oliver?'

I knew he would bring that up later; he would be upset that she had called him 'our Oliver', like her relationship with him was in any way equivalent to the one between us.

'I don't need your approval,' Oliver said. 'Either of you.'

'Well, of course not, but I want to know if he's a decent person,' Cat said.

'He is,' I said. 'I like him, and he seems to treat Oliver well.'

'He does,' Oliver said. 'He cooked me a three-course meal a few days ago for no particular reason at all. It was heavenly.'

'Oh my god,' Cat said. 'If only Henry would ever do that!'

'I would hate to be heterosexual,' Oliver said.

'Oh, shush.' Cat playfully slapped him on the arm with a smile, and he laughed. 'Is it really so bad, Lolo?'

'Being heterosexual? I wouldn't know.'

'No, being with a straight man. It isn't, is it?'

She still had that nonchalant glint in her eye, but I wondered if there was something else behind those words. They seemed so pointed.

131

'It's not so bad,' I said. 'But it's nothing compared to being with another woman.'

I watched Cat's face carefully, gauging her reaction. I hadn't said it suggestively, not with Oliver right next to us, but she must have caught my meaning because she smiled softly.

'Have you heard about the orgasm gap?' Oliver said. 'According to this study, straight women come much less than straight men do, but lesbians orgasm much more frequently.'

As he spoke, Cat looked down at the floor. I thought I saw her gently bite her lip.

'Of course I know that,' I said. 'I don't know why they'd need to conduct a study.'

'I suppose it makes sense,' Cat said, looking at me rather than Oliver.

I winked at her. It felt bold, but it also felt like she'd most likely take it as a joke.

She chuckled, and Oliver looked briefly confused. I didn't say anything to explain.

If she'd been upset with me, I was fairly certain she wasn't any more.

11

Oliver spent the night. I always let him, being familiar with the high cost of Ubers. We didn't wake up until eleven and then we went to brunch.

He devoured his plate of pancakes, while I was a little too hungover to be enjoying myself. I poked at my food, regretting what I had got myself into.

'I saw you and Chloe got along last night,' he said, his eyebrows raised with a whole lot of meaning.

'We did, I suppose.'

'Did you get her contact details or do you want me to give them to you?'

'I've already got them.'

He started dancing. I never understood how he could be so cheerful this soon after waking up.

'I knew it,' he said, bobbing his shoulders. 'I fucking knew it.'

'Come on,' I said. 'It doesn't mean anything.'

'Doesn't it? Doesn't it?'

'No.'

'Well, then it should.'

I moved the food around on the plate with my fork. 'I don't know.'

Chloe was attractive and funny, and she was into me. We'd probably have fun together. Probably end up sleeping together, and god knows I wanted that after all the time I'd spent exclusively with Alistair having such heterosexual sex.

It wasn't the fact that he was a man; it was the fact that the intercourse was so heteronormative. Always me going down on him longer than he did on me, always ending it with penis in vagina. No strap-ons or turn-taking, no foreplay that lasted longer than about ten minutes.

But Chloe had seemed like such a sweet and good person, and I would hate to disappoint her or lead her on. The real problem, however, was Cat. There was a part of my brain that still liked to remind me that she and Henry had broken up before, that their relationship was unstable right now and might end at any moment. What would I do if I was involved with Chloe at that point?

'I don't want to give her the wrong impression,' I said.

'What do you mean?' Oliver spoke with his mouth full of pancake. 'I bet Chloe is DTF.'

'But is she DTFIL? Because you know I'm not.'

'I have no idea what that means.'

'Down to fall in love.'

'You make me feel old.'

'Don't. I just made it up.' I wiped the corner of my mouth with a napkin.

Oliver nodded. 'Don't you ever think that you're a bit too strict with that no-dating rule?' he asked. 'I mean, you don't plan to keep it up for ever, do you?'

'I do,' I said. 'I don't believe anyone needs a relationship to live a happy and fulfilling life.'

'Of course not, but it does add something to any life. It's quite enjoyable.'

'I know you think so,' I said. 'Is that why you've had so many?'

He threw one of his strawberries at me.

'In my experience, what relationships add isn't something

134

good,' I said. 'It's usually quite the opposite. I know that's not the case for most people, but I'm not most people. I know myself enough to know that.'

But when I said it out loud, I imagined waking up next to Cat in the morning and it gave me butterflies in my stomach.

Oliver brought his shoulders up to his ears. 'What does that even mean, Louise? You can't have a relationship because, what, you had a bad experience when you were younger? Because you're autistic?'

I cringed at the fact that he had boiled Maisie down to that one phrase: a bad experience. He didn't know, but she had been so much more than that. Maisie was the only person who had ever truly understood me. I would never find someone else like her.

'No,' I said. 'Because I love too intensely. I get too involved.'

So stop thinking about Cat's smile, and stop playing her laughter on repeat in your head.

'That's a good thing,' Oliver said.

I shook my head. 'It's a good thing in moderation, but I just said I don't do it in moderation. I overdo it to the extreme. You know all this already.'

And I knew it too, so why did my heart start beating faster when I thought about Cat?

'Yes, but I still don't quite believe you.'

Did I even believe myself any more?

'You don't have to,' I said. 'Just leave it, all right? I don't need to have a relationship.'

I forced myself to remember Maisie. *Is that what you want again?* I asked myself.

No, I didn't.

Oliver rolled his eyes. 'Fine.' He pointed at my plate. 'Are you going to finish that?'

I had a whole pancake left and his plate was so empty I wondered if he'd somehow licked it clean without me noticing.

'No,' I said, pushing my plate towards him. 'You have it.'

They had to break up.

And if I had to, I would make it happen.

When I got home later, Cat was on the couch reading. Her laptop and notebooks were spread out across the coffee table. When she looked over at me, I saw that she had a black eye.

'Hello,' she said, smiling.

'What happened to you?'

She touched a hand to her eye as if she had forgotten. 'This?' She chuckled. 'I drank a bit too much last night and managed to bang my head against the edge of the bed.'

'You weren't that drunk,' I said.

'No,' she said, 'just tipsy and clumsy. I don't need alcohol to injure myself.'

I knew this to be true. Cat often walked around with a minor injury, like a broken toenail from dropping a tin on it or a small cut on her finger from cooking. Still, I wasn't sure I believed this story. Who could bang their head against the edge of a bed hard enough to leave a bruise? But if Cat didn't want to share, I wasn't going to pry.

'You're not upset with me, are you?' she asked.

'Why would I be?'

'It seemed like you were.'

'I thought you were upset with me.'

'Well, I'm not. So let's be friends again?'

'I didn't know we'd ever stopped,' I said.

She smiled happily. 'Come. Sit down.'

I sat down.

'I should have told you this earlier,' she said. 'Thank you for telling me about Maisie. I know that can't have been easy for you. I'm sorry I wasn't in the right mindset to offer you sympathy at the time.'

My heart pounded. I managed to shrug. 'It's OK,' I said. 'It's been years. I've had enough sympathy.'

Cat looked me in the eyes. 'Have you?'

I opened my mouth and I realized I'd lied. I'd never had much sympathy from anyone. At the time, my mum had been almost more devastated than me. There had been so much crying and so much hugging and asking about my feelings at every turn. She couldn't look at me without tearing up. Of course, I hadn't been able to tell her how I really felt. And since then, well. No one else had ever known. A bad experience, that's what Oliver had called it. I suddenly craved Cat's sympathy intensely.

'I thought so,' she said, her voice quiet. 'I think you've been bottling this up more than you should have. And trying to ignore pain is like trying to ignore a twisted ankle. You keep walking on it and it gets worse. If you go on for too long, the damage . . .' She shook her head. 'Well, it becomes irreversible eventually.' She gave me a sad, weak smile. Her voice almost broke there at the end.

'Have you?' I whispered. 'Have you bottled something up until it becomes irreversible?'

Her mouth twitched. 'Now's not the time to talk about me. Lolo, you don't have to keep this to yourself. I'm here if you need to let it out. What you experienced was so awful and so traumatic, and it never should have happened. You didn't deserve that.'

She put her arms around me. I lost my breath at the feeling of her skin against mine. *Don't cry*, I told myself, *don't cry*.

I relaxed into her shoulder and inhaled the smell of her shampoo. She was right. I'd waited seven years for someone to tell me these things, and I hadn't even known. Cat had, though.

She also knew what to do next, that it was time to stop dwelling on this and that I needed to feel normal again.

'Do you want to study together?' she asked.

Cat always knew.

We still didn't agree. I had most recently read Hume, and he offered a solid argument against psychological egoism, which I recounted to Cat.

'He gives an example,' I said, 'of a mother who attends to her sick child with such dedication that she completely disregards her own well-being and stops taking care of herself, causing her own health to decline. Her child dies and then she dies. How can that ever be motivated by self-interest?'

'Because she loves the child,' Cat said. 'We've gone over this before. She'd be devastated to lose her child.'

'I don't think that's a satisfactory answer,' I said. 'It's not in her best interest to love another person that much, is it? It's not to her advantage to love so strongly that it kills her.'

It's not to anyone's advantage. I knew that better than most.

'It's to her advantage to raise a child to take care of her in old age,' said Cat, 'to be her companion throughout life.'

'She could have another.'

'Which it is not in her best interest to do, especially at the time Hume was writing. Pregnancy is taxing and risky, and so is childbirth.' Cat shrugged like she was confident she had solved the issue. 'Altruistic actions are always means to selfish ends.'

'I don't think you were telling the truth when you told me you were happy to be proven wrong,' I said.

She laughed and wrapped her arms around my neck, planting a kiss on my forehead and squeezing me tightly. 'No one ever wants to be proven wrong,' she said. 'That's human nature.'

That weekend Alistair drove us to the next town over. We had been to all the nearby hotels already, and we never went to the same place twice. A young woman and a rich-looking man twice her age sharing a double bedroom – it was preposterous to return to the same hotel.

I was scrolling on my phone in the passenger seat. Chloe had sent me a message.

Hi! It was really nice meeting you. Hope you don't think I'm weird and creepy for this! Smiling blushing emoji.

Because I didn't know how to respond immediately, I went to her account instead. Her feed was very aesthetic, filled with books and gorgeous pictures of her in a number of scenic locations all across the world, always with florals in the background. Her captions were all in both English and Cantonese. She had more followers than me, which is a very low bar, but less than Cat. I sighed. I might not be the best at social etiquette, but I knew I needed to reply to her at some point.

I was still thinking about what to say when Alistair spoke up.

'You're going to have to show me how to use it,' he said. 'I'm not very good with technology.'

He didn't need to clarify that he was referring to the vibrator in my handbag.

'That's all right,' I'd said. 'You have other strengths.'

139

I slipped my hand in between his legs as he drove, and I put Chloe out of my mind for the time being.

The hotel room was not as nice as the last one we'd been to, but Alistair was more likely to mind that. His standards were higher than mine. He took off his jacket and tie, and I unzipped the back of my dress.

'I have an idea,' I said. 'I think it could be fun.'

His face perked up at that, his eyes alert. Alistair loved variety.

'You know about role-playing?' I asked.

'I'm open to it,' he said.

We'd never attempted anything like it, presumably because we were already living one of the most clichéd role-playing dynamics. What would we role-play – that I was his wife? He came over to me and helped pull the straps of my dress down over my shoulders.

'I'd like you to call me by a new name,' I said. 'I want you to pretend I'm someone else.'

'I see,' he said, smiling. 'What do you have in mind?'

'I want you to call me Cat,' I said.

He frowned. 'Like the animal?'

'No, like Catherine. I'm not a furry, Alistair.'

He laughed lightly at that. 'OK, OK. Cat. I can do that. And what about me? What should my name be?'

I wanted to tell him that his name should be Louise. It almost slipped out of my mouth before I thought better of it.

'How about Henry?' I suggested, reaching for his belt.

He leaned in to kiss me. 'Are we role-playing the Tudors?' he said amusedly.

'If you say so,' I said.

12

My mother wrapped her arms around me. 'Louise. Why don't you do this more often?'

Because of this, I thought. I couldn't keep track of the number of times we had discussed my aversion to hugging. I had expressed to her so many times how uncomfortable it made me. When I was little, I would cry – I would actually cry – and then she would cry too. 'Why won't you hug your own mother?' she would say. 'Why won't you love your own mother?'

So despite how much I cried, she would pull me in anyway, just like she did now. I stood there with my arms against my sides and waited for it to be over. If I explained to her again, she would nod and smile and tell me how difficult that must be. But then she would take a breath and look away from me and talk about how much more difficult it was for her not to be able to hug her own daughter, with tears barely suppressed in her eyes.

'But I understand,' she would say. 'If that's how it has to be, I understand.'

Which of course meant that it would not be how things would ever be. In the end I would always feel guilty enough to say that I supposed it was fine. Just a few seconds, what's that? But every hug seemed to be longer than the last after I'd started university. Which led me to delay the next visit, which led her to hug me even more. A vicious cycle.

'I'm so busy,' I lied. 'It's a master's, you know. That's not exactly a part-time commitment.'

'I know,' she said. 'I know, I know. My daughter is so accomplished and successful; you don't need to remind me.'

She gave me a look and a smile. I knew I was meant to laugh, so I invoked a humble smile and an awkward chuckle.

Mum was satisfied. 'I'll put the kettle on,' she said, like she always did.

'Great,' I said.

Before I followed her into the kitchen, I inhaled deeply and gathered all my strength. The lounge was to my right. On the mantel above the fireplace she still had several of my old drawings, framed and displayed like objects far more valuable than the unsophisticated doodles of a teenager. They depicted people I'd considered important back then, actors from my favourite shows that I could barely name any more. The drawing of Maisie was at the far corner, half hidden behind another, as if Mum knew it made me uncomfortable to see but didn't care enough to remove it completely.

I squeezed my hands into themselves. I stepped into the kitchen ready with a smile in case she turned around. She pottered around, collecting crackers and mugs and teaspoons, forgetting once again where she'd put the sugar.

We sat down with some tea. I never drank tea at Cat's; it wasn't something I ever craved, not anything I ever looked at in the shops and thought to buy. If someone offered, I would say yes, and if someone was offering, it was usually my mother.

'How's your dissertation going?' she asked.

'It's going great,' I said. 'I really enjoy the fact that I can choose what to write about.'

'You know, I tried to do that with my students, when I was younger and dumber. I assigned them an essay of a certain length and told them they could write about whatever they wanted. Didn't quite work out. I figured they need a bit more guidance at that age.' She smiled. 'But of course you don't. You've done all that boring stuff now, haven't you?'

'There's still plenty of boring stuff,' I said.

'Especially when it comes to Kant,' Mum said.

She supposedly knew about Kant from her own under-grad a very long time ago, but I suspected it was more likely she had read his Wikipedia entry after I started studying philosophy. I knew I should probably consider that to be sweet, but it felt more like desperate to me. And misguided. It wasn't as if Kant was something I was particularly keen to discuss with my mum.

I told her I wasn't doing Kant any more, and then got stuck explaining psychological egoism. Mum nodded politely, but I didn't think it was likely she was taking much of it in. When I was in the middle of a sentence she suddenly stood up and said, 'Goodness, I forgot about the honey. Don't you take honey in your tea?'

She went away and got the honey. I haven't taken honey in my tea since I was twelve years old.

'Thanks,' I said.

'How's Oliver?' Mum asked.

She had met Oliver twice and absolutely loved him. After the first time he was shocked to find that she had sent him a friend request on Facebook.

'He's good,' I said. 'He has a new boyfriend, and I think it's going well.'

'I'm happy for him,' Mum said. 'What about you?' She angled her chin downwards and peered at me through her lashes, a suggestive smile on her face. 'Do you have a new boyfriend? Or girlfriend?'

'Nope,' I said.

'Anyone you're talking to?' she asked. 'Isn't that what you say these days, before you're dating someone? Talking?'

'I guess so,' I said. 'But no, I'm not. You know I'm not very interested in that.'

Mum shook her head and smacked her lips. I wasn't quite old enough for her to start asking for grandchildren, so I suppose she still held out hope. Maybe when I reached thirty, things would start to change and she would get a bit frantic, but for now her questions were never too invasive and her comments not unbearably judgemental.

'How's Cat?' Mum asked.

'Excellent,' I said. 'Isn't she always?'

She nodded. 'She's still with Henry?'

A week ago, when I started mentally preparing for this visit, I expected my answer to be no.

'Yes,' I said. 'She is.'

'They're a beautiful couple,' Mum said. 'Just gorgeous. He's nice to her too, though, isn't he?'

'As far as I know,' I said.

'Sometimes,' my mum said, 'the couples that look the happiest are the ones trying the hardest to appear that way. Do you know what I mean?'

'I think so.'

'When something goes wrong, it's always that couple about who everyone says, "Oh no, I never expected that to happen – they were so happy!"' She took a sip of her tea. 'Of course I'm not saying Cat and Henry are like that.'

'Of course,' I said.

When I was finally free from that conversation, I said I wanted to go upstairs and get myself settled in the guest bedroom. The room that used to be my bedroom. I've heard of parents who leave their child's room untouched for decades after they move out, endlessly hoping they will return, but Mum had given up on that game long ago. In the beginning she kept reminding me I still had that room to come back to. *In case it isn't your thing*, she would say. *There's no shame in changing your mind*, she would say. She never believed I would be able to live by myself, attend university like a normal person, lead an independent existence.

I never considered studying closer to home, though. I'd waited for years to leave by that point. Living with Mum had always felt like living with a random flatmate you found online, that you briefly tried to make friends with but quickly realized you had nothing in common with. Eventually you just coexist in the same space, making small talk when you accidentally run into each other, arranging movie nights to watch films neither one of you wants to see but believes the other one does.

My room no longer looked the way it had when I lived there. I had kept the walls busy, choosing a patterned wallpaper and covering it with posters. The walls were grey now. The wardrobe was empty aside from a few boxes of my old belongings on the upper shelf. It was all so clinical and impersonal, like a hotel room. It was an Airbnb, of course. That was why the bed was always so perfectly made when I came to visit, usually with a towel folded at the end of it. The last visitors who had stayed in here were a German couple that my mum introduced to scones and *Strictly Come Dancing*.

I took out my cosmetics bag and the book I was currently reading and put them on the bedside table. I still slept on the same side of the bed every time I visited. Switching would have felt odd at this point, like putting your shoes on the wrong feet.

The truth was that I was glad the room looked so different now, that it was a guest room rather than my old bedroom. I don't know how it would have felt to return here and have everything be the same, all the old memories so close by. If it had been too similar to when I was sixteen, if I lay down in bed and looked at my phone, I would almost be able to think I was waiting for a message from Maisie. Better, instead, to have it so unrecognizable that I could pretend I was staying in a hotel somewhere. Not in my childhood home, not even in my home town. Only psychopaths want to be sixteen again.

This was where we kissed for the first time. I remembered that as I sat down on the edge of the bed. Despite the time that had passed and how different the room looked now, she felt so close by in moments like that.

Mum made meatloaf for dinner. When I was little, I wanted to eat meatloaf every day and we would always have fights about it. She would try to explain to me how nutrition works and how a varied diet is important. She would give up and cry that she didn't want to have bloody meatloaf one more time, for god's sake; she was tired of it. That was usually around the time Dad would get up and go to the pub instead, muttering that we were both insufferable. Now that I had grown up, she made meatloaf every time I came home to visit.

'Remember when this was the only thing you wanted to eat?' she asked that night, smiling as if at some kind of shared secret.

'I do,' I said.

'Is it still your favourite?'

'I don't think so,' I said. 'My tastes have changed a little bit, I think.'

'Is that why you no longer watch that ghost-hunting show?'

'Partly. Also the fact I'm not twelve any more.'

She settled back with her fork in her hand and a melodramatic expression. 'I can't believe how fast time passes,' she said.

It was inevitable for this moment to come; it did every visit.

'I know,' I said.

'Sometimes it feels like I wake up and you're another five years older,' she said. 'Like I'll wake up tomorrow and you'll be married with two children and I'll be sitting here saying "Feels just like yesterday you were visiting me while you were doing your master's and you were still so sure you were never getting married." Imagine that, eh?'

I nodded disinterestedly. 'Imagine that.'

We ate for a while, Mum taking occasional breaks to talk to me about something or other. I watched her plate as I finished my own food, wishing she would stop talking for a moment and finish hers so the meal could be over and I could finally go to bed and recover from the day.

'I bumped into her mum at the shops,' Mum said eventually, her voice lowered.

She didn't say the name. She never said the name. But I knew from the tone of her voice, the cautious look in her eyes, the use of the pronoun 'her'. Just *her*, like there was no one else she could be referring to.

'OK,' I said.

'She asked how you're doing,' Mum said. 'And I told her you're doing great. You are, aren't you?'

'Of course I am,' I said. 'I live in a great place, I have great friends, I'm doing my master's.'

'Well, yes,' Mum said. 'But I mean, with your mental health and stuff. With the recovery. With the . . .' Her voice drifted off.

'I'm doing excellent,' I said.

And I was, was I not? My therapist might say otherwise, but Susannah didn't live in my head.

Mum smiled, exhaled, looked relieved. 'You should reach out to her some day, you know,' she said. 'I think she would appreciate it. I think she's expecting it.'

I took a deep breath. I must not cry in front of Mum. That was not something I had done in many years. I suspected that if I ever shed a single tear in front of her she'd send me back to the inpatient unit, just in case I was about to lose it again. I had done a great job so far on this visit of convincing her that I was a functioning member of society.

'I don't think that's a good idea.'

'Louise. You said you're doing excellent.'

'And I am. But I don't want to stop doing excellent, you know?'

Mum was silent. Her lips were pursed in thought.

'I don't want to go back there,' I said with finality. 'And I don't want to keep talking about this right now. Can we not?'

'Yes,' Mum said. 'Of course. Would you like some dessert?'

Maisie. My first girlfriend. My only girlfriend.

Her mum was always very kind to me. Mum was probably telling the truth, telling me that Carol wanted to hear from me. They didn't know we were dating, not back then, but I imagine they figured it out at some point. Carol knew

148

there was no one closer to her daughter than me, that we shared her in some inexplicable, intangible way that outsiders would never be able to understand.

I didn't understand it either at the time. It wasn't until I was an adult that I could see it clearly. Maisie didn't have other friends either. Her social anxiety was intense. She had panic attacks when plans changed. When she was nervous, she'd start scratching herself, or line up all her pens on her desk. When she was happy, she'd spin in circles.

'Do you ever get tired of it?' she asked me once. 'Being a person. Smiling and nodding and making facial expressions and making sure you do what you're supposed to.'

'I didn't think anyone else did,' I whispered back. 'I thought it was just me.'

In bed that night I thought about Carol. I wondered if I should reach out. I decided two things: that I should, and that I wasn't going to. Carol was a good woman, but I wasn't ready to put her comfort above my own. She wanted to reach some sort of catharsis, and good for her, but she would have to do it without me. Catharsis requires facing things in a more intense and final way than I was willing to do.

Oh god. I was crying.

I made sure to keep it quiet, to press my face against the pillow and muffle the sobs so Mum wouldn't hear. It wasn't her fault she had brought Carol up. But did she really have to do it every time? Was she never going to let me move on?

I let myself cry for a bit. It was another thing about visits home that tended to be inevitable.

My phone buzzed with a notification. I wanted it to be Cat, telling me she missed me, though I had barely been gone a full day yet and would be back the next day. It wasn't

Cat, though. It was a message from Chloe; surprising, since I'd forgotten to reply to the first one.

Hi, what are you up to?

I replied with *You sound like a fuckboy*. Because it would be rude not to respond, but it would be giving her false expectations to reply in any way positively and encourage this.

She responded with a succession of the laughing/crying emoji.

I couldn't sleep. I tossed and turned for hours before I gave up and turned on the bedside lamp. When I was little, I used a torch under my duvet to draw myself to sleep on nights like these. I was old enough now that I didn't need to hide from Mum any more.

I pulled my sketchbook out and lay on my side to draw in bed. After all that talk of Maisie, I couldn't think of another subject. It had been a while since I had last ensured I still remembered her face. I might as well.

I drew, squinting at the paper in the half-light. A few times I had to use a rubber to erase something or other. No matter what I did, something just wasn't right. I had half a face in front of me, but it didn't look like Maisie. It looked like what a police sketch artist might have conjured up with a description of her.

Was it the placement of her eyes? Were they too close together or too far apart? The shape of her chin? I couldn't have forgotten. I'd never forgotten before.

I ended up getting out of bed and sneaking downstairs with the sketchbook. I held it up beside the drawing of Maisie on the mantel. As soon as I saw them next to each other, I knew what was wrong.

My new drawing had Maisie's round face and wisps of

unruly hair. It had her freckled nose. But it had Cat's oval eyes and curled lashes. It had Cat's full lips leading into Maisie's dimples.

When I climbed back into bed, I ripped out the page and threw it in the bin.

13

One night at Mum's was more than enough, and it was good to be back at the flat again. The mice woke up at the sound of my voice because they hadn't received any attention the night before. Cat wasn't home, but she called me at midday.

'Lolo,' she said, panting over the phone. I could hear cars in the background and it sounded like she was walking. 'Can you do me a favour?'

'Of course,' I said.

'I'm just about to head into a seminar, sorry – I forgot I had a date with Henry in a few hours. My schedule is absolutely full and there's no chance I'll be able to make it home before, but I need an outfit. Can you get some clothes from my closet and meet me somewhere?'

'I don't know,' I said.

My heart was racing at the idea of this. She probably expected a perfect date-night outfit from me, and how was I meant to put that together? I couldn't have her judging my taste if I picked the wrong colour shoes for a certain dress.

'Hi,' Cat said, sounding fake, her voice directed away from the phone. 'No, I'm fine, just give me a moment. Louise?'

'I'm here,' I said.

'Can you, please?'

'What clothes do you want?'

'I don't have time. I really have to go now, but can we meet in, like, an hour or so at the library? It's the only break

I have. I'll text you when I get there. Thank you! I love you so much.'

And, just like that, she hung up on me. She hadn't told me where in the library we were meeting. I hadn't even said yes. An hour? I looked at the time. It wasn't as though I was doing anything in particular, but I hadn't been planning to go out. I took a breath. I didn't have a choice. You usually didn't have a choice with Cat. I couldn't remember the last time I had asked her for a favour, but she requested them often. Like I was a personal assistant she continually forgot to pay. It wasn't like I could say no, though, after all the expensive things she'd bought me, and the fashion and make-up tips she gave me, and the fact that she barely charged me rent.

I walked into her bedroom. The bed was unmade and one of the drawers of her bedside table was wide open.

I opened the closet. Cat generally kept her room tidy, so I hadn't been prepared for what I would see as I slid open the doors. There was no rhyme or reason to the way her clothes were organized. Her going-out dresses hung next to blouses and jeans. Nothing was folded. Her shoes were in a large mess on the floor, piled on top of each other. There were too many for them to be organized next to each other in any sort of orderly fashion. The chaos of it all made me feel slightly nauseous.

It was a date; I needed to find a date outfit. But what kind of date was it? In a few hours – that meant it wasn't lunch or brunch, but it was also going to be too early for dinner. What kind of date did one have in the middle of the afternoon? An art gallery, perhaps? Henry seemed the type of person who would take her to an art gallery and then stand there telling her everything he had googled about the art pieces right before they arrived. I didn't know what you wore to an art gallery.

I took out one of her dresses. It was blush pink and lacy. It reminded me of fairy tales and Regency-era fashion. Probably too nice for an art gallery. But maybe not for Cat; maybe for Cat it wasn't nice enough. It seemed like something she might wear during a regular day. I could see her pushing a trolley around the shops in that dress. Actually, no, I couldn't see her pushing a trolley around the shops in any outfit. How did Cat get her groceries?

I held the dress up in front of my body and turned towards her full-length mirror. I had seen many outfit selfies she had taken in this very mirror. The fabric felt harsh in my hands. I tried to determine if this was a suitable outfit and what else I might add to it. What shoes should I take? Jewellery? Would a cardigan be appropriate to dress it down a little? Did I want to venture into the mess of her shoes? Surely she could make do with the ones she was wearing.

The colour of the dress complemented my skin tone. Not as well as it did Cat's tan, but well enough, despite how pale I've always been. I wondered how it would look on me. And then it dawned on me that I didn't have to wonder; there was no reason I couldn't try it on. I had a bit of time. I got out of my jeans and took off my top. The dress was tight, hard to pull down, the sleeves digging into my armpits. I knew I wouldn't be able to zip it up at the back, but from the front it looked nice. It was so short I felt self-conscious about it; I would be fine to take a picture in it, but walk around? What if there was wind? But it did make me feel like a princess. I twirled around and watched the skirts fly up in the mirror.

I took it off and sat down on the floor in my underwear. I found the label and looked up the brand on my phone.

Goodness. Their dresses were usually over two hundred pounds, a month's rent for me. I couldn't find this specific model, and maybe it was for the best.

I took out another dress from the closet and put it on. It was more appropriate for everyday wear, a simple denim body-con dress with a zip at the front. It was stretchy enough that I managed to do it up. I looked at myself in the mirror. It didn't look as good on me as it would on Cat. I knew that. I had too much stomach and not enough cleavage. But I straightened out my posture, trying to stand more like she did. It helped a little. I didn't check the brand of this dress, nor did I try to search for it online. It would be at least a few hundred pounds. Cat always said that good quality is worth it.

I went back to the closet, attempting now for real to find something I could take to her. The jean dress might be good for a date in the middle of the day, but I honestly didn't know how to style it. I came across one of her bras. Even the fabric felt luxurious. It was purple with lacy pink detailing. I unclasped my own bra and slipped it on. The cups were much too large, and my breasts weren't enough to fill them out. It made me laugh. I checked the mirror, and I looked ridiculous. Before I put the bra back, I held it up against my nose and sniffed it. I did it without thinking, before I allowed myself to recognize how odd it was. It smelled vaguely like her, vaguely like sweat. Then I realized what I had done. I quickly shoved the bra back, taking great care to place it the way I had found it.

'Oh my god, Louise, you're a lifesaver!'

Cat was already tearing into the bag of clothes I'd brought. In the end, I'd settled for some smart chequered trousers and a white V-neck blouse.

'No worries,' I said, though I did, in fact, have several worries.

'Wow,' she said, holding up the trousers. 'I don't know if I've ever worn these. I think I completely forgot they existed.' She looked at them in silence. She did not look impressed. The bruising around her eye was only the faintest greyness now, covered with makeup.

'Are they good, though?' I asked.

She smiled at me and took too long to respond. 'Of course. It looks great. Thanks again. Come with me.'

We walked into the toilets on the ground floor and Cat handed me her bag and entered one of the cubicles.

'Where are you going, anyway?' I asked.

'We're going to this double feature at the cinema,' she said. 'I can't remember what we're seeing. It was Henry's idea. Grabbing dinner afterwards, I think.'

Shit. Of course she'd looked at the trousers for that long. Of course the glance I'd seen was one of disappointment. This was not a cinema outfit. This was a museum outfit, a day-in-the-office outfit, even.

'It's very hard to pick out a date outfit if you don't know what the date is,' I said.

'I *completely* understand that,' Cat said. 'I should absolutely have told you.'

I appreciated the fact that she hadn't outright told me that the outfit was bad. I appreciated that she was still changing into it, despite the fact that the T-shirt and jeans she'd already been wearing seemed much more appropriate.

'Well, I hope it's fun,' I said.

She came back out of the cubicle in the outfit I'd brought. It looked even more out of place with the trainers she was wearing.

'I wish I had a necklace with this,' she said.

'I didn't want to go through your jewellery,' I said. 'Sorry.'

'No, no,' she said. 'That's fine.' She held out her arms. 'How do I look?'

Absolutely gorgeous, I thought. She looked like the hot secretary the boss is having an affair with in a porn video. She looked like the teacher you badly want to be punished by.

'Great,' I said. 'Really nice.'

She walked over to the mirrors over the sink and checked her make-up, leaning close in, ruffling her hair a little.

'Yeah,' she said, almost to herself. 'Yeah, I look fine.'

Was it meant to be pointed? Was the word 'fine' supposed to signify just that, *fine*, as opposed to great or gorgeous or beautiful or nice? I didn't ask; I didn't want to know the answer.

She turned back to me, beaming. She held out the plastic bag into which she had put her old outfit. 'Would you mind –'

'No, it's fine,' I said. 'I'll take it back home.'

I spent the rest of the day studying or wasting time on my phone. Cat posted a picture on her story from inside the cinema. The theatre looked much fancier than any cinema I had ever been inside, and I wondered where on earth they were. Another picture of her hand in Henry's. It made my stomach turn.

Later in the night more pictures came in from their dinner. She tagged some expensive Italian place in photos of their pasta and herself holding a glass of wine, her eyes closed, her mouth smiling, her head turned to the side.

*

They came home late, but I was still awake. They were laughing and talking. She sounded a bit tipsy. I thought I heard her falling, a bang against the wall, followed by both of them laughing again. His soft voice in an admonishing tone.

Within minutes of entering her room they were having sex. The bedframe banged against the wall rhythmically. I put my head to the wall and I could hear her unrestrained moans. That was what I focused on. That was what I listened to as I lowered my pyjama bottoms and put my hand between my legs.

'Oh my god,' she said. 'Keep going, keep going.'

I could practically feel the wetness spilling out of me at those words. I loved the idea of her enjoying herself this fully, the thought of Cat so undone by pleasure. Her face would look like it had during our threesome. Her hair would be tousled, maybe held in one of his fists. Her skin would be slick with sweat and that little rose tattoo would be rocking back and forth with the motions of his fucking.

I imagined that I was the one doing it to her. When I touched my clit, I pretended it was hers. When I heard a whimper, I went harder. My breaths came faster. I slid a hand up to one of my breasts and touched it, closing my eyes and bringing myself back to the shape and size of Cat's gorgeous tits. I wanted to kiss them, lick them, flick them, make her cry out just from that much toying with her. My hand moved faster. I could hear Henry grunting too. *No, I* thought, *don't finish too quickly. She's so close now, Henry. Make her come really hard. Don't you dare stop.*

Maybe she was thinking the same thing. *If it was me, I* thought, *you wouldn't have to worry about that.* I would make her orgasm ten times over if that was what she wanted. I wouldn't roll over the second I was done and consider the job finished. I wouldn't stop until she couldn't take it any more.

I continued to touch myself, moving my hand faster as their rhythm increased. I kept my eyes closed and thought about her body instead of my own. As best as I could, I pretended Henry wasn't there.

'Henry,' she said breathlessly.

I knew from the way she said it that she was about to finish. Two seconds later, I heard her scream. I remembered the way she had convulsed and bucked under my tongue, the way her eyes had rolled back into her head when I made her come. The orgasm was powerful and instantaneous. It left me spent and catching my breath, just sitting there against the wall.

14

I hadn't been on a date with a girl since the beginning of my undergrad. In preparation I asked to borrow the denim dress I'd seen in Cat's closet. I styled it ten different ways before I put on a pair of cream knitted thigh-highs and a choker and asked for Cat's expert opinion.

'You look beautiful,' she said without hesitation.

Which meant it was true. Cat once said, for no reason whatsoever, that the outfit I was wearing looked off. That exact word: 'off'. No attempt to cushion the impact. I never wore that outfit again.

Chloe had suggested a place that did vegan junk food. I wasn't very experienced with or enthusiastic about vegan food, but it comes with the territory if you want to be able to date lesbians. Our table was next to the window.

'You're stunning,' Chloe said. 'Oh my god.'

'Thank you,' I said. 'You look really nice.'

She smiled awkwardly. It's difficult to tell, when you're two women who like other women, whether you're complimenting each other the way a man who wants to fuck you does, or whether it's the kind of compliment you get from straight female friends.

'Have you been here before?' Chloe said.

'No,' I said. 'But it looks great.'

'It is great. The food is so good. I hope you'll like it.'

'I'm not picky,' I lied.

I was sure we had probably talked about more things the

first night we met than that vampire show, and that I should know something about her, but I couldn't remember anything. I didn't know what to talk about. The menu proved an excellent deterrent to conversation. I picked it up and started scanning the list of foods. I already knew I would likely leave the restaurant hungry. That part was fine – I could deal with it later – but I didn't want Chloe to sit there wondering why I was leaving behind a plateful of food. I had always hated the texture of tofu, and everything on that menu had some variety of tofu.

Chloe shook her head at her own menu. 'I'm struggling,' she said. 'There are too many options. I want everything.'

'I know, right?' I said.

Up until the waitress came to take our order, we chatted about the menu and spent long periods silent under the pretext of concentrating on our options. When the fateful moment came, I ordered two of the sides instead of a main course.

'I'm starving,' Chloe said. 'I didn't have time to eat breakfast.'

'Oh no,' I said, and thought, *Then why didn't you get up earlier?* That was a rude thing to say out loud. I knew that. Not everyone has the same time-management skills I have.

'My supervisor always schedules our meetings in for really early,' she said.

'That sucks,' I said. 'Who do you have?'

'Susan.'

'I've got Robert.'

'Aw, lucky you.'

I didn't know what to say to that. We sat there smiling at each other like idiots. Nothing of substance had been said so far. Words had been spoken, but it had all amounted to nothing.

Dates with Alistair were different. There was almost a script to them, which I had written for myself a long time ago. There was a personality I put on like a mask for him, the persona I knew he wanted and liked. It was harder to do that in a situation like this, when I didn't know what she expected of me. We hadn't spent hours over text laying out the rules of our relationship and going over each other's kinks.

'So.' She cleared her throat. 'What are you writing your dissertation about?'

That, at least, was something I knew. I launched into the old explanation of psychological egoism I had said almost word for word several times now. Chloe nodded along. I worried I might have gone on for too long, so I asked about hers in return.

She groaned and laughed. 'Ugh. I'm doing extended mind theory. Do you know what that is?'

'Yes.'

'Well, then you know it's a bitch. Not really, but, like, I don't care enough about it to dedicate this much time and effort and brainpower to it, you know? So I really regret it, but it's way too late to change now.'

I nodded my sympathies and didn't tell her that I'd done exactly that a couple of weeks prior. I didn't want to make her jealous.

Before the food arrived, I excused myself to go find the toilets. They smelled very strongly of incense.

I didn't need to use the toilet, but I did need some time. It was a bad idea for me to have come on this date in the first place. I had been doing just fine without trying this. God, I hated meeting new people. It came and went in waves, the way I had been as a child, unable to understand what one was meant to do with other people. Sometimes I knew perfectly well and I could hold a conversation, I could enjoy spending time with Oliver, and I saw exactly why people did it. But sometimes there it was again. I was sitting in a restaurant with a hot girl who liked me and I was an alien. An actor who'd forgotten her lines.

Susannah liked to tell me that everyone feels that way sometimes, that everyone gets socially anxious and feels a bit different. Oliver had said something similar once. He'd told me that he was convinced no one actually liked him and when he left the room they would all start talking shit about him, so he couldn't leave the room, and he couldn't stop talking and let them hear their own thoughts, and he couldn't stop making fun of himself. If he did it first, they would know he was already aware of everything about him worth making fun of.

I felt for him. I did. But what he and Susannah were talking about was on an entirely different level from what I experienced. They would never understand it. They would never fully grasp the feeling of sitting down opposite someone and feeling as if they spoke not only a different language but way beyond that. A language can be learned. This can't. This doesn't go away.

Maisie alone had understood.

I took deep breaths in front of the mirror and checked my make-up. I looked normal, at least. Sometimes I wished I didn't, so no one would expect me to act it.

'Fuck,' I said to myself.

I checked the outfit. The dress fitted me all right, but it would have looked much nicer on Cat. Cat had never been awkward a day in her life; she always knew exactly what to say. What would Cat do if she was here right now?

I stopped. I knew what Cat would do. Why not do that? Instead of trying to figure out what personality Chloe wanted from me, I could just give her Cat's. Everyone liked Cat.

I went back to our table without adjusting the dress and without looking around the rest of the room. That's what Cat would do: walk in a straight line to the table with a long and confident stride, not once looking behind her or down at her feet to see if she had stepped on some toilet paper.

Chloe looked up when I sat. Our food had arrived.

Cat wouldn't wait for Chloe to start eating first, so I didn't. I grabbed one of my chips and dipped it in the vegan mayo. Chloe followed my lead and took a bite of her burger.

And that was when Louise would have asked how Chloe's food was and got us stuck in an awkward conversation about it that neither of us would have enjoyed or learned anything from. I refrained from doing so and asked myself what Cat would have done.

'How long have you known that you're into girls?' I asked.

Chloe laughed in surprise, gesturing at her mouth full of food and taking a few seconds to swallow.

'Sorry,' she said. 'That was surprising. Uh, I don't know. Probably since I was about eight, watching *Kim Possible*.'

'Shego?'

'Absolutely. I think I still have a crush on her.'

I shook my head apologetically. 'I'm sorry I can never be her.'

Chloe shrugged. 'You'll do. What about yourself?'

'Who says I'm into girls?' I said. I used the bland and serious tone that always made Cat laugh.

Chloe stared at me for a second, her eyes wide and her mouth slightly open.

'Kidding,' I said, smiling.

She burst out laughing. 'Jesus,' she said. 'I thought you were about to tell me this wasn't actually a date.'

A date? So it is a date? I would have said. Cat wouldn't, though. She would already know it was a date. She would already know Chloe wanted her, that everyone, on some level, wanted her.

'Definitely a date,' I said.

Everything went so much better after that. There wasn't a single awkward silence, and not because Chloe was leading the conversation. I was doing that. I couldn't remember the last time I had. We didn't touch on the weather or our studies or talk about how good the food was. I brought up interesting topics, second-date subjects. We talked about the way we identified: I told her I was bi; she said she was a lesbian. Though she had been with a guy, just once, she admitted. She vented about how terrible it had been and I expressed my condolences and told her about the worst sex I'd ever had with a guy. I made her laugh so many times. On one occasion she spurted Coke out of her nose from laughing so hard. She kept apologizing, hiding her face, wiping the table with napkins. It was odd to be the one who wasn't nervous. I reached across the table, grabbed her hand and told her in the most comforting voice I could muster that everything was OK.

She taught me how to pronounce her Chinese name, which no one outside her family really used for her. We talked about whether the fact that she didn't force white people to use it had something to do with internalized racism or if it was some kind of resignation to white British narrow-mindedness. We talked about what we wanted out of life. Chloe wanted to be an academic, which wasn't unexpected. Most people don't waste time and money on a philosophy master's unless they plan to actually use it. I told her I didn't know what I wanted, that I was just planning to let life take its course and see where it would lead me. Exactly the kind of thing Cat would say.

I paid, even though it stung, because that's what Cat would have done too. And after that, when we stood outside, I didn't suggest meeting up again or say that I would call. I waited for Chloe to make the decision and pretended like it didn't matter to me at all.

'Do you want to go dancing?' she asked.

And I said yes. We went to a Latin bar with a dance floor, got ourselves one shot each and started dancing. Louise would never dance on so little alcohol, but I wasn't Louise. Cat was never self-conscious about her dance abilities. It worked so well, being Cat. It worked well enough that by the end of the night we were kissing on the dance floor, pressing our bodies against each other.

It was incredible how confident I had been as Cat. I woke up the next morning feeling like I could do anything.

I had too much energy to waste the day. I messaged Alistair to see if he wanted to meet that week; he did. After breakfast I worked out in my room and took an everything-shower, washing my hair and shaving every hairy part of my body. I tackled the cleaning before Cat had even woken up, and when everything looked as tidy and shiny as a show-room, I decided to do the things all adults pretend to do but none of us actually bother with. I cleaned the windows. I wiped down the insides of the cupboards in the kitchen, and the rag came out dirtier than I would have liked.

Like a Disney princess minus the singing and wild-animal companions, I went through the flat with a duster, pulling one of the dining-table chairs with me to climb up on and reach the surfaces I'd never bothered to touch before. I took the Hoover out and lifted the couch cushions to vacuum underneath them.

And that's where I found it.

A phone. Henry had told us he'd lost it at our place on the day of the threesome. I'd forgotten about it because he'd been carrying a new phone around within a few days. The old one had been here all along. It's so easy for a phone to slip between couch cushions, after all. And it's very typical of rich boys like Henry not to even bother to lift a cushion.

Cat had not emerged yet, but I knew I should hand the phone over to her as soon as she did. She could give it back to him. But that was when the idea hit me.

Being Cat felt so powerful. It was possible to achieve anything – anything – this way. Including getting her to realize what a terrible boyfriend she had.

I slipped the phone into my back pocket and got rid of the surprising amount of filth and dust that had been hiding under our couch cushions. Then I decided that I was done with the cleaning, and I put the Hoover back and went to my room.

Henry's phone had long since run out of battery, but one of the chargers in the mess of my bedside table drawer fitted. I plugged it in and tried to convince myself to do something else while I waited for it to turn on. Instead, I just walked around a circle in my room and came back to the charging phone. Maybe he'd wiped it remotely when he realized it was missing. I shouldn't be getting my hopes up, but I still inhaled quicky when the phone finally had enough battery that the screen lit up.

It didn't take me long to figure out his PIN; it was his birthday. I rolled my eyes.

The phone hadn't been wiped. I almost couldn't believe my luck, but I could also very much believe it. Rich people didn't think about details like that. It wasn't a big event for Henry to lose something as inconsequential as a phone.

At first I really did only plan to go through his phone and find something incriminating. *Do you think he'd pass up the opportunity to fuck someone else?* Oliver had said. Of course he wouldn't. Henry was a Stirnerian egoist. He was Henry the Eighth, for god's sake. He'd put his cock in a jar of peanut butter if it looked at him the right way.

I was surprised to find nothing when I went through his texts. It was almost sad, really. There weren't many people he messaged regularly, and even with them the conversations were far from being intimate and friendly. Always short and to the point, never about emotions. There was nothing flirtatious about his texts with the few female friends he had. It had been over a month since he'd last been in contact with his dad, and that was just Henry giving him the Netflix password. The person Henry spoke to most was his grandmother; I'd long suspected, piecing it together from the stories of his childhood and his family he'd told me, that she was the closest family member he had.

I would get nothing from his texts or call history. Fine. I looked for dating apps instead. He had all the apps I'd expect – investment apps, workout trackers, banking, every social media known to man – but no Tinder, no Bumble, no shady, super-kinky dating app the general public would be shocked to learn exists.

Getting slightly more desperate, I started going through his social media messages instead. Those were even sparser than his texts. He wasn't active on any of them, and no one was sliding into his DMs. Nor was he sliding into anyone else's. Could it be that Henry was actually loyal?

Of course not. He hadn't wanted to date me because he didn't like the idea of commitment or the restricted freedom that comes with being in a relationship, which had suited me perfectly. Henry wanted to be able to do whatever he wanted, whenever he wanted. He'd told me so himself. Even Cat couldn't have changed that mindset, not for someone as self-assured as Henry. He might have agreed to a relationship, but no way was he going to keep himself from straying. But I had no proof of this, so I would have to find another way to convince her.

It was a bad idea from the start, but I did it anyway. I started following every female social media model I could find from his account. It's easy enough. You follow one and the algorithm will recommend more for you. The more suggestive their pictures, the better. I liked their posts. I left comments on the dirtiest images, all heart eyes and fire emojis. Every woman has seen enough gross men be creepy online that they know exactly how to replicate it.

This was obviously not enough. I dallied, staring at the screen. *This is wrong*, I told myself. *But it's for the greater good.*

I went to Cat's account and started following girls she followed, girls who had much more normal numbers of followers and who had our uni or our town in their bio. A lot of them might have been her friends, but Cat and I have very different definitions of friendship; mine involves having more than two conversations with someone.

These were the girls I actually messaged. Simple but

non-platonic things like *I don't usually do this, but I think you're very beautiful*, or *Hi! Are you single?*

I was still doing this when I got a notification that one of the girls had reacted to the message I'd sent her. I immediately closed the app and turned off the phone. My heart hammered. It was too late. I couldn't undo it.

I wondered if I could still give the phone back and pretend I had just found it. It would be too easy to pin everything on me, though, if you looked at the timing of the messages. It was best not to risk it. He'd already bought a new phone anyway.

I put the phone at the bottom of the bedside table drawer and shut it.

15

I woke up to a bang. It wasn't the sort of wake-up where you doze in and out of consciousness for a while, slowly becoming aware of your surroundings. I was awake in an instant, my heart pounding.

They were shouting. I heard her voice first and then his, much louder, much angrier. She sounded more sad than angry, pleading with him, as his voice drowned out hers. I couldn't make out what they were yelling. But I knew something was happening, so I got out of bed and started pulling on a pair of trousers. The yelling was replaced by his loud footsteps making their way through the lounge, him fiddling with the lock and the front door slamming shut. It shook the picture frames on my walls.

I slipped out of my room. The door to her bedroom was open, and I looked in. Cat was sitting on the edge of the bed with her head in her hands.

'Go away,' she said softly.

It wasn't a command; it was a request.

'What happened?' I asked. 'Is everyone OK?'

She inhaled slowly and deeply, the air getting caught in her nose. 'Everyone's fine,' she said, her voice wobbly.

I didn't know what to do, so I just stood there in the doorway. Everyone was not fine. She, at least, was not. Henry hadn't sounded very fine either.

'Please go,' she whispered.

She stood up and walked across the room, keeping her

face down and her eyes to the floor the whole time. She put her hand to the door when she reached me, and that was when she first looked up, that was when I first saw it.

'Cat,' I said. I could hear the surprise in my own voice.

She tried to push the door closed, but I caught it with my body and stopped her.

She started crying. 'Please,' she said.

She gave one final shove at the door, but I didn't move. She sank to the floor and her body convulsed with sobs. Her face was bruised again. Even in the darkness I could see the shadow of it on the left side, down from her forehead to her cheek, a spot of blood underneath her nose.

I sat down opposite her in shock. 'What happened?'

Cat didn't answer. I reached out my hands, holding them out like an offering. She took one. She looked up at me again and I could see it more clearly. It was bad, like she had walked head first into a wall. But I knew she hadn't done that.

Every time a man hurts a woman, everyone who knows him says they're surprised. They say he would never do something like that. They say he's the kindest guy in the world. I was not surprised. Nothing about this seemed out of character for Henry. He had never hurt me. I'd never heard him raise his voice. He'd never been violent towards me, though he had enjoyed being rough in bed. He'd choked me and pulled my hair; doesn't every man these days? But still, he was Henry. No one was more important to him than himself.

'Did he do this to you?' I asked.

Her cheeks were lined with tears. She was wearing her pyjamas and she looked so incredibly young. I felt suddenly protective of her.

She nodded once, quickly, a very small movement.

I wanted to run outside and catch up with him. I didn't know what I would do once I reached him, but I wanted to so badly. She needed me more, though. I had to stay with her.

'Oh, Cat,' I said.

This set off another burst of sobs from her. She scrunched up her face and struggled to catch her breath.

'This isn't the first time, is it?' I asked quietly.

She shook her head.

'Is this why you broke up before?'

If she nodded, I didn't manage to catch it.

'I'm sorry,' she said.

'Why are you sorry?'

'Because of this. I'm sorry. I woke you up. You don't have to take care of me. I'll be fine. Please go back to bed.'

'Absolutely not,' I said. 'Stop apologizing, Cat. This isn't your fault.'

'But I went back to him, didn't I?'

I didn't know what to say and I took too long to answer.

She snorted and looked off to the side. 'You think I'm stupid,' she said.

'I don't.'

'But I am, aren't I?'

She pulled her hand back from my own and clasped it over her mouth. There was so much pain in her eyes I almost couldn't bear it. I hadn't seen so much pain in another person since—

It disorientated me. I was suddenly dizzy. I hadn't seen so much pain in another person since Maisie.

'Please don't tell anyone,' Cat said. 'Please, not ever.'

'I wouldn't,' I said.

'Not even Oliver. I mean it.'

'Not even Oliver,' I promised.

'I know he already thinks I'm vapid and stupid and ridiculous,' she said, drying her face with one of her sleeves.

This came as a surprise to me.

'Of course he doesn't,' I said.

'Yes, he does,' she said. 'He doesn't like me, I know that. No one likes me, Louise. No one actually likes me. I don't have any friends.'

I don't have any friends. It stung. It stung so unexpectedly it felt as though I'd been punched in the chest.

'That is not true,' I said. 'You have so many people who love and care for you.'

Cat shook her head. 'No, they don't. They just care about me because I have money and I can buy them stuff, or because they want to sleep with me. They like me because I'm always happy and funny and smiling and up for a good time, but they don't want to see this. They don't want me to stop smiling. They'd run away if I started crying in front of them. They'd all leave if they knew I was such a fucking fool I let my boyfriend hit me and then took him back and let him do it all over again.'

I moved in closer to her and wrapped my arms around her, pulling her towards me. She allowed it to happen, which I hadn't expected. She kept crying. I was close to tears myself.

'I'm not running, am I?' I said.

'No, because I let you live here for two hundred a month,' she said. 'You can't run. And do you know why I do that? Because if you weren't living here I'd be so alone. I'd be so fucking alone.'

'Cat,' I said, 'I am not here only because you let me

176

live here for next to nothing. I'm here because I am your friend.'

She clutched one of my arms in her hand, hard, using her nails. 'I shouldn't have yelled at him,' she whispered. 'I started the fight. It was my fault. I saw this text on his phone and I –'

I froze. 'What kind of text?' I asked, hoping she wouldn't notice the panicked quiver or too-high pitch to my voice.

'From a girl.' Cat swallowed. 'He was trying to chat her up. He didn't even try to hide the notification.'

This was my fault. This was all my fault. But I hadn't meant for this to happen. Cat was supposed to get angry at *him*. She was supposed to break up with him. He wasn't supposed to get angry back. He wasn't supposed to *hurt* her.

'It doesn't matter if you yelled at him,' I said.

'Are you really not going to leave?'

'Of course not. Not ever.'

She sank her face into my chest and pressed her forehead against my bare skin. 'I think you're the only real friend I have.'

And that was why I'd done what I did. I'd done it because I cared about her. I'd done it with good intentions.

'I don't know if that's true,' I said. 'But you do have me, whatever else you believe, whatever else you do or don't have. You do have me.'

'I don't have any friends,' Maisie had also told me once, her arms wrapped around legs that were pulled up to her chest. 'I keep trying, but I just never know the right thing to say. I feel like there's something wrong with me that every-one else can see. I feel like I keep starting conversations that no one is interested in continuing.'

*

I used Cat's phone to take pictures of her bruised and battered face in the bathroom. She had said she wouldn't report it to the police, but I had insisted that we needed to take pictures in case she changed her mind.

She looked even worse in the bright yellow lighting of the bathroom. Her face was all shades of green, blue and purple. Her nose was sore, the blood under it dried. Her lips were swollen. I forced myself to look at her, to take all of it in. This was all my fault. Had it been worth it? Had I gone too far?

It couldn't be too far. Not for Cat. I would do anything for Cat.

She washed her face, wincing, as I put one of the dining-table chairs against the door handle of the front door.

'He won't come back,' she said. She'd come out behind me while I was doing it.

'Better safe than sorry,' I said.

'I'm very tired.'

'Let's go to bed, then.'

She looped one of her fingers with one of mine. 'Will you sleep with me?' she whispered, like she was afraid of saying it too loudly in case I said no.

'Of course,' I said.

She fell asleep quickly and I lay wide awake, staring at the ceiling and listening for any suspicious sound. Every time her phone lit up, I looked over at the screen to see if it was a message from him. It never was, and I was glad. He'd better know to stay away. He'd better know he wasn't welcome.

Cat flinched in her sleep.

'I'm sorry,' I whispered.

She'd told me I was the only real friend she had. I believed her. No one else had been there during the break-up. No one else was there to clean her up that night. But I was. I always would be. I was a real friend. I would always put her first. I would do anything, I told myself, to keep her safe and happy. Especially now. I would do anything to make up for what I'd done.

'Can I ask you a question?' I said to Susannah.

She raised a brow. She looked surprised. I never asked questions. I never started a conversation.

'Of course,' she said.

'Why do abused women go back to their abusers?'

Susannah's eyes widened, her mouth slightly open as she fumbled with her pen. 'Did something happen to you?'

'No,' I said. 'Nothing happened to me. To a friend of mine. You don't need to worry.'

There was a drawing of Cat's battered face in the sketch-book in my backpack. I'd drawn it earlier that day when I was supposed to be studying. It was the only way I could make it leave my mind. All night, every time I closed my eyes, she'd been staring at me with those dark bruises and teary eyes. I knew my drawing was a perfect likeness. I'd remembered every single scratch and mark.

With a sceptical glint in her eyes, Susannah nodded cautiously. 'Well, there are many different reasons. A lot of them tell themselves that they deserved it. Many abusers are good at convincing them that it won't ever happen again. And in a lot of cases I think it's about the love that still remains for the abuser. It doesn't go away just like that. Especially not for women who don't value themselves enough to feel like the abuse was unforgivable.' She smiled. 'Does that sound like your friend?'

I shrugged. 'Maybe.'

There was a time, not long ago, when I would have said absolutely not. Cat was not that type of woman. She was the most confident person I had ever met, carrying herself with the self-assurance of someone who had never doubted their own value. Now I wasn't so sure.

'That's a difficult situation for you to be in,' Susannah said. 'How does it make you feel?'

I ignored the question and met it with one of my own. 'How do you help someone in that situation? What do you do with someone when you're worried they might go back again?'

'If they want to go back, you let them go back,' Susannah said. 'I know that's not the answer you want, but you stay by their side no matter what. You're not going to convince them to leave for good. That's something they have to do themselves. And there's value in that, you know. There's autonomy there that they lost because of their abuse, and you don't want to take that away from them by telling them what to do. So no matter how frustrating it can be, you need to stay. Because if you leave, if they lose their support system, it's going to be even more impossible for them to get out of that situation.'

He was like an ant infestation. You can kill as many ants as you want, you can block off every possible entrance to the house you can think of, and you can get rid of anything that attracted them in the first place. Put the poison out. But if a single ant survives, they return. Just like Henry did.

Less than twenty-four hours had gone by, but he was at our flat when I came home from therapy. There was a vase with a giant bouquet of flowers on the coffee table, and I knew. I knew before I heard the laughter from the kitchen.

I walked in, and, despite myself, I was actually hoping it would be Paul. Rather Paul than Henry the Eighth.

How did I not think about that when I gave him the nickname? Henry the Eighth was an abusive piece of shit. He had two of his wives decapitated.

Cat was standing behind him with her arms around his neck. There was something sizzling in the frying pan on the stove and the oven was on, the extractor fan on the highest setting, buzzing something awful. He turned around, bringing her with him.

'Hello, Lolo,' Cat said, smiling.

It had been such a short time since she was crying on her bedroom floor about this man. Her face still looked a mess, the bruises darker in colour. They must still be sore to the touch. But here she was, her arms wrapped around him, smiling. She looked so disgustingly happy.

'Hello,' I said. It came out a little confused and hesitant.

Henry smiled. I wondered if he knew that I knew. He was docile and compliant; under her grip he reminded me of a patient uncle with an annoying child insisting on a piggyback ride. He was a straight-A student. He was his grandmother's favourite. Not someone who would ever harm another human.

'Hi,' he said.

It was the same voice I had heard shouting last night, but at the same time it wasn't. It was so far removed from that tone and that volume I suddenly thought I might have dreamt everything. I might have, except for the bruises on Cat's face. He couldn't fucking know that I knew or he wouldn't be looking so smug, meeting my eyes with such confidence. I wanted to gouge his eyes out.

'Henry's making me dinner,' she said.

Wasn't that what abusers did, apologize with grand romantic gestures? Wasn't that what Susannah had said, that some of them are awfully good at convincing the victim that it won't happen again? Standing in that kitchen, even I had a hard time understanding that it could happen again. He tilted his head to the side and managed to angle it so he could kiss her cheek. You could have put them in an advert with how in love they looked.

'That's nice,' I said. I could hear that I had failed to keep the venom out of my voice.

'I'm very nice,' Henry said. 'I am incredibly nice.'

Cat laughed like this was an inside joke.

'Cat,' I said, 'could I talk to you about something?'

'What?'

'I need to borrow tampons. Or pads. Whatever you have.'

'Of course.'

She walked with me out into the lounge and went past me to lead the way to the bathroom. Henry stayed in the kitchen, humming a song and moving the frying pan around. She pulled out one of the drawers of the bathroom cabinet. 'I thought you knew where these were,' she said.

'I do.'

Her smile faded. 'What is it, then?'

'Do you want me to get him to leave?' I asked, keeping my voice low.

'Why would I want that?'

The loud volume of her voice made my heart beat faster. I wanted to tell her to keep it down.

'Are you OK?' I asked. 'I mean, are you really?'

'Of course I am,' she said.

I could hear him whistling in the kitchen. 'Are you sure about this?'

She looked in that direction. 'Stop treating me like a child,' she said.

'He hit you.'

She stared at me. 'I never should have told you. We had a fight, but I think you misunderstood something. He didn't actually hit me.'

'Then why does your face look like that?'

'I tripped, Louise. I slammed my head against something. Do you think Henry would fucking hit me?'

I knew she wasn't going to admit anything. I could have stood there arguing all night and she would have maintained her story. Did she believe it herself? I didn't think so. Her face and her voice were too desperate for that. She was much too intent on convincing me.

'OK,' I said. 'I suppose he wasn't trying to cheat with those girls he was texting either, then.'

Her eyes turned into dark, narrow slits. 'Why would you bring that up?'

'Because it's another example of Henry being a great boyfriend and me misunderstanding things.'

Cat shook her head slowly. 'He got hacked,' she hissed.

The laugh escaped me before I could stop it. That's what he was going with? And she believed it?

She snorted. 'I'm glad this is funny to you.'

I'd done it again. I'd been myself and forgotten how to be a competent human.

I reined myself in. 'It's not,' I said. 'I'm sorry, Cat. I'm just trying to help.'

'I don't need your help,' snarled Cat, and stormed out of the room.

I wandered to my bedroom in a daze. They were laughing in the kitchen. I clenched my jaw hard to keep myself from marching in there and throwing punches. According to Susannah, I shouldn't do that. Cat was mad enough at me.

Breathing heavily, I pulled out my desk chair and opened the sketchbook. I drew Henry, smiling and gorgeous, perfect. The world disappeared around me, the sounds from the kitchen drowned out by the pen against the paper.

I let my anger flow down through my arms and covered his eyes with two thick black Xs. I moved the pen back and forth across his neck, pressing hard, the lines growing darker and stronger until the pen broke through the page.

For the moment, it was enough. I unclenched my jaw and sat back, catching my breath.

I remembered the day Maisie had showed me the scars on her arms. I'd seen them on others. I knew people did it. But I had always seen thin white lines so light they were barely noticeable. Hers were dark and wide and ugly, so much worse than I could ever have imagined. There was such determination there. There must have been so much pain and self-hatred for someone to push that far past their self-preservation instincts, when every cell in their body would tell them not to press the knife deeper.

'I didn't know what else to do,' she had cried quietly. 'I didn't know what else to do.'

I'd felt like I was about to be sick. I had wanted to save Maisie so badly, but I had failed.

I couldn't let that happen again. I had to save Cat.

16

Oliver slammed his books on to the table in front of me so suddenly that I flinched.

'Christ,' I said.

'*Entschuldigung*,' he said, sliding into the seat opposite me. 'I didn't realize you were so completely engrossed in your own thoughts.'

'My thoughts are very interesting,' I said.

He unwrapped an ice lolly instead of opening his books. 'Tell me about them.'

'Does caring about other people mean psychological egoism isn't true?' I asked. 'Or does it mean their interests just become yours too?'

Oliver nodded. 'Yeah, sounds like you're having fun.'

'I'm going to rip my hair out.'

'Try it. You could pull off the bald look.'

I groaned and put my head in my hands. I had something of an introduction, about five hundred words. It might as well be nothing . The truth was I hadn't been thinking about my dissertation at all.

'Aren't you going to ask me?' Oliver said, wriggling excitedly in his seat.

'Ask you what?'

'Why I'm so excited.'

'Oliver, you know I'm not good with facial expressions. If you're excited, you have to tell me you're excited.'

He rolled his eyes. 'Fine,' he said. 'I'm excited because Mateo's meeting my parents.'

'Wow,' I said. 'That's a big step.'

He nodded. 'Yeah, I know.'

None of the others had ever got quite so far. Maybe I'd been wrong about Mateo. He was sticking around, it seemed.

'Congrats,' I said. 'Do you think it's going to work out?'

'Oh my god,' he said, and sighed. 'I have no idea. I'm terrified. Mum's going to be fine, I know she is, but Dad? It's not been that long since he accepted the whole having-a-gay-son thing. I keep worrying that he's only OK with it in theory, but when reality hits and he actually has to meet someone who's, you know, fucking his son, he might freak. Is that weird?'

'I think that's perfectly reasonable,' I said.

'What's new with you?' he asked, putting the lolly in his mouth.

I had to tell him something that wasn't about Cat and Henry. 'I went on a date,' I said.

His eyes widened.

'With Chloe,' I said.

He gasped. 'Louise!'

'Yes!'

'You're actually doing it,' he said.

'Well, I'm doing something. It's not going to turn into anything serious.'

He raised a brow. 'But it went well?'

I smiled. 'It did.'

'Did you . . .?'

'No.'

That wasn't the most exciting piece of news I had, and I played with the idea of telling him the rest of it. It moved in waves inside me, pushing open my mouth, threatening to overflow and run out of me. *I had a threesome with Cat and Henry. I tried to get them to break up. He hits her.*

Tell me what to do, I wanted to say. But I didn't, because I knew exactly what he would say. *Move out. Leave them behind. Wash your hands of the whole mess.* It was probably the sensible thing to do, and I knew that. *See, Oliver*, I wanted to say. *For once I do know what the right thing to do is. I've got that much covered.*

'I'm writing the best man speech in my head right now,' Oliver said. 'Can I release doves at your reception?'

'Oh my god.' I shook my head and laughed at him. 'There's not going to be a reception. Ever.'

He didn't look at me. He exhaled with a huge smile on his face and a dreamy look in his eyes, directed up at the ceiling. 'I love being in love,' he said.

I'll kill Mateo if he messes this up, I thought.

'I have a weird question,' I said.

He looked back at me and cocked his head.

'Would you ever hang out with Cat?'

He frowned. 'Why would I do that?'

'Why not?' I said. 'You'd get to know her better.'

'I know her well enough,' he said sceptically. 'Why do you want me to hang out with Cat?'

'I think she'd appreciate it.'

He narrowed his eyes at me in confusion. 'Cat and I aren't exactly friends. You know I don't like her.'

'Yeah, because she's rich and pretty and outgoing,' I said. 'There's more to her than meets the eye, though. You of all people shouldn't be so prejudiced.'

'Of all people?'

'You're a Black gay man. You know not to judge a book by its cover.'

187

He rolled his eyes. 'Look, I know you really care about her, and you can be friends with Cat all you want, but I have no interest in that myself. Her energy is too intense and I don't think she's genuine. I don't like people who aren't themselves.'

I could have asked him then why he liked me, when every single word I said to him was carefully chosen, every facial expression an act, my personality a crafted character.

'I think you would like her if you knew her better,' I said instead.

He peered at me suspiciously. 'Is something going on with Cat?'

'No,' I said. 'Not at all. I just –'

'Henry,' Oliver said matter-of-factly.

'I don't believe it's a very good relationship, and it would probably be easier for her to leave if she had more friends to rely on.'

'What are you talking about?' Oliver said. 'Cat has tons of friends. I wish I had as many friends as she does.'

I bit my lip. I had reached the limit of what I was able to say without divulging way too much. She had trusted me.

'Never mind,' I said. 'It was just an idea.'

Chloe wanted to cook for me, and I wanted to get out of the flat. It was the perfect solution.

Chloe and I didn't greet each other with a kiss, but we did hug. I didn't like it, but Cat always hugged. It was over quickly anyway.

Meeting someone after the first time you've kissed is always awkward. *Am I a terrible kisser?* I wanted to ask. *Did I do anything embarrassing without even realizing?*

'We're alone, by the way,' she said. 'Straight male flat-mate is out.'

'Good,' I said. 'I couldn't stand having a straight guy here making jokes about threesomes and asking us if he could stay and watch.'

Chloe laughed. 'He's usually pretty cool about it, actually. His sister is pan, I think.'

In the kitchen there was a pot on the counter pushed back against the wall, with something mouldy inside it.

'Not cool about doing the dishes, though,' I said.

It made me appreciate Cat more than usual. I'd had to clean up after her plenty of times, but she wouldn't go that far. And it wasn't as if she didn't bring something to the table in return. In our first couple of weeks together we'd gone shopping for our mandatory reading, and she'd paid for all the books I needed for my courses. There'd been plenty of times I'd opened a kitchen cupboard to find that she'd stocked up on more of the noodle flavours I liked, or anything else she'd seen me eating.

Chloe rolled her eyes. 'Yeah, I know. I'm refusing to take care of it on principle, so it's been about two weeks now. I don't know how much longer I'll be able to hold out.'

'No, now you have to,' I said. 'He needs to learn his lesson and you've already committed to teaching him.'

'But it's driving me insane.'

'I won't let you give in. Do you need me to restrain you?'

It slipped out so easily when I was pretending to be Cat; it rolled off my tongue with such casualness and ease.

Chloe turned around, and her eyes were wide. She blushed and laughed, and I smiled back.

She made us a vegan roasted-pepper pasta, which was surprisingly good. As we ate she told me about how

Parmesan isn't even vegetarian and made me vow never to buy non-vegan Parmesan again. Then she told me about her family and the fact that she had a brother. Her dad was the CEO of some gym chain, and I was astonished but pleased to finally find out where to place her in the socioeconomic hierarchy. Rich girl.

She opened a bottle of wine and we started sharing it. We ran out of food but we didn't, luckily, run out of things to talk about. I never considered telling Chloe anything real about myself. Instead, I told her I had one brother who was currently living in Australia on a working-holiday visa. I told her my parents were still married and that my mother had once been a model and my father was in business, just like hers; he was an entrepreneur who had set up a few different companies. It wasn't hard to pretend to be Cat, not when I knew her so well. I could've done a quiz about her family and got every question right. I skimmed over the details and brought my attention back to Chloe. It makes people feel special when you do that, and Cat always makes you feel special.

When Chloe said she felt like she needed a holiday, I asked her if she had ever been to the Riviera. She said no. I then told her about my latest trip there, taking inspiration from everything that Cat had told me. Chloe said she was jealous. So was I, I suppose. The only time I'd ever been abroad was when my parents took me to Mallorca right before the divorce. I'd been too young to retain any real memories.

As I got tipsy, it became easier to embody Cat. I added my own details to Cat's Riviera stories and I didn't care if they matched up with reality or not. If you say something confidently enough, no one will doubt you. And Chloe showed no sign of doubting me.

'I wish I was like you,' she said.

I was stunned silent by this, even in my talkative drunken state. I didn't think anyone had ever told me that before.

'You have such an easy time meeting people and making friends,' Chloe said.

She had just interrupted the story about how Cat, or I, had run into a group of drunken British girls outside a club one night and ended up going skinny-dipping with them and adding most of them on Instagram. This was not a story I had ever doubted; it sounded exactly like something Cat would do.

'I don't think any of my friends like me,' I said.

'Why would you say that?' Chloe said, her forehead furrowed in such obvious concern.

'They only like me because I'm pretty and I have money,' I said. 'They either want to sleep with me or for me to buy them stuff. And they only like me because I'm always fun and smiling and they want to have a good time, but they don't rush to my side when I'm upset.'

I knew deep down that I was taking it too far. But in the moment it seemed the closest I could get to the truth without ending the charade. It was also the best way I could make my Cat as full and convincing as the real one was.

'That's not true,' Chloe said. 'I don't believe that for a second.'

I smiled at her. 'Why not?'

'Because I can't imagine anyone not liking you. Like, how could someone get to know you and decide you're not for them?' She shook her head. 'That's unbelievable.'

I knew she wasn't actually talking about me, but I let myself absorb it and take the compliment to heart anyway. My chest felt warm. I was smiling unintentionally, which never happens.

People don't believe me when I say that, but it's true. A smile is not a natural reaction I have to feeling happy. I do it to signal something to the people around me. But I did smile spontaneously then, and I was surprised to realize it.

I kissed Chloe.

She melted into it, moving after me when I pulled away.

'I want to get a tattoo,' I found myself saying.

This was news to me, and not something I had ever wanted as Louise, or when sober.

'Do it,' Chloe said.

'I want to get a tattoo of a rose,' I said.

Chloe pulled up her sleeve. She had scars, the same scars Maisie had had. Hers were faded in a way Maisie's had never had the chance to be. I forced myself to look away, to the tattoo on her bicep. It was a bunch of lavender, the purple splashed in with a watercolour effect.

'Why lavender?' I asked.

'The Lavender Menace.'

I laughed. 'That's amazing.'

'Thank you! I'm glad you know what I'm talking about.'

'Of course,' I said.

Oliver was an expert on queer history and he had taught me everything I knew. My knowledge before him had been limited to knowing the sexualities of certain famous people and the vague understanding that male homosexuality had stopped being illegal in the UK sometime in the sixties.

Chloe spent some time showing me her other tattoos. She had a Pokémon on her thigh, a quote from a poem she liked on the other arm, a rabbit on her shoulder. I avoided looking at the scars as much as I could. The last thing I wanted to think about in that moment was Maisie. Chloe took her top off entirely to show me the Cantonese on her ribs.

'This is the best I can do without taking the bra off,' she said, locking eyes with me, lifting the band.

'Why don't you take it off?' I said.

The sex was good, but it wasn't what I wanted. I wanted *her* to be Cat now. I wanted her to be the confident Cat that I knew, who'd told me exactly what to do and who'd perfectly known the hold she had over me.

Chloe wasn't like that. She wanted me to push her into her pillows and smack her arse. She wanted me to hold her wrists in one of my hands and to tell her to get down on her knees for me. I did it, of course. It was the energy I had embodied all night. But it left me unfulfilled. A little bit disappointed. Still hungry.

17

Dishes in the sink again. I took a deep sigh and prepared my oats. While they were in the microwave, I started loading up the dishwasher. I had to take out some of the stuff that was already in there and rinse and scrub the old food off it. I thought about Chloe's flatmate and reminded myself that it could always be worse.

'Good morning,' Henry said.

He strolled in, barely looking at me, not as if he was avoiding me or felt too ashamed to meet my eyes, but more like he just didn't care that I was there.

He took out a box of eggs, cracked some into a bowl, and began whisking them as I stared at him.

'Making breakfast?' I said.

He looked up. 'Uh-huh.' He continued beating the eggs.

'Trying to make up for something?'

My tone was sharp enough that he could tell it wasn't a joke.

He looked vaguely confused. 'No,' he said, smiling casually. 'Just being a thoughtful boyfriend.'

I bit my tongue.

He turned his back to me and put a frying pan on the hob. 'And also needed a break from dissertation writing.'

I frowned. We didn't have casual conversations.

I looked at the microwave. There was still a minute left until my porridge was done.

'I'm writing a defence of Stirner,' Henry continued.

'I think his views have long been oversimplified and he's simply not been taken as seriously as he should be. He makes some valid points.'

I've been told I'm oblivious to social clues, but no one is as oblivious as a straight white man to the signs that someone doesn't want to talk to you.

I clenched my fist. 'What part of Stirner do you think needs defending?'

'Well, his conception of freedom, essentially. I think no person is truly free unless they can act however they please. Anything that imposes on that prevents us from being free.'

In my mind an image briefly flashed of smashing the frying pan against the back of his head. It felt satisfying. I imagined what the crunch of his skull cracking would sound like, how he would flop on to the floor.

'What if I wanted to be free to murder someone?' I asked.

Henry turned around, his expression one of faux surprise. 'I didn't mean that freedom is always a good thing,' he said, almost purring. 'But yes, if you wanted to murder someone and you weren't able or allowed to, you wouldn't be free.' He cocked his head to the side. 'I suppose we'd better hope you don't want to murder anyone.'

With one final crooked smile and a glimmer in his eye, he returned to the food preparations. He started humming something, and it was the most annoying sound I'd ever heard.

I inhaled deeply, then grabbed my porridge from the microwave and left.

I made the phone call at my desk.

'Hello?' said a suspicious voice.

'Hi,' I said. 'Mara? It's Louise.'

A moment of silence followed. I should have gathered as much; I had met Cat's mother only once, and I had the impression that she was a very busy person with an extremely active social life who had a lot of names and faces to remember. Me, her daughter's tenant, was probably not a priority.

'I'm sorry . . .?'

'Louise who lives with Cat,' I said.

'Oh, right,' she said. 'Terribly sorry, my dear. How are you?'

'I'm great,' I said. 'I was calling to talk to you about Cat.'

'Is she all right?' She said it casually, like she was asking how the weather was over here.

'I think so,' I said. 'But I'm worried. Just a little.'

'Did something happen?'

'No,' I said, which felt like the wrong answer to give. 'Maybe.'

I took a breath and tried to gather my thoughts. What was I hoping to get out of this call? I was being desperate. I was grasping at straws and now I had a straw in my hand and I didn't know why I had wanted it in the first place.

'Louise,' Mara prompted.

'Have you ever had a bad feeling about Henry?' I asked.

A second passed. 'A bad feeling?'

'I mean, do you like him, or have you ever had the sense that something was off? That there's something not great about him?'

'I don't know why you're asking that,' Mara said. 'I think Henry's grand. He's never given me any other impression.'

'But what do you think about their relationship?' I asked. 'Do you think it's healthy, or have you ever been apprehensive?'

'Isn't he always taking her out on dates and buying her presents?' Mara said. 'I'm so confused right now. Did something happen between them? Have they broken up again?'

Of course, Mara knew about the break-up. That was why I had assumed Cat might have told her something else too. Not that Henry hit her, obviously, but that something was wrong. At the very least Mara should have been suspicious. How could she talk to Cat as often as she did without noticing this?

'No,' I said. 'But do you know why they broke up last time?'

'Well,' she said, 'sometimes young people are just unsure about what they want. I imagined that's what happened with them. Though I'm not sure I would even call it a break-up given it lasted less than a month, to be perfectly honest.' She chuckled, like she was trying to lighten the mood.

'Right,' I said.

'Why are you calling me?'

'I don't know,' I said.

Cat and I went on ignoring each other. She was barely home that week, and when she was she remained in her room. I followed her days on social media, staying glued to my phone, my notifications turned on for all her accounts. Cat posted as if nothing was wrong. Every day there was something new on her stories: a cinnamon bun in a café, an aesthetically pleasing notebook on a desk, a friend with a drink in her hand.

And then came a new post on her feed. A picture of her and Henry. His face was barely visible, but I could tell it was him. She had one arm wrapped around his neck and she was smiling into his face like they were about to kiss.

I love you, the caption said.

To help her avoid me, I resolved to stay out too. Chloe and I went out for lunch together; she showed me a tattoo artist in town who did a lot of fine-line floral work that looked exactly like the style of Cat's, and she told me about tattoo aftercare.

She took me to a vintage clothing fair where you paid for clothes per kilo instead of per item. Nothing was my style. I wandered after her aimlessly and pretended to pay attention to the clothes on the rack, while she picked out a denim jacket, a pair of flared trousers, a shirt that looked like it came from the seventies and more and more and more.

I was astonished her arms didn't break under the weight of it all, but Chloe wasn't frail. She did weightlifting, and she was always vaguely condescending about my weight-free home workouts.

'Are you not finding anything?' she asked, turning back to me.

I looked down at what I was currently touching. Some kind of lacy top I had no interest in.

'Not really,' I said.

'I love vintage shops,' Chloe said. 'I only shop second-hand these days. I don't want to contribute to fast fashion.'

I hummed and nodded my agreement as we continued along the clothing rack. I stopped in front of a glittery skirt with sequins. It wasn't anything I would normally wear. I didn't quite know how to style something like that, or what occasion I could possibly wear it for. It would look garish

and tacky on me. On Cat it would look beautiful. The skirt
was so her. She would shine in this. She would get so many
compliments.

'You should buy it.'

I flinched. Chloe was suddenly standing right behind me.
I hadn't heard her approach.

She put her chin on my shoulder. 'It would look good
on you,' she said.

I cocked my head to the side. 'Would it?'

'Yes. Beautiful.'

I took it off the rack to look at it more closely.

An item like that requires confidence. It looks ridiculous
on someone who isn't sure about wearing it. But Cat had
the self-assurance to wear a skirt that shimmers like freshly
fallen snow when the sun hits it just right, and as far as Chloe
was concerned, so did I. Maybe she was right. Maybe when
I was Cat, the skirt wouldn't look so out of place on me.

'And you've been looking at it for ages,' Chloe said. 'You
clearly want it. Why not just grab it?'

That's how rich people look at the world, I suppose. If
you want something, there's no reason not to take it.

'Is that Cat?' Chloe said.

The name came so unexpectedly out of her mouth. It
sounded wrong in her voice. When I looked up, I still didn't
understand quite what she'd said, because she couldn't possibly be referring to *my* Cat, who definitely wasn't present.

Except she was. That hair always made her so easy to
identify. A few racks down, across an ocean of people, there
she was. A beacon.

'Let's go and say hi,' Chloe said.

My chest contracted. I couldn't let Cat see me with
Chloe. Cat was not meant to know about whatever was

going on between Chloe and me. She definitely wasn't meant to know about the person Chloe thought I was.

'She wouldn't want to interrupt,' I protested.

'I don't mind,' Chloe said, grabbing me by the arm.

I could have excused myself and run out of there, but the only thing worse than meeting Cat with Chloe was to let Cat meet Chloe without me. There were so many things she might let slip: the fact that I'd been to the Riviera, that my brother was in Australia, that my family had a summer home in Barcelona. All things Cat knew very well not to be true, because they actually described her.

One of her friends was with her, a girl with dark hair, on the other side of the clothing rack Cat was standing by, laughing at something she'd said.

'She's probably busy,' I said.

'We'll just quickly say hi,' Chloe said. 'Come on, you live together. I want to talk to her.'

Chloe had suggested that we hang out at our place that day, but I'd made up an excuse about not having tidied my room or having any food and suggested we should go out for lunch instead. I'd been trying to avoid exactly what was now about to happen.

Before I knew it, we were a few steps away from Cat.

'Cat?' Chloe said.

Cat turned her head and her eyes were wide and blank for a moment, and then her mouth slowly spilled into a smile.

'Hello,' she said. 'I'm sorry, I can't seem to recall your name.'

'Chloe. I don't think we've met properly.'

I couldn't stop thinking about the fact that she was holding my arm, that we were standing so close. I watched as her eyes drifted down, but the smile didn't fade, and she looked at our linked arms for just a second before she faced Chloe again.

I wished she wasn't still smiling. I wished I knew what she was thinking.

'I think we have,' Cat said. 'You were at Henry's birthday party, weren't you?'

She had an excellent memory for faces.

'I was,' Chloe said. 'We didn't really speak, though.'

'I'm sorry about that. I'm a terrible hostess, aren't I?'

Chloe smiled. 'There were a lot of people.'

Cat turned to me, our eyes meeting. I hoped my face wasn't too pained.

'How do you know each other?' she asked, as genially as if those weren't the first words she'd spoken to me in days.

'We met at the party,' I said, before Chloe could tell her we were dating.

Cat could draw her own conclusions. Hopefully ones that weren't correct. Who was I kidding? Cat had perfect intuition. She already knew.

'Lovely,' Cat said. 'Did you find something?'

For a moment I thought she was asking if we'd found something with each other. I almost couldn't breathe.

'No,' Chloe said. 'I'm auditioning for the role of clothes rack in a few days, so I wanted to get some rehearsal in.'

That was not funny. Had Chloe ever been funny? I hadn't paid enough attention before, but now it was embarrassing.

Cat laughed anyway. It sounded shrill. It burrowed into my brain.

'What about you?' Chloe said.

'Well, I'm having the same problem,' Cat said. 'I just came in to buy a pair of shoes, but I seem to be on the completely opposite side of the room from the shoes.'

'They're over there,' Chloe said.

'I know.'

And they both laughed again. I was nauseous. I didn't want them to be laughing together, but it was much better than talking about anything else. About families, or holidays, or hobbies. Or pulling me into the conversation, when I had one way I spoke with one of them and one way for the other, and whichever one I chose one of them would notice that something was wrong.

'What about you?' Cat said. She nodded to the skirt, which I had completely forgotten I was still holding.

'I was just looking at it,' I said.

'I think she should get it,' Chloe said. 'What do you think?'

Cat's eyes wandered across the skirt and then seemed to move elsewhere. Over the rest of my body, scrutinizing, then upwards to my face, where they stopped. Like there was something she wanted to say. I wanted to leave so badly.

'It's gorgeous,' she said. 'Just like you. You should get it.'

The word echoed around in my head, bouncing from one end to the other. *Gorgeous, gorgeous, gorgeous.* I suddenly needed the skirt.

'I love your top, by the way,' Cat said to Chloe.

'Thank you,' Chloe said. 'I love your bracelet.'

Cat raised her arm and touched the gold bracelet around her wrist. 'This?'

My heart immediately sank. I already knew what she would say next.

'I got it on the Riviera a few weeks ago.'

My lungs were no longer working. My throat was too tight to let in any air. I looked over at Chloe and it felt like I was watching a train wreck as she opened her mouth slowly. *Please don't say it*, I thought. *Please, please, please.*

'How lovely,' she said, smiling brightly. 'Did you go together?'

She looked at me as she said this, and then back at Cat.

Cat's eyes met mine for just a second. She cocked her head to the side. 'What do you mean?'

My legs bent, as Chloe opened her mouth to reply. The only thing that stopped me from falling was that she was still holding on to me. She helped me down. 'Louise,' she said, sounding alarmed.

I planted myself on the floor and inhaled. I was dizzy and there was a high chance I would be sick.

'Are you OK?' Chloe asked.

Cat remained standing in the same spot, staring down at me silently. Her face hadn't changed in the slightest. I wondered if she would have been this stoic if I'd been bleeding, vomiting, fainting, dying. I suspected so.

'I'm fine,' I said. 'I just felt a bit weak.'

'We should probably go home,' Cat said airily. She lifted her phone and started tapping on the screen. 'I'll get us an Uber.'

'I can take her,' Chloe said.

'Don't be silly.' Cat smiled again when Chloe turned to her. 'We're going to the same place, and I should go home and work on my dissertation anyway.'

Chloe rubbed my arm. It felt painful to me. I wanted her to go away.

'What happened?' she said.

'I think I didn't get enough sleep last night,' I said.

'Now you definitely deserve the skirt,' Chloe said.

She bought it for me. She insisted. Cat ordered the Uber. She also insisted.

The smile was gone as soon as Chloe was, and we sat

quietly next to each other in the car. I'd been silly to imagine anything else, to fantasize about Cat taking care of me, making me some food and tucking me up in a blanket on the couch, sitting there next to me and talking things out.

Minutes passed, and we just sat there. I held the new skirt in my lap; I hadn't brought a bag, and Chloe hadn't bought a plastic one for me. Cat was looking out of the window and I, whenever I felt brave enough to do so, was looking at her.

She spoke without turning to me. 'Is that my dress?'

'Yeah,' I said. 'It's the one you said I could borrow.'

'You know, when I said you could borrow it,' she hissed, 'I meant actually *borrow* it. Which means fucking returning it afterwards.'

'All right,' I said. 'I'll return it.'

She had never asked anything like that before, but I didn't want to argue with her right now.

We got home, left the car, walked up the stairs. She put the keys on the hook and said, 'You should stop trying to be me.'

'I'm not trying to be you,' I said.

'Yes, you are. You're always taking my clothes.'

'Friends borrow each other's clothes.'

'Oh yeah? And how would you know what *friends* do?'

'What do you mean by that?'

She glared at me. 'Don't pretend to be stupid.'

She walked into the lounge. I followed her before the door could close between us, still not sure what she was talking about.

'I know you talked to my mum,' she said. 'Why would you do that?'

'Because I'm worried about you,' I said. 'I didn't tell her anything.'

Cat shook her head. 'You're not worried about me.'

'We've talked about this before,' I said. 'Sometimes people do actually care about others. I don't need to have an ulterior motive.'

'But you do,' she said. 'You want us to break up, don't you?'

'Of course I do,' I said.

She held out her hands. 'Why are you so obsessed with us?'

I couldn't make myself any clearer than I already had without saying something really bad. It was probably best if I didn't.

'I should go,' I said.

'No, you should explain to me what's going on,' Cat said. 'Because this is weird. You keep taking my clothes and getting involved in my relationship and talking about Henry.' Her voice was louder now. She paused, inhaled. 'If I didn't know any better,' she said, 'I'd think you wanted my boyfriend.'

I stared at her, wondering if I should laugh.

'I asked you if you were fine with it,' she said. 'I asked you if there was anything serious between you two, and you said it was just sex and that you didn't care. So why do you care now? Have you been holding out hope this entire time?'

I laughed. I couldn't help it. I'd had her boyfriend, so I don't know what there was to want.

'Why the fuck would I want your boyfriend?' I said. 'He's a piece of shit.'

'Do you think I don't know that? Do you think I want any of this?'

And then I realized that Cat wasn't angry – she was sad. Her eyes changed. She shook her head and sank on to the couch dejectedly.

'Cat,' I said, surprised.

'You can have him,' she said, a tear rolling down her cheek. 'I know you don't want him because who the fuck would, but you can bloody well have him, because god knows I don't. I'm not an idiot.'

'I know you're not an idiot,' I said quietly.

'No, you don't, though!' Cat cried. 'You think I'm making the worst choice ever, but did you ever think that maybe I don't have a choice? If I did, do you think I'd actually choose to stay? Do you really believe I would just let him do this to me? You should know better.'

Her voice was not admonishing me. It was disappointed. And I couldn't deny what she'd just said. From the very start I had been focused on how to make Cat leave Henry. I hadn't thought that the issue was making Henry leave Cat.

'I'm sorry,' I said. 'I didn't know.'

She looked up at me. Her face was lined with tears now, her mascara running.

'He won't go away,' she said. 'Of course I've tried to break up with him, but no matter what I do, he won't go away. He comes back like a boomerang until I can't say no any more.'

'Why can't you say no?'

Cat wrung her hands and swallowed hard. 'Because I think he might . . .' She sobbed. 'He's not going to quit, Louise. You haven't seen how insistent he gets when he wants something. He says he's never going to let me go. He says that as long as we live, I'm going to be his. So what am I supposed to do with that?'

Oh god, I thought. I was just staring at her, not quite sure what to say. I knew exactly what she meant.

'He wouldn't,' I said.

She looked me directly in the eyes. 'He almost did once,'

she said. 'He choked me until I passed out. When I woke up, he said that he'd do it again if he had to. That it had been easier than he thought it would be. That he wouldn't stop next time.'

I could see it. I *had* seen it. In the memory I was naked underneath him, his hands around my throat, his eyes not even focused on me. For a second I'd wondered if he would stop in time. Afterwards I'd decided I was being silly.

When I had declared that he was Henry the Eighth, I'd called her Catherine Howard. I hadn't thought twice about the fact that Henry the Eighth had had Catherine Howard executed.

'You have to tell the police,' I said.

'And what are they going to do?' she said. 'Give me a restraining order? That's a piece of paper. It's only going to make him even angrier.'

'We took those pictures,' I said.

She shook her head. 'He deleted the pictures. He knows my password. He goes into my phone sometimes. He was very upset about the fact that the pictures existed at all, by the way, so thank you for that.'

'I'm a witness,' I said.

'You haven't witnessed him do anything,' Cat said. 'And do you even know how the justice system works? A trial would be months, even years, in the future. That whole time he's going to be walking around free to come here whenever he so wishes, to punish me for doing this to him.'

'You can move,' I said. 'We can both move. He doesn't have to find us.'

'And hide and hope for the best for ever?' She threw out her arms. 'Even if this went to trial, he'd get acquitted. Because the closest thing I have to evidence is the fact that you heard him yell at me. His dad's a bloody MP. They have lawyers in the family. People like that don't go to prison.'

'There has to be something we can do,' I said.

'There isn't, Louise,' she said. 'I'm stuck in this. So stop bloody judging me for it.'

I sat down on the floor in front of her. Everything she said made so much sense, but I couldn't accept it.

'We'll figure something out,' I said.

Cat slowly shook her head. She looked at me, not with anger or desperation or sadness. She looked at me with pity, like she knew something that I was too simple to wrap my head around.

'There's no way this is going to end before one of us dies,' she said.

18

One day when I was sixteen, Maisie didn't come to school. I tried to call her during one of our breaks, but there was no response. I asked one of the teachers if Maisie had called in sick and she told me no and then waved me off, like she couldn't care less.

I came home to find my mum crying at the kitchen table. Somehow I knew it was connected to Maisie. I immediately assumed that whatever illness she had was worse than I had anticipated, that maybe she was in hospital. It even crossed my mind that she might have hurt herself, or that she'd attempted to end her life. People always say it comes as a surprise when that happens, but it didn't, not to me. I knew Maisie was in pain.

There was one thing I didn't even consider, though. It didn't occur to me, until Mum said it out loud, that she wouldn't just have attempted it. It didn't seem to be a possibility that she would've been successful.

I lost the love of my life at sixteen. I have never referred to her as such out loud. People believe that kind of thing is silly teenage love. Those relationships so rarely last. But Maisie and I were different. She was different. We fitted together like I've never fitted with anyone since; she understood me like no one else ever has. There are so many things I stopped saying out loud after I lost her, because all I would get back would be bewildered stares. When I had said those things to her, she had always nodded, and she'd always known exactly what I meant. She'd always experienced the same thing. Maisie was like me. She was the only one like me. Nothing else would ever compare to that.

It wasn't the knife in the end. It was her antidepressants. She took all of them. Her mum was out that night and didn't know. I was at home just a few streets away, texting her until the very end. We were talking about such mundane things, like the test we had the upcoming week, the fight she'd had with her mum that day, what the weather was going to be like the next day. If I hadn't been the way I am, I might have caught on to the fact that something was wrong. I've scoured those conversations a hundred times since then, but I still can't find anything indicating what she had already done. We kept messaging until she said she was tired and had to go to sleep. Her last text said she loved me. I messaged the same thing back. It was never read.

'I'm tired of waiting,' she had told me once, when she was past crying and just staring at the ceiling again. 'I'm tired of waiting for things to change. I feel like I've been waiting my whole life. I feel like I'll always have to keep waiting.'

She didn't leave a letter. Maybe she was just feeling distraught and took too many tablets. Maybe she had planned it. Maybe it was a spur-of-the-moment decision. Maybe if she'd been as lucky as me and got diagnosed, she would've understood why she felt the way she did.

Maybe then she would've lived.

I woke up the next morning with eight missed calls from Alistair. At first it made my heart sink with dread. I had completely forgotten that the reason Chloe and I had gone out for lunch was because Alistair and I had been meant to have dinner that evening. After the fight with Cat I hadn't been able to think about anything else.

Then I got annoyed. Eight missed calls was far too many for anyone short of your spouse or child, or perhaps a grandparent with dementia.

I called back anyway.

'She's alive,' he said, as if he had never doubted this at all.

'I'm so sorry,' I said, still rubbing the sleep out of my eyes. 'Something happened last night, and time just got away from me.'

'What happened? Are you all right?'

His tone was perhaps a bit apprehensive now, like he was ready to take everything back if I revealed I'd been in a car crash or got mugged or something equally dramatic.

'It doesn't matter,' I said. 'I'm fine. It was just really chaotic.'

This wouldn't be a satisfactory explanation for my no-show, but it was better than talking to Alistair about feelings. Not just for my sake. Alistair didn't pay me to have feelings, and definitely not to express them to him.

He sighed on the other end of the line. 'Of course it was,' he said.

He left that sentence hanging in the air, giving me time to fully take in the fact that he hadn't said anything approximating 'It's OK.'

'How about we try again on Wednesday?' I said.

I was at the tattoo studio a few days later. I was lucky that the artist Chloe had recommended had a cancellation and could fit me in so quickly. If I'd had to wait longer, I probably would have backed out.

The tattoo artist was a young person with green hair and a body covered in tattoos. Their voice was very soft and sweet, which was slightly at odds with their appearance. I filled out a short form about allergies, medical conditions and other things, promising to follow the aftercare and that I had eaten in the last few hours.

I'd drawn the tattoo myself and emailed over a picture a few days earlier. They'd printed it out, and it looked exactly like it was supposed to. I hadn't even needed to look for photographs to be able to replicate Cat's rose tattoo.

'Where did you want it?' the artist asked.

'On my hip,' I said. I pointed at the exact spot through my clothing. 'Right here.'

'Cool,' the artist said.

They held the piece of paper against that spot and asked me if I felt it was the right size. It was a bit smaller than Cat's tattoo, so I asked if it could be made slightly bigger.

I lay on the tattooing bed with my jeans at my ankles and one side of my underwear pulled down, stoic against the pain of the tattoo needle.

'Are you OK?' the artist asked.

'Yeah,' I said.

'It's funny,' they said. 'I did a rose just like this in the exact same position on another girl a while back.'

'Huh,' I said.

'What a coincidence, right?'

Afterwards I waddled over to the mirror with my jeans hanging low and looked at the tattoo. I barely even looked like myself any more. The change was minuscule, invisible when I wore clothing over it, but in my eyes it was radical. I felt like Cat.

'Spill the tea,' Oliver said.

He had his hands deep in the pockets of one of his long

coats. He was wearing mascara and he had glitter on his cheekbones.

'About what?'

'Chloe, of course. What's going on?'

'It's great,' I said.

He eyed me even harder, one eyebrow raised.

'It is,' I said.

'Just great? Nothing else to it?'

The queue to the club moved ever so slightly. It wasn't insanely long; there aren't a lot of gays in our small university town. Even if every single one of them had lined up for the club that night, we still would've managed to get inside at some point.

I was wearing another one of Cat's dresses. I hadn't asked if I could borrow it this time, which I knew was wrong. I sneaked in while she was out and went through her closet, going to the back, where I could find the clothes she'd worn last year and would never put back on again. She probably wouldn't notice it was gone.

The dress was pretty. There were cut-outs so you could see parts of my waist and hips. Much paler than Cat's, and not quite as smooth and thin. But I'd sent a couple of mirror selfies to Chloe and she'd assured me I looked lovely. Oliver had said I looked amazing, and he's too honest to lie about something like that. He'd never tell me if I looked terrible; he'd just neglect to say anything about my appearance at all and let me draw my own conclusions.

'I don't know what you want me to say.' I laughed. 'It's been a few dates, all right? It's not anything serious and it never will be.'

'So there are no feelings involved at all?' he asked doubtfully.

'None whatsoever.'

'Not on her end either?'

I pulled my lips into my mouth. I hadn't asked, and I wasn't planning to. My version of Cat, the person that Chloe was dating, would never initiate that conversation. And if Chloe did, she would say that she was only looking for something casual. That was one of the few things about her that was true of me too.

'Not everyone falls in love with every person they go on a date with,' I said.

'I don't do that,' Oliver said.

We shuffled onwards. We were now only a couple of people away from the bouncers, and we could hear them chatting to the guys at the front.

'How many first dates have you been on that were only one date and nothing more?' I asked.

'Stop judging me,' Oliver said. 'I'm a romantic.'

'How many?'

'Well, two.'

'And the only reason one of them didn't become a second date was because –'

'You were convinced he was a serial killer.'

'He *was* a serial killer.'

'You could've given me the opportunity to confirm for myself. Who knows, he could've been lovely.'

'And you could've been murdered.'

He shrugged. 'Or I could've found love.'

I rolled my eyes at him, making sure to include affection in the gesture.

'She seems like a really sweet girl,' he said.

'Chloe? She is, yeah. She's lovely.'

'And that doesn't make you feel anything?'

'Not at all,' I said.

'You can't just stop yourself from falling in love,' Oliver insisted.

'*I* can.'

'Are you honestly telling me that ever since you made that stupid little resolution of yours, you've never once found someone that's made you go "Oh shit"? Just for a moment?'

I thought about Cat. Smiling, laughing Cat. Charismatic and popular, bubbly instead of solemn, loud instead of quiet, the centre of attention instead of withdrawn. Was it any wonder I had fallen for her?

'Yes,' I said. 'I'm honestly telling you that. Not even once.'

The bouncer waved through the last two people who were in front of us and asked for our IDs. Oliver asked him how his night was going and smiled, and the bouncer huffed and looked at his ID without meeting his eyes. When he said, 'Go ahead,' Oliver said, 'Have a great one!' and he didn't respond.

'You know you don't need to flirt with everyone,' I said as we made our way inside, raising my voice to keep it audible over the loud music.

'I wasn't flirting,' Oliver said. 'I'm a taken man.'

'Well, you don't have to make friends with everyone, then.'

'I just wanted to brighten his day a little.'

'I think you made it worse.'

The club was packed with bodies, mostly male, mostly topless. Bare skin glistened with sweat in the erratic light that kept changing colour and rhythm. I was overwhelmed within seconds.

It wasn't a good time to be going out. I knew that. I should have been working on my dissertation. My last meeting with Robert had been a disaster. He'd asked me about my argument, and all I had managed to say was that we can help people we don't care about and still feel good about it, because it earns us praise from others or makes us feel like we're good people. Which means the motivation isn't empathy, after all. Which means the fact that we care about people isn't a good argument against psychological egoism.

'I'm sorry,' Robert had said. 'I thought you were supposed to be arguing *against* psychological egoism.'

So I'd told him I just needed to understand the arguments for it better first, to know my opponent. I tried to appease him by saying that I'd started writing my introduction, and he said he wouldn't advise me to start writing that without first having a clear outline of the dissertation. He reminded me how little time I had and that I wouldn't want to finish this the night before the deadline. He insisted on another meeting in a week to check up on me again.

He even asked me how I was doing. He said he knew it was hard to manage your mental and physical health alongside the workload of a dissertation, but it was important to take time for yourself. And really, wasn't that what I was doing? I needed a night of not thinking about morality.

'Shots?' Oliver shouted into my ear.

'Shots!' I shouted back into his.

I wasn't overly drunk when I came home, but I wasn't completely steady on my feet either. I paid careful attention to where I placed them with every step, making my way from the Uber up to the front door. For a few moments I gathered myself together inside, the floor spinning below me. Someone came bounding down the stairs and I looked up, just in time to see that it was Henry.

He took the steps two at a time, like he always did, and

he was dressed somewhat like an old Etonian from the early twentieth century, in a tweed jacket and a white shirt.

'There she is,' he said.

I watched him, waiting for him to stop blurring. 'Been looking for me?' I asked.

Henry was standing in front of me now, his dark brown eyes staring into mine.

'And if I have?' he said, smirking slightly.

I rolled my eyes and made to move past him.

He took a step to the side and blocked my way. 'I've been meaning to ask you about something,' he said.

He was too close. I blinked and took a step back.

He followed. 'Remember when I lost my old phone?'

I shrugged, desperate not to betray how hard my heart was beating. 'Why would I remember that?'

'I thought someone must have taken it off me,' he said. 'Or found it when I left it behind somewhere, and then sold it for the parts, or removed the SIM and sold the whole phone.'

His eyes remained intently focused on mine. I reminded myself to swallow.

'But then the weirdest thing happened,' continued Henry. 'Someone hacked my Instagram. *If* they hacked it, that is.'

Eye contact has always been uncomfortable and painful for me. It had never been this bad before. It felt like someone was drilling into my eyes.

'What do you mean?' I asked.

He put his arms on either side of me and pressed me back against the door, too quick for my inebriated mind to comprehend what was happening. His head cocked to one side and he brought his face closer to mine.

I sucked in a breath. I felt way too sober, way too suddenly.

'I mean,' he said, 'maybe someone got into my phone.'

I put both my hands on his chest and pushed him backwards. Henry frowned.

'What does that have to do with me?' I said.

He grinned. 'Nothing,' he said.

I walked past him and made sure to bump my shoulder against him, sending him stumbling slightly to the side. I rushed up the stairs as fast as I could without making it obvious that I was hurrying.

'It's just funny,' he said. 'Because for a while there, I was completely convinced I'd lost it at your flat.'

I looked back down at him from the top of the stairs. He was smiling again, like nothing was wrong, like it was all one big game.

I could hear the piano before I opened the door to the flat. I stood there for a moment, pressing my forehead to the door, listening. She would stop, as always, the moment I came in, but I wanted to savour this. The piece sounded so complex and intricate. It also sounded incredibly tragic.

When I was ready, I unlocked the door. The music continued as I took off my shoes on unsteady feet, as I hung up my coat, even as I opened the door to the lounge. She must have heard the door, but she still did not stop. I stood in the doorway and for the first time ever I saw her fingers gliding across the keys. Moving so smoothly it was like they had been created for this and nothing else, like she had been doing this all her life.

'Hello,' I said.

The music died.

She turned her face to me. 'Hi,' she said. 'Where have you been?'

'I went clubbing with Oliver,' I said.

'Has the new boyfriend broken up with him?'

'No, they're still going strong, actually. I think he just wanted to get out for a bit.'

'That's nice,' Cat said. 'I'm glad to hear romance isn't quite dead.'

'Speaking of which.' I nodded my head in the direction of the front door. 'I met Henry downstairs. Are you all right?'

'Of course,' she said immediately. 'Don't worry. We didn't have a fight.'

I opened my mouth, but I couldn't tell her what had happened downstairs. She couldn't know that I was guilty of what Henry had accused me of. I hadn't thought much about the phone since I'd shoved it into my drawer, because Cat never went into my room anyway, but it wasn't Cat I needed to worry about. I was suddenly acutely aware of all the time Henry spent in our flat, a lot of it while I was out. It would be so easy for him to enter my room and test his hypothesis.

Cat looked back at the piano and I couldn't see her face any more. I wondered if it was intentional, if she didn't want me to see whatever expression she was making now. A single key made a high note.

I was torn between sitting down next to her and running to my room to check that the phone was still there.

Cat won. If Henry *had* found his old phone in my drawer, that wouldn't become a bigger problem in the next ten minutes.

I sat next to Cat and left a distance between us about the width of an adult hand, but she put her head upon my shoulder and closed the gap. There was no one, no one except Maisie, who I had ever felt this comfortable with.

To my surprise she started playing again. This piece was

slower. The touch of her fingers on the keys was so soft it almost wasn't there.

'I was wondering,' she said, 'would you come away with me to Barcelona for a few days?'

'Cat, I don't think I can afford it.'

For a few moments she didn't speak; she just continued playing. Her hands were even more mesmerizing this close. I could see the veins on the back of them. I could feel her hair against the skin on my neck.

'What if I paid for it?' she asked.

'I couldn't ask you to do that,' I said.

'You didn't. I offered.'

I imagined those fingers on my skin instead of the keys, soft and warm, stroking and rubbing. Gliding across my stomach, cupping my breasts, circling a nipple. Coming up over my throat, holding it in their grip.

'If you're sure,' I said.

She turned her head and nuzzled deeper against my neck, so that I could feel her warm breath, so that her lips were painfully close.

'I'm sure,' she said. 'Here.'

She grabbed one of my hands and placed it on the piano. I allowed the other to follow and settle alongside it. She put both her hands above my own, her fingers slipping into the gaps between mine.

'Just follow me,' she said.

Her fingers holding firm, she lifted my hands like they were her own and put the right one down on one side of the piano. Then she let it drag across the keys, the sound deepening. It would be so easy, in that moment, to reverse the grip she had on my hand and take control over where hers went. To guide it down between my legs.

'There you are,' she said. 'You're playing the piano.'

I smiled. I let her play holding my hands, putting them wherever she liked. We played a short tune together. I wondered if she would stop me if I leaned in for a kiss.

'Barcelona,' she said.

My crotch was throbbing at the memory of the way she had touched me once, these very fingers finding the right spot, and I ached to rub myself against something, to feel her in that way again.

'Yes,' I said breathlessly. 'Let's do it.'

'Really?'

'Really.'

'There's no way this is going to end,' she'd said, 'before one of us dies.'

I felt like I'd stepped through a hole in time. I'd spent years watching Maisie suffer, completely unable to do anything about it, full of dread for the inevitable crescendo. There was no chance I was going to let it happen again. This time, no matter what it took, I was going to stop it.

'What are you thinking about?' she asked.

'Barcelona,' I lied.

My heart nearly beat out of my chest as I opened my bedside table drawer.

Nothing was out of place.

The phone was still there.

19

I ran my hand down her torso and put my face close to hers.

'What do you want?' I asked.

She was breathing heavily, her hands restrained over her head and her crotch moving upwards as my hand approached.

'I want you to fuck me,' she whimpered.

When I leaned in, she did the same, her mouth begging for mine. I left her hanging and smiled instead.

'How badly do you want it?' I whispered.

'So badly,' Cat said. Her voice trembled. 'Please.'

I moved my hips forward and pushed the tip of the dildo against her clit. She pushed back harder and laughed briefly in frustration.

'Please,' she begged.

'Only because you asked so nicely,' I said.

I took my hand off her and used it to guide the strap-on towards her pussy instead. I entered her slowly, just the tip, and she gasped and stiffened underneath me. We stayed for a moment, her heartbeat matching mine.

'More?' I asked.

She nodded, biting her lip. I pushed the whole dildo inside her, and put my thumb on her clit at the same time. Her breath shuddered and her eyes rolled backwards. I kept my pace steady and slow in the beginning, rubbing her as I fucked her, and watched her clenching the bedsheets harder and harder.

'Fuck,' she whispered. 'Keep going.'

I sped up a little as her breathing did the same, becoming jagged and uneven. Cat closed her eyes. Her eyelids fluttered. Her neck was taut, a vein standing out, her back beginning to arch. Her fingers fumbled for the sheets. I pushed as deep inside her as I could.

'Yes!' she cried out, and her whole body shook.

I kept going anyway, not letting myself slow down, fucking her through the entire orgasm until she screamed and came again. That was when I let her fall back down on to the bed and released her. Her chest was shining with sweat. I kissed her forehead as I pulled the toy out of her and she smiled, still catching her breath.

'That was amazing,' she said.

I now had to confront the fact that she wasn't Cat. I reminded myself of this carefully, worried I would otherwise call her by the wrong name. Chloe. She was Chloe.

'So were you,' I said. 'You're incredibly hot.'

She blushed and covered her face. Definitely not what Cat would've done.

I wriggled out of the strap-on harness and lay down next to her to recover. I felt quite exhausted and delightfully spent. Chloe turned on to her side and threw one arm across my chest, planting her chin on my shoulder and giving it a little kiss. I didn't like it, of course. It was as painful as hugging a cactus. But I told myself that I was Cat, and she would never be appalled at physical contact. We'd just fucked, for god's sake. What was a cuddle compared to that?

'When are you leaving again?' Chloe asked, tracing circles on my ribs.

'Sunday.'

'I'm going to miss you,' she said.

'It's only a few days.'

'Still, I'm going to miss you.'

She looked up at me and smiled. I knew then that this wasn't the sort of "I'll miss you" that you said out of politeness and obligation. She meant it. Christ. We'd only been on, what, four dates, and she was already going to miss me when I went away for a few days. Not even a whole week. This wasn't even a full relationship. It gave me a feeling of suction inside my stomach, like an empty space. I couldn't have her go falling in love with me, but I didn't want this to end. Being Cat was nice.

'I'm going to miss you too,' I lied.

How do you tell someone that you aren't ever going to fall in love with them?

'No, you won't,' she said.

For a dreadful moment I thought she was on to me, and then she poked her tongue out at me and I realized she was being silly.

'You'll have plenty of fun in Barcelona,' she said. 'And I'll just be stuck over here, doing the same old.'

'The same old is underrated,' I said.

'We can do video calls,' she said.

I held myself back from saying that it was hardly worth video-calling for four days apart.

'Of course we can,' I said.

She smiled and looked away, tapping her fingers against my chest.

'Is Cat straight?' she asked.

Even I could hear that it wasn't as casual as she probably meant it to be.

'Yes,' I said. 'Why do you ask?'

Chloe shrugged. 'No reason,' she said, her voice unnaturally high. 'Just wondering.'

I closed my eyes and tried to rest.

'She's very pretty,' Chloe said quietly.

'She is,' I said.

Something was hanging unsaid in the air. I can usually tell when people want me to say something particular, when they're trying to coax something out of me. I've never been able to tell what, though. We lay there in silence.

'I hope you have fun,' Chloe said eventually.

'Oliver,' I said, holding the bag of mouse nuggets. 'Are you listening?'

He was sitting on my bed, dangling his legs like a school-girl and smiling at his phone.

He looked up. 'Sorry,' he said. 'What's that?'

I rolled my eyes. 'Mateo?'

'He's just so sweet,' Oliver said. 'He's going to go out and buy coffee so there's one ready for me when I get back home.'

'Home? Since when do you live together?'

'We don't – officially. But when you spend four nights a week somewhere, it starts to feel like home.'

'Were you?' I asked.

He blinked.

'Listening,' I said.

'Of course,' he said. 'That's the food. I give them three each every day.'

'No,' I said. 'Three in total every day. They're almost the size of their heads; they can't eat three of them each.'

'I could probably eat three meals the size of my own head every day.'

'Thank you for watching them,' I said. 'I'm sorry. I'm just nervous. I've never left them with someone else before.'

Oliver smiled. 'I understand that. They're your babies. As much as I absolutely don't get it, I get that much.' He nodded to the cage. 'Who's that?'

I turned around and saw that Squeak had emerged from the nest.

'That's Squeak,' I said. 'Want to say hi?'

'God, no.'

I bent down, opened the lid and put my hand out for her. Squeak climbed on immediately, having no idea where she was going but happy to come along for the ride. I presented her to Oliver in the palm of my hand. 'See? She's not so bad.'

He looked at her with his nose wrinkled. 'She's not,' he said. 'It's just the tail I can't deal with.'

When I tried to put her closer to his face, he pulled backwards and shook his head. I laughed at him and gave Squeak a stroke. She walked in circles round my hand, looking for a way to get off. Her attention span was very short, and she was always bored of something within two minutes.

'What will you do if one of them gets out of the cage and you have to pick her up?' I asked.

'I'll just go into witness protection, thank you very much. I'll miss you terribly, of course, but it can't be helped.'

I smiled and shook my head at him. I gave Squeak a kiss on her back and put her down inside the cage again.

'I wish I could go to Spain,' Oliver said. 'I need to brush up on my Spanish.'

'As if you have any Spanish in the first place,' I said, because he knew the absolute basics of probably ten different languages and was conversational in none of them.

'I should get a sugar daddy too,' he said.

'Or a rich friend.'

'Hmm, no,' he said. 'I'm good. Are you sure she's actually bought you a plane ticket?'

'I am,' I said. 'She sent me the confirmation.'

'But are you sure she won't abandon you somewhere without a wallet or roaming on your phone? And are you sure she doesn't plan to kill you and dispose of the body somewhere in international waters?'

'I'll just stay off any boats, then. Problem solved.'

Oliver sighed. 'I'm only a teensy bit worried.'

My mother had expressed the same sentiment but less tactfully and a lot more dramatically.

'You've never been abroad without me,' she said. 'Is your passport even still valid?'

'It's valid,' I said.

'Don't forget you can't take any liquids over one hundred mills on the plane,' she said. 'And have you checked what vaccinations you need?'

'I'm going to Spain; I don't need any vaccinations.'

'But you have accommodation sorted, right? And have you looked up public transport? Do you know what to do if you get lost? Have you checked that your debit card is activated for purchases abroad?' She sounded like she was hyperventilating.

'Mum,' I said, 'I'm an adult. I moved out years ago. I can go abroad. I'll have Cat with me the whole time.'

'I know,' she said. 'I know, I know. I just worry.'

'It'll be OK.'

'I know,' she said. And then, after a pause when I dared to believe it was over, she added, 'Do you have enough of your medication to last you the whole trip? You know you won't be able to get hold of your prescription over there.'

I didn't want to have that same conversation with Oliver,

so I sighed. He looked at me with an expression that was slightly apologetic.

'Why are you so worried about me travelling with Cat?' I asked. 'She's not evil.'

'I don't think she's evil. I just think she's . . . rich and self-centred.'

I raised my brows at him.

'I don't think she's going to kill you,' he said, holding up his hands. 'I just don't know if she'd help you if anything were to happen. Like, if you got hit by a car, she'd probably abandon you in the hospital so her holiday wasn't ruined.'

'Well, I wasn't planning to get hit by a car.'

Oliver groaned. 'You know what, I hope she does kill you and dispose of the body in international waters.'

'But then you'd be stuck taking care of the mice for the rest of their life,' I said, and he laughed.

Cat had laid out two large suitcases and one small cabin bag on the floor of the lounge. She seemed to be in the process of trying to fit her entire wardrobe inside them. She had booked hold luggage for both of us, even though I had already told her I would be fine with my cabin bag.

'Are you OK over there?' I asked, watching her push one of her flouncy dresses on top of a mountain of clothing in one of the suitcases.

'No, I'm not,' she said. She sat back on to her bum and sighed. 'I don't have enough space.'

'We're only going for four days,' I said. 'And there's a washing machine anyway, isn't there? You could take two outfits and wash them halfway through the trip.'

She stared at me. 'Lolo,' she said, 'it's a holiday. I'm not going to wear the same outfit more than once.'

'No, of course not,' I said. 'But you've packed more than four outfits anyway.'

'Well, that's because we might go out for dinner somewhere fancy, so I would need a nice dress, but then I'd also need the shoes to match. And I have to take my pillow. I can't sleep on anything else.'

'Give me the dress,' I said. 'I'll put it in mine.'

Cat shook her head and threw out her arms. 'It wouldn't make a difference. I've got so much else I need to fit in as well.'

'How many suitcases do you own?' I asked.

'Too many.'

'Then pack another one, and we can check it in as mine. I'm only using my cabin bag anyway.'

Her eyes twinkled and she smiled. 'Would you really? Louise, you're an angel.'

'I'm not,' I said.

'And you're sure you'll be fine with just that tiny little bag?'

'Perfectly.'

'I don't know how you do it. I wish I was more like you.'

My heart floated in my chest. I prayed I wasn't blushing.

'Well, you're taking the whole flat with you anyway,' I said. 'There's nothing I'll need that you won't have in one of those.'

'And then you'll be very grateful and maybe you won't judge me so much for it.'

I rolled my eyes.

She looked down at her suitcase and hesitated for a moment, swallowing hard. 'Just to let you know, Henry's coming over tonight.'

I bit back what I really wanted to say. 'Right.'

I'd sold his old phone to a second-hand electronics store in town. I'd been a fool to keep it for so long and that conversation with Henry on the stairs had made me see it. There was no way I could have gone to Barcelona without getting rid of it, with Henry having the run of the flat while we were gone. Now, no matter what he believed, he'd never have any proof.

'He wanted to say bye before we leave,' Cat said.

I held my tongue. I didn't want her to become angry with me and stop talking to me again, like the last time I had tried to talk about this seriously. Getting her to Spain for a while would be good for her. The distance might bring her some clarity on what to do. At the very least she would be far, far away from him.

'Of course,' I said.

My phone started ringing at just the right moment. I took it out of my pocket, expecting it to be Mum with yet another reminder about something I needed to do before getting on the plane. It was Alistair.

I went into my room and closed the door to take the call. I cleared my throat to make my voice sound right and spoke softly enough that Cat wouldn't be able to hear me.

'What are you up to?' Alistair said. 'Busy?'

'No,' I said. 'Just packing.'

'Yes. That's what you usually need to do before you go off gallivanting across Europe with no notice whatsoever.'

'I did give you notice.'

'It's not very like you, is all.' He paused. 'It makes you seem very different to be this spontaneous and adventurous.'

'I'm trying something new,' I said.

'Don't let it turn into a habit, will you?'

'I don't think I can afford that.'

I managed to draw out a short laugh from him at that.

'And here I was,' he said, 'thinking you were too busy with your dissertation and that's why you had no time for me any more.'

'I very much am,' I said. 'But I've decided to give the dissertation a miss for just a few days.'

'Right.'

He didn't sound convinced. As much as he was joking, and as much as his tone didn't tell me any different, I could sense that he was upset. He hadn't been entirely happy with me on the date we'd had to make up for the one I had missed. We hadn't spoken much during dinner and the sex had felt – off. I'd been so preoccupied, thinking about other things. We had been meant to go on another date during the week that I would now be in Barcelona.

'Look,' I said, 'I know it's inconvenient. But my friend is going through something at the moment, and she needs to get away. She needs a distraction. I figured going to Barcelona all by yourself isn't much fun, is it?'

'I suppose not,' he said. 'But you're right – it is inconvenient. I am vaguely disappointed.'

'I understand. It's just sometimes friends have to take precedence. I'm sure you can understand that. I'm sure your wife would take precedence over me if she needed you.'

'I don't have a wife.'

'Then one of your friends.'

Alistair sighed heavily. 'I will ask that you make it up to me.'

I smiled. 'I wouldn't expect anything else. I quite look forward to it, actually.'

'Of course you do.' For a moment I could hear the wetness of his mouth as he moved his tongue around. 'How do you plan to make amends?'

I wasn't very keen to get into anything at that moment, but I knew I was on thin ice. Also, I would need to ask for even more money from him that month if I was going to spend any money in Barcelona and still be able to survive when I came back home. And just then the doorbell rang and I heard Cat shuffle across the lounge to get the door, so I knew Henry had arrived. I might as well stay in my room.

'Well,' I said, 'what I have in mind starts with using my tongue.'

20

Cat was gorgeous even at six in the morning. I had no idea how she did it. While I felt like a gremlin that had just rolled out of bed and managed to pull some actual clothes on, she was dressed in a loungewear set and making coffee in the kitchen. I wondered how early she must have got up to put on a full face of make-up and curl her hair. There was no stress in her. She drank her coffee out on the balcony and kept an eye out for the taxi while I rushed to pack my remaining belongings, forgetting one thing and then another, scarfing down my breakfast standing upright because I didn't have time to sit down.

'Taxi's here!' Cat called in from the balcony door, not at all in a hurry to get down and prevent us from being charged extra for keeping the driver waiting.

I filled my bowl with water in the sink and made a note to ask Oliver to wash it at some point. He'd be coming over once a day for the mice; he'd outright refused to have them at his in case one of them got loose and sneaked into the walls.

Cat started lugging her suitcases to the door. 'Have you got your toothbrush?'

'No,' I said. 'Shit.'

I scrambled around like a headless chicken getting my toothbrush into my cosmetics bag while she met the driver downstairs and brought him up to help with the suitcases. I was surprised to see him at the door. I'd never dare to ask a driver to go up a full flight of stairs to help me carry suitcases; I'm fairly certain it isn't part of their job description. He seemed happy enough to be doing it, though, and he chatted easily with Cat, making her laugh.

We left only five minutes later than planned, but I was still worried about how long the lines would be at check-in and security. How long did it take to check bags in anyway? I fidgeted with my hands to calm myself down, and Cat firmly took one of them in her own and smiled at me without saying a word. My heartbeat returned to a normal pace. She leaned her head on my shoulder and sat like that for the full journey to the airport, and I felt perfectly at ease the whole time. No one had been this good at calming me down since Maisie.

Cat was an easy traveller. On the plane she put her headphones in, placed a travel pillow around her neck and closed her eyes. She slept the entire flight, while I sat there trying to read one of my moral philosophy books and fought against the urge to yell at the child behind me who kept kicking the back of my seat.

But it was too noisy and disruptive, and there was too much turbulence, so I gave up on my attempts to read. I turned my head to the side and looked at Cat. She slept the way pretty girls do in films. Not with her mouth open and drooling, not with one tit hanging out of her tank top and her hair a frizzy mess. She slept with a relaxed expression, a closed mouth and a soft smile.

I replaced my philosophy book with my sketchbook and drew her just like that, capturing every detail of her on the page.

Her family's flat in Barcelona wasn't quite as luxurious as the one she lived in at university, but it was still far nicer than anywhere I had ever lived before I met her. We stepped into an open-plan apartment with a kitchen in one corner and a lounge in the other, right next to a large terrace. The stone floors were cool and felt wonderful against the soles of my tired feet when I took off my shoes and socks. The hot Spanish air was already making me sweat, but it felt more bearable here than it had in the taxi. Amazingly enough, but not at all surprisingly, Cat had not a single drop of sweat on her face or even a stain under her armpits.

She dropped the suitcase she'd been dragging to the floor. I'd been given responsibility for the two others, of course.

'Oh my god,' she said. 'I haven't been here since I started university. I can't believe it still looks the same.'

She walked across the room and opened the door to the terrace. I didn't feel like that would make much of a difference, since it was even hotter outside, and there wasn't even the semblance of a breeze in the air.

'I need to turn on the AC,' Cat said. 'It's boiling in here.'

I sat down on the couch and rested my head against the back of it. I would've liked to nap for the rest of the day, but Cat seemed too energetic for that. She was running back and forth, turning on the AC and the fridge and freezer and checking that the lights worked in every room, or whatever else one does with a home no one's been in for several months.

'Is there WiFi?' I asked.

I needed to tell my mother I had arrived safely as soon as possible or she might have a heart attack, and I wasn't going to pay any roaming charges unless I absolutely had to.

'Of course,' Cat said. 'I think the router is over there by the window; the password is on the back.'

Mum had already messaged half an hour ago to see if I had

arrived. Chloe had texted me good morning and said that she missed me. Oliver had already replied to my text about the bowl in the sink with a gif of someone rolling their eyes.

Robert had responded to the email I'd sent him about being away. He'd worded it as kindly as he could while still remaining stern. It was clear he didn't think it was a very good idea for me to go on holiday right now, with the dissertation deadline so close and with so little of it having been written. He reminded me again not to take this so frivolously. I'd already told him I was taking my laptop and planned to get at least some writing done while I was over here; I hardly thought Cat had something planned for every hour of every day. She had a dissertation to be writing too, didn't she?

I looked up from the couch. She was unpacking now. I'd never seen someone start unpacking so quickly after arriving at their destination. I was planning to live out of my bag the whole time we were there.

She noticed that I was looking at her. 'Did you manage to get on the WiFi all right?'

'Yeah,' I said. 'I do need to do some work on my dissertation while we're here, by the way. I hope that's not an issue. I've got Robert breathing down my neck about deadlines.'

'No, that's fine,' she said. 'Me too, technically. Have you started yet?'

'What do you mean? Have you not?'

'Not properly. I've been reading a lot, though, and putting my thoughts together. It won't take long to write it all down.'

I smiled and felt immediately comforted. She was so relaxed about the whole thing, speaking as casually about it as if she was talking about missing a bus when there would be another one along ten minutes later. Cat had never missed a deadline, so if she said it was fine when she was even more behind than I was, then it was fine.

'I forgot to tell you,' she said. 'There's only one bedroom. There's also the couch, of course, but I figured you wouldn't mind sharing.'

My heart skipped a beat and I swallowed. The first time I had shared a bed with her, she had touched me. We'd never talked about it again. We'd acted like it had never happened. But now, not for the first time since she had brought up the idea of going, I wondered if something was going to happen again while we were in Barcelona. In the end, that was probably the biggest reason I had said yes.

'That's fine,' I said. 'I don't care.'

It was better than telling her I was extremely excited.

'Do you want to go out to the pool?'

'There's a pool?'

'The building has a pool. We can use it.'

I had a fresh tattoo and had been expressly forbidden from going swimming for the foreseeable future, but I couldn't tell Cat that. She would ask about the tattoo. In the end, the only excuse I could come up with was silly.

'I didn't bring swimwear.'

The truth was I didn't own any. I hadn't gone to a swimming pool since I was a child.

'We can buy some!' Cat exclaimed, her face lighting up. 'Let's go and do some shopping.'

'Sure,' I said. Even though I wouldn't be doing much shopping, because I wouldn't be able to fit much more in my bag on the way back, and hers were full already. 'Can I shower first?'

*

Cat had already unpacked her cosmetics and put everything in the bathroom. She'd brought along the shampoo, conditioner and shower gel she used at home.

I sniffed the shower gel after pouring it into my hand. It smelled just like she did. Lathering myself with it all over felt like rubbing her on to my skin. When I left the shower, I smelled like her. I put my nose to my arm and inhaled deeply.

I could hear her talking outside, and when I came out of the bathroom in a towel she was holding her phone in front of her head and moving it across the room.

'And here's Louise,' she said as it panned over to me.

'Hello, Louise,' Henry's voice said from the phone.

I bit down hard. 'Hi, Henry.'

'Behind her is the bathroom,' Cat said. She walked past me to open the bathroom door again as I walked away. 'Pretty basic, but nice.'

I didn't want to hear them any more. I'd thought we were planning to spend the whole trip pretending Henry didn't exist. Even if she wasn't, I was certainly still intending to do exactly that. I went to the bedroom and locked the door to get dressed. I was pretty sure Cat wouldn't open it without knocking, but not entirely. There was no chance I was ever letting Henry see me naked again.

After getting dressed, covering myself in sunscreen and putting on enough make-up to make me look more awake, I went back out to the lounge. Cat was sitting out on the terrace now, still with her phone in front of her and Henry's face on the screen. She was laughing. I left her like that. I put my phone on charge and lay down on the bed to wait for her to come and tell me she was ready to leave. I might have dozed off.

There was a knock on the door. 'Lolo?' she said. 'Are you ready to go?'

'Yes,' I said, forcing myself to get up. 'I was waiting for you.'

'And I was waiting for you.' She laughed. 'Come on. If we go now, we'll make it before the shops close for the siesta.'

Cat tried to order an Uber into the city centre, even though I assured her the walk wouldn't be that bad. Luckily for my wallet, there was no driver that accepted our request. Cat grumbled under her breath and we started walking. She was wearing open-toe sandals, which looked a lot more comfortable than my old trainers in this heat. I told her this, and she said I should get some. I hummed in agreement, even though I didn't have the money to buy new shoes or the luggage space to take them back home with us.

The sun was beating down on us. Cat told me we should also buy sun hats, and in my mind I could see all the expenses piling up on top of each other already. Cat crouched down to greet a dog that was walking past us, cooing at it in her baby voice, and it immediately turned to her and began wagging its tail, letting her stroke its face and massage its ears.

'Careful,' I said. 'Might it not have fleas or worms or something?'

'It's not a stray,' Cat said. 'They let them walk around like this the way we do with cats. I'm sure this little one has a home. Don't you?'

Cat loved animals. She owned a horse because she'd been convinced it was her life's calling a decade earlier, and of course she couldn't just take classes like a normal teenager. I don't think she'd seen her horse in years.

She gave the dog a kiss on the top of its head and we

continued walking. It took us half an hour to get into the city proper, the housing areas replaced by long pedestrian streets full of restaurants, cinemas and shopping centres. There were plenty of people out and about.

'Do you want lunch?' Cat asked.

'Sure,' I said.

We found a small place that looked local, where the menu was only in Spanish and Catalan, and the waitress, though she smiled and nodded at everything we said, didn't seem to fully understand what Cat was talking about when she asked for specials or recommendations. I had something with rice and seafood. Cat had a salad. She took pictures of our food and it went both on her social media stories and straight to Henry's messages. He replied a few seconds later, as if he'd been waiting by his phone. She spent the rest of lunch taking occasional bites while messaging him, as I finished my food and sat there waiting for her.

After lunch, we had about an hour to do our shopping before the siesta would start. We found a nice little boutique with swimwear that I found cute, until I saw the price tags and swooned.

'Can we go somewhere cheaper?' I asked.

'The cheaper stuff doesn't last half as long,' Cat said. 'Trust me, this is cheaper in the long run. You pay for actual quality, you know. This is cute.'

She held up a small maroon bikini in front of me.

'I'd prefer high-waisted,' I said. 'To hide my stomach a bit more.' And not expose my tattoo.

'Louise, you don't need to hide your stomach. You barely have one. You're so beautiful.'

I blushed. 'Thank you,' I said. 'But I prefer having more coverage.'

Cat shrugged. 'Suit yourself.'

I managed to find something in the end, and decided when I paid for it that I would not open my bank app for the next few days.

Even though Cat bought herself a new bikini to add to the one she'd brought from home, she dragged me into more shops and started piling things into her arms, ending each shop visit with a trip to the dressing room. I patiently sat outside and waited for her to come out and show me each item, posing for me like a model in a photoshoot.

Cat was a miracle. Every single item fitted her. Women's clothing is an inconsistent nightmare and I felt very confused about the EU sizes, but this didn't matter to Cat. No matter what the tag said, she could hold out a piece of clothing in front of her and tell whether it would fit or not. Nothing pinched or looked unflattering on her. Nothing was baggy in any weird spots.

Despite the fact that we'd gone out to buy me a bikini, Cat was the one who ended up with the most bags by the time the siesta hit. This time we managed to get an Uber back to the flat.

'What do you want to do now?' she asked.

'I'm very tired,' I said, because the heat and the early start had me feeling like I was about to pass out. 'Do you mind if I take a nap?'

'Of course not,' she said. 'We can hang out at the flat for a little while.'

I fell on to the bed and was asleep almost instantly.

When I woke up, Cat was sitting out on the terrace with a book. I felt disorientated and out of sorts, the way I always do after taking a nap in the middle of the day.

'Hello,' she said when I emerged. 'Are the Spanish on to something when it comes to the siesta?'

'I think they are,' I said. 'I don't understand why it hasn't caught on everywhere else too. What are you reading? Studying?'

She grinned sheepishly and showed me the cover of her book, which said *SWF Seeks Same*.

'What's that?'

'Ugh,' she said. 'It's a silly thriller from the nineties. Don't tell my supervisor. I know I should be reading something more academic, but I figured I should get at least one day of a proper holiday before I do.'

I sat down in the lounger next to her. It was hot from the sun.

'What are holidays for if not reading trash?'

'Exactly,' Cat said. 'I knew you wouldn't judge me.'

I was pleased with this. It was good that she knew. She closed the book and put it on her lap. I checked my phone and made myself respond to Chloe, who had double-texted.

What's the weather like? she'd asked.

Cat glanced over at my phone casually. 'Who are you texting?'

'It's just Chloe,' I said.

'Are you dating?'

'No,' I said immediately. 'We're just friends.'

I didn't make the choice to lie; it just happened.

'What a relief,' Cat said.

My chest fluttered. 'What do you mean?'

She was quiet. The seconds stretched out, unbearably long. Why was she relieved? It couldn't be what I thought. I knew that. And yet . . .

'I wanted to be nice,' she said eventually. 'You know, if she was your girlfriend. But I don't like her.'

This surprised me. Cat had been so friendly when they'd met at the clothes fair, smiling and laughing. I'm not good at these things, but there had been no indication at all that she didn't like Chloe.

'Why not?'

'She just seems to try so hard,' Cat said. 'What with all the "I only shop second-hand" and being vegan and all that. I have nothing against vegans, but it's the fact that she had to bring it up. I didn't ask. She talks to you like she thinks she's better than you.'

I hadn't thought about that before, but it wasn't untrue. The very first time I'd met her she'd been lecturing Oliver about queer representation as if he wasn't a six on the Kinsey scale. On our first date she'd made me promise not to buy Parmesan – and what kind of person messes with a woman's cheese consumption?

'Yeah,' I said. 'Yeah, she does do that.'

'Look, I'm not saying anything,' Cat said. 'But it always makes me suspicious when people are like that. If someone is trying too hard to convince you they're a good person, they're usually not.'

I nodded.

'And you deserve the best,' she said.

I tried to decipher the expression on her face, but it was so neutral, and I'm so autistic.

It was at dinner that night she first brought it up. Over tapas and wine we had got ourselves a bit tipsy. There were candles on our table shining in the dark, and her face was red from the alcohol.

I'd waited for the topic of Henry to be broached. He was like a bad smell hanging in the air that it felt impossible to ignore but rude to bring up. I wanted to be able to breathe again. I wanted to find a solution to the problem he posed.

'Sometimes I wish he would die,' Cat said. 'Is that a terrible thing to say?'

It shocked me, but only a little. He was a terrible person, after all. It didn't seem so very unusual to me that a victim of abuse would think this way about their abuser.

'No,' I said. 'I don't think it is.'

Cat looked off into the distance, swirling the wine in her glass. 'I just feel like things would be better if he was dead.'

21

I woke up the next morning with her hair in my nose. Her shampoo smelled like bubblegum. I wanted to devour her. We had fallen asleep with more distance between us, but I had moved across to her side of the bed in the night. She was so close to the edge she was almost falling off it.

I went outside on the terrace in my nightie without feeling in the least bit chilly. While I waited for Cat to wake up, I tried to be productive. I sent some nudes to Alistair that I'd taken weeks earlier and saved for a time when I couldn't be bothered taking new ones. I did some reading for my dissertation but struggled to focus. There was no breakfast, so I used my phone to locate the nearest shop and went over there. I found milk and cereal and came back to Cat sunbathing on one of the loungers on the terrace.

'Good morning,' she said.

'I bought breakfast,' I told her.

'Did you get coffee?'

'No, sorry. I wouldn't even know what to get. You know I'm not a coffee person.'

'That's fine,' she said. 'What's the plan for today?'

'Studying, I suppose.'

She sighed and rolled her eyes. 'Do you want to go down to the pool first? It's too hot to study.'

I felt very exposed in my new bikini. I've never much liked having my body on display, available to be assessed by others.

My stomach never flat enough, the cellulite always too visible. It was even worse when the person doing the assessment was an otherworldly deity like Cat, who never seemed to even bloat. I stayed in the pool and let the water hide me from her judgement. She remained firmly planted on the lounger, wearing her sunglasses and working on her tan.

I paddled around in the water. It smelled of chlorine and the surface shone with the reflection of the sunlight. It was delightfully refreshing compared to the oppressive heat of the air. I rolled over on to my back and closed my eyes, letting myself float around. No one else had come out to the pool yet, and it was our own private little oasis.

When I opened my eyes again and looked over at Cat, her head was angled in my direction. Through the sunglasses I couldn't tell what she was looking at, but I suspected that it was me. It made me want to cover myself up. I wondered if the plaster I'd covered my tattoo with was visible. The air was too hot not to take advantage of the pool, and I'd figured the plaster should be enough to protect the tattoo. It was also easier to explain if Cat saw it – I'd come up with a story about cutting myself rather badly while shaving. I adjusted my bikini bottoms anyway.

'What are you looking at?' I asked, and tried to sound like I didn't care.

'Nothing,' Cat said. 'You sure you don't want to work on your tan?'

'I don't tan. I burn,' I said. 'Why don't you come in here instead?'

She considered this for a couple of seconds and then removed her sunglasses. 'Why not?'

She put her legs in first and lifted herself off the edge with both arms, sliding into the water and disappearing below the surface. When she came back up, her mascara was running. It was the sort of thing Cat wouldn't care about at all. That was one of the many reasons I loved her.

She pulled the hair back over her face and opened her eyes again. 'This is so nice,' she said.

'I know.'

She swam up next to me and placed her hands on my waist. It made my breath hitch. Our legs paddled right next to each other. *Now*, I thought, *now is the moment she kisses me*. My heart drummed with anticipation. For a moment I forgot to keep myself afloat and almost sank. Cat smiled at me. Her hands felt so soft against my skin. She was utterly, utterly perfect. I swallowed.

Then she pulled me underneath the surface. I had just enough warning to take a breath and close my mouth before I went under.

She released me quickly and was laughing when I resurfaced.

'You arsehole,' I said.

She grinned at me.

I splashed some water at her face and she laughed harder, splashing me back with one hand while protecting her face with the other. We swam in circles around each other, throwing water at each other and laughing, grabbing for each other's legs and bodies to pull each other down again.

We didn't study at all that day. After the pool, Cat suggested going back into the city, so we spent several hours exploring, going into interesting shops and visiting museums. I didn't think about Henry the whole day. Instead, I told myself that tonight I was going to do it. I was going to make a move. It might not be a kiss, I wasn't sure I was bold enough for something that unambiguous, but I would try something. I had to. We weren't going to be in Barcelona for ever.

But in the evening, when I came out of the bedroom planning to ask if she wanted to watch a film, Cat was already on the phone with Henry. They were gossiping about people they both knew, names I recognized but had no faces to connect to. I slowly retreated back to the bedroom and replied to Oliver's messages instead.

He'd sent me a picture of Squeak sitting on his shoulder. *I can't believe I'm letting her do this!* he'd written.

I ignored some messages from Chloe. She'd sent me selfies. She'd sent me texts about how much she missed me and other texts asking about what I'd been up to. I ignored my mother too, who wanted to know I was still alive and was asking the question with such seriousness I almost thought she must have a real reason to believe I was not.

Cat slept longer than I did. I lay in bed watching her. She was so beautiful it was impossible not to. Her eyebrows were dishevelled. Her mouth was slightly open and her lips looked so soft. She had pushed the duvet down so it was only covering her lower half. Her tank top had slid so precariously to the side she was almost exposing herself. She wouldn't care about that, would she? I had seen her naked. I watched her chest rising and falling slowly with every breath she took. I put my head on the hair that flowed on the pillow beside her. It was the only part of her I knew I could touch without waking her up.

I got up eventually, dragging myself out of bed at ten because I was too hungry not to. Back at home Cat had a laundry basket in her room, a wooden one with a lid on top. Here the only hamper was in the bathroom and it stood uncovered in a corner. There was hardly anything in it, but at the bottom lay a pair of her knickers.

I knew I shouldn't do it. That was what I told myself as I brushed my teeth and kept glancing over at them, fighting against the temptation. Temptation won. I took her knickers out of the hamper and straightened them out. They were light pink with black stripes. They weren't very sexy, not the kind of underwear you'd wear to a date where you were hoping to get lucky. That made them feel even more intimate and valuable. This was what she would wear on a regular day.

I shoved them deep inside one of the small compartments of my bag and hoped she wouldn't discover they were missing. Knowing Cat, she probably never would.

I made coffee the way I had watched her do it, pleasantly surprised that I didn't manage to make the coffee maker explode in the process. I poured her a bowl of milk and cereal and woke her up with breakfast in bed. She rubbed her eyes and sat up, her hair an absolute bird's nest at the back and her eyes squinty and sleepy.

'You're the best,' she said. 'Thank you so much, Louise. What time is it?'

'Twenty past ten,' I replied.

'Would you mind if I slept a bit longer?' she asked.

'Oh, no,' I said, 'of course not.'

Back in the kitchen I placed her coffee on the counter and ate her cereal before it went soggy, annoyed but not planning to say anything to her. I put on clothes and stuck my earphones in my ears and went for a walk. Chloe called me and I let it go to voicemail. I knew I should feel bad about it, but I just didn't have the energy to do all the pretending that speaking to her involved. It was oppressively hot even this early in the day. I saw some lizards on the walls of the building. I walked until I made it down to the beach and took off my shoes. The sand was too warm, so the shoes went back on.

I went back home a different way and came back almost an hour after I had left. If Cat was still sleeping, it would be a good opportunity to get some work done. I opened the bedroom door slightly, just to see if she was awake. She'd thrown the duvet off entirely and her hand was in her underwear, her back arched. Her eyes were closed. I could see her nipples standing up underneath the tank top. The other hand was slowly stroking up her stomach.

It was the single most alluring thing I'd ever seen in my life. My knees were weak. I swallowed hard and it took everything I had in me not to enter the room. I closed the door as quietly as I could. There was a taste of blood in my mouth. My heart was beating intensely.

I took my laptop out on to the terrace and sat there staring at the screen for a while. Not a single new word was added to my dissertation. Every time I blinked I saw that moment again. Eventually I retrieved my sketchbook from my bag and drew her from memory.

That night, as we walked home from the restaurant where we'd had dinner, Cat veered down to the beach.

'What are you doing?' I asked, following.

'I need to feel the sand between my toes,' she said.

True to her word, she took her sandals off as the asphalt turned to sand and we walked down the path to the beach. It was dark already and the place was deserted, probably due to the late hour and the cold breeze.

Cat spun around in front of me, her white dress flowing,

while I wrapped my arms around myself and wished I'd brought a jacket.

'It's so peaceful,' she said. 'So quiet.'

She reached for my hand and clasped my fingers. I allowed her to take them and lead me down the beach towards the water. We stopped far enough from the shore that I didn't worry about the waves reaching us. The sea was unsettled and foamy.

'Can I ask you something?' Cat said, turning towards me.

'Of course.'

'How did Maisie die?'

My breath caught in my throat.

'You don't have to tell me,' Cat said.

And she meant it. Her mouth was softly inclined upwards, though it wasn't quite a smile. She was looking directly into my eyes.

I didn't have to tell her, but I wanted to.

'She killed herself,' I said.

It was the first time in seven years I'd said it out loud. The words seemed so strange, like when you repeat something so many times that it loses its meaning.

Cat hugged me. 'Oh, Lolo.'

I closed my eyes. 'It was an overdose,' I said. 'I don't know if that means it was painful. Sometimes I want to look up what an antidepressant overdose feels like, but I can't bring myself to.'

Cat said nothing. She breathed on to my neck.

'I wish she'd left a note,' I said.

'You don't know why she did it?' It was a whisper.

'I think I do. I think she thought her life would always be the way it was back then. That it was never going to change or get better.'

Cat released me from the hug. There were tears in her eyes.

I blinked, half convinced I must be imagining them, but the wetness remained. 'Cat . . .' I said.

'Let's swim,' she said.

'It's cold.'

'Come on.' She grabbed me by the hand again. 'We're on holiday.'

'We don't have our bikinis.' And I didn't have a plaster over my tattoo.

'Louise. Live a little.'

She was right. We were on holiday. And, god, I wanted to be more like her, spontaneous and unafraid, ready to dive into unknown waters without first thinking about every single thing that could go wrong.

When Cat started getting out of her dress, I took off my shorts and top. I hoped she couldn't see in the dark that my pants didn't match my bra. I pulled them up high enough to cover the tattoo. She ran ahead into the waves so effortlessly that the cold took me completely by surprise when I went after her. I gasped at the shock. I was only a few steps in, but the waves were up to my knees.

'It's freezing!' I said.

Cat turned around, smiling. 'I know,' she said. 'Isn't it wonderful?'

She dived, submersing her whole body. I fought against my survival instincts and waded out further, focusing on my breathing, trying to keep my teeth from chattering. Cat re-emerged in front of me like a mermaid, her hair in front of her face. She pushed it back, opening her mouth to inhale.

The water reached my chest now, higher every time a wave burst against me.

Cat stood back up, her skin slick. She looked at me. 'It means a lot that you would trust me with that.'

I gave her a small, frozen smile.

'You make me feel that way, you know,' she said. 'The way you said she made you feel. Like someone finally understood you. Because you make me feel like – like someone finally sees me for who I really am.'

She stepped closer, and I was so focused on her words that I forgot to feel the cold.

'It's a stupid thing to complain about,' she said. 'But I feel like I spend most of my time figuring out what everyone around me wants me to do. What they want me to say, what they want me to look like.'

It felt like she was describing me. Ever since I'd been in the inpatient unit, everything I had been and done and said had been entirely determined by other people's expectations. I had never been me. It had only ever been a role I was playing.

'But you,' she said, so close, so very close we were nearly touching, 'I think you only want me to be myself.'

There were goosebumps on her arms. There was water on her soft full lips.

'I do.' I barely got the words out.

'Sometimes that's the hardest thing to be, though. Isn't it?'

I nodded. *I understand*, I wanted to say. *I understand all of it.*

She put her fingers gently on my arms. 'I have a confession,' she said.

I forgot how to breathe. My heart stilled. I didn't feel the cold any more.

Sometimes change takes you by surprise. Other times your entire body is aware that your whole life is about to change, that past this second nothing will ever be the same.

This was one of those moments.

I made myself nod again. Words were beyond me.

Cat opened her mouth and I leaned towards her.

'I didn't want the threesome,' she said.

I stopped mid-movement. It felt like being right at the edge of a ravine, your toes across the edge, balancing to keep yourself upright, a fraction of a second from disaster.

'But Henry did,' said Cat.

'And . . .'

'Yes.'

Neither of us had to say it out loud.

'I didn't want the threesome,' she said again, smiling this time, 'but I'd do it all over again in a heartbeat.'

22

On our last night in Barcelona Cat wanted to go to a jazz bar. I hadn't brought anything for the occasion, so I borrowed one of her dresses. We got ready together and she put her face close to the mirror in the bathroom, parting her hair with her fingers.

'Are my roots very obvious?' she asked.

'What do you mean?'

'I should've got them done before I left,' she mumbled.

I saw what she meant now. The hair that was growing out of her scalp wasn't red – it was blonde.

'You dye your hair?'

She looked at me like I was supposed to know this already. 'Yes,' she said. 'Or, well, my hairdresser does it. I'm not a natural redhead.'

I'd never seen her without this hair colour. I'd never caught her walking around the flat with her hair bundled up under a towel smelling of ammonia. But this made sense; Cat wouldn't do her own dirty work.

It felt special. It felt like exactly what the purpose of this trip was: to get to know her better. To deepen our bond. Did Henry know this? I doubted he would have noticed.

'All yours,' Cat said, moving aside.

I looked at myself in the mirror, turning from side to side.

Cat put her arms around me from behind and kissed me

on the cheek. 'You look beautiful,' she said. 'Stop staring at yourself. You're just finding new faults.'

'It's the same old faults as always,' I said.

'Every time I stare at myself in the mirror,' she said, 'I find something new to be ashamed of. Another dark hair growing from a mole. Another spot of cellulite. Another pimple.'

I looked at her, stunned. Of course I knew she wasn't actually perfect, but I figured she didn't care. I had never imagined that Cat noticed these things.

'What?' she said.

'You don't have any faults.'

'Don't be ridiculous,' Cat said. 'I'm full of faults. You're the one who's completely without them.'

I laughed. It was such an absurd statement.

Cat threw her hands out and smiled. 'And you don't even know it,' she said.

I felt all warm on the inside.

Barcelona was beautiful by night. Despite the late hour we were able to walk around in dresses that didn't reach our knees without any jackets at all. The city shone, golden, alive with people, packed with groups of both tourists and locals, Spanish and Catalan carrying across the air and mixing with other languages. Cat gave money to a street performer. There was so much music everywhere.

The jazz bar was in a basement, and the whole thing reminded me of a speakeasy in the US. It was dank and dark. The place seemed entirely populated by locals, and no one was carrying a camera or wearing one of those souvenir T-shirts that mark you out as a tourist.

'How did you find this place?' I asked Cat.

'Someone I know recommended it to me,' she said. 'You know Manolo?'

She was always dropping names as if I was supposed to know who she meant. No doubt Manolo was also at our university, so of course I should know him – never mind that there were thousands of other students and that Cat and I moved in very different circles.

'No.'

'Well, he's from here. And he's a musician. So I trust him to recommend the best local music.'

She ordered drinks for us by leaning across the bar to make herself heard by the bartender, holding up two fingers to clarify that we needed two drinks. There was a band with four members on the stage: a singer, someone on drums, someone on the guitar, someone on what looked like a bass. The singer sang in a sweet, deep voice. I had no idea what the words meant but he used his hands as he sang and his eyes were wet.

We sat at one of the tables. Cat had ordered cocktails. I could barely taste the alcohol, which I greatly appreciated.

'He's very hot, isn't he?' she said, looking at the singer.

I hadn't thought about it until she said it. He had blue eyes and dark curly hair. I suppose he could be considered attractive. The look in her eyes made something chafe inside me, like a cheese grater on my bones.

'You have a boyfriend,' I said.

Somehow, saying that made me feel no better at all.

'I know,' Cat said, rolling her eyes. She said it as if she had a loving boyfriend and a healthy committed relationship and she'd been a bit naughty and I'd teased her about it. Not like she was trapped in a strange battle to the death that I would never understand and she had every right to fantasize about other people. 'But he's not here, is he?'

She looked at me. She had a curious half-smile on her face and a glint in her eye. It sounded inviting.

'How's the drink?' she asked.

'It's surprisingly good,' I said.

Cat laughed. 'I know what you like, Lolo. The music's pretty good too.'

I nodded. 'I've never been to a jazz bar before.'

'Can I be completely honest with you?' She leaned across the table like she was about to tell me a secret. 'Neither have I.'

We sat at the table for a while, listening to the music and finishing our drinks. Cat reached for me underneath the table and took hold of my hand. Mine felt so dry and chapped in comparison to her smooth skin. Some of the songs were more upbeat than that first one, causing Cat to start dancing in her seat, bobbing her shoulders and moving her head from side to side. She didn't stop looking at the band, as if she wasn't even aware she was doing it.

Then she stood. 'Let's dance.'

I was usually fine with dancing, but not in front of her. Never in front of her. She was effortless and beautiful, and I was a graceless ogre who could barely move my hips. 'No,' I said.

'Come on,' Cat said. 'It'll be fun, I promise.'

She held both hands out for me, her rings catching the light from the lamps above us. I sighed and allowed her to pull me up from my chair. No one else was dancing. They were all sitting down. We would look ridiculous if we did this, so out of place. I suspected there was something of convention about this. There are rules to every social situation you can find yourself in, and doing the wrong thing makes you stand out. I have never been very good at those rules, but I have spent years trying to figure them out. I knew enough to know that dancing here would feel like dancing in the aisle of a supermarket.

'I'm not drunk enough to be any good at dancing,' I said.

'You're full of shit,' Cat said.

She was smiling. Of course, she didn't care. But Cat was more socially successful than I was. She had more friends, she had more experience, and she never seemed to embarrass herself. Maybe she was right. Maybe I was wrong. I decided to trust her.

We danced tight together, her hands on my body, running up and down. I almost wanted her to stop. It was too much to have her this close but not quite mine. She put her head on my shoulder towards the end, one hand on my waist and the other in mine, and led me into a slow dance. We swayed against each other, so close, hand in hand. And she'd been right: no one looked at us. I caught myself thinking that I wouldn't have minded if they did.

Her breath was warm on my bare skin. I was convinced I felt her plant a kiss there.

We walked home arm in arm, delightfully tipsy, taking a detour to the waterfront. Cat led us to the fence that separated the street from the drop down to the sandy beach and let go of me. She put her arms on the fence and I found myself doing the same, following her gaze out to the sea. The waves were beating against the shore. The sea was dark, but there was a light out there far away on the horizon, a ship of some kind.

'I wish we didn't have to go back,' she said.

'Me too,' I said.

I wanted every night to be exactly like this: just her and

me and a small amount of alcohol in my system, the music from the jazz bar still playing in my head.

She closed her eyes. Her hair was blowing in the wind.

'We should kill him,' she said. 'Get rid of him.'

'Slip a bit of poison into his drink,' I said.

She grinned at me. 'Too hard to get hold of poison. Let's stab him.'

'Too much blood,' I said. 'Let's push him off a building.'

'Too hard to get him up there,' she said. 'Let's hit him with a car.'

'Too big a risk he wouldn't die,' I said. 'Let's smother him with a pillow.'

She opened her mouth as if she was about to speak, and then she burst out laughing instead.

I laughed too. But the truth was that for just a moment she had sounded sincere. The look on her face had been serious.

My heart had picked up pace and I had doubted her. The laughter came as a relief.

I've never been good at telling when something is a joke.

Back at the flat, Cat flopped on to the couch and said one of those outrageous and completely unexpected things that only she could get away with.

'I'm so horny.'

I laughed awkwardly, still taking off my shoes. That was one sentence I'd never been taught the proper reaction to.

'That's practically the only reason I miss Henry,' she said. 'I mean, my trusty hand is pretty good, but it's not good enough. And I just wish I could get some release.'

'Just download an app,' I said, trying so very hard to make it clear in my voice that it was a joke.

'God, no,' Cat said. 'I don't like sleeping with strangers. It makes me feel weird, you know?'

I nodded in agreement. I wasn't sure if I was ready to verbally reveal anything about my sex life. It felt like a slippery slope when she looked so gorgeous.

'Do you like one-night stands?' she asked.

'Not particularly,' I said. 'I mean, it's usually not very good the first few times you have sex with someone new.'

'That's so true,' she said.

She stretched her arms above her head. She was more tanned than she had been when we left England. It made her eyes pop and her teeth look even whiter. 'And you never know beforehand who's going to be terrible, do you?'

'No,' I said. 'Though I find that it's a safer bet with girls. They're at least guaranteed to find the clit.'

She laughed, and I felt pleased with myself.

'I think you're right,' she said. 'I've only been with one girl, but I have to say it was pretty good.'

She smiled. I felt myself blushing and my mouth closed itself on me. If I had tried to speak, I would've stuttered helplessly. I turned around and walked over to the kitchen section, opening the fridge.

I took a deep breath. 'Do you want some orange juice?' I asked.

'No, thank you,' Cat said.

I didn't want orange juice either, but it was the only thing I could think of to do that would get me away from staring straight at her. She was only messing around, of course. She was only a little tipsy.

I poured myself a glass and took a sip of the cold orange juice. It had pulp. I despise orange juice with pulp. I could barely swallow it. When I turned around, Cat was still look-ing at me.

'Are you hot?' she asked.

'Hmm?'

'Your cheeks are very red.'

I touched one cheek. It did feel warm.

Cat smiled. 'Sometimes I think about the way you ate me out when I touch myself.'

I didn't know what to say, so I said nothing.

'You're so good at it,' she said.

She moved one leg outwards and then the other, until she was almost in a straddle on the couch. I couldn't see her underwear because of the shadows cast by her dress. I put my glass on the counter and got down on my knees, slowly enough that she could tell me no if she wanted to, hesitantly enough that I didn't appear over-eager. I was still in disbelief that this was happening. I tested out the waters. I sat on both knees and looked at her.

'Come closer,' she said.

I crawled on all fours. My crotch was aching. I was already painfully wet. I wanted to know if she was wet too. I wanted to taste her again. I wanted to know what she would be like without Henry here.

She leaned over and took my hair in one hand, angling my face towards her own. She licked her lips. My breath was coming so fast and so shallow there was no way she couldn't tell how badly I wanted her.

'What do you want?' she whispered.

You, I thought. *The only thing I've ever wanted is you.*

'Please,' I said.

She smirked. 'Let's go to the bedroom.'

I nodded and she took my hand and led me to the room.

When the door closed she turned around and began kissing me. I put my hand on her thigh and began moving it upwards. Her skin was so soft and smooth. When I reached her underwear I pressed and she moaned. She moved against my hand and I began rubbing her slowly through the thin fabric, and her kisses stopped and were replaced by her forehead pressing against my own. I kissed her neck, sucking at the skin, hard enough to leave a mark. I wanted Henry to see. I wanted everyone to see. I wanted to claim her as my own and for the whole world to know just how she had trembled in my arms.

Holding her upright, I continued doing what I'd been doing and her breathing began to sound strained. I slid a finger inside her knickers and she gasped. She was wet. It made me crave her something fierce to see how desperately she wanted me, how I'd managed to reduce her to this.

She pulled my hand away. 'Wait,' she said.

She grabbed me by the shoulders, turning me around and then dropping me backwards on to the bed. We both laughed. She climbed on top of me and looked into my eyes, trailing one hand down my torso.

'I want to make you come first,' she said. 'I want to know what you taste like.'

She left a lingering kiss behind, pulling my bottom lip with her. She moved down so she was straddling me lower on my legs and then she lifted up my dress. Her hands touched my skin, so hot and so soft and so hers. My need for her felt so urgent my entire pelvic region was a dull throb.

Then she stopped, her expression thoughtful, her head cocked to the side. My dress was pulled up to my waist. She was looking at my right hip. She reached her hand out and touched my skin cautiously.

I'd forgotten about the tattoo. I'd been so desperate for

her that I hadn't stopped to think that she would see it.

'This is my tattoo,' she said, her voice neutral and blank, her thumb resting on the stalk of the rose. 'Why did you get my tattoo?'

'I thought it looked nice,' I said.

'Louise.'

I felt like I was in an interrogation room with a police officer. I looked away.

'What the hell?' Cat said loudly.

She lifted her leg over mine and stepped on to the floor.

I felt ridiculous lying there with my underwear exposed and I pulled my dress back down, trying and failing over and over to say something that made sense, starting sentences that I didn't know how to continue.

'That's weird,' Cat said. 'It's really weird, Louise.'

'Plenty of friends have matching tattoos,' I said.

'That they get with each other's knowledge! It's like you're —' She shook her head. 'It's like you're trying to be me, or something.'

I shook my head violently. 'I just liked your tattoo and I wanted one like it.'

'And if that's completely normal, why didn't you tell me?' She had her hands on her hips.

I sat on the bed and looked down at the sheets.

'You know this isn't right. It concerns me.'

'There's nothing to be concerned about,' I whispered.

'It's obsessive.'

My mouth gaped like a fish as I stared at her in desperation. I wished I knew the right words, but nothing I said seemed to matter. And she was right, wasn't she? There was a reason I hadn't told her about this tattoo. It was nothing like a matching friend tattoo.

'Don't you see that this is creepy?'

And I did see that, I did. But I couldn't let her know that. My only recourse was playing dumb and pretending that this had been a silly little faux pas, just an autistic person making a mistake when it comes to relationships and social cues.

'No,' I said. 'I thought you'd think it was sweet.'

She laughed.

'Please,' I said. 'If this is odd, I'm sorry.'

'It is odd. It's not sweet. Why do you have to do everything that I do?'

'I don't.'

'But you do, don't you?' I watched her jaw tighten and clench. 'You keep taking my clothes. You changed your dissertation topic to the same one I'm doing.'

'It's not the same as yours. It's the opposite.'

'You got the same bloody tattoo as me!' She took a deep breath. 'Henry told me about this.'

It felt like she'd thrown a rock at my chest.

'He couldn't have,' I said. 'He doesn't know about the tattoo.'

'Oh, for fuck's sake,' Cat said. 'Not that. He told me you were obsessed with me and that I should be cautious around you. He told me there was something unhealthy and strange about it.'

I clenched my fists. The prick.

What's the first thing every abuser does? They alienate their victim from their friends and family, the people closest to them, anyone who could see that anything was wrong. I should have known that he would drip poison into her ear about me. None of this would be happening if it wasn't for that. If he hadn't planted this seed in her, the tattoo could have been explained away more easily, possibly even dismissed and laughed at and turned into a moment of bonding.

Had he told her more? Had he told her what he suspected about his missing phone? I shouldn't have messed around with his social media. I should have left the damn thing to gather dust under our couch cushions. Cat wouldn't have believed him, of course. Now she might.

'Why would you believe *him*?' My voice was getting louder. 'He's an abusive piece of shit.'

'But now I know that you're also seriously messed up,' she said. 'You have to see how fucked this is. How can I trust you now? You're the one person in the world I thought I could depend on, and I can't even fucking trust *you*.'

I could feel that I was crying now. It was the first time she had ever seen me cry, but she didn't come rushing to my side with a hug and a box of tissues and reassuring words. She looked at me like I was a dead rodent her cat had dropped on the floor in front of her, with my intestines hanging out and my blood staining her floors.

'I'm sorry,' I said.

'I'm sure you are,' she said. 'I'm sure you're really sorry you can't keep staying at my place practically for free.'

'That's never been part of it,' I said.

'Do you think I fucking care? Just get out of here.'

I stood up on shaky legs. 'Please,' I said, my voice breaking.

'Now,' Cat said. 'You're lucky I'm not calling the police.'

I went out into the living room.

She closed the door behind me and the lock clicked shut.

23

I slept on the couch that night and we didn't speak the entire trip home. I followed her outside when she left and climbed into the Uber behind her, but she didn't even look my way. We walked through the airport like we didn't know each other. She got through security faster than me; I'd forgotten to put any of my liquids in a plastic bag and the agent spoke to me in frustrated broken English, rolling her eyes, as I watched Cat's red hair disappear.

I found her outside our gate with a cup of coffee in her hand. Her carry-on was on the seat to her right and there was an old man sitting in the one to her left. She didn't move her bag for me. I sat further away and willed her to look at me. If she did, I could mouth to her about how sorry I was. This time it might work. This time she might listen to me.

She didn't look over once. Then she treated me like a stranger as we boarded and for the entire flight as we sat next to each other.

She watched a film she had downloaded on to her laptop. I stared at one of my open philosophy books. I had, of course, done no studying in Barcelona. I also, of course, got no reading done on the plane home.

At one point I went into the toilet and cried quietly, getting knocked into the wall by the turbulence.

Henry was at the flat when we came home. He was waiting for us in the lounge. Cat ran up to him and wrapped her arms and legs around him. He carried her like that and spun her around. She looked at me over his shoulder and I had never wished more that facial expressions were understandable to me.

Oliver was in my room, sitting on the floor next to the cage.

'*Buenos días!*' he said.

'I didn't expect you to be here,' I said. 'I could've fed them today.'

I hoped my voice sounded normal. I hoped my eyes were not still red.

'I know,' he said. 'I wanted to say goodbye to them.'

'Goodbye? You're here at least once a week anyway.'

'I know, but it won't be the same,' he said.

'You've grown surprisingly fond of them.'

He shrugged. 'They stole my heart. They even made it worth the fact that I had to awkwardly talk to Henry when he showed up. Which is weird, right? Like, he doesn't live here. He said he wanted to be here when Cat came home, that they'd "missed each other".'

I sat down on the floor next to him as he spoke and rolled his eyes. His arm was hanging down into the cage and I could see something moving up and down inside his sleeve. I smiled as Squeak popped her little face out. Pip was eating oats from his hand. It was their favourite treat.

'Something on your mind?' he asked.

I heard them laughing outside. 'No, nothing.'

'How was Barcelona?'

I wished I could tell him everything. At this point I even wanted his judgement. I wanted him to tell me what on earth I had got myself mixed up in.

'It was lovely,' I said. And burst out sobbing again.

He blinked and reached out for me, but then thought better of it.

I pulled my legs up to my chest and wrapped my arms around them and buried my face against my knees. I was so grateful that he had remembered not to touch me. I was so embarrassed that I was breaking down in front of him. He'd never seen me do this before. I don't like needing people. I never have. People are fickle and unreliable. I'd needed someone once and it had nearly killed me.

Now I was crying in front of him. Like a baby. Like an overdramatic idiot. I hated the fact that he was seeing me so weak.

'What's wrong?' he asked. 'Did something happen?'

I tried to breathe, to stop myself from sobbing for long enough to speak.

'We had a fight,' I managed to say.

It felt so insufficient. It didn't at all describe what had happened. I'd had everything in my hands, everything. I'd had Cat on my tongue, in the bed, between my legs. I'd had her and I had lost it all.

I wanted to tell him all of this. That there was something wrong with me. That this was the reason I didn't do love and romance any more. I always ended up overdoing it, and I always ended up heartbroken and alone. I always ended up destroyed.

But I told him nothing. Oliver was a romantic, but he wouldn't understand why I had her tattoo on my hip. He wouldn't understand why I had her knickers in my suitcase. I didn't understand it myself.

'What did she do?' he asked.

'Did it occur to you that maybe I was the one who did something?'

He blinked, unyielding. 'No.'

'You know, you could try a little harder to like her. She's my best friend.'

I knew what I'd said the moment it left my mouth, but by that point it was too late. *She's my best friend, not you.* I hate words. They can cause so much damage in just a moment, and no matter how many times you apologize, you can never undo it.

'I know,' Oliver said.

He was good to me, better than I deserved. He stayed there as I continued crying and he didn't insist on talking. We were so quiet we could hear Cat and Henry speaking in the next room. They sounded serious, their voices hard. She was probably telling him about me.

I cried harder.

After he left, I lay on the bed and listened to the fight or the parts of it I could catch. I'd known it would come. They were both shouting this time, and every time I blinked I could see Cat's face the way it had looked when I was the one she was angry at.

'Fuck you!' she yelled. 'Get the fuck out, Henry!'

'I'm not done talking to you!' he shouted back. 'I'm not done –'

And the words became unintelligible. I had no sense of how long it went on. Sometimes I wasn't sure I was entirely there. I was in my bed, but I was also crying myself to sleep on the couch in Barcelona. I was in my bed, but I was also in the room with them, putting my hands around his neck. Shoving a knife into his stomach. Bashing his head in with something heavy.

I went over that night again and again in my head, that

moment out by the water. After I had suggested the poison, it had seemed like a joke. She'd responded with a glint in her eye and a smile. But when she had first said that we should kill him – I could've sworn she was dead serious. I'd told myself it was just me being autistic. Oliver had needed to explain his sarcasm and deadpan jokes to me so many times. I'd been ridiculous, that was all. But what if I hadn't been? What if it wasn't a bad idea? I imagined a world without Henry. A world where there was only Cat and me. Where no one would ever hurt her again. I would take care of her. I would protect her. She would forgive me.

There was a bang.

I sat up. I would kill him. If he had hurt her again, I would kill him. But there were no more loud noises, there was no more shouting. When they started speaking again, they were so quiet I couldn't make it out any more.

I went across the room and put my ear against the wall. All I could hear was murmuring and the occasional word, not enough to put together any complete sentences.

Eventually Henry left and I waited for a few minutes to see if he would be back. Part of the fear I felt was at the idea of seeing her again. I dithered until I couldn't any more and carefully opened my bedroom door.

The suitcases were sprawled across the floor in her room and one of them was open. She was unpacking. As if nothing had happened just now. She glanced at me, a bundle of clothes in her arms, and moved across to the wardrobe without looking back again.

'Cat,' I said.

'What?' she said, her tone sharp.

'Did he do it again?'

If he'd hit her, he hadn't done it in a place where it

showed. There were no bruises on her face or bare arms. She looked like herself.

She put her hair behind her ear and bent down over the suitcase again. 'You should leave,' she said.

'OK.'

'Not just my room. I mean the flat.'

She had to give me sixty days' notice, didn't she? It was a ridiculous thing to be thinking about right then, but it was the only thing that came into my mind.

'What if he comes back?' I said.

Who was going to protect her then? Who was going to keep him from killing her?

'Of course he'll come back,' she said. She raised herself up and looked straight at me. 'He's my boyfriend.'

My mouth opened helplessly.

'I don't want to go,' I whispered.

'I don't care,' Cat said.

I went back to my room. I looked around and thought about how much I loved this place. I loved how much light the large windows let in on those rare sunny days. How big the bed was and how I could spread out as much as I wanted without reaching the edges. How I could lie awake in the mornings and listen to the sound of Cat getting ready: the shower running, the sound of her feet on the floor, the grinding of the coffee machine.

I took her underwear out of my bag and pressed them to my nose. They didn't smell like much. They didn't smell like her. Frustrated, I shoved them under my pillow.

My room. My lovely, lovely room.

My Cat. My lovely, lovely Cat.

I pushed the bookshelf out from the wall and watched it crash to the floor with a loud bang that rattled the window frames and sent Pip rushing across the cage in a panic. It wasn't enough. I pulled out one drawer after another from my chest of drawers and smashed them. They were light enough that I could break them. I could make the bottoms crack and the hinges bend. I watched all of this as if it was just happening, as if it wasn't something I was doing.

It wasn't until I saw a smear of blood on the floor that I realized I was bleeding.

Chloe hugged me tightly. She smelled overwhelming. Her hair tickled my face. Her arms felt like they were rubbing against my ribs inside my chest. I wanted her to stop. I wanted to crawl out of my own skin. Instead, I let her do it, and I let her kiss me, and I made myself smile and slip back into the version of me that she knew and liked.

'I missed you,' she said.

I knew she had. She'd messaged me every day and I'd only occasionally responded, making up excuses about lack of service or data. I was grateful that she'd never pursued the idea of a video call. I suspect she was waiting for me to do that.

'I missed you too,' I said.

I hadn't. I'd just needed somewhere to go.

In the Uber on the way over I'd ignored a message from Alistair. *I believe you're back on British soil now. How about catching up tonight if you have time for me now?* It wasn't that I didn't consider it; it was that I didn't want to be myself right now, even if it was his version of me.

It was easier to be Cat instead.

'Come,' Chloe said. 'Come in.'

The TV was loud in her lounge. She grimaced at me as we walked towards her bedroom. Her flatmate was yelling something. The sound was almost unbearable. Everything was almost unbearable.

We sat down on Chloe's bed and she pushed herself right up next to me, her leg against mine.

'Tell me about Barcelona,' she said.

It annoyed me how she said it the Spanish way, lisping on the 'c' and trying way too hard.

'It was great,' I said. 'I had a lovely time.'

'What did you get up to?'

I thought about dancing with Cat. I thought about seeing her touching herself. I thought about getting on my knees for her. I thought about the absolute mess that I had somehow got myself into and the fact that I couldn't go home.

'Not much, to be honest,' I said. 'We spent a lot of time at the pool, and we visited this little jazz bar last night.'

'Sounds great,' Chloe said. 'I wish I'd been there.'

Her voice was different to Cat's. It was lower and not quite as sing-songy. She needed to shut up. I leaned over and kissed her, grabbing her face in my hands. She let out a giggle and kissed me back.

When I opened my eyes, it was Cat's face I was looking down on.

'I missed you so much,' I said.

I pushed her down on to the bed.

Cat would have loved to know about this. She would have felt so justified that she was right. The truth was that I had never cared about Chloe's emotions, only my own. I had done it simply for my own selfish desires. But then isn't that what we always do when it comes to relationships? Do you ever love someone for their sake, or do you always do it because you get something out of it?

278

But I'm not heartless. I had been in love. And I think I would have done anything for Maisie, no matter what it did to me in the process. If I could have died in her stead, I would have. I wouldn't have hesitated at all.

I rarely thought about it any more, but I reminded myself of this whenever I thought I was incapable of loving another person. Of course I was. After I lost Maisie I felt like I'd lost everything. That included the will to live. I strung a belt around the clothes rail in my wardrobe and wrapped it around my neck. For a few seconds I was about to join her. In my sixteen years on this earth I hadn't found a single other person who understood me the way Maisie had. I'd already known I wouldn't find someone new after her. There would be no one else who would ever get it the way she did. No one else who felt exactly the same.

The clothes rail didn't hold. I went crashing to the floor, and Mum heard and came running upstairs. That was me off to the inpatient unit for I can't even remember how long. I was so out of it, on so many different pills that made me lose touch with reality and lose track of time. Sometimes I was practically catatonic. Sometimes I wouldn't stop crying for hours.

That was why Mum still had me in therapy, obviously. That was why I was still on medication. And it was also why I had promised that I would never, under any circumstances, fall in love again.

But I'd been wrong. I had found someone who understood. I had found someone who felt everything I felt. *No one actually likes me*, she'd said. *I don't think she's genuine*, Oliver had said. And he was right. Cat wasn't herself; she was what everyone around her expected her to be. She did what everyone else wanted her to do. Just like I always had.

I both loved and hated her for the spell she'd put on me. I'd made a vow. I'd been committed for so many years and had avoided falling for so many different people. She'd ripped me wide open. That was how I knew I was the one who was right about psychological egoism. Because it had never been in my best interest to fall for her. It had done nothing but bring chaos and havoc to my life.

And that's when I finally found the direction for my dissertation. The biggest piece of evidence against psychological egoism is the fact that we fall in love.

24

'In the end, it does nothing for you, does it? It's not in our own interest to do something as risky as falling in love. What we actually enjoy is being loved by others.'

Robert opened his mouth as if he wasn't entirely sure.

'But we can get that without loving them in return,' I continued. 'We can go through the motions of loving them and get all the attention and affection without any of the risk. We can reap all those benefits just by pretending to love without actually doing it. Falling in love just makes us vulnerable to being hurt.'

Falling in love just means that one day you might be lying on the floor of your wardrobe with a belt around your neck, gasping for air.

Robert cocked his brows. 'You're saying you can just have someone else be in love with you and provide you with all the love and affection you want without ever asking for anything in return?'

'No,' I said. 'I'm saying that you can give them everything they want from you without actually loving them. You can pretend without actually putting your own heart at stake.'

'You're talking about faking it.'

'Yes. Isn't that the most logical thing to do?'

'That argument has been made,' Robert said. 'We can fake cooperation with the people around us to reap the benefits of cooperation without actually contributing to it. But that's incredibly risky, isn't it? You might get found out.

Plus, it's hard work, so you still put in the effort with more risk. The easiest way to reap the benefits of a social cooperative is just to cooperate; that's easier than faking it. The same goes for love. Would you really say it's easy to fake being in love with someone in a way that's convincing and reliable?'

'It doesn't matter if it's easy,' I said. 'What matters is that it's safe.'

Robert put his hands together. 'It's certainly an angle I don't think I've seen anyone else take. But I really don't know if it works. Wouldn't most people agree that falling in love is actually in our best interest?'

'Why?'

'Because it's a good thing.'

'It's not,' I said. 'When you fall in love, you give someone the absolute power to destroy you. If they hurt you, you'll never recover.' I inhaled. 'They don't even need to do it intentionally.'

Robert smiled. 'You might be right that falling in love is risky,' he said, 'but love is usually considered valuable in itself, rather than because of the benefits it might bring us. It makes us feel good. It lets us see the world in a new light. It lets us experience happiness and joy along with the person we love when they're happy.'

I nodded, pretending to genuinely consider his viewpoint. 'Right,' I said. 'Those are good objections to consider.'

Robert shook his head. 'I'm not trying to give you objections to address. I'm trying to deter you from going down this route. It's going to be a minefield, and it's going to be very difficult, and it's far too ambitious for a master's dissertation. You could write a whole book about this without managing to make a convincing argument.'

He smiled at me, exasperation in his eyes. He probably

had no idea what to do with me at this stage. The desperation was palpable, even for me. We were so close to the deadline and the only direction I had managed to come up with was one he was convinced would never work. I really should reconsider, if only to spare his heart. One more piece of distressing news from me and he might die on the spot. And, yes, I didn't have much time, and I didn't have a very high word count to address all these points. He was right about all of that.

'Do you have any literature to recommend about whether love has intrinsic value or not?'

I didn't ask Chloe if I could stay. I just did it – one night and then another. Chloe didn't ask me to leave; she seemed happy that I was there, and I played into it. I pretended that the only reason I didn't go home was the fact that I had missed her so much I didn't want to leave. If we'd been straight, she might have questioned things. But lesbians do this all the time. She was probably wondering why I hadn't moved over all my possessions yet.

We worked on our dissertations together at the kitchen table. Or I should say that she worked and I sat next to her. She was on the conclusion and I was still reading my sources, with nothing but a half-baked introduction. I didn't get any further with her there either. Chloe would drop random questions into comfortable silences, like a wrecking ball into my productivity.

'Did you ever have a crush on Cat?' she asked.

I turned my head and stared at her. There was nothing I could think to say that a look couldn't say just as well.

'I mean, she's so pretty,' said Chloe too quickly, keeping her eyes fixed on her laptop.

I was probably meant to interpret this as casual. I suspected it was anything but.

'Why would I have a crush on her just because she's pretty?'

'Not just because she's pretty. But, like, doesn't every non-straight girl have a crush on her straight best friend at some point? Isn't it a rite of passage?'

I remembered how she had asked about Cat's sexuality before I went to Barcelona and thought about the clingy desperation to her texts while we were over there.

'Are you jealous of Cat?'

Chloe snorted and made a silly face, as if this was the most ridiculous thing she'd ever heard. 'No!' she said. 'I was just asking a question.'

'OK.'

It was a natural conclusion to the conversation. I tried to write some more, but Chloe's keyboard remained quiet.

'Why would you think I was jealous?' she asked softly. 'Is there anything to be jealous of?'

Some things to be jealous of: the fact that when she was out or in the shower I drew Cat in my sketchbook; the fact that every time we had sex I was imagining Cat; the fact that she would never compare to Cat.

'No,' I said. 'Of course not.'

Oliver took care of the mice. I gave him my keys as if it was some kind of illicit drug deal. I could tell he wasn't happy about going into Cat's flat when she was there and I wasn't, but he pursed his lips and didn't tell me this out loud. I assumed he'd texted her to let her know about his visits, but I didn't want to know. I promised him it was a temporary arrangement, because that's what I was telling myself.

There was no point convincing an Uber driver to take the mice in their car and to lug their cage across town to Chloe's if I was going back home any day.

'I just can't go back right now,' I said. 'I can't.'

'What happened?' he asked.

I shook my head, and he, bless his heart, didn't ask again, even when the question was obvious in his eyes. He must think Cat had done something horrid for me not even to be able to face her.

Let him think what he wanted. I was too tired to worry about that.

I cancelled another date with Alistair that day, because I couldn't think of a reason to be out all night that I could give Chloe. *Of course*, he'd replied. *You have other priorities*.

When I wasn't studying, and when Chloe and I weren't being disgustingly couple-like, I was usually drawing. When I was doing that my brain could be silent. Chloe started taking an interest, though; she wanted to see my sketchbook, and I couldn't show her because I had so many drawings of Cat, then she asked if I would draw her, which I didn't want to. The one time I tried, the drawing had morphed into Cat and I had to rip out the page and scrunch it up and say I'd made a mistake. I stopped drawing when Chloe was around.

I spent a lot of time on social media. I refreshed my feeds hundreds of times during the day, checking for what Cat was up to. Very little came up except for a repost of some quote about feminism on her story. I analysed it to death, wondering if it was in any way directed towards me, considering whether I should like it or respond to it or do anything. This led me to spend an hour thinking about messaging her.

I drafted a text. I deleted it. I drafted another and thought it was better, but then deleted that one too. I didn't even know if I was allowed to go back home. And if she didn't want me there, what would she do about it? I did have a rental agreement. She couldn't kick me out without notice; I was fairly certain of that. She probably couldn't call the police either; I hadn't done anything illegal. But she could be angry at me. She could yell at me. She could give me the look she'd given me in Barcelona, and that would be so much worse.

And then there was another picture from the hair salon. Cat was smiling with her hairdresser behind her like they were best friends. The salon was tagged.

I booked an appointment immediately, pledging to spend more money than I actually had, and I arrived with reference pictures from Cat's feed where you couldn't see her face.

They got the colour almost exactly right.

I'd been staying with Chloe for three days when she shook me awake in the morning. She was saying something, but I wasn't conscious enough to catch it. I rubbed my eyes and opened them; she was sitting up next to me in her small pyjama top. Her hair was still tousled by sleep.

I could finally make out what she was saying.

'Who's Alistair?'

I looked down at her hands. She was holding my phone. Her expression was almost pleading, like she didn't want to be right.

'No one,' I said. 'Stop going through my phone.'

I sat myself up.

'I'm not going through your phone,' Chloe said. 'I wanted to check what time it was, and you have a message from someone named Alistair.'

Of course I did. His messages were getting more frequent and increasingly passive aggressive. The day before, he'd written, *If I didn't know better, I'd file a missing person report about now.*

'What time is it?' I asked.

'Do you have a boyfriend?' she asked. 'Is Alistair your boyfriend?'

'Not exactly.' I snatched my phone out of her hands. 'We're not exclusive or anything.'

'So he's your fuck buddy? Like I am? Is that what I am?'

'No.'

She threw her hands out. 'Is that all you're going to say? What are you even saying no to, that he's your fuck buddy or that I am?'

'I don't know what you want me to say,' I said.

'I want you to tell me what's going on,' Chloe said. 'I thought we were dating.'

'Well, we are, but it's not like we've talked about this. I didn't know that you expected exclusivity already.'

'Do I have to say it out loud?'

Neurotypicals never fail to confuse me about these matters. If something was this important to her, then, yes, she should have said it out loud. How else did she expect me to know?

'I would have appreciated it if you had,' I said.

'I would have appreciated it if you'd told me Alistair existed,' she said. 'Who the fuck is he?'

I sighed. 'He pays to spend time with me.'

There was a moment of silence.

Her mouth was wide open. She blinked slowly. 'You have a sugar daddy?'

'Your words, not mine.'

'So you don't have sex with him?' she said, frowning.

'I didn't say that.'

'You're a prostitute?'

'I'm not a prostitute. I don't have anyone else except him, and he pays for more than the sex.'

'It's the same thing, isn't it?'

I shrugged. 'I don't think it is, but feel free to draw your own conclusions.'

'Don't you find it gross and exploitative?'

Cat had been right. Chloe was clearly one of those feminists: all for a woman's right to choose, until she chooses to do something Chloe doesn't like.

'No,' I said. 'I find it nice to be able to afford rent.'

'By selling your body?'

I rolled my eyes. 'Do you work, Chloe?'

'No,' she said, straight-faced. 'My parents are supporting me until I graduate.'

'Right,' I said. 'So you have no idea what it's like not to have rich parents who can pay for everything you need.'

'Your parents have money,' she said.

Right. Because I was Cat to her, not Louise.

'You're not fucking poor, Louise,' Chloe said. 'Your dad has plenty of money.'

'They . . .'

I was beginning to develop a headache. Was there anything I could say to fix this? Probably not. But I couldn't tell her the truth either. I had to salvage some of the persona I had created for her. If I told her that I'd made up everything about myself, then there was every chance someone else was going to find out too. Including Oliver. Including Cat.

Chloe stared at me. 'They what?' she said, her voice harsh.

'They're homophobic,' I said.

288

She couldn't know that I didn't know where my dad was, that my mother was a teacher, that I didn't have a brother.

'You could get a job,' she said.

'When would I have time for a job?'

'Plenty of students have time for a job.'

'And if I was a bartender, would I not be selling my body too? Would I not be using my body to replace kegs and make drinks and serve people?'

'You'd be fully clothed when you did it.'

'You don't usually want me to be fully clothed.'

She sneered at me. 'Women aren't meant to be sex objects for rich men.'

'Well, I believe women aren't meant to be tools for capitalists.'

'You're talking to me like I'm an idiot,' she said. 'You can't tell me it's empowering.'

I nodded. 'It doesn't matter what you think about me. I'm going to leave, and you don't have to see me again and be so disgusted by me.'

Chloe stood up. 'You're just going to leave? You really don't care?'

'No,' I said. 'Why would I?'

'Because we're . . .' She looked very small and deflated, and she flopped her arms out. 'We're dating. Are you just going to step away from that without even trying?'

I knew I was supposed to say something else, but I was tired of lying to her. I couldn't even muster the energy to make my face appear sad.

'Yes,' I said.

'But I fucking like you, Louise,' she said, looking distraught. 'Do you not care about me at all?'

'Not particularly,' I said.

It came out a little too fast.

She laughed incredulously, just once. 'You know what? Fine. Fuck you.'

'I hope you have a nice life,' I said, trying to be polite.

It felt like the right thing to say.

I sat on the kerb with my one suitcase and waited for my Uber to Oliver's place. It was the only place I could think of to go. I opened up our chat to let him know I was coming, but I just ended up staring at the messages. He'd told me to check his socials. When I didn't respond, he'd sent me a screenshot of his profile. His relationship status had changed to *In a Relationship*. It set something off inside me. The full extent of everything I had fucked up and thrown away.

I took a deep breath to stop myself from crying. A car that matched the app's description pulled up beside me. I stood up as the passenger-side window was rolled down.

The driver asked if I was Louise.

'Could I change the destination?' I asked.

'Sure,' he said. 'But it will also change the price. Where are we going?'

I didn't care what Cat would say. I just needed to go home.

I took my shoes and jacket with me into the bedroom instead of leaving them by the front door as I usually did, trying to hide the fact that I was home from Cat. She was in the shower when I sneaked in; I got lucky.

My bedroom was still the mess I'd left it in, the bookshelf on the floor and wrecked drawers sprawled across the room. No wonder Oliver had been so worried, walking into this disaster every day. I was still too tired to clean it up.

I lay in bed, afraid to make a sound. She went about her business in the lounge and in the kitchen, singing some old Celine Dion songs to herself.

Her voice was so beautiful. I closed my eyes and listened to it.

25

'Louise,' Susannah said, 'tell me honestly. How are you?'

It took a moment for me to bring myself back to the present and remember where I was. I hadn't slept well my first night back at Cat's. It had been several weeks since my last therapy session.

'I'm fine,' I said without thinking about it.

I didn't want to ask myself if I was fine. I didn't need to know that.

Susannah looked at me, concerned. Her forehead was full of worried wrinkles. 'You don't look very fine.'

'Thanks,' I said.

'No, I'm serious. You look upset.'

I had been five minutes late to this appointment because I'd had to wait for Cat to leave the flat and then be far enough behind her that we wouldn't run into each other. If she hadn't gone out, I suppose I would have been cooped up in the room all day. Not even able to go to the bathroom.

'Do you need a refill of your prescription?' Susannah asked.

'No,' I said. 'I'm fine.'

It was such a routine question by this point; it seemed she was always asking me about my medication. It didn't occur to me that I should have thought about my answer more carefully.

'OK,' Susannah said. 'You should have run out a week ago, according to my calculations?'

Shit, I thought.

'Actually,' I said, 'I didn't check today, so maybe I'm close to being out.'

'You shouldn't be close to being out. You shouldn't have anything left.'

'Maybe your calculations are wrong.'

Susannah sat back and stared at me in silence, as if she expected me to cave if she did that for long enough.

'How long ago did you stop taking them?'

'I didn't stop,' I said. 'Maybe, you know, I've been a bit inconsistent. I've missed a day here and there, but that's just because I have a lot on my mind, and you know I'm forget-ful sometimes. But, I mean, just a day here and there, not for any prolonged stretch of time.'

'Hmm.'

She didn't believe me.

It made my head swim. Did she have the right to decide if I should take my medication or not? Would she be able to have me sectioned if I didn't? I was filled with dread.

I couldn't go back to the inpatient unit. I didn't want someone to tell me when I should eat, when I should wake up and go to sleep, when I should take my pills. I didn't want to live like that again, surrounded by all those people, not even able to go to the toilet without bumping into another person.

One day I had woken up in that place and decided I couldn't do it any more. I never again wanted to deal with the condescending tone people spoke to me with, the pity with which they looked at me. That was the day I pulled myself together. I became 'high-functioning'. I'd spent enough time watching my mother and the people around me and on the TV. I could make my face do the things theirs did, make my voice sound like everyone else's.

A week later I was home, and Mum was crying and hugging me, telling me how much better I seemed. I didn't get reprimanded a single time that day. So I kept it up.

I talked to people. I went to school and raised my hand in class. I gritted my teeth when the supermarket lights bothered me. I laughed when Mum made jokes. I pushed the overwhelm down, down, down until I was alone. I went to university and got a degree.

I put on the act of a normal human being every single day. Of course I could put it on for an hour of therapy.

I smiled. 'So, yeah,' I said, 'I should probably renew my prescription. I will probably be out soon.'

'I don't want to undermine your ability to make your own decisions about these matters,' Susannah said. 'But if you were to ask me if you should stop taking your medication, I would tell you that I don't recommend it.'

'I have no plans to stop,' I said. 'I promise.'

I stocked up on some food that didn't need refrigerating. I didn't want to see anyone, not even Oliver. The only other place I could go was the library, but the idea made me feel nauseous. I hadn't written a word on my dissertation since I'd got back from Barcelona. It had been nearly a week now. Robert had sent me another of his biweekly emails that morning, and I'd deleted it without opening it.

I stood on the street outside and looked up at our balcony for a while; the door was closed and I didn't see any shadows moving on the other side of the window. Hoping Cat wasn't home, I slipped inside as quietly as I could and checked for her shoes and for her keys on the hanger. No keys. I put the food in my room, used the bathroom and then shut myself in my room.

I checked my bedside table. I was right that I hadn't run out; there was enough medication to keep me going for another two weeks. That hadn't been intentional. I was fine, though, wasn't I? I felt absolutely fine. Peachy, even. Having the time of my life.

I cried for a while. I stayed holed up in my room for hours, eating cold macaroni straight out of the tin. I opened up my dissertation and then spent hours refreshing social media until there weren't any new posts to see, trying to find out where Cat was. It was evening when I finally figured it out. She put up a picture of her food at a restaurant. A restaurant in London. She was over there, then, presumably visiting her parents. I wondered if Henry was with her, but he was never active online.

I breathed a sigh of relief that I could stop being so paranoid. If she was in London, she wasn't coming home that night.

When it was time to sleep, I went into her bedroom. It was messy, the evidence of her packing for an overnight stay everywhere, the closet doors open. I crawled into her bed and slept there.

In the morning I had another email from Robert. I again deleted it without reading it and got up to get ready. Cat had left her toothbrush behind in the bathroom and I brushed my teeth with it, using her toothpaste. I had breakfast and then I did my make-up using her products. I played the loudest, screamiest metal on her speakers and brushed her eyeshadow on to my eyelids, applied her mascara to my lashes and chose a deep red lipstick to slather across my lips. It felt like kissing her.

There was nothing I could do now to save our relationship

and so I made the most of it. I rooted through her bed-side table drawers. The top drawer was filled to the brim: painkillers and melatonin, birth control pills and thyroid medication, Lemsip and antihistamines. There was Vaseline, moisturizer, some pregnancy tests. In the drawer below were more interesting things. Nestled among a pack of cards, a random assortment of cables and an old tablet with a cracked screen, I found rope, lube and her vibrator, a massage wand-style toy.

I used it to masturbate on her bed. Even on the lower settings, it was more powerful than mine. I writhed on her sheets and pressed my nose to them, pretending she was here with me, that it was her hand holding the wand, and came fast and hard, twice.

The music was making my ears ring. I put on one of her dresses. It wasn't my usual style to wear a dress quite so frequently, but I would never be able to fit into a pair of her jeans. I looked at myself in the mirror. I couldn't remember the last time I had looked so pretty. Normally I avoided mirrors like the plague; I never wanted to catch sight of myself unposed and with a facial expression I hadn't planned or executed consciously. Stomach protruding, eyes awkward and staring, my butt flat. No, I hate mirrors, but with this dress and my new hair colour and Cat's lipstick on my face, I felt beautiful. I couldn't get enough of the sight of myself.

Still in her clothes, I went back to my own room and opened my laptop. I was finally able to write. I wrote like a maniac, producing a thousand words in only one hour, not using a single reference in the process. I'd put that in later. It was fine. I'd be able to reference everything I was saying, make all of it sound academic and professional and trustworthy. For now I just needed to write. And the words poured out of me like water in a stream-of-consciousness dissertation about psychological egoism and why we fall in love and whether it's intrinsically valuable or not.

Answer: it's not. I don't recommend it.

The front door opened during a break between songs. I never would've been able to hear it otherwise. I snapped back into reality and scrambled to turn off the music. It was a disaster. Not only would Cat realize that I had come back home, she would see me wearing her clothes and make-up and realize my hair was the same colour as hers.

But the steps in the lounge weren't Cat's; they were too heavy and loud.

I looked around for the heaviest object I could find; it was a statuette that had been on my bookshelf when I moved in, which was now on the floor with everything else. It would have to do. I grabbed it and sneaked out of the room as quietly as I could.

Cat's bedroom door was open. I could hear someone moving around in there. My heart was beating very fast. I peeked in through the doorway. I could see the back of a man, rifling through Cat's open chest of drawers.

Henry. Of course.

I contemplated my next move. I could always claim that I had genuinely thought it was an intruder. I could always hope that this small but heavy object was weighty enough to crack a skull. My grip around it tightened.

'Henry,' I said.

He turned around without straightening himself up, still with his hands in her drawer. He didn't look surprised to see me.

'Hello,' he said.

'What are you doing?' I asked.

'What are *you* doing?' he said, nodding to the statue in my hands.

'I thought we were being robbed.'

'Louise, I don't need to rob you.'

The fact that he sounded so casual and unafraid of me when I'd been considering bashing his head in just a few seconds earlier made me reconsider my decision not to. He returned, unbothered, to going through his girlfriend's belongings.

Her belongings – I'd put everything back where it was supposed to be, hadn't I? It was hazy to me now, but I was sure I could remember placing her things back where I had found them.

'Then why are you here?' I asked. 'Where's Cat?'

'She's with her parents. I'm just looking for a pair of socks I think I might have left in her laundry.'

She must not have told him about our argument or about anything that had been said. He didn't even appear to have noticed that I was wearing something of hers, and he had said nothing about my hair colour.

'Do you usually go through her things?' I asked.

He shook his head and laughed a little, amused. 'I'm not going through anything important, am I? I'm just looking for my socks.'

'You're not looking for fucking socks, Henry. Why would you need to come all the way over here, when she's not even home, for a pair of socks?'

Henry shrugged.

'I don't know if anyone's ever told you this, but just because she's your girlfriend, it doesn't make you entitled to do certain things.'

He turned around and leaned back against the chest of drawers, looking at me.

'Fine,' he said. 'You got me. I'm not looking for socks.'

'Then what are you looking for?'

His expression remained unchanged. 'Her nice lingerie.'

I snorted. 'Creep.'

'I'm not a creep,' he said. 'I wanted to know if she'd taken her nice lingerie with her to London, because there would only be one reason she'd do that.'

'Did she?'

That wasn't the right way to respond to this situation. But it was exactly what I was wondering.

'No,' he said.

Despite myself, that did make me feel relieved.

'I guess she's not cheating on you, then,' I said. 'Which makes the snooping creepy again.'

'No,' Henry said. 'I know she's cheating, which is exactly why I'm here. I guess it just isn't with someone in London.'

He cocked his head to the side and smiled. I wondered what I was supposed to glean from that smile.

'How can you know that?' I asked.

'She told me.'

Something caught in my throat. If she had told him that much, she might also have told him who it was with. He was already suspicious enough of me, judging by that conversation about his phone. And I knew Henry wasn't opposed to a bit of violence.

'She didn't,' I said.

'You're right,' he said. 'She implied it pretty strongly, though, when we were having a fight.'

'I would know if she was cheating on you. I live here too.'

His eyes narrowed. 'I'm sure you would say that.'

His gaze was so focused I couldn't move. I was utterly alone with him, this man who had a habit of hurting women. I might be holding a statuette, but he was taller than me, and he spent so much time at the gym.

'Do you think it's me?' I said.

'Is it?'

'Of course not. Cat is straight.'

'She didn't seem very straight that night we had our little . . . *ménage à trois*.'

There is nothing more annoying than a non-French person who feels the need to say *ménage à trois* instead of threesome. It doesn't make it sound any nicer or fancier.

'Do you not think I've seen the way you look at her?' Henry said.

I took a deep breath. 'I don't know what you think,' I said. 'But you're wrong. And I don't think you should be in here going through her things.'

He stood up to his full height. 'Really?' he said. 'You mean you've never gone through her things? You paid for that dress yourself?'

I took a step back. He didn't come towards me, but the stance he'd adopted made it seem like he wanted me to know that he could if he wanted to. I thought about Cat's bruised face. I'd never taken a single self-defence class.

'I borrowed it,' I said, trying to keep my voice from shaking.

'Yes,' he said slowly. 'I'm sure you did.'

I was closer to the door than he was. I could probably get back to my bedroom before he caught up with me. That wouldn't help me much, though; there was no lock.

I clenched my hand around the little statue I was still holding. I wondered if that was still the better option. He glanced over at my hair very obviously.

'I don't like your new hair,' he said. 'It's a good colour, but it doesn't suit you very well.'

I held my tongue. Bashing his head in definitely felt like the best option again.

Henry held his hands up, like he was showing me that he didn't have a weapon. 'Will you let me leave?'

'I'd love to,' I said.

When Cat came home that night, I was sitting on the couch waiting for her. She stopped in the doorway and looked at me with her duffel bag thrown over her shoulder.

I spoke before she could ask why I was back.

'We should do it,' I said. 'We should kill Henry.'

26

My phone buzzed and buzzed. I took a deep breath and answered. 'Hi, Mum.'

'Hello, my love,' Mum said over the phone. 'How are you?'

I was smiling even though she couldn't see me, putting on the performance even though she would have no idea. It had become so automatic over the years. I looked at the kitchen knife in my hand. 'I'm good,' I said, making my voice sound chirpy and upbeat.

'I mean . . . mentally. Emotionally. Are you feeling all right, Louise?'

The blade of the knife caught the sunlight and the grey gleamed and sparkled. I twisted and turned it, looking at the way the colour changed with the light. I'd never paid quite so much attention to our knives. It looked expensive. The sharpness was indicative of Cat regularly sharpening it, which didn't surprise me in the least.

'Never better,' I said in a short tone. 'Why do you ask?'

I wondered if Susannah had spoken to her. I wasn't legally entitled to privacy if she was worried enough about me. I decided to make more effort at sounding extremely happy and content and not at all like someone that should be sectioned.

'It's almost the anniversary,' Mum said softly.

I hadn't even realized. I usually meticulously kept track of the anniversary of Maisie's death. One year since she died. Two years. Four. Seven now. Seven whole years without her.

'Right,' I said. 'Right, I completely forgot about that.' I put on a laugh.

'Honey,' my mum said, 'are you sure you're fine?'

'Positive.'

'It isn't like you to forget.'

'Maybe it's a good sign,' I said.

There was silence as she chewed this over.

'It means I don't think about her all the time any more,' I said.

Mum inhaled. 'And don't you?'

'No,' I said. 'I don't.'

When she was thoroughly satisfied I wasn't going to kill myself, and when I was thoroughly satisfied that she hadn't spoken to Susannah about my precarious mental state, we hung up.

I clasped the handle of the knife. One of my pillows was in front of me on the bed. I raised the knife above my head. I pretended the pillow was Henry's chest and I brought the knife down. It went through the pillowcase and into the soft insides. I slashed downwards and opened a large gash.

Would it really be that much harder to do it on a human being?

'You have to do it.'

It had been the first thing Cat had said to me. She hadn't looked surprised or horrified, and she didn't say, *What on earth are you saying?* She didn't even say, *What the hell are you doing here? We just had a massive fight.* With a voice that did not tremble and a face that did not flinch she had looked straight at me and said, 'You have to do it.'

I hadn't felt like anything was real. I couldn't believe the words I had just said, even less the ones she'd responded with. It had to be some weird nightmare I was in.

'I don't think I can,' I said, my voice breaking.

'I'm the significant other,' Cat said. 'I would be the prime suspect.'

I couldn't argue with that. She would be the first one they looked at, especially if they found out he'd been abusing her.

'I need a watertight alibi,' she said. 'And to be very far away from . . . where it's going to happen.'

She was right. Still, I could barely think about doing it without bile rising in my throat.

'If you do it,' I said weakly, 'we can say it was self-defence. We can make it look like self-defence.'

Cat shook her head. 'What if they don't believe me? We have no evidence he ever abused me. Everyone apart from you will testify that he was a great boyfriend. He has no criminal record. His family will do everything they can to convict me.' She took a breath. 'I told you before. The law is always on the side of people like him. It doesn't believe women. It doesn't believe that outwardly perfect and successful rich white boys can be bad people. I might spend the rest of my life in prison. I can't take that risk.'

'But what if I spend the rest of my life in prison instead?'

'That won't happen, Lolo. I won't let it. You're an outsider; you have no stake in the game. There's no reason they would ever suspect you, and even if they did, they would have to work much harder to connect you to it.'

'But I'm not,' I said. 'We . . .' I closed my mouth.

'Who would tell them?' Cat said. 'You weren't official. It was hardly well known.'

I stared at her. I tried to picture her in prison: bright, radiant Cat forced into a life of routine and monotony. It was impossible. She could not be contained in a cell. She could not be kept hidden from the world.

Cat shifted her weight. 'Hold on,' she said. 'I need to put this down; it's heavy.'

I didn't understand how she could sound so casual and matter-of-fact about the whole thing. As she walked over to her bedroom and deposited the bag, I looked down at my hands. I read somewhere that you should make it a habit to count your fingers. Do it enough and you'll start doing it in your dreams too. That's how you'll be able to see if the number of fingers you have isn't right, and that's how you realize you're in a dream. I counted my fingers now, and there were ten of them.

Cat sat down next to me on the couch. 'Louise,' she said. 'You can't believe how relieved I am. If you hadn't suggested this, I don't know what I would have done. I don't know what *he* would've done.'

Henry the Eighth killed Catherine Howard, I told myself again.

'He'd never let you go.'

'He wouldn't.' She scooched closer. 'And, Louise, he deserves to die. If we don't do this, he'd just go on hurting more women in the future. No one ever holds a man like that accountable. If he ever went to prison, he'd get back out and then he'd return to normal. He could ruin so many lives without anyone ever making him pay for it.'

'We'll make him pay for it,' I said. 'We'll stop him from being able to hurt others.'

There were tears in her eyes. She snivelled.

'Cat,' I said, reaching out for her.

She smiled. 'I'm going to be free of him.'

She leaned forward, putting her face in her hands and

starting to cry. I moved in towards her and, with just a little hesitation, put one hand on her back. She didn't yell at me to get away. She seemed to lean into it instead. It was enough. I wrapped my arms around her and let her cry.

'I'm sorry,' she said between sobs. 'I just – we have to do it. I can't stand the idea of the rest of my life being like this.'

I thought about Maisie. She must have been so afraid in those final moments, so very alone. And now she was gone. I hadn't been able to stop it from happening. I hadn't been able to help her. But this, this I could do. It wasn't going to happen to Cat too.

'It's OK,' I said.

I kissed the top of her head. I held her tighter and pressed her against me. Hugging another person had never felt so good. It had never been something that gave me any pleasure or enjoyment at all. With her I just couldn't get enough of it.

'I'll do it,' I said. 'I'll do it.'

I sat at the foot of her bed as she undressed in front of me. She unbuttoned her blouse and threw it to the side. She leaned over as she pulled her trousers down, giving me the best possible view of her breasts. When she was only in her underwear, she put her legs on either side of me and sat on my lap. She stroked my neck and ran her hands down my body. She rubbed her face against the side of mine and she kissed me. Her hand in my pants. Her chest against mine.

She undressed me tenderly, kissing me as she went: my neck, my breasts, my stomach, my thighs. Her hands explored me, up and down, her tongue licking me in tandem. She stroked my rose tattoo, then leaned down and kissed it. She looked up at me. Her eyes told me she understood now. She wasn't angry or afraid of me any more. The tattoo didn't mean I was unhinged. It just meant that I loved her. It meant that we were the same.

She put her fingers on my clit and rubbed. I came faster and harder than I ever had before, my entire body becoming stiff and taut and then exploding. Sparks behind my eyelids. I couldn't breathe. I collapsed in a mess and could do nothing but roll my head from side to side as she smiled at me and teased me with her tongue and looked oh so very pleased with herself.

She ran her hand through my hair. 'I like this colour on you,' she said. 'It's like mine.'

I nodded. 'It's like yours,' I whispered.

We're the same, I thought.

I placed myself on top of her, positioning my leg between hers and squeezing myself as close to her as I could. She looked up at me with an open mouth and desire in her eyes, her hair flowing around her head like a crown. I stroked her cheek. She turned her head and took my thumb into her mouth, closing her eyes and sucking it down.

I moved my hips. From the way she gasped, I knew that I had managed to find the right spot. I moved back and forth, rubbing myself against her, the slickness sliding down our thighs and sticking us together. She was so beautiful. I would remember this for the rest of my life. I put my hand around her neck and squeezed softly. She exhaled a soft 'yes' and I pressed harder.

When she came, she dug her nails into the skin on my back so hard that it was painful. She screamed like she was in pain too. I didn't stop until she fell back on to the bed and stopped convulsing. She was panting, her chest heaving.

I leaned down and kissed her. Smiling, she allowed herself to be kissed.

In the aftermath we curled up naked next to each other, as close as we could get, like a proper couple. One of her legs was draped over me. Her head was on my shoulder and her arm was across my chest. I traced the birthmarks and freckles on her upper back. Cat kissed my collarbone softly. The tenderness of it carried so much love.

'I think the best way would be to stab him,' she said.

It was difficult to imagine myself doing that. I didn't think it would be quite as easy as films made it seem. His body would be hard and I would have to push deep. The knife would get stuck and there would be blood everywhere. I didn't mind blood, but it would require so much cleaning if it ended up on me or I would be instantly incriminated. That's what I told Cat too.

'I know,' she said. 'But I still think it's the best option.'

'What about poison?' I asked. 'I could put something in his drink.'

'Do you know anything about poison?' Cat said. 'Because I don't. We'd need something that wouldn't change the taste or appearance of his drink. And we'd need something that would act fast enough that you wouldn't have to wait around for days, preventing him from going to hospital. And something that would definitely kill him and not just give him the shits.'

'Strangulation?' I suggested.

'With your bare hands? We can't take anything there. You'd have to use something at his flat so it can't be tied to you. I can't think of what you could use to strangle him, but he obviously has knives in the kitchen.'

I *hmm*ed at this. I couldn't think of a better solution.

'I don't know how to stab someone.'

'You can practise,' said Cat. 'It can't be that hard, can it?'

'Where would I do it?'

She put a hand on the left side of her chest.

I nodded. It was the obvious spot: quick, easy, deadly.

'You're right,' I said. 'I'll stab him.'

27

I didn't want to go anywhere or see anyone but Cat, but Alistair was impatient. We still hadn't had a date since I'd come back from Barcelona, and it was probably the longest I'd gone without seeing him since our relationship began. The messages hadn't stopped coming, and ignoring them hadn't helped. I could tell he was annoyed with me when I sat down at the table; he barely looked up from his phone, simply giving me a quick nod. I was annoyed right back. I'd spent a long time on my make-up and dragged myself out of Cat's very comfortable bed for this.

'Are you angry with me?' I said, pouting my lips.

'Just busy,' he said, typing.

I expected it to be a quick text, but he kept typing and typing.

I sighed. 'Come on. Have I not been giving you enough attention lately?'

I put my foot against his leg. It was something he usually liked. And it did the trick.

He finally looked up, an eyebrow cautiously raised.

'You've changed your hair,' he said.

'Do you like it?'

'No,' he said.

He put his phone down on the table so aggressively the sound made me flinch.

I pulled my foot back from his leg.

'You're right,' he said. 'You haven't been paying enough

attention to me. Do you know how long it's been since I last saw you? Do you know how many dates you've cancelled? For the past month I've barely been able to get more than a word from you. We haven't even done our calls.'

'I know,' I said.

I knew better than to put on my sexy apologetic voice, the playful one used for imagined infractions and minor disagreements, when we were both aware we were playing a game. The way he spoke was not a game. He was angrier than I had ever seen him before.

'I've been incredibly busy with my dissertation,' I said. 'But it's almost done now, and then we can go back to normal and I'll be able to see you as often as you want me to.'

'Your dissertation, is that it? And flying off to Barcelona, of course. Can't forget about that.'

'I don't know what you want me to say,' I said.

'We had an agreement,' he said. 'One date every two weeks. That isn't much.'

'You knew I was a master's student. You knew there might be periods when I would be busier than usual.'

'Louise, I'm not your boyfriend. This isn't the sort of relationship that can take a back seat when you're especially busy. We are both here for one thing and one thing only. Don't lie. Don't lie and say you see me because you want to. You see me for the money. You see me because I pay your rent and buy everything else that you want. Why should I keep doing that if I don't get anything in return? If you were one of my employees and you just never showed up to work, I wouldn't keep paying your wages. That's not how the real world works.'

I sat silently and stared at him. Alistair never lost his

temper. I felt like I had been admonished by my mother or by a teacher, like I was a child who had misbehaved.

'I said I'm sorry,' I said.

He held out his hands. 'And what do you want me to do with that?'

'I think you're being unreasonable,' I said. 'Sometimes things get in the way temporarily and you have to change your priorities.'

'I know,' he said. He lifted his wine glass and took a sip. 'That's why I've been so understanding and patient with you. I've allowed you to blow me off and ignore me for months.'

'Allowed me?' I couldn't help but laugh. 'You can't allow and forbid me to do things. I'm an adult, Alistair.'

He shook his head and waved his hand. 'I'm not going to argue with you about word choices. There's a hundred other girls out there who would kill for the opportunity I've given you.'

'But they're not me,' I said. 'They don't know how to talk to you the way you want. They don't know how to fuck you the way I do.'

He smirked at me across the table. 'They can learn,' he said. 'You're replaceable.'

'Piss off,' I said.

Alistair laughed in surprise. 'I thought we'd be able to have a civil last meal together,' he said. 'But somehow I don't think either of us is going to enjoy ourself.'

He stood up from the table. 'Get anything you want,' he said. 'Let me know when you get the bill and I'll transfer you the amount. Just remember it's the last money you'll ever get from me.'

He walked away.

I looked around. People at other tables were glancing over at me, subtly looking away when I caught their eye. I didn't know how much they'd been able to make out of our conversation, but they must have heard the tone, and now they were seeing me sitting at the table all by myself. I took a deep breath to compose myself.

'Miss.' A waiter was standing next to me now. He smiled. It looked so apologetic and sympathetic. 'Are you ready to order?'

'No,' I said. 'I don't want to order anything, actually. I think I'll just go.'

It didn't matter that I no longer had Alistair.

Not when I finally had Cat.

We spent most of our days planning, talking of little else and barely leaving the flat. We ran out of food and Cat started ordering takeaways for all our meals. Whenever she left me for a couple of hours to see Henry, I sat around aimlessly waiting for her to return. She didn't leave often; she pretended to be busy with her dissertation and made sure only to make plans in public or at his place.

We didn't work on our dissertations. We fucked in her bedroom over and over again, marking her sheets and using up all the battery in her vibrator, living in a constant state of sweaty bodies and wet pants.

It all came together so fast. I couldn't do it at the flat, of course. I had to do it at his place. But I also couldn't message him to make any plans to that effect; we were both convinced he would say yes if I invited myself over, and we laughed at this, but then our messaging history would be right there for the police to read. In the end we agreed that I should go over unannounced. I needed to be dressed sexily and he would let me in; it was guaranteed. Cat would make plans with him first, though, to ensure he'd be home and that he'd be alone. He'd be waiting around for her, but she would cancel at the last minute.

'I can injure myself,' she said. 'I can burn myself with the curling iron as I'm getting ready to go and see him and make it bad enough that I have to go to hospital. Then there'll be so many witnesses to corroborate. Impartial witnesses.'

I nodded enthusiastically.

She didn't need to tell me about the layout of Henry's place, but we went over it anyway since it had been so long since I was last there. She made sure I knew exactly how to get to the kitchen knives. We made a list of the things I needed to take in my bag: a change of clothes, a plastic bag, cleaning wipes to get rid of the fingerprints. It seemed so straightforward. We considered every possible thing that could go wrong. I couldn't believe it was so easy to get away with murder.

We talked and talked and talked in the lounge, and in the middle of it all the doorbell rang. We looked at each other. Even though there was no way someone would be able to tell what we had been discussing, I felt nervous.

'I'll go,' I said.

I got up and pressed the buzzer to let in whoever was downstairs. It was Oliver. He was extremely wet. His curly hair was soaked through and his jacket had turned dark with the moisture. His chest heaved up and down. His facial expression was distraught.

Cat kicked into host mode sooner than I did. 'Oh my god,' she said. 'Come in. You're drenched.'

His eyes flicked between us several times and his mouth was open. He no longer seemed upset so much as surprised.

315

'I'm just here to see Louise,' he said stiffly, giving me a look.

I wished more than ever that I could make sense of looks. He couldn't know, could he? How on earth could he know what we were planning?

'Are you OK?' I asked.

'No,' he said.

'Come in.'

His timing was terrible and I wanted him to leave, but I knew that was what I had to say. I wasn't the excellent actress Cat was, and I didn't know how long I would be able to put on a convincing performance of an innocent normal person. I stepped aside to let him in, and wondered how I could get rid of him as quickly as possible.

'I'll take your jacket,' Cat said, already lifting it off his shoulders. 'I'll check if Henry has any clothes here that you can borrow.'

'That's all right,' Oliver said. 'You don't need to do that.'

I had known that Oliver didn't like Cat, but he was good at pretending and he always acted like they were the best of friends. None of that charm was utilized now. He wasn't smiling at her or shrieking at the sight of her and yelling compliments about her outfit.

'If you're sure,' she said.

He looked at me again and his eyes were wide and clearly screaming something that I couldn't hear at all.

'I'm sure,' he said.

'Come,' I said.

We went to my bedroom and I closed the door.

Oliver stood in the middle of the room, dripping on to the carpet.

'I'm sorry,' he said. 'I don't want to sit down and get your bed wet.'

'I appreciate that,' I said. 'What's going on, Oliver?'

'We broke up,' he said.

'Oh my god,' I said. 'I'm so sorry.'

I expected him to start crying; he always cried when his boyfriends broke up with him. But he didn't cry. He looked bewildered, like someone who didn't quite know where he was.

'I just wanted to see you,' he said. 'I didn't know where else to go. I'm sorry.'

I shook my head. 'Don't be sorry. Of course you can come here. Do you want anything to drink? A hot chocolate? Some vodka?'

I smiled at him, but he didn't react to my attempt at a joke. His brows were furrowed. 'Louise,' he said, 'what's going on?'

I chuckled nervously, my heart pounding. 'What do you mean? You're the one who's shown up here with no warning. I should be asking you what's going on.'

Oliver immediately shook his head. 'No, this is really creepy. You look like her. You look exactly like her.'

I didn't know what I had expected from him, but it wasn't that.

I frowned. 'What are you talking about?'

'You look like Cat,' he said. 'When I saw you next to her, I realized you look like Cat. You're wearing the same clothes she does. You've done your make-up like she does. You've dyed your hair the same colour as hers.'

I looked down at what I was wearing. It wasn't a particularly extraordinary outfit, I admit; it was just a pair of leather trousers with a sweater tucked into the waist. Everyone wears clothes like that.

I told him this.

'No,' Oliver said. 'Not you. You don't dress like that.'

'Well, I do now,' I said slowly, confusedly. 'And my hair doesn't look that much like hers. It's just a similar colour. I wanted a change.'

'Why are you doing this?'

'I'm not doing anything,' I said, my voice snappy now.

I didn't have answers to the questions he was asking me. I was being forced into a corner and he just kept yapping at me, and there was no way I could escape.

'This isn't normal,' he said.

'You know,' I said, 'you don't have the right to judge me. Your life is just as fucking messy as mine. I'm not the one who showed up soaking wet at my friend's flat begging for help with yet another break-up. I'm not the one getting constantly heartbroken by people I barely know and shouldn't have become so emotionally dependent on in the first place.'

Oliver said nothing. He looked very small, his shoulders hunched. There was a puddle of rainwater beneath him. He just stared at me.

Is that enough? I wondered. *Is that enough to make him go?*

'What?' I yelled. 'What do you want from me?'

He smiled. 'You're right,' he said. 'I shouldn't be so upset about it, should I? I should stop caring so much about people who don't care about me.' He started walking to the door.

'Oliver,' I said.

'No, it's fine,' he said. 'I'll leave you alone. I'll stop being so emotionally dependent.'

He opened the bedroom door. He stayed in the doorway, looking into the lounge.

'Do you want to know why we broke up?' he asked.

'Sure,' I said dejectedly.

He turned his face back to me. It was pained, like he was finally about to start crying, the way I'd expected him to. Something about it made my chest hurt. There had to be a way back from the things I'd said. I had been there for him enough times for this one failure not to count. But the way he looked at me now made me doubt that, and I was afraid that I'd done something I could never undo.

'He cheated on me,' he said.

Like a reflex, I almost said I was sorry. That's what a good friend would have done. A good friend would've hugged him too. I clearly wasn't one of those. I didn't want to be. I still needed to get him to leave, even if it meant that he'd probably never come back.

'Let me lend you an umbrella,' I said softly.

'No,' he said. 'Don't bother.'

He slammed the door shut behind him, and I walked back into the lounge. It was still raining outside and he would be trudging home in the cold and wet.

Cat was peeking out from her room. 'What's up with Oliver?'

'Another break-up,' I said.

'Hmm,' Cat said, coming back to the sofa.

I caught a small roll of her eyes. 'What?' She sighed, but I pressed on, 'What was that?'

'I don't want to ruin your perception of Oliver,' she said, 'but I don't think it's fair that he always does this to you. He keeps getting himself into these situations and then he comes to you to pick up the pieces and comfort him until he does it again.'

I sat back down next to her. 'It isn't his fault,' I said gently. 'He got cheated on. I can't blame him.'

'*If* he got cheated on.'

I stared at Cat.

'Come on,' she said. 'Do you actually believe him every time one of these things happen? The last time he got cheated on. The guy that stole from him. The one that made that racist joke. How much bad luck can one person have?'

'You think he's lying?'

'Not about all of it,' Cat said, 'but some of it seems unbelievable. Look, I don't think he's a bad person or anything. I think he just likes the attention.'

I couldn't think of a single counterargument. She was right; this had happened a few too many times. And he was always equally devastated afterwards, as if the guy he'd had a relationship with for two months was the love of his life.

'Maybe,' I said.

What would my life look like without him? I wasn't going to dwell on that thought. I would be fine either way. With Cat I would always be fine.

The day before I was going to do it, we went out to dinner together on Cat's insistence. We were both wearing dresses of hers and she'd put her own jewellery on me. I wore the necklace like a badge of honour next to the hickey she had left on my throat.

We ordered pasta at an Italian place, but I could barely eat anything.

I didn't want to think about Henry or what would happen the next day. Instead, I wondered if this was a date. Friends didn't dress up this nicely to go to dinner together. Friends didn't hold each other's hands over the table or slide a leg up each other's dresses underneath it. There was a candle in the middle of our table that lent some romantic ambience to the meal. The bill wouldn't be split but paid by Cat, which was also such a date thing to do. I looked at her tapping on her phone and asking the waiter for some more water, smiling, her nails perfectly manicured. I thought about what that lipstick would look like all over my inner thighs and I squeezed my legs together.

Cat's phone rang once before she picked it up.

'Hi, honey,' she said.

I instantly struggled to breathe and was brought back to the reality of our lives. There were bigger concerns than whether this was a date or how to remove lipstick stains from white bedsheets.

'No, it's just me and Louise,' Cat said.

So he'd already seen the pictures on her Instagram. It couldn't have been more than five minutes since they had been posted.

Cat laughed. 'No, it's really good. Like, really good. We should come here together some time.'

It seemed to me such a ridiculous thing to say to someone who would die the next day. But she lied so easily, and it amazed me. Every word that came out of her mouth and every expression that showed on her face seemed so genuine.

'I love you too,' she said. She smacked her lips together and made a kissy sound at the phone. 'Love you more. Goodbye.'

She put her phone down and dug her fork into her pasta, twirling strands of spaghetti around it. 'Henry says hi,' she said.

'Does he?'

'No,' she said.

*

We walked home arm in arm. It reminded me of our nights in Barcelona, though it was darker and chillier here. The cold didn't bother me with her by my side.

'I miss Barcelona,' I said.

Cat smiled. 'We can go back.'

'Can we?'

'When this is over, we can go anywhere we want.' She put her head on my shoulder. 'Where would you want to go?'

I liked the idea of this. I had been to so few places, seen so little of the world. Without Cat it wouldn't have felt worth the money or effort to travel. But with her I would enjoy anywhere I was and whatever we were doing. And I wanted to do *everything* with her. I wanted to see the world through her eyes, experience all the places she'd told me about and visit all the cities she'd recommended to me.

'I've never been to France,' I said.

'You can think bigger than that,' said Cat.

So I did. 'We can go to the Bahamas,' I said, thinking about white beaches and blue water and Cat in one of her little bikinis.

'And New York,' she said.

'And Japan.'

We continued like that, naming places I'd never dreamed of going to before, so far away that they might as well not have been real. I never would've had the means to do any of this without her. But life was spread out before us now, so much of it, and there was such a big world for us to see.

'Do you realize I've proven you wrong?' I asked.

She turned to me and lifted one of her brows.

'About psychological egoism,' I said. 'I'm acting in your best interest right now, while risking my own.'

She nodded and was silent for a moment.

'Yes,' she said. 'Yes, I suppose you are.'

'It's all for you,' I said. 'It's entirely for you and not for myself.'

She squeezed my arm. 'I know,' she said. 'And I love you for it, Louise. I think you might be saving my life.'

We looked into each other's eyes. Her lipstick was a little faded after all the pasta she'd been slurping. Her gaze drifted down to my mouth as well. I thought she might kiss me, but then she looked away.

28

I put on the nice lingerie that I had bought for our three-some. It felt like a lifetime ago now. Cat helped me pick out a small, slutty dress from her closet. She zipped it up for me. She did my make-up, as effortlessly as she did her own. My eyelids tickled as she applied the eyeshadow. The final look was a light smoky eye with tinted lip gloss. She put her hands through my hair and ruffled it.

'How are you feeling?' she asked. She was pouring me a shot of vodka for courage.

'I don't know,' I said.

Things I did know: my hands were steady. The world around me was slightly out of focus. I was cold. My throat was dry. I was aware of every breath I was taking.

I wasn't quite sure what conclusion to draw from that.

She passed over the shot glass and I took it, throwing the vodka back into my throat before I could think about the taste. It went down fast and it burned and tasted awful. Cat leaned over and kissed me, moving some of my hair behind my ear. The lip gloss had transferred over to her, just a little bit, and made her lips look shiny.

'I love you,' she said.

She was saying it differently to how she used to, back when we were nothing but platonic friends. When the way she would sound during an orgasm was only something I fantasized about hearing. When the idea of what she looked like under her clothes was just an idea and not a certainty.

I felt like a robot being wound up, like a machine with buttons being pressed to determine my next move.

Cat sat down at her dressing table and plugged in her curling iron. We both watched as it heated up, waiting in silence, until it let out a ding. She picked it up and I held her shoulder. She inhaled deeply and put the iron to her neck. I could hear it sizzle. For the first few seconds she didn't make a noise, but I felt her tense and I increased my grip. Then she let out a whimper. I could smell burning flesh. She pulled the iron away and let out her breath, starting to pant and wince.

'Jesus,' she whispered. 'Jesus, fuck.'

The mark on her neck was red and angry and looked very sore. It stood out sharply against her skin tone.

'Does it look bad enough to warrant a visit to A&E?' she asked.

'Yes,' I said. 'It does.'

She met my eyes through her dressing-table mirror. She clasped my hand and formed an odd, unhappy smile. Her eyes were teary.

It was time.

'Hello?'

Henry's voice over the intercom was short and confused-sounding.

'Hi,' I said. 'It's me. Louise.'

Static crackled for a few moments. I almost thought he'd left.

'What do you want?'

'To come in,' I said. 'Can I?'

'Uh. Sure.'

The intercom buzzed. When I got up to his flat, Henry

was standing in the open door. He wasn't dressed for company. He was wearing joggers and a T-shirt, which I'd never seen him in before. That was how he dressed around Cat, I supposed. I felt ridiculous standing next to him in that dress.

'What's going on?'

'Nothing. I just wanted to see you.'

His eyes flicked from me to behind me and then back again, like he thought this must be a trick.

'Look,' I said, 'we didn't part on the best terms, but I think we should talk about something.'

'All right,' he said hesitantly. 'Then come in, I suppose.'

He stepped aside, and I went into his flat. Henry had lived by himself for as long as I knew him. Supposedly he had lived in a flatshare during his undergrad, but he couldn't find any flatmates he thought he'd get along with this time around, so his dad agreed to pay for an entire one-bedroom just for him.

'Do you want anything to drink?'

'No, thank you,' I said. 'I'm all right.'

He sat down on the couch in the middle of his open-plan living space, leaning against the back and crossing his legs. 'Have a seat,' he said.

I sat down next to him. Not close enough for my intentions to be immediately obvious, but close enough that it wasn't the way I would sit if I was just a regular platonic friend here for a regular platonic catch-up.

'You look nice,' he said. 'I feel underdressed.'

'You are,' I said.

He laughed. He had always liked my bluntness. Once, he'd told me it transferred into the bedroom. I didn't dance around the topic. I would grab him by the cock and tell him

I wanted him to fuck me. He'd nearly burst as soon as I said it, if I recall correctly.

'I didn't expect you,' he said. 'I had the impression that you're not my biggest fan right now.'

'Well,' I said, 'you don't need to like someone to want them.'

He cocked his head to the side and looked at my face. 'No,' he said. 'I suppose you don't.'

He leaned across the space in between us and put his hand on the side of my neck, with his thumb right beneath my chin, stroking softly. I leaned my head back almost on instinct, exposing my throat to him.

Henry chuckled. 'Has Cat not been obliging lately?'

'I –'

He interrupted me by grabbing my hair and pulling my head back. It stung.

'Don't lie to me, Louise,' he said. 'If you want me to fuck you, I want you to tell me the truth.'

He eased his grip on my hair and removed his hand completely, sitting back again.

'The truth isn't always what you want it to be,' I said.

'I'm well aware.'

I swallowed. 'You're right. We have been sleeping together.'

Henry closed his eyes and smiled softly. It was such a strange reaction to a confirmation that you had been cheated on, but I suppose it was in character. As long as he was right, he was happy.

'For how long?' he asked.

'Since Barcelona,' I said.

His eyes widened in surprise. 'Really?'

'Really.'

He nodded. 'And why are you here, then?'

'Because we had a fight. And I'm very angry with her right now. And I'd like to get back at her.'

'What was the fight about?'

'You, actually.'

Henry grinned and looked down at the couch. 'She's meant to leave me for you, isn't she?'

'That was the plan,' I lied. It wasn't so far removed from the truth.

He angled his eyes up at me again. 'I'm very sorry,' he said, 'but you know that isn't going to happen, don't you?'

'No,' I said. 'I don't know that.'

He cleared his throat like he was preparing for a monologue. 'What Cat and I have is special. It's beyond silly indiscretions with other people. It's something that can't be broken by anyone.' He shrugged. 'Not even ourselves.'

There's no way this is going to end, Cat had said, *before one of us dies.*

'What's so special about it?'

'It's hard to put your finger on things like that, isn't it? But I know she's meant for me. As I'm meant for her. Like we were always drifting towards each other.'

'No offence,' I said, 'but that sounds ridiculous.'

He laughed and then he leaned over again, reaching for my mouth with his own. I pulled my head back before he could touch me and he stopped.

'What's wrong? Isn't that what you're here for?'

'Do you really think the best way to turn a woman on is to tell her how you're soulmates with someone else?'

'Not working for you?'

'No. And, Henry, just because you think you're destined to be together or some bullshit like that, it doesn't mean you have the right to hit her.'

329

His smile faded. His face moved away from mine. He sat himself back down and stared at me. 'I don't know what you're talking about.'

'You're not going to achieve anything by playing dumb.'

For a moment he was silent. He had never been violent towards me, but for a second I glimpsed that anger again. It frightened me a little.

His jaw settled. 'It isn't quite like that,' he said.

'Really? Then what is it like?'

He smiled, but it was weaker now. 'You know Cat. She's not the easiest person to be around, is she?'

'Are you saying you only abuse her because she deserves it?'

'We all deserve it sometimes, don't we?' he said. 'Our fights can get heated, I'll admit that, but I think you'll find that she starts most of them.'

I snorted. 'Maybe she starts fights because you're a piece of shit who doesn't care about anyone except yourself.'

'Maybe if it bothered her so much, she would have left me,' Henry said. 'Did you never think about that? Yes, I have hit her. But she knows as well as I do that all couples have arguments. She knows that what we have is worth the pain we sometimes cause each other. And she's hurt me too, hasn't she? We've done terrible, terrible things to each other. Because love is pain, Louise. It hurts. The way that I love her, it hurts. But that just means it's real.'

I thought about the aftermath of Maisie's death. About lying on the floor of my wardrobe, crying, because missing her was simply too painful. About all the times in the in-patient unit that I had screamed because of how much it hurt.

And maybe Henry was right. Because Cat hurt too. I had ached for her for so long. I ached with her because she was in pain. I loved her. Which was exactly why Henry couldn't be right and exactly why he couldn't live.

'There's a world of difference,' I said, 'between cheating on someone and actively abusing them. I've seen the way you leave her. That's not love.'

The corner of his mouth curled upwards. 'And how would you love her, then?'

'I'd never hurt her,' I said. 'I'd never raise my voice to her. She would never have to be afraid of me. I would hold her when she needed me to. I would kiss her when she was in pain. I would tell her everything she needed to hear, do everything she needed me to do.' I took a deep breath. 'And I will. I will love her just like that. And I will do everything she asks of me.'

He looked so very smug with that little smirk of his. His teeth showed through it, straight and whiter than any teeth should be. 'And what has she asked you to do?'

He tipped his chin down to his chest and peered at me, an amused twinkle in his eyes.

His eyes. Those eyes were going to be dead soon.

I'd never seen a dead body before.

I thought about the way I had practised on that pillow. In my head I went over the route I would have to take to the kitchen area to grab one of the knives. I knew it perfectly.

'To free her,' I said. 'To free her from you.'

I was going to take his life. A life. It had never before felt like such a tangible thing, like something real. Here one moment and gone the next. I thought about the vacuum Maisie had left behind, a space in the world where she had belonged, like someone who's been edited out of a group picture. I didn't like Henry, but he would leave a vacuum too.

'I don't know what you're expecting,' Henry said, 'but it won't be as easy as you think, I can promise you that. If you get Cat, you're going to regret it. You're going to see her for exactly who she is.'

'I do see her for who she is,' I said. 'I know there are depths to her that no one else has seen. I know she feels alone and unappreciated. I know she puts on a smile like others put on clothes in the morning. So I do know what I'm getting myself into. I know exactly what to expect, and I will love every part of her.'

Something shifted in his eyes. The amusement gave room to something else – I couldn't tell what it was. It was dark, blank. It was vacant.

'Oh, honey,' he said. 'That's not what she's like at all.' He licked his lips. 'Cat eats people,' he said. 'That's the only way I know how to describe it. She knows what you want from her, and she becomes that. And then she eats you. She gobbles you up whole and spits you out when she's done with you.'

He was wrong. He hadn't seen Cat the way I had. The tears in her eyes on the beach in Barcelona that night. The way she had sobbed in my arms after he had hit her. Yes, Cat became who people wanted her to be – but so did I.

'That's why Cat and I are meant for each other,' he said. 'Because I know that's what she's like and I don't let her use me. She hurts me, and I hurt her back. I hurt her, and she hurts me in turn. But neither one of us gets ruined. Neither one of us gets to harm someone innocent.'

'You're full of bullshit.'

'Of course you'd think so,' he said. 'Why did she ask you to come here?'

I blinked and was speechless for a moment. I hadn't expected the question.

'Come on,' he said. 'Why did she ask you to come here?'

'She didn't,' I said.

'That's not true. Is it just a coincidence that I was here at home waiting for her and she had to cancel? Is it a coincidence that you showed up instead?'

'I didn't know you had plans.'

'You did, though. I should have known from the beginning. From the moment you stole my phone, at least.'

My mouth instinctively opened to deny this. There was no point, though. It didn't matter that he knew. He'd take everything he knew with him.

'How did you know?'

His smile grew ever so slightly wider. 'I didn't. I suspected it, though. Come on, I lose my phone at your flat and then someone uses my social media to message girls?' He shook his head. 'No, deep down, I knew. I was just wrong about the reason you did it.'

I frowned. 'Why did you think I did it?'

He held out his hands. 'Call me self-centred,' he said, 'but I was fool enough to think it was me you wanted. I thought that's why you wanted to break us up.'

I couldn't help but roll my eyes. 'You're right,' I said. 'That does make you sound pretty self-centred.'

He laughed softly. 'Well, at the time I wasn't aware of the way you felt about her. If I was, I never would've agreed to the threesome.'

'What do you mean?' I asked. I could hear my own pulse racing.

'I mean that she obviously suggested the threesome so that your obsession with her would grow,' he said. 'So that

333

her hold on you would strengthen. And this is what she wanted, isn't it? This is the end of the road she was leading you along.'

My head was full of such an abundance of Cat that it made me dizzy. Cat smiling, Cat's voice, Cat's hands.

'She didn't suggest the threesome,' I said. 'You did.'

Henry shook his head slowly. 'That's what she told you, is it?'

'Why shouldn't I believe her?'

'I've told you every reason you should need to doubt her,' he said. 'But I suppose it's too late.'

I had to do it now. When I looked at him, I forced myself to think about the way his body would look when he was dead. Lying on the floor cold, blood pooling around him. His life extinguished. His voice gone, his mannerisms lost, the light in his eyes disappeared. I shook the image out of my head. I thought about Cat instead. Her bruises, her tears. Her hand in mine, her arms wrapped around me.

I stood up. It felt like I was drunk. The floor was moving beneath me, but I stepped towards the kitchen anyway, watching my own feet, making sure I didn't topple over them. I could hear my own heart pounding. He needed to die.

'Water,' I said. 'I'm just getting some water.'

I stumbled towards the kitchen, gripping on to the counter to keep myself upright. He wasn't afraid of me. Of course he wasn't. He didn't even get up from the couch.

Maybe he was right not to be afraid of me. When I looked at the knife block, I suddenly didn't know if I would be able to do it.

He was a person.

A bad person, I told myself. He was an abuser. He was an

334

egotistical narcissist. He was a spoilt rich boy who was used to getting everything he wanted.

But he was close to his grandmother. He had a complicated relationship with his dad. He had been a child once. Another train of thought derailed.

Cat had been a child once too, I told myself. She was a person too, with as much right to exist as he had. More right. She didn't cause harm like he did.

I inhaled and exhaled. I stared at the knives.

'Louise,' he said from the couch, 'what are you doing?'

29

I woke up in Cat's bed, but she wasn't next to me. I was sweating and my heart was beating rapidly; I'd had a nightmare. One in which Henry lay motionless and bloody on the floor, his eyes blank, his head bent. And then he was staring straight at me and his hand was around my throat.

The curtain was slightly open, letting some of the daylight in. I had no idea what the time was. I'd been in a state the night before, crying and screaming, trembling like a leaf until I fell asleep. I was sure I had vomited at one point by the taste in my mouth. But I was home now, and the bed smelled like Cat. She had held me. She had kissed me and run her hand through my hair and put her nose to my neck. I'd fallen asleep to the sound of her whispering, 'It's OK, it's OK, it's OK.'

In the light of day I was surprised to find that it did feel OK.

I slipped out of bed, catching sight of myself in the mirror and looking away. I was a mess: make-up dried and smeared all over my face, wearing nothing but my underwear.

There was a clean nightie neatly folded at the foot of the bed. Such a Cat thing to do. I pulled it on and stepped out of the bedroom. The lounge was too bright. There was the sound of something frying in the kitchen. I followed it. Cat was at the hob wearing a cream-coloured jumpsuit, her hair in a bun on her head.

She turned around, her cheeks delightfully rosy. 'Good morning,' she said, smiling.

She was cooking something. The sight didn't make sense to me; it was far too normal for a morning like this. I stared at her and then at the frying pan and back again.

'I figured you needed the sleep,' she said.

I still didn't know what to say, so I just stood there. Were we not going to talk about it?

'Do you want some?' Cat asked.

She was still smiling, with the spatula in her hand like a modern Stepford Wife. Something about the smile was too tense. It didn't feel like her.

I managed to nod. Maybe it had been a bad dream. Maybe it had all been a bad dream. But we were going to have to talk about it.

Cat put the spatula down and came over, laying her arms on my shoulders. She kissed me, first on the mouth and then on the nose. I closed my eyes and let my head fall on to her shoulder, pressing my cheek against hers. She embraced me, squeezing perhaps just a little too tightly.

'I'm sorry,' I said.

'Why?' she asked, her tone sharp.

It couldn't be a genuine question. I raised my head so I could look at her, but her face didn't seem like that of some-one who was joking. She stared back into my eyes as if she was waiting for the answer.

'Are we going to talk about it?' I asked.

Cat blinked. She didn't stop smiling. She cocked her head ever so slightly to the side.

'Talk about what?'

I took that as a no.

*

338

It felt terribly domestic to have Cat serving me breakfast. I waited for her to say something, but she moved around in silence, slamming my plate down on to the table so hard I flinched. I looked up to see if she was angry at me, but her face gave nothing away.

She had made some kind of breakfast hash with potatoes, sausages and meat, topped with eggs, served with a glass of freshly pressed orange juice. I hadn't even known we had a juicer. I tried to force the food down, but it tasted like nothing and got stuck in my throat.

Something was wrong.

It was the fact that she was so uncharacteristically quiet. It was the fact that the smile seemed to have become her resting facial expression and remained there endlessly. It was the fact that something clearly needed to be said. There was a fucking elephant standing on the table in between us and she was just leaning to the side and peering at me through its legs.

I looked down at my plate to find that it still looked almost the same as when I'd started eating. The texture of the meat was all wrong, slimy and full of fat, and there was pulp in the orange juice, and the yellow of the egg was too runny.

'Do you want to do face masks?' Cat asked.

The day passed by in a daze. We did face masks and sat on the couch with them on, watching some old comedy show that only Cat laughed at. I miraculously remembered to feed the mice; they were still asleep, hidden in the nest. Later we sat at the kitchen table with our laptops, under the pretence of writing our dissertations.

When she finally spoke, her tone was firm and direct. 'How's it coming along?'

'It isn't,' I said. My voice didn't sound like my own. I couldn't believe we were talking about our dissertations. 'Yours?'

'Oh, I'm at about, what, eight thousand words.'

I simply stared at her. Hadn't she been telling me until very recently that she'd done no work at all on her dissertation?

'I thought you'd barely started,' I said.

Cat waved her hand. 'I hadn't. But, like I said, it comes together fast when you do.'

She was next to me when I fell asleep in her bed. She was gone when I woke up in the morning.

This time I didn't find her in the kitchen. The bathroom was empty. I tried to call her and stared at her smiling face on my phone screen until I was sent to voicemail. I couldn't find anything on social media.

I messaged her. *Where are you?* I added a smiley face to make it look less serious.

She'll be home soon, I told myself.

I tried to sit on the couch but couldn't remain still for too long. I took a shower instead, my mind racing. The water was still draining the dye from my hair. I watched it running red down my chest and my legs.

I thought about calling Oliver, my finger hovering over his name in my contacts. We hadn't spoken since the disastrous day he and Mateo broke up. How could I explain what had happened the night before? Did I *want* to explain it? I had no one else, but I thought about what Cat had said and I felt like I didn't know him. Cat was good at reading people. She'd been right about Chloe. And I hadn't exactly missed Oliver. I'd barely thought about him. I didn't need anyone but Cat.

Cat hadn't responded yet. I sent her a question mark as a follow-up. Cat was always on her phone; she always replied quickly.

I went to get some breakfast, more out of habit than any real need for food. I didn't think I'd ever be hungry again. Henry was plaguing my mind. It made me nauseous and antsy. In the fridge I found a box of leftovers from the breakfast I hadn't finished yesterday. I needed to eat something, and this was the option that required the least effort. I took it out and opened the box.

And stared. And stared.

There was something in the food like a thick strand of hair. I furrowed my brow and reached in to remove it, still not comprehending what it was. It was the feel of it in my hand that made me realize.

It was a tail.

I held it in my hand and thought, *No, no, no.* It couldn't be. It couldn't.

I dropped it to the floor and ran back to my bedroom. I still felt some implausible hope that I was wrong. I'd unravelled more than I'd realized. I'd misinterpreted what I'd seen. I'd hallucinated.

I opened the cage and lifted out the little wooden box the mice usually slept in. Their nest of tissue paper was empty. I lifted all their toys and didn't find a single trace of them. I dug my hands into the bedding and looked for hidden tunnels and dens they might have dug themselves into.

They will be so upset when I find them, I thought. They were always grumpy when you woke them up.

There was nothing soft and round and warm in the bedding. I tipped the entire cage on to its side and shovelled the bedding out on to the floor. Nothing.

341

I ran to the bathroom and was sick in the toilet, retching and crying. It should have been more difficult to believe, but it wasn't. Cat and I were the only ones who'd been in the flat. The cage had been closed; the mice wouldn't have been able to get out by themselves. The tail had been in the food that Cat had cooked me. I remembered waking up in the night to find the bed empty. I'd sat up in confusion, then she had sneaked back into the room and slid into bed next to me.

'I just went to the bathroom,' she'd whispered.

I had no idea how long she'd been gone. I wondered how she had done it. Had it been quick or drawn out? Had they been afraid? Had they been in pain? I hoped they hadn't, but I'd never known Cat to be merciful.

I didn't wonder why she had done it; I knew the answer to that already. It was a punishment. She had made me breakfast and hugged me, but I had known that something was off.

I did wonder how she'd been *able* to do it. How had she looked at their innocent little faces and ended their lives?

And more importantly, if she'd been capable of that, what else was she capable of?

They came around midday on Sunday. I'd been awake for a few hours when there was a knock on the door. Somehow they'd made it inside the building and up the stairs. I hadn't buzzed anyone in.

I felt like I was wading through water. I grabbed the door handle and took a deep breath. It was two police officers, a man and a woman.

'Louise Wilson?' the man said.

'Did something happen to Cat?' I asked.

A glance passed between them. I hoped it hadn't been an odd conclusion to draw. They'd knocked on her door, looking for me. Why else would the police be looking for me if it wasn't to do with Cat?

'Could you come with us to the station?' the woman said gently.

'Is Cat OK?' I asked.

'Do you know someone named Henry Johnston?' the female officer asked.

It was the first question after they had taken my name, birthdate, address and contact details. She had introduced herself as Detective Murphy, he as Detective Lewis. The room we were sitting in was colder than it should have been for late summer.

There was a small table in between us, two chairs on their side and one on mine. It was hard and uncomfortable. I twisted and adjusted my position, with no success.

'He's my flatmate's boyfriend,' I said.

She nodded and they both scribbled in their notebooks. They wrote for too long, writing something much longer than that one sentence.

'And your flatmate's name is?'

I scratched myself. My fingers were still black from the fingerprints they'd taken when we arrived.

'Catherine. Catherine Collins.'

'And how do you get along with Mr Johnston?' she asked.

'I . . .' I took a deep breath. 'We don't have much of a relationship. We rarely talk and never hang out. He's just around sometimes because he's dating my flatmate.'

More scribbling. The sound of the pens against the paper was so loud.

'Where were you on Thursday night?' Detective Murphy asked.

My heart stopped dead. My mind raced around for an answer, but there seemed to be nothing I could say that would make sense. And the more time passed, the more suspicious my answer would seem.

'I was at home,' I said.

She looked up at me from her notebook and then glanced at Detective Lewis.

'Are you sure about that?' he asked.

I nodded.

'Would anyone be able to verify this?' he asked.

I was sweating. 'No,' I said.

'Catherine wasn't home?' he said.

'She went to A&E. She was gone for a few hours.'

'Why did Catherine go to A&E?' Detective Murphy asked.

'Because she . . .' My tongue became too big for my mouth. 'She burned herself. On a curling iron?' I could've cringed; that was supposed to be confident, not a question.

'How long was she gone?' Detective Murphy said, still writing.

'Um.'

I hadn't been to A&E since the time I had tried to hang myself. How long did you usually have to wait these days? I had no idea.

'I don't know,' I said. 'I went to bed. She was back when I woke up.'

Detective Murphy peered up at me from her notebook, her eyebrows slightly raised. I had the feeling that I'd said something terribly wrong.

Detective Lewis's shoe scraped against the floor as he repositioned himself. Neither of them said anything.

'Is Cat OK?' I asked again. I didn't know how many times I'd already asked that.

'Catherine's OK,' said Detective Murphy.

'Then why am I here?'

'Henry is dead,' Detective Lewis said.

I stared at him. I only had a second to go through all my knowledge of human behaviour and figure out how a normal person would react to that sentence.

'He is?'

'He died on Thursday night,' Detective Lewis said. 'That's why we need to know where you were.'

'I was . . .'

They were both staring at me, pens in their hands, their faces serious and devoid of smiles. What the fuck was I supposed to say?

'I was at home,' I said weakly.

'And there was no one else there?' Detective Murphy asked.

I shook my head.

'There's no one who could vouch for where you were while she was gone, then?'

There wasn't. Of course there wasn't. But this was what we had agreed to, when we thought that Cat was the one who was going to be suspected. The plan didn't work if it was me.

'Why am I here?'

They looked at each other. Detective Lewis gave his colleague a small nod.

Detective Murphy turned back to me. 'Your fingerprints were found on the murder weapon,' she said. 'Would you care to explain how that might have happened?'

'I don't know,' I whispered.

'When's the last time you were at Henry's flat?'

I shook my head. A dull ache had begun behind my temples. I'd had those cleaning wipes in my bag, and I hadn't used them. In the chaos, it had never even crossed my mind. I'd barely been able to walk straight, even less think about evidence. My fingerprints were there. Could I make them believe there was a good reason for that?

'Last week,' I said. 'I think it was on Tuesday, maybe Wednesday. We had dinner.'

'Dinner?' said Detective Murphy.

Let them think that I'd been seeing Henry behind Cat's back. That wasn't a crime. That was the only way I could get out of this.

'He cooked,' I said. 'And I did the dishes. That must have been how my fingerprints ended up on the knife.'

Detective Lewis straightened his back and grew taller. 'How did you know the murder weapon was a knife?' he asked. His voice was almost soft.

'Am I a suspect?' I said.

I was charged with murder in the interrogation room, based on the fingerprint evidence and my relationship with Henry, plus the fact that I'd lied about it. Lying had got me in enough trouble. I stopped talking.

They told me I was entitled to speak to a lawyer, but I refused. I would speak to no one, let this get no further. *Cat will sort this*, I told myself. Cat could sort anything. She was angry at me, but she wouldn't let this happen.

At the prison I was allowed one phone call. I couldn't possibly choose anyone but her.

The phone rang. The guard next to me looked away, as if that would constitute enough privacy. I waited. The phone rang. They had searched me, their hands all over my body, making me wince and close my eyes. I'd thought I might be sick again. The phone rang. I wondered how similar prison would be to the inpatient unit, just how miserable I would be. The phone rang until it didn't any more.

'*This is Cat's voicemail,*' her voice said. She sounded so young, so carefree. She sounded so far away. '*Tell me why I should call you back. Make it worth it!*'

A beep. She was gone. I put the phone back on the receiver and fumbled with the keys to dial another number. Oliver would pick up. He'd be able to get hold of her.

'Sorry,' the guard said. 'Only one call allowed.'

'I didn't have my call,' I said. 'She didn't pick up.'

'Doesn't matter,' she said, grabbing me by the arm. 'It still counts as your call.'

It's OK, I thought, letting her lead me away. *Cat will sort it. Cat has to sort it.*

If I thought it enough times, maybe I would start to believe it.

Mum was the first visitor I received. She was already crying when she came into the visitors' room.

I looked behind her. She was alone.

'Where's Cat?' I asked.

Mum opened her arms to hug me. I wasn't going to allow it this time. I had no patience left for her. When she moved in, I moved to the side.

She stared at me, dejected.

'Have you spoken to Cat?' I asked.

'No,' Mum said.

'I need to talk to her.'

I'd said the same thing when I woke up the first morning

347

and they opened the door to my cell, and on the second one: *I need to talk to Cat.* Whatever they said to me, that's all I would say back. *I need to talk to Cat.*

'Louise,' my mum said.

There was nothing else. Her mouth hung open.

I pulled out my chair and sat back down. She staggered over to the other chair, moving like an old lady in a way I'd never seen her do before.

'She'll sort it all out,' I said.

After everything we had been through, Cat wouldn't leave me in here. Cat would find a lawyer to make my story believable. They only had some fingerprints, after all. We could explain that.

Mum was silent now, the tears still streaming down her face. I held my tongue. It almost made me angry the way she was the one who was upset. I was in prison. I had been arrested for murder. But she couldn't stop bawling and I was having to make the arrangements.

'You need to speak to Cat,' I said. 'Her family has money. They have lawyers. She'll help.'

'I'm looking for a solicitor for you,' Mum said.

'She'll have a better one.'

Mum shook her head and inhaled.

'Stop,' I said. 'Stop crying. It's going to be fine. I'm going in front of the magistrate in a few weeks; it's going to be fine.'

Mum folded over, her arms wrapped around her stomach. She closed her eyes. I couldn't believe my first visit was being wasted like this.

'For fuck's sake,' I said. 'It's going to be *fine*, Mum. They can't convict me of a crime I didn't commit.'

30

That night, as I leaned against Henry's kitchen counter and stared at his knives, I heard him rise.

'What are you doing?' he repeated.

I turned around. He was walking towards me.

'She doesn't love you,' I said.

He stopped. He made an exaggerated face of surprise, like I'd told an ill-timed joke.

'No one loves you,' I said. 'Your mother doesn't love you. That's why she left. Your father doesn't love you. That's why he doesn't have time for you.'

Henry rolled his eyes and continued approaching. 'Is that so?'

He was standing very close to me now. I could hear his breathing, a sound I was supposed to silence for ever. He put his hands on the counter on either side of me, pinning me in, as if we were going to kiss.

'You can't make someone love you out of fear,' I said. 'You can't make someone stay with you because they're afraid. And she is afraid of you.'

'Cat isn't afraid of anything,' he said.

'Are you?' My voice was low. 'Aren't you afraid that your hold on her is fragile? Control through fear is unreliable. It doesn't last. You're going to lose your grip, and when you do, she's going to be gone.'

Henry leaned in. He smiled. 'You don't need it,' he said. 'Whatever it is you think she's going to give you, you don't need it.'

Not that much earlier I would have said that he couldn't possibly have any idea, couldn't know what it was like to be me, to be so utterly alone you could disappear without ever being missed. To not have a single person in the world who understood you. To feel like the last specimen of an endangered species, living and dying in captivity.

But now I saw him for who he really was.

'I'm not the one who needs her,' I said. 'That's you. Because without her you don't have any friends. Without her you're boring. Without her your life is empty. Without her you're nothing but a pathetic, lonely man-child who will never get someone to genuinely care for you.'

'Well,' Henry said, 'I suppose it's a fair trade, then. Because without me she's nothing but a pretty face who's fun at parties but who no one would ever dream of calling back the next day.'

I spat in his face and the slap was immediate, like a reflex. My cheek burned, my jawbone loose as if it had popped out of place. I put a hand to it. I'd never been struck by someone before.

'Who the fuck do you think you are?' Henry sneered.

'I think I'm someone who's got under your skin,' I said.

His voice was low and dark. 'I think you're someone who needs to be put in her place.'

When his hands closed around my throat, I wasn't even scared; I was surprised. I gripped on to his wrists to prise him off, but it was like trying to pull a tree from the ground. It was like trying to move concrete. That's when I got scared.

'I know why you're here,' he murmured, his teeth clenched. 'You're not as pretty as her.'

I opened my mouth, but I couldn't breathe. I gasped for air and nothing came. My heart was suddenly beating twice as fast as usual, pounding in my chest. I tried to hit him. I put all my strength into it and watched my hands flap helplessly at his chest. He didn't budge; he didn't even flinch.

'You're not as smart as her.'

Like an animal caught in a trap, I dug my nails into his arms, scratching as hard as I could. It made him squeeze harder. I felt light-headed.

'You're not as likeable as her.'

The knife. It was the first rational thought I'd had since it started. I twisted my arm around for the knife block. I had no idea where it was or how far I would need to reach. My eyes darted in that direction, but I couldn't see it, and my head was held too firmly in place to move.

'You're not as memorable as her.'

His voice was quieter now, muffled, like it was coming from far away.

'And the saddest part is,' Henry said, 'that she wouldn't miss you if I killed you right now.'

He let go. It happened so suddenly I could barely register that it was real. He was going to let me live. I inhaled once. I lifted my leg with as much force as I could muster and drove it straight into his crotch.

Henry didn't shout; he just let out a loud wheeze. He stumbled backwards. My hand found the wood of the knife block and suddenly I was holding a knife. As he looked up at me, I put the tip of it to his throat.

He became very still.

I breathed heavily. The steel of the knife was touching his skin, right above his Adam's apple. I could push it straight in. I could rid the world of the plague that was Henry and no one would be worse off.

'Do you think she'd miss you?' I said.

I don't know how intimidating I sounded. My lungs still ached and my legs felt like they were made of jelly.

He swallowed hard. His eyes were big and wide and his arms hung rigidly by his sides.

You don't need it, that's what he had said. *Whatever it is you think she's going to give you, you don't need it.* He would never understand. I wasn't doing this because I was hoping she would give me something for it. It was the opposite of that. This wasn't for me; this was for her. It was in her best interest, not my own.

I thought about the way Cat had cried to me. I thought about the bruises I had seen on her and the fear I had felt just now – how many times must she have experienced the same thing? I imagined it was her neck he was squeezing, her eyes bulging and her hands scrabbling at his arms. Her beautiful nails digging into his skin. Her gorgeous mouth gasping for air. I'd never so badly wanted to hurt someone.

But his eyes were full of fear and I knew who he was now. He could've killed me if he wanted to, but he hadn't. He'd wanted to scare me, because he was scared. He'd wanted to hurt me, because I'd hurt him. Henry wasn't evil. He was pathetic and small.

His breath quivered, and I didn't hate him. I felt sorry for him.

I was frozen in place. Even if I tried, my arms wouldn't move.

I'm sorry, Cat, I thought. *I'm not a murderer.*

'You're a piece of shit,' I said. 'And you're not worth the effort of putting this knife through you.'

'I didn't kill him.'

My defence lawyer arrived the day after my mum, and

those were the first words I said to him. But I didn't greet him with them. I met him with silence and maintained it for five minutes.

'Hello, Louise,' he said as he sat down. 'My name's Amir. Your mother has employed me as your defence solicitor.'

He was too young; he couldn't possibly be more than ten years older than me. Had he ever worked a murder case before? Cat would never have hired someone this young.

He smiled at me. 'Do you have any questions about what's happening?'

I blinked.

He cleared his throat and his smile looked slightly uncomfortable. He told me I was going in front of the magistrate, which I knew. He explained what would happen on the day, which I didn't want to know. There were pauses and there were questions I was meant to answer.

'Do you understand what that means?'

I didn't respond. There was no point. Cat's lawyer would replace him soon.

He told me bail might be granted if we could prove I would be no harm to anyone else, but that the prosecution was going to make this difficult. He spoke fast. He didn't make eye contact very often, his gaze drifting over to me briefly and then returning to the papers he kept fiddling with. It was probably the way I stared at him. I didn't care.

'You'll need to tell me what happened,' he said. 'I'm going to do all I can, but I'm only able to do that if you tell me everything that happened on Thursday.'

'I didn't kill him,' I said.

Amir moved back, almost startled. His hands stilled.

'That's all you need to know,' I said.

'Louise,' Amir said patiently, as if he was speaking to a child, 'you need to talk.'

'I'll talk to Cat,' I said. 'No one else.'

It took two weeks. Two weeks of standing at my cell door every morning saying 'I need to talk to Cat.' Two weeks of sitting opposite Amir at that table watching him grow older before my eyes. He didn't have bags under his eyes or that wrinkle on his forehead when we first met, did he? By the end of those two weeks he did.

I heard women in the other cells crying at night. I watched them crying at breakfast. I looked on as they pleaded desperately with the guards. One sat next to me at lunch and burst into tears over the chicken nuggets, telling me it was her children's favourite. Prison was such a sad, desperate place. Everyone had either a wild and untamed look in their eyes that begged for release or one that was resigned and always slightly wet from tears, practically dead.

Everyone except me. I was calm. I was waiting. On the outside Cat would be pulling all the strings she could, and there are so many strings available to someone like Cat. If there was anyone who could do this, it was Cat. Cat was the smartest person I knew. She would find a solution. Cat would tell them any story she needed to, and they would believe her. Cat was beautiful, wealthy and put together. She was an excellent actress. She was friendly and amiable and could charm her way through any situation. No one doubted her word.

She loved me. She'd told me so.

I dreamt about her at night. I thought about her during the day.

Henry was dead. Henry had been the biggest problem.

The fact that I was suspected of his murder was a minor detail, not significant at all. We could get past that. After all, they couldn't possibly pin it on me. They couldn't find evidence for something I hadn't done.

I spent most of my days in my cell, even during free time, when most people walked around or hung out in the common room. One thing you don't expect from prison is that you have a small TV in your cell. I only had the most basic channels, but I stared at that screen compulsively. Almost every time the news came on, they mentioned Henry. They showed pictures of him where he looked like the ideal man. They showed pictures of me where I looked deranged. There were pictures of Cat too, though they rarely referred to her as anything but the victim's girlfriend. I'd rush across my cell to the TV and touch the screen before she disappeared. I was allowed a sketchbook, but I was already running out of pages. I had nothing to do but draw her, to bring forth every aspect of her face from memory so I never forgot.

I waited for the day she would give some sort of press conference and tell everyone I was innocent. But she never spoke to the press. All I saw was footage from outside Henry's building and ours, and interviews with people I went to school with and hadn't spoken to in years. *She was always odd*, they said. *She was always on the outside looking in.*

Oliver came only once. The moment I saw him, I knew Cat had been wrong, and I couldn't believe I had ever doubted him.

'Thank you for coming,' I said, and for the first time ever I wanted to reach across the table between us and take his hands.

'Of course I came,' he said, and he made a sad attempt at a smile.

'How are you?' I asked.

He nodded awkwardly, swallowing hard. 'I'm good,' he said. 'I'm good. I've gone back home for now. It's been a bit much. Not that it's not overwhelming having Mum treat me like an invalid, but you know. At least I get food out of it.'

We looked at each other and I made myself smile. I wasn't sure what else to say.

'And you?' he asked eventually. 'How are you holding up?'

'Not so bad,' I said.

And we went quiet again. We'd had many moments of silence before, hours spent studying together or sitting in the same room on our phones without saying a word, but this was different. This felt like speaking to a stranger. What should I say to him? What might he be interested in?

'You don't know anyone named Nathalie, do you?' he asked.

I searched my mind. 'Not really,' I said. 'I might have sat next to a Nathalie in a seminar at the start of the year.'

'I figured,' he said. 'She got in touch and said you were close friends and she wanted to know what was going on. Turns out I have a lot more close friends than I realized. I might need to delete my social media. My phone's going to die from all the notifications I've been getting.'

'I'm sorry,' I said. 'That sounds awful.'

'It's been bad. Everyone pretends to be horrified and outraged, but they talk about it so much you start to suspect they're secretly enjoying it. I've been offered a lot of money to talk to reporters.'

'Did you take it?'

He furrowed his brows. 'Of course not.'

'You should've. You could've made up some really nasty stories about me.'

He snorted. I was proud of that. It felt almost like the old days.

'You would've been completely justified,' I said. 'I'm sorry I wasn't there for you when Mateo cheated on you. I'm sorry I was so mean.'

Oliver smiled softly. 'I know you are.'

His smile made my chest hurt.

'Do you hate me?' I asked.

'Of course I don't hate you,' he said.

My eyes stung. It felt like I'd had a rock on my chest which was finally gone.

'I don't think you're a bad person,' he continued. 'I think you're dealing with a lot. I think you've done the things you have because you're troubled.' He stopped speaking and looked at me as if he'd said something wrong.

I frowned. 'What things?'

He didn't respond in words. The way he pursed his lips said enough. My breath hitched. For the entire conversation we'd managed not even to allude to the fact that I had been accused of murder. We were so close to acknowledging it now.

'Oliver,' I said, 'are you asking me if I did it?'

'No,' he said too quickly.

But I felt no relief, because he didn't need to ask. Not because he knew I was innocent. He didn't ask because he believed I was guilty.

'I didn't do it,' I said. My voice was harsh.

He flinched, only slightly, but it was enough. Enough that I saw the fear in his eyes for a moment, the bob of his throat as he swallowed. The way his foot moved as if he was preparing to get up and run.

'I know,' he said, and it was the most obvious lie I'd ever heard.

The worst part was that I couldn't even blame him. The last time we'd seen each other, I'd been cruel and heartless and deliberately inflicted pain on him. I'd been exactly the kind of person who could kill someone.

'I think maybe you should go,' I said quietly.

Days before my appearance at the magistrates' court, I received my final visitor. I knew it wasn't Mum, because two guards stayed with me in the visitors' room while I waited. No one supervised my visits from Mum or Amir. My heart started beating faster.

Her face appeared in the door window. I felt like I'd been wandering through a desert for days and had finally spotted an oasis.

The door opened and I stood up.

One of the guards immediately stepped towards me as Cat took a step back, the door closing a little. 'Sit back down,' the guard said.

Cat remained behind the door, unmoving.

I sat.

Another moment passed, the guard nodded and Cat came in. She wasn't wearing make-up, but she'd never looked so beautiful. She didn't weep at the sight of me, though her eyes were red. In one hand she was holding a crumpled tissue, like she'd been crying into it. But when she looked at me, her eyes were completely blank.

'Cat,' I said.

She said nothing. She blinked at me with those strange, empty eyes. The guards were right there. She had always been so good at pretending.

'I missed you,' I said.

She pulled out the other chair slowly. She sat down

without pushing it back towards the table, maintaining the distance between us.

I waited for her to speak. She was always the one who started our conversations; she was always the one who carried them.

I cleared my throat. 'What's happening?'

'What do you mean?' she said quietly.

Her voice. Her soft, beautiful voice. It had told me she loved me. It had reassured me everything was fine. I could've cried at the sound of it. Whatever anger I'd felt dissipated. I had spent a lot of time wondering how I would feel when I saw her, if all I would be able to think about were the mice, or if I'd be scared that she'd left me behind, but that wasn't the case. I was thinking about our nights in Barcelona, about lying next to her in bed. Cat wouldn't abandon me.

'What's happening with the case?' I asked. She must have found a lawyer by now.

She looked over to one of the guards, her brows furrowing. 'You're going to appear in front of the magistrate,' she said. 'They're going to ask how you plead. And then you're going to the Crown Court for the trial.'

'That's not what I meant,' I said. 'This isn't going to trial, right? We're going to stop it, aren't we?'

She stared at me as if I'd spoken a foreign language.

'Cat,' I said, 'I forgive you. I know I messed up first, and I forgive you.'

That was what she wanted to hear, wasn't it? That I was still hers. I always would be. That was what she needed. Maybe she'd been worried that I'd be throwing *her* under the bus, and that's why she hadn't come earlier, that's why she hadn't got me a lawyer yet. Yes, of course that was it. But I wouldn't. The entire time I'd been in prison I'd known and I hadn't said anything.

'Forgive me for what?'

'The mice.' I couldn't make myself say the rest of it out loud.

I'd scrubbed my mouth so many times, but I still sometimes felt like pieces of flesh were stuck between my teeth.

But Cat was the only hope I had. If I had to learn to live with what she'd done, I could do it. I could learn to live with anything if it meant being with Cat.

One day I would forget. One day I would forgive.

'Please,' she said. 'Please calm down.'

'I am calm,' I said, and realized it was too loud and lowered my voice. 'I am calm.' I took a deep breath. 'Did you tell them I didn't do this?' I whispered.

But no matter how quietly I spoke, there was no way I could prevent them from hearing everything I said. I wanted these strangers out of the room. I wanted her to myself.

'Why would I lie to the police?' Cat said slowly. 'That's a crime.'

'It's not a lie,' I said. 'I didn't do it. I didn't kill him.'

Her eyes were very big and her voice was very slow. 'But you did,' she said. 'I thought you were finally going to admit what you've done.'

I gaped like a fish. I told myself it was fine; we were being listened to. Whatever she was saying, it had to be for a good reason.

'There's another plan, isn't there?' I said.

There had to be. We'd been so careful. Cat never would've done it without a plan.

'You can make this go away,' I said. 'Please tell them I didn't do it.'

Cat stood up, and her chair squeaked against the floor as it moved back. The worst part was how she looked at me, like

I was a stranger. Like I was dangerous. It was the complete opposite of how she had looked at me in the days leading up to his death. Her eyes had been so full of love and desire, always holding in a smile, always on the verge of laughter, always sparkly. Like I was someone special.

'I didn't do it!' I yelled as she turned around.

It didn't stop her. She went towards the door, one of her hands going up to her face.

I wanted to run after her. I wanted to grab her. I wanted to strangle her. I wanted to kiss her.

'You *know* I didn't do it!' I shouted.

She already had a hand on the door handle, ready to leave. She turned for a final time, her eyes watery, her lip wobbling.

There was no one else who knew with absolute certainty that I hadn't done it. There was only her.

'I'm sorry,' she said.

When Amir came, I looked up from the table.

'What's going to happen?' I asked.

He halted mid-movement, surprise replacing the usual despair on his face.

'I heard that you saw Cat,' he said. 'The prosecution was hoping it might make you talk.'

I repeated the question. 'What's going to happen?'

Amir sat down, placing his documents on the table and straightening them out. 'When you go in front of the magistrate, they're going to go through the charges,' he said. 'The sentence won't be given yet, because it's a murder case. They're going to ask you how you plead, and you'll plead guilty or not guilty.'

'I'm going to plead not guilty,' I said.

361

'Then you'll go to trial,' he said. 'If you plead guilty, you would receive a sentence without a trial. Probably a lower one. It might even be psychiatric help instead of prison.'

And it would make less work for you, I thought.

'I'm not going to plead guilty to something I didn't do,' I said.

He peered at me and nodded. 'I'm going to be honest with you,' he said. 'I'm here to advise you legally, and I must say that a trial is not the course of action I would recommend for you. I don't think it's very likely that you would win. You might get life in prison.'

'Why wouldn't I win? They can't have evidence.'

His gaze was unwavering. He observed me like he thought I wasn't all there and maybe didn't understand what he was saying. The way you look at a child when you know you're going to have to explain something to them that they're not going to believe.

'They have plenty of evidence,' he said.

I was cold with the realization that I should have asked about this earlier. I'd been so convinced there couldn't be any evidence, apart from the fingerprints they'd told me about.

'Your phone location places you in the area of the crime,' Amir said. 'You have no alibi for when he was killed, and you lied about where you were.'

'I didn't,' I said. 'I was at home.'

'You weren't,' Amir said. 'Catherine says you left around ten and were out for hours.'

'She wouldn't know. She was at A&E.'

'Catherine didn't go to A&E.'

'She did.'

'Louise.' Amir looked me directly in the eyes. 'She says

she was home all night. There are no medical records for this supposed visit to A&E.'

All I could hear was his voice. I could no longer hear my breathing or the sound of his papers as he moved them.

Amir looked down as he read. 'His DNA was found under your fingernails. The knife he was stabbed with had your fingerprints on it. There were no other fingerprints in the flat that shouldn't have been there. You stole his phone. It was sold to a tech store and the sale traced back to you.'

I blinked and saw Cat's face, her expression as she had looked at me that last time. They wouldn't question the fact that her fingerprints were there. She was his girlfriend, after all.

I shook my head. 'I didn't steal it. He lost it. I found it.'

'But you didn't give it back, did you? And then there's the matter of your past.' Amir looked up from his documents. 'You spent months in a psychiatric unit once. It wouldn't be hard to convince the jury that this had something to do with your . . . mental health issues.'

'But . . .'

I had called her Catherine Howard once, a long time ago. How silly of me. She was no Catherine Howard – she was Catherine Parr. The survivor. The only one left standing while the rest of us went down.

'But what would have been my motive?' I said weakly. 'Why would I have killed Henry?'

'The current line of inquiry,' Amir said, 'is that you killed him out of jealousy. You had some sort of obsession with your flatmate and her relationship with him.'

I shook my head as he spoke.

'Was that not the case?'

'No,' I whispered. 'No, it wasn't like that.'

363

She had kissed me. She had fucked me. She had told me, the night that it all happened, that she loved me. But she'd said the same thing to Henry, hadn't she?

'They found her underwear in your room,' he said. 'Under your pillow. They've heard disturbing stories from Catherine about the way you would act around her. Stories she said made her fear for her life when you were around. Stories that have been collaborated by a third party.'

Oliver. I remembered his bewildered look when he'd turned up at the flat. He'd told me I looked just like her, that it was creepy. If I hadn't treated him like shit then, maybe I would've had a single person who would defend my character in court.

'Did you or did you not,' Amir asked, 'get a tattoo identical to hers to make yourself more like her? Did you not dye your hair to look like hers? Did you not steal her clothes and her underwear?'

Oliver had seen what everyone else would see. That I was crazy. I hadn't been taking my pills or picked up my new prescription. I had her knickers under my pillow. My room was a bashed-up mess. I had a history of mental illness. I didn't make eye contact the way I should and I smiled at the wrong times. I was exactly the type of person who would do something like this.

'One of the main witnesses is a woman named Chloe Wu,' Amir said. 'She says you were dating. Is this true?'

My heart gave an extra beat. 'Yes,' I said. My throat felt dry. 'Briefly.'

'She says you told her a lot of things that weren't true,' Amir said. 'Such as things about your family and what they do. Things that correspond to Catherine's family. Is this also true?'

I closed my eyes and took a breath. I opened them again.

Amir was looking at me as if he was expecting me to say something, but I didn't have anything useful to say. I kept my mouth shut.

Amir sighed. 'In your initial interview,' he continued, 'you lied to the police and said you had no relationship with the deceased. You were dating him before Catherine was, weren't you?'

Cat eats people, Henry had said. *She knows what you want from her, and she becomes that. And then she eats you.*

I didn't correct Amir that we'd never dated. There was no point.

'If he rejected you for her,' he continued, 'that would explain why you were trying to become like her. And if he rejected you again, despite all that, that would explain why you killed him.'

'I didn't.'

She had told me so many times, hadn't she? Cat didn't believe in altruism. She didn't believe we ever did anything that wasn't in our own best interest. She believed that we were all selfish. And getting rid of Henry was in her interest. Keeping me around was not.

And of course, I had wanted Henry gone too. I had wanted her to be mine. I had wanted her to be free of him. So had she been wrong? Or had she been right all along?

'I didn't say you did,' Amir said. 'I'm saying there's very strong evidence that you did, and it's going to be very difficult to prove that you didn't.'

I sat there, staring at the wall. I heard Cat's voice in my head again. *There's no way this is going to end before one of us dies*, it said. *I'm the significant other. I would be the prime suspect.*

I already knew the answer to the question I was about to ask.

'Why did they suspect me?'

There must have been a reason they came to get me from the flat that day, that they took my fingerprints, that they checked my phone location.

'Catherine told them she thought you'd done it,' Amir said. 'The day she found the body and called the police, she told them to look into you.'

I saw her in the flat with her duffel bag over her shoulder. *I might spend the rest of my life in prison*, she'd said. *I can't take that risk.* The only way to avoid that risk was to make sure someone else was convicted.

'And then there's this.' Amir pushed a stack of papers across the table towards me.

The top one was a scan of my drawing of Henry. His eyes had been covered with Xs. There were black scratches across his throat.

I already knew what the rest would be. It started off with normal drawings of Oliver, of strangers, of the mice, of celebrities. Cat was interspersed throughout. Then she was more prevalent. Then she was the only face that appeared. Cat smiling. Cat laughing. Cat from the side, looking pensive. Cat naked. Cat asleep. I got to ten consecutive drawings of Cat before I couldn't look any more.

'You need to make a decision,' Amir said. 'You need to decide if it's worth fighting this or if you're ready to confess. And if I'm completely honest with you, I wouldn't suggest the first option.'

There was one final way I could show Cat that psychological egoism is false.

If I chose to plead not guilty, there was a chance, however small, that we'd somehow manage to explain away all the evidence and raise reasonable doubt, that I'd be free. Taking the blame wouldn't benefit me at all. There was no chance it would work out to my advantage. There was no reason I would choose to do that unless I was doing it for her. Unless I was doing it to make sure no one ever suspected her. That would be the ultimate selfless act. That would be for no one's benefit but hers.

I looked down at my sketches. Ten versions of Cat's face were looking back at me, smiling. She was still the most beautiful thing I'd ever seen.

Acknowledgements

Thank you to my wonderful editor, Madeleine Woodfield, to whom I owe my entire career.

To Emily Glenister, who helped make the book into what it is now. To my wonderful copy-editor, Jennie Roman, and my incredible cover designer, Lauren Wakefield. To everyone else at Michael Joseph who had any part in bringing this to the shelves, especially the assistants I've never spoken to and who never get acknowledged enough.

To Phoebe, who has left her mark not only on this book but on all my writing. To my old friend James, who believed in me before anyone else did. To Kashish, whose friendship I'm incredibly grateful for.

To my family: my mum, my dad and my sisters, for always cheering me on. None of you are allowed to read this one, I'm afraid.

To Diego, the love of my life, for reading this novel before it was anywhere near as good as it is now and somehow enjoying it anyway.

Thank you.